Ain't No River

Ain't No River

Sharon Ewell Foster

Multnomah® Publishers *Sisters, Oregon*

AIN'T NO RIVER
published by Multnomah Publishers, Inc.
© 2001 by Sharon Ewell Foster

Published in association with the literary agency of
Sara A. Fortenberry, 1001 Halcyon Avenue, Nashville, Tennessee 37204

International Standard Book Number: 1-57673-628-8

Cover image by Corbis
Cover image of woman's face/David Bailey Photography

All Scripture quotations, unless otherwise indicated, are taken from
The Holy Bible, King James Version

Multnomah is a trademark of Multnomah Publishers, Inc.,
and is registered in the U.S. Patent and Trademark Office.
The colophon is a trademark of Multnomah Publishers, Inc.
Printed in the United States of America

For information:
Multnomah Publishers, Inc.•Post Office Box 1720•Sisters, Oregon 97759

Library of Congress Cataloging-in-Publication Data
Foster, Sharon Ewell.
Ain't no river / by Sharon Ewell Foster.   p.cm.   ISBN 1-57673-628-8 (pbk.)
1. Afro-American women—Fiction. 2. North Carolina—Fiction. 3. Teenage girls—Fiction. 4. Grandmothers—Fiction. I. Title.
PS3556.O7724 A75 2001   813'.54—dc21   00-011347
01 02 03 04 05 06—10 9 8 7 6 5 4 3 2 1 0

Only You knew that I would actually make it to the end of this second book. Much of the time, it was You and I alone. So, again, I lift this book up to You, Lord. Thank You for Your Word and Spirit that sustain me. Bless the words and each page that they might in turn bless the readers. Not my will, but Your will be done. No hearts will come unless You draw them.

I offer *River* not as one perfected, but as one who struggles daily to be more like You. May You teach me and sustain me with the grace to walk worthy of Your calling.

I also dedicate this book to my grown children—my first editors—and to my family and friends.

Many thanks to the ministers who keep me fueled, especially Bishop Howard Oby, pastor of Beloved Tabernacle of God, my spiritual father and confidant. Also, Joyce Meyer Ministries, T. D. Jakes Ministries, and Daughters of Rizpah Ministries. I also dedicate this book to the great visionary, Rev. Dr. Walter Scott Thomas, pastor of New Psalmist Baptist Church and to the New Psalmist family.

Blessings and thank you to Jenniemaew, LizrdLpsKW, CrzyNanc, HOST OPRH Yerf, AuntieD11, and all my other friends and supporters on the AOL Oprah Christian fiction chat line.

Blessings to Baby Jakes, his mother, and all my fellow writers. Thank you to Zenus Newby for helping keep my head and hair straight.

This book is for Mary and Rahab's daughters (and sons), for Tamar's daughters (and sons), for Esau's sons (and daughters), for Samson's sons (and daughters)—for all of us who are less than all He wants us to be. May you find here healing, sweet treats, and blessings—whatever you need. And may you find in His Word bread, water, and life everlasting. If you already know Him, I'll see you on the other side. If you have not met Him, if you have avoided Him because you do not feel worthy—come, the door is open—take the water of life freely.

Acknowledgments

Thanks to all those who helped me the first time, especially Major Brooks and all the good souls of the Defense Information School.

Thanks and blessings to the Kingdom Women of New Psalmist Baptist Church, especially Minister Mary and Queen Mother Angela.

Thank you to the Cape Fear River Assembly—http://www.cfra-nc.org/index.htm

Thank you to 1898 Centennial Foundation—http://www.spinnc.org/spinsites/1898/default.htm, 1898 Foundation, Inc., P.O. Box 1205, Wilmington, N.C. 28402.

Thank you to the American Lung Association Big Ride Across America—http://www.bigride.com/

Serve the LORD with gladness: come before his presence with singing. Know ye that the LORD he is God: it is he that hath made us, and not we ourselves; we are his people, and the sheep of his pasture. Enter into his gates with thanksgiving, and into his courts with praise: be thankful unto him, and bless his name.

PSALM 100:2–4

Cast of Characters

Big Esther—beauty shop owner, Garvin's longtime friend from Jacks Creek

Carmenone—of Monique's high school friends

Garvin Daniels—attorney, Meemaw's granddaughter

GoGo Walker—Meemaw's personal trainer

Dr. Hemings, Brian—litigant in Garvin's case

Inez Zephyr, Sister Inez—a customer a Big Esther's beauty shop

Jonee Rainat—Garvin's lawyer friend at Winkle and Straub

Josephina—one of Monique's high school friends

Lacey—one of Monique's high school friends

Matty Zephyr—Sister Inez's niece

Meemaw, Evangelina Hightower, Miz Hightower—Garvin's grandmother

Miz Maizie—cleaning lady at Garvin's law firm

Miz Moline the dinner lady—sells dinners at the beauty shop

Monique—Meemaw's young friend in Jacks Creek

Mr. Green—grocer in Meemaw's neighborhood

Ramona—Garvin's fight-for-you friend from D.C.

Smitty—GoGo's longtime friend

Prologue

◆

Monique

The girl looked through the rusty bars. Crusty orange had over-taken what had once been new, black, and shiny. Her hands first touched the bars tentatively, as if they might burn her like battery acid. Then she grabbed them and held on as she looked to the other side. The voices that rose to her from there were light, care-free, singsong. At one time she had felt that way. Monique was only fifteen, but her time of innocence, of freedom, seemed long gone. She gripped the bars more tightly, as though she yearned to pull herself through them. Orange-brown smudges covered her fingers. Sunlight played across the tip of her small nose and a single tear traveled from one of her eyes through the shadows that covered the rest of her face. Monique turned from the bars and looked in what she knew was the direction of Miz Hightower's house.

GoGo

GoGo slid behind the wheel of his red convertible BMW with an immaculate cream-colored interior. He opened the glove compart-ment, reached in, pulled out his leather-bound appointment book, and scratched through an entry on the list of names. That one had gone well. He looked to the next name: Hightower. She was always his favorite. Miss Evangelina Hightower.

GoGo smiled and slid the appointment book back into the glove compartment. He had an hour before his meeting with her…just enough time to refuel with some lunch.

He rubbed his hand over his shaved head, then looked in the rearview mirror as he rubbed his hand over his clean-shaven, dark-skinned face. GoGo looked down, turned the ignition key, shifted from neutral to first. It was a good life. Red-colored dust flew up from his wheels as he quickly shifted from second to third. He tilted his head back and let the sun kiss his face, then sped away, leaving a large, well-appointed house behind him. A very good life, for sure.

Garvin

"Hello."

"Hello, Meemaw. It's me, Garvin. Like you wouldn't know, of course." There was no response. "Meemaw…Meemaw… *Meemaw!*"

"Sorry, baby."

"Meemaw, where were you? What are you doing?"

"Oh, sugar, I had to get my leg warmers."

"Leg warmers?"

"Mm-hmm. GoGo says I need them. You know, those things you children were wearing in the eighties. GoGo says that they help keep my muscles from getting cold. Helps keep them warm, loose, and supple."

"Supple? What? Meemaw, what are you talking about? Who is GoGo?" All Garvin could see in her mind was an image of her grandmother in leg warmers and a long sweatshirt with the number 1-800-U-GO-GIRL printed on the bottom in hot pink letters. She shook her head to clear the image. "Meemaw, what's going on? Who's GoGo?"

"Oh, I thought I told you about GoGo. Didn't I tell you about GoGo?"

Obviously not! Garvin held her tongue. "No, Meemaw, you

never mentioned anyone named GoGo. Is she some dancer or something?"

Garvin thought it sounded as though her grandmother had taken the phone away from her mouth. She could hear her laughing. "Oh no, honey." Meemaw's voice was clearer again. "GoGo's not a she, he's a he. He's my trainer."

Garvin pressed her free hand to her forehead and rubbed one of her temples with her fingertips. "Your what, Meemaw? Your trainer?"

"Um-hmm. He is the sweetest, most wonderful man. Just the cutest young thing!" Garvin could imagine her grandmother waving her hand in the air while she talked. "He is teaching me how to work out and just enjoy myself, get toned and everything. 'You have to make yourself, your happiness, and your well-being a priority, Miss Evangelina.' That's what he calls me, 'Miss Evangelina.' Don't you just love that? I love the way that sounds, *Miss Evangelina.*" Meemaw was giggling.

Garvin rubbed her temple harder; it felt like a migraine was coming. "Meemaw, what are you talking about?"

"GoGo is doing wonders. Since I came back from that T. D. Jakes Women's Conference in Atlanta, I've been working out. My doctor say I got the blood pressure and the bone density—I think that's what he said, bone density—yes, that was it, the bone density of a much younger woman." Meemaw certainly sounded pleased with herself.

Bone density was fine, but Garvin didn't even like the name GoGo. "Meemaw, are you taking your medication properly? Are you being careful?" She thought she heard her grandmother giggle again. "Meemaw, you have to be careful. Who is this GoGo? You know there are all kinds of people out there. Men who just wait to prey on lonely, older women. Especially at some fly-by-night gyms and places. They try to trick older women into buying expensive gym memberships, and then—"

"Gym? Oh no, baby. I didn't meet him at no gym." There was no doubt about it, Meemaw *was* giggling. In fact, she was laughing out loud. "Oh, I knew his grandmother for years. She and her husband used to be big people in the AME church around the way. Speaking of church, did I tell you I saw your old high school friend Esther? She used to go to my church, too, but not so much since her husband died."

"That's fine, Meemaw, but we weren't talking about Esther. We were talking about that guy. Why doesn't that give me any more comfort to know that his grandmother used to go to church there, Meemaw?"

"Probably because you don't never go there so you can get some comfort," Garvin's grandmother quipped.

"This is not about me, Meemaw." Garvin took her hand away from her forehead and put on her take-control voice. "I'm trying to look out for you. You must know there are bad men in the church, too."

"In Jacks Creek? I don't think we have enough people here to qualify for a bad man." Meemaw laughed at her own joke; Garvin was not amused. "Besides, baby, I wasn't born yesterday, no matter what you think. GoGo is a fine young man. 'Bout your age." Garvin could hear her grandmother's doorbell in the background. "Wait just a minute, baby. I think that's him now."

She heard the phone drop. Garvin stood up, ready to take control of things...even from six hours away. Over the phone, in the distance, she could hear her grandmother talking and laughing. Garvin thought she could make out a man's voice. There was no telling what was going on.

"Meemaw," she spoke into the receiver. "Meemaw. Meemaw!"

Garvin could hear the cord rattle as her grandmother picked up the phone.

"Oh, I am so sorry, baby. I forgot you were on the line. Well, Meemaw has to go, now. I will call you back later…just a minute, Garvina." It sounded like a hand had gone over the mouthpiece. Garvin could hear her grandmother's muffled voice talking. It was hard to make out, but she thought she heard her say, "Just a minute, GoGo!" Then there were more giggles.

Garvin's free hand flew back to her forehead. "Meemaw. Meemaw? I told you I don't want you to call me that. I told you I changed my name…Meemaw?" She didn't believe her grandmother was listening. Her grandmother's voice sounded muffled again.

"I'm coming, right now!" she thought she heard her grandmother say. "Stop now." More giggles, then the mouthpiece was uncovered. "All right now, sweetie. Meemaw will call you back later." *Click.*

Garvin glared at the mouthpiece. She hung up the receiver, stared at the designer telephone, then moved her gaze to the stack of files on the desk in front of her. The Hemings files. First the case, now her grandmother…what else could go wrong? Her career was unraveling, and Meemaw sounded like she was losing it—if she hadn't lost it already. It was Meemaw who had always been her foundation, who had been the one solid force in her life, a spiritual light in the community. And now…

Garvin began to believe someone was out to get her.

One

ow or later. Banana.

The sticky, yellow candy wrapper blew northwest across Lafayette Square, caught in a gentle summer breeze. Impatient Washington, D.C., traffic stopped, started, stopped, honked, and dodged bicycle couriers—but the banana-colored paper, creased with grime and dirt, drifted and bobbed with the current. As if caught on a wave, the sheath ebbed and flowed, finally affixing itself to a curb in front of the Decatur House. While business shoes, walking shoes, and jogging shoes sprinted by, the three-inch heel of a hot pink, nonsensical pump punched through the tiny bit of paper and carried it north on Seventeenth Street to K.

Alternately shaking her foot and dragging her heel against rough, grimy, gray concrete, Garvin Daniels managed to finally shake the confection wrapper just outside of the revolving door of the executive building that housed the offices of her law firm. Leaning against the building, she removed her pumps and replaced them with a more acceptable pair. The pink ones she pushed deep into the dark at the bottom of her large shoulder bag.

Just inside the smoky, teal-colored glass doors and wall-sized windows, Garvin nodded at the round-shouldered, gray-haired guard. She boarded the elevator to the fifth floor, exited when the door opened, turned left, and pushed through the heavy glass doors that opened into the Winkle and Straub offices. Walking past pink marble pillars, her sensible shoes clicked on the tiles that eventually led to her cubicle. Once seated, she went immediately to work on the stack of folders in front of her.

It was too early in the morning to be so irritated. Garvin had barely finished her second cup of coffee, and the morning light—having fought its way from a window office into the hallway—confirmed her feelings: It was far too early to already be ready to kill.

Garvin slammed the drawer. In the instant she heard the cream-painted metal desk drawer start to impact the metal of the desk, she was sorry. Sorry she gave them an indication of how angry they had made her. She usually kept her composure. Never let them see you sweat or anything. The vultures would pick up on any sigh, any sound, any nuance. They would be glad to know how mad they had made her. That they had gotten to her. She knew better.

When her stomach was lurching, when her heart was pounding, she always kept a calm, practiced exterior. *Placid. Stoic.* They were the words she reached for every morning when she swung her legs out of bed. *Alone. Composed.* Those were two more good words.

Garvin looked around her cubicle area, subtly trying to watch the watchers. She was on the lookout for anyone who might have heard her reaction.

So what? Just so what? Who cared anyway? After all the work she had done. After all the work she had put into this bleeping company. Forget them, man. Garvin opened the drawer and slammed it again for good measure. There, let them take a big bite out of that one.

She sat back and crossed one lean, brown leg over the other. Her skirt was contemporary, executive length: just above, just grazing the knee. Garvin took a deep breath, but silently, so the listeners couldn't hear. Couldn't listen and tell how uptight she was. As the only African American lawyer in the large firm, Garvin knew all eyes were on her. She reached her arms up and stretched—did her best cat stretch. She felt her DKNY suit flex with her in the way only an expensive tailored suit can. Let them eat that, she told herself, hoping the watchers would see. Hoping her body language would tell them just how unconcerned she was…and how good she knew she looked. It was all about the show.

Garvin ran one of her hands through her hair. Long, sassy; every hair was in its intended place. Her fingers rubbed the roots; she could push it two more weeks before she would need a touch-up. She took one sugar brown hand and flipped her hair, the whole bouncin' and behavin' mass of it, to one side. *They're all wannabes.* The texture of her hair felt good. It had held up under the coloring. Brown, just like she wanted, not red-brown, just straight brown.

Yep, they're wannabes. Like the song from the Spike Lee movie, they wannabe me. Wish they could be. Wished they had the court record she had accumulated—new kid on the block that brought home the win every time. More important, she brought home the money every time. This year, her fifth year litigating first chair, her first year with Winkle and Straub, she had already brought home more than twenty times her own salary. Partnership was in her view. After all, it just made good sense—at least it made good sense to Mr. Straub. He had recruited her, had taken an active interest in her career, had mentored her. Straub had hinted to her that she had the qualities—and the firm had the desire—to get her where she wanted to be. The others may not have wanted her, but Straub was set on her.

None of Winkle and Straub's homegrown, pampered babies could boast such a record. They were too scared to take the risks it took to win big like she did.

Garvin shook the gold-plated snow globe she kept on her desk. Watched the flakes slowly drift through the water to cover the little church inside. Her mind drifted with the imitation frozen droplets, and she laughed to herself. Meemaw would have a fit if she knew this was the closest Garvin had been to a church in years. But there were enough hypocrites right here in the office to last her all week long—she didn't have to go to church looking for them.

She shook the globe again. The bubbles...something... reminded her of the river.

Garvin lowered the globe and leaned forward in her seat. The water dispenser sat to the right of her cubicle; she could hear the muffled giggles of several of her colleagues. She could make out Mindy's and Tod's voices. Typical. Too insecure to face off against her, but stupid enough to gather like jackals, to laugh at what they must have hoped would be the end of her career.

She stared at the four folders that lay on the desk in front of her. For two weeks she had been carrying them back and forth between her home and the office. She had a bad feeling about them. Garvin tapped her well-manicured, bronze-painted nails on the cover of the top folder. Each of the folders was thick—too thick. Career killers wrapped in manila. She unstacked them so that she could see all the content labels at one time. "Hemings vs. Wade and Sommers Medical Services—one of four" on the first. "Two of four," "three of four," "four of four" on the other three folders. No doubt about it, career busters. She tapped her finger-nails again on the thickest folder, then restacked them. For sure someone at Winkle and Straub, someone powerful, must be out to get her. Someone didn't want her playing in his or her yard, and sure didn't want her winning.

Rising from her desk, she walked past her row of cubicles out to the main hallway, past oak doors with engraved nameplates. Garvin turned her head just as she passed the door labeled "Gooden." He had a window office—golden sun, mahogany wood, thick carpet. She saw Gooden and two other individuals gathered inside—the three of them stared out into the hallway at her. Someone was out to get her; it could be one of them…maybe all of them.

Jackals, she thought to herself, but smiled and nodded anyway as she moved past the office.

"Garvin." A voice caught up with her just before she could escape into the ladies' room.

She turned and looked at the man in front of her. Tried to keep the anger out of her eyes. Gooden looked so sincere, which only made it more difficult to keep cool.

"We broke from the meeting so quickly. I just wanted you to know, Garvin, that you can come to me if you have any difficulty with this case. Any doubts, any questions about the law. I know this isn't your specialty. But we thought…knew you were the one to handle this."

Garvin stared at a shiny spot on his forehead, just above his brow.

"I'm here for you, Garvin. We all are." He motioned to the other two men in his office.

Yeah, right. Instead she said, "That gives me so much comfort." She could speak with forked tongue too.

"Well, I'm certainly glad that you know where I…where we stand, Garvin."

"No doubt about it," she quipped, her hand still on the ladies' room door.

"Good. Good. And if you should decide you don't want to

handle this case, for whatever reason, we would be happy to forward your concerns up the chain."

Garvin wondered if Gooden painted that smile on his face each morning after he overdid the daily bronzer.

"I'm sure that there would be no negative inferences drawn, none against you, if you decided to decline the case. However, we—" he pointed again at the other two attorneys in his office— "thought this was the perfect time in your career for you to try on something like this. Get a little pro bono work under your belt." Gooden's smile broadened.

"Right." Without looking, Garvin slid her passkey into the slot and pressed the bathroom door inward. She didn't think Gooden could look any more like the Cheshire cat than he did at this moment. But maybe she was wrong; he had fooled her before. "Thanks." She nodded her head toward the bathroom.

"Oh, don't let me stop you."

"No problem. I know that thought never occurred to you."

Inside the bathroom, an old lady wearing rubber gloves that matched the putrescent green of her polyester uniform moved in and out of doorways, pouring similarly colored green toilet bowl cleaner into the last four commodes in the line of stalls. Her green uniform, juxtaposed with the salmon-colored décor in the bathroom, could kill an appetite really quickly.

The old woman's back looked permanently stooped. Her hair looked like it had seen one too many home relaxer kits. What was left of her tresses was mostly gray and was obviously held in place by some beauty preparation that was a close relative of Dixie Peach or Royal Crown hair pomade. The dark skin on her face, and that peeking out of her uniform sleeve, was seamless, creaseless. But her back and her hair were her age giveaways.

Garvin walked past the woman without speaking, without

acknowledging her, and settled into the first stall. She heard the lock of the stall door next to her release, heard the door slam, the faucet turn on and off, then the ladies' room door banged shut.

"You ain't fell in, has you?"

Garvin could hear the ring on the old woman's hand, muffled by the rubber glove, knock on her stall door.

"You let me know, now. I'll call for some help." The "I'll" sounded more like "Iya" and the "help" sounded more like "hep."

"No, Miz Maizie, I'm still above rim."

"You know, Garvin, I heard of lots of little children—" Garvin heard *chirren*—"falling into them old-fashioned outhouses, and you ain't too much bigger than they were." The old woman laughed to herself. "Don't eat enough to keep a little pup going. Um-um-um," She laughed one of those Sunday church sniggles again. "For sure, it don't look like you got no food at home. A man look at you, he know you can't cook. If he for serious, for sure he gone run the other way.

"On the other hand, a man look at a woman like me," the old woman cackled and Garvin imagined her patting her fleshy hip, "he know he done come up on a woman that know her way around some ribs and chicken. Yes, sir." Miz Maizie laughed again, like it was getting good to her. "You sure you ain't fell in that toilet, girl?"

"No, I just wish I had. But then again, maybe I did."

"You are one pouty child, Miss Garvin." The older woman laughed. "Yes, you are. One pouty child."

Garvin exited the stall and moved to a face bowl and began to wash her hands. "You don't know what I've been through, Miz Maizie." It felt good to slip into the language, the rhythms of her grandmother's generation. "All this plottin' and cloak and dagger stuff."

"What you mean, I don't know, child? You know if *anybody* know, I know. Everybody talk everything in front of me, like I'm not even there. Honey—" Garvin liked the way Miz Maizie wrapped her tongue around the word…the sound reminded her of hot cornbread sopping butter mixed with molasses—"you know I hear it all."

"I know you do. I hoped you would be in here, Miz Maizie. You know they are trying to kill me. That case they gave me, you know they are trying to kill me. What do I know about EEO law? Nothing! What do I know about unemployment discrimination law? Nothing!"

"Um-um-um," Miz Maizie responded. "You think they're out to get you?"

"They're just trying to ruin me." The rate of Garvin's speech accelerated. She lost the easy rhythm. "They know I lose any way the case comes out. If I lose, my record is ruined. They know it. They can't compete. Which one of them can say they haven't had any losses? None of them. So they give me this, knowing that it's almost impossible to win an EEO case in this social climate. They're *hoping* I lose." Garvin stomped her foot, and Miz Maizie shook her head while she wiped down the countertops.

"Even if I win, I lose. Just by my association with the case, people will start to look at me like I'm some sort of militant, some sort of modern day Eldridge Cleaver in pumps and lipstick with a law degree. My career is over! And if I decline the case, I still attract attention. Negative attention from the guys upstairs. It's over. And for what?"

Garvin checked her hair in the mirror, then folded her arms across her chest and watched Miz Maizie clean. "A lazy, complaining man. A throwback that thinks the whole world owes him something because he's black. Somebody that couldn't cut it and wants to holler EEO so he can get a promotion he doesn't deserve…at my expense!"

Miz Maizie sprayed a generic window cleaning spray on the mirrors. "Beg your pardon, sweetie, but did you ever think the whole world don't revolve around you? Maybe this man needs your help."

"Right." Garvin smirked.

"Maybe he got a good case. Maybe somebody trying to do him in."

"Right."

"You read the files yet?"

"No, Miz Maizie, I haven't. And, no disrespect to you, I don't *want* to read it. All that stuff is over. Please! The new millennium is upon us, and they are still walking around marching and having sit-ins. You know what, Miz Maizie? I made it and I didn't have a silver spoon in my mouth. I'm black too!"

Miz Maizie smiled and kept wiping. "Do tell?"

"All that stuff is in his mind and in all those other *protestors'* minds. And you know what? Even if it's not, it's not my business. I've got my own life to lead."

Miz Maizie kept wiping the mirrors like it was a fine work of art she was painting. "That may be. But the Lord might have something else in mind for you, something other than your plan."

"Maybe so, but He hasn't asked *me* about it. Miz Maizie, me and the Lord haven't talked to each other in a very long time. Right now, I've got too many issues of my own… It's over!" Garvin tossed her hair.

"Um-um-um, don't let me get you started. Let's change the subject before your lid blow off right here in this bathroom." Miz Maizie kept wiping, and Garvin thought she heard her add, "…or before the Lord sends a lightning bolt in here."

"Did you say something, Miz Maizie?"

"Me?" Miz Maizie kept wiping.

Garvin unfolded her arms and placed her hands on her hips. "I'm sorry, Miz Maizie. They've just worked me up." Garvin turned and looked into the mirror. Checked her lipstick. Tousled her hair and threw it over her shoulder and walked toward the bathroom door.

The older woman shook her head and pursed her lips. "You don't owe me no apology. You not hurting *me*." Miz Maizie kept wiping, silent for a few seconds. "You just look in your lower right-hand drawer before you leave here today. Might be a little something in there for you."

Another attorney walked in then, so Garvin turned and walked out.

For the rest of the morning, Garvin flipped the covers of the folders open and shut. Took pages out, stared at them, then replaced them without reading them. At noon she restacked the folders, picked up the phone, and dialed from memory.

"Good afternoon, Technical Solutions. Ms. Robins speaking. May I help you?"

"Good afternoon, Ms. Robins," Garvin returned the cordial business tone. "Ramona Kingston, please."

"I'm sorry—" ice waves started to pulse through the telephone line—"Ramona is on sick leave. *Again*." Ms. Robins didn't offer to take a message.

"Thank you." Garvin hoped her own tone would put the woman back in her place. Let the receptionist know that she should not assume too much about the person on the other end of the line. Garvin hung up quickly, snatched up her purse, and headed to lunch.

As she walked down K Street, Garvin thought about Ramona.

Why had she even bothered to call? She always ended up feeling the same way. Ramona was a living stereotype. Talked too loud, hands on hips, neck jerking, eyes rolling. Garvin closed her eyes for a second and tried to blot out the image of her friend.

For all of who she was or was not, Ramona was her friend. Every airbrushed, bright orange-painted, acrylic-fingernail-wearing inch of her. Ramona was her friend and yet every time she thought of Ramona—especially Ramona at work—Garvin felt pressure in her chest. Her own lawyer's sensible-but-fashionable heels struck the downtown D.C. pavement at steady, strong, predictable intervals.

So what if Ramona didn't come to work? What does it have to do with me? Garvin could just imagine, just visualize the looks on Ramona's coworkers' faces. Could just hear their offhanded remarks when Ramona called in sick. *Again.* She could just imagine their coffee-break humor when Ramona's hair—hair her girlfriend bought—stood almost a foot above the top of her head, when her earrings were almost three inches in diameter.

The pressure had started to squeeze now. Just a little, but a definite squeeze. Garvin watched groups of well-dressed, business-attired people trade almost imperceptible glances with each other as they moved past walking, sitting, standing stereotypes. Glances that promised conversations to come. Lunchtime humor, cocktail icebreakers, teambuilding exercises featuring recollections of people like Ramona.

Sometimes Garvin caught their eyes to let them know that she knew. Tossed her hair, squared her shoulders to confront their beliefs, their jokes. To let them know that she knew what they were thinking, what they were doing, and that she was a walking contradiction, a slap in the face to all that they still clung to, to their conviction that they really were better by birth.

Sometimes she did it to make her own place, her own room. But sometimes, she did it in defense of Ramona. To slap back a world that could not, would not see who Ramona really was. To stick it in the face of a world that hired Ramona just to say that they had—to pretend that they had welcomed her inside—then tried to change everything about her or made fun of her.

Garvin squeezed her eyes shut again, then opened them. She tousled her hair while she looked in the window of her destination. Enough. That was enough. Her image reflected back to her from the blackened glass pane. She wasn't responsible for Dr. Hemings and she wasn't responsible for Ramona either. Garvin pressed the door handle that let her walk through the smoked door panel and into the restaurant.

She liked Nino's. It was quiet inside the expensive restaurant. She paid to be pampered, and got her money's worth. She ordered her usual, and the waiter served it to her quickly.

Garvin moved the bitter green leaves, the goat cheese, and the blueberries around on her plate. She wasn't sure why she ordered raspberry vinaigrette dressing. She didn't like it, but definitely she wasn't going to be tempted to overeat with it on her plate.

"More water?" The waiter asked as he bent to carry the salad plate away.

"Yes, with another slice of lime." She didn't like lime or water, either. Garvin crossed her legs, reached into her purse, pulled out her cellular phone, and dialed Meemaw's number.

The phone rang, but there was no answer. Meemaw was always home…until this GoGo person had appeared on the scene. Garvin felt a knot forming in her stomach and reached in her purse for ibuprofen to fend off the headache she could feel coming.

Two

acey started dancing as soon as the air hit her face. Her blond hair, pulled into two loose, brushy ponytails tied with bright colored ribbons, flopped every time she shook her head. Monique followed her friend through the heavy, metal double doors, happy to be leaving school and fascinated by Lacey's lack of inhibitions. Didn't she know everyone was watching? Lacey danced right past groups of students huddled in threes, fours, and fives. Danced like she heard a beat that would not let her go, and her feet made a whisking scraping sound as she moved. Her big blue eyes were shut tight at times while she bent and jerked and spun. Lacey's khaki pants looked like they could fall off at any moment, but it didn't seem to be on her mind. Her arms jerked back and forth while her feet slid and scuffed. But somehow, all together, it was a dance.

Monique ran her hands over her own kinky, curly, sandy blond hair while she observed the students watching Lacey, glad that the attention was not on her. She wore her hair like a mistake. Monique followed Lacey as she bopped down the sidewalk, under the breezeway, past the other double doors and the second building that made up the other half of Rogers High School in Jacks Creek. The only high school in Jacks Creek.

"Hi, Britney!" One group of girls called out to Lacey as she danced by. Lacey didn't stop moving. She just smiled and nodded in their direction.

Monique tried to bring her friend back to reality. "Don't you get it, Lacey? They're making fun of you."

Still dancing, moving past several large ornamental flowering bushes, Lacey shook her head, "I don't care. I like Britney Spears and some day I'm going to be like her—dancing and making videos. Who cares what they think?"

Monique reached down and tugged at the back of her loose-fitting jeans so that she wouldn't continue to step on the cuffs.

"¡Hola, muchachas!"

Monique turned to see Josephina and Carmen heading in their direction.

She lowered her book bag from her shoulder to the ground. "What did you say, Josephina?"

In a tone that said Monique should have known, Carmen answered, "She said, 'Hi, girls' You better bone up on your Spanish, girl. That final is going to tear you up." Carmen chewed on the end of one of her braids; most of them were caught up in a multicolored scrunchy.

"I might have to hire you as my interpreter, girlfriend." Josephina bumped hips playfully with Carmen. With her hair pulled smoothly back into a ponytail, it was easy for Monique to see the beautifully painted cloisonné earrings she wore.

Carmen bumped back. "Yeah, like you need an interpreter. We're running neck and neck in English class for the best grade." She pointed with two fingers in between Josephina and herself. Then she turned her attention on Lacey. "Girl, you dance more than anybody I've ever seen." Carmen turned toward Monique. "You're going to have to do something with your friend. She's going to dance a hole in the ground."

Lacey reached out to grab Carmen's arm. "Come on, Carmen, dance."

"Not me, girl!" Carmen sidestepped Lacey's grasp. Josephina laughed, while Monique stood observing the other three girls and those who passed them.

"Hey, Monique! You going to Sol's party?" A group of boys called to her and nudged each other as they walked past.

Monique wrapped her long, unbuttoned, blue plaid shirt around her so that her navy blue T-shirt no longer showed. "Hi. I'm not sure...I..." She stopped before she said she hadn't been invited...yet. Monique squinted her eyes against the afternoon sunlight, then looked down and hoped the other girls weren't staring at her. She looked up at her friends. "Are you all going?"

"Me? Are you kidding?" Josephina swung her book bag to her other shoulder, then adjusted her Tommy Hilfiger designer eyeglass frames on her nose. She laughed. "About all I do is *look* cool." She adjusted her tinted glasses again and shifted her weight to one hip. "You know what happens at Sol's parties, and my grandmother ain't having none of that!" She laughed and switched hips. "She wasn't having it in Piedras Negras and she's definitely not going to have it here. YaYa didn't bring me to this little town for me to do stuff she wouldn't let me do in the city. She would string me up by my ankles!"

"You know everybody's going to be there. Randy, Kent, Ricky..."

Lacey stopped dancing and turned as though to listen to Monique, then turned to look at Carmen. "What about you? You like to dance."

"Girl, you know Sol's party is not about dancing. And my mama is just like Jo's grandmother; my mama would hang *me* up by *my* ankles. No offense to anybody, but I'm not trying to go there. Besides, we got Saturday morning band rehearsal next weekend. Our big end-of-the-school-year concert is coming up—and you all better be there. As a matter of fact—" she held up a clarinet reed in her hand—"I'm on my way to band now."

Josephina looked at Lacey. "What about you, Miss Spears? You going?"

"Very funny, Jo. Ha ha." Lacey looked at Monique. "I don't know. I haven't made up my mind yet. It might be a good party."

Carmen pursed her lips. "Whatever. See you all." She popped the reed into her mouth and began to suck it—sometimes the contour of the reed, when she tongued it, distorted the shape of her jaw—as she headed toward the band room. "Later," she called back over her shoulder.

"Yeah, me too. I've got lots of homework, you guys. I swear, I think the teachers are trying to kill us before the school year is out." Josephina held up two fingers. "Peace!" Her ornately patterned shirt billowed out behind her as she loped in the direction of her home.

Lacey's shoulders began to twitch as though she were about to start dancing. She could never seem to be still for long. "Are you going, to Sol's party? I mean, if Ricky's going to be there, I mean, I'll probably go."

Monique felt a sinking. "Maybe…maybe not. Who cares anyway? It's just another party." Lacey looked confused. "Just keep dancing, Lacey, okay? I gotta go." Monique turned and started walking south on Eden Rock Road, her eyes focused on the sidewalk in front of her.

She held her head down and scuffed at the gravel with her shoes. Even the sound of bees hovering near a hive in a tree near where she walked only distracted her for a short time. Monique had been stung once, and she did not want to experience it again. She stepped off the gravel sidewalk onto the road until she passed the insects, then her mind went back to Sol, back to the playground, and back to her destiny.

At Courtney Street she stopped, switched her book bag, looked down the street, and told herself she would not go there. She would not torment herself—at least not this afternoon. She turned and kept walking up Eden Rock, past Big Esther's Beauty Salon, in the direction of Miz Hightower's house.

"Oo-oo-oo! That child looks like a ghost!"

Sister Inez stood manning her post in the storefront window of Big Esther's—pronounced *Esta's*—Beauty Salon. "Look at her," Inez called to some of the other patrons. "She always was pale, but she just looks washed out now."

Big Esther used her foot to pump the metal bar on the chair in front of her. The chair responded; Esther had good understandings—her daddy's kind-funny way of saying she had large feet, feet that suited the rest of her. She needed to raise the client up about six more inches so she could place the rollers in her kitchen just right. Pink rollers on the crown, black ones on the side, and green ones in the kitchen. The rollers at the nape of the neck were the hardest for Esther to place, for some reason. "Inez, if you minded your own business as good as you mind other people's business...I guess that's an impossible dream." Esther's movements were languid, like she didn't buy into the hype, like she knew big girls could have sexy for a middle name, too.

"You know they never said for sure who her daddy was, but look how light she is. Those funny eyes and hair. I know that child is mixed for sure." Inez was pressed against the wall, hidden behind a potted tree and a hanging plant with purple flowers. She peeked out between the leaves. Big Esther thought the CIA had missed a prime candidate in Inez. "Her mama's family was light, but that child is way lighter than the rest of them; I know she's mixed."

"So what, Inez?"

"So, those things are important. And you know about what else they say. You know about the baby. I don't know all the details, but they said it was messy. Something about a pickle jar." Inez's face was flat, round, and worrisome. It was expressionless. From a distance, and up close for that matter, trouble and joy looked just the same.

"Inez, stop spreading rumors!" Esther shifted from foot to foot, sometimes using a hand to swat at a worrisome fly that kept buzzing her face.

"Look, I didn't do it. But one day she was and next day she wasn't—"

"Inez!"

"Look!" Inez nodded at the window. "Look at all these Mexican children coming. They are taking over."

"Inez, how could three people be considered *all*? Besides that, who says they're Mexican? Those children look Argentinean to me. But the bigger question is, aren't you supposed to be trying to avoid being a respecter of persons—"

Before Esther could finish speaking, Inez's head turned like radar. "Look who's coming now. GoGo, child! That red car and that black man…um-um-um. And you know where he headed—straight for Miz Hightower's. Poor old woman. You know a man like that ain't up to no good in a little town like this. Why he want to move from L.A. to Jacks Creek? He must have used up all his *opportunities* there." Inez leaned forward to see better, her flowered polyester dress pulling at the seams.

She looked at Big Esther. "Somebody need to do something about it. I would, but you know Garvina never cared for me. You know she wouldn't believe me. But if I was her friend—" Inez looked pointedly at Big Esther—"I would tell her about that man and her grandmother before it was too late. I see him with other old women sometimes, but he is on Miz Hightower like cops on crime. You know when her husband died he left her the house and everything."

Sister Inez paused, as if she were allowing that tidbit of information to sink in, giving time to allow the inferences to be drawn. "If Garvina knew that man was after her Meemaw, I believe she would come on down here and do something, even if she has lost her mind over that big-time job she got in D.C." Inez turned her head back to her post. "Look! He just stopped right beside that poor little washed-out child. He's good-looking, but he is a dirty dog!"

Big Esther shook her head and counted to ten. Inez was enough to rupture a blood vessel. "Inez, if you don't sit down somewhere, you gonna have to leave out my shop."

Sister Inez looked offended and moved to sit at a vacant dryer. "You don't have to talk to me that way, Esther. Don't yell at me 'cause you feeling guilty. Somebody needs to do something."

Monique heard a car approaching. She stopped to look both ways before crossing to the opposite corner and noticed the red BMW convertible that pulled to a stop beside her. The driver nodded—silent, dark sunshades covering his eyes—then pulled away. She had seen his car at Miz Hightower's before. He must be on his way there—it wasn't as if there were a lot of possible destinations on Eden Rock Road. Funny, a man like that settling here in Jacks Creek. She walked on, destiny on her mind.

When Monique reached Miz Hightower's house, sure enough, the red car was parked in the driveway. She waved at the older woman, who stood just inside her house about to shut the door.

Miz Hightower waved back. "Hello, baby! When you coming to see me? It's been a few days."

"I know, Miz Hightower." Something about the older woman, her porch framed in flowers, pushed the troubling thoughts away. "I'll come by sometime when you don't have company. I promise."

"You make sure you do." The woman continued to wave.

Monique kept walking, and in the distance she heard the snowball truck. Maybe things were going to look up after all.

Meemaw watched the girl's back as she walked down the street. Poor thing. Somebody needed to do something. She could give her cookies and hugs, but Monique needed a more energetic woman. She looked across the room and smiled at GoGo; come to think of it, she still had a lot of pep left in her. Still, if not more energetic—at least a woman closer to Monique's age. If only Garvina lived closer, she would be a good match for the girl. Garvina would understand her. In fact, the relationship might help both of them. Yes, indeed! It might be good for both of them. She would have to think of something.

Meemaw, Evangelina, looked across the room at GoGo. She would get right on it, but right now, she had her own business to tend to. "Come on, darlin'—" she reached out her hand to him— "let's not waste any time!"

Sister Inez wiggled in the dryer seat, clearly tired of sitting. "People today are selfish, just looking out for themselves. Friendship don't mean nothing, they too busy to even pick up the phone and send a warning call." She said the words out loud, but as if to no one in particular.

Big Esther put down her comb, put one small hand on one of her heavy hips, and turned in Sister Inez's direction like she was about to explain something up close and personal. Just then, the door cracked open and Miz Moline the dinner lady stuck her head inside the shop.

"You all hungry?" Miz Moline the dinner lady wore a hair net tight down over her little head. "I got fish and I got chicken."

"You a little late, ain't you, Miz Moline?" Big Esther kept staring at the hair net, and wondering, like always, just where Miz Moline got her never-ending supply of nets. Of course, she knew not to ask Miz Moline about her nets because the little, tiny, dark-skinned woman would cuss you out first, then ask Jesus to forgive her later. No need to get her started.

"I said I got fish and chicken."

Sister Inez leaned forward to see better. "How you, Mother Moline?" She waved at the little woman. "I believe I'm gone pass, the truck ought to be coming by anytime. and I don't want to overdo it."

Miz Moline stared at Sister Inez briefly, held her mouth like there was something bitter on her lips, then turned back to Big Esther. "You want some dinner? I got fish and I got chicken."

"Yeah, Miz Moline, I'll take three—I'm not gone feel like cooking dinner when I get home. What kind of fish you got?"

The expression on Miz Moline's face said Big Esther should have known. "Spot. What you want with them?"

"What you got, Miz Moline?"

"Greens."

Big Esther couldn't resist asking, "What else you got to go with the fish?"

"Greens."

Big Esther smiled and shook her head. "Okay, three fish dinners with greens. I'll just stop by your house and pick them up on my way home."

Miz Moline the dinner lady nodded, then closed the door behind her. Sister Inez slid from her chair and back into position. "Poor old dried-up thing. She works hard though, scraping by selling those dinners. Funny—" Sister Inez turned her full gaze on Big Esther—"I don't see Mr. Fancy Red Sports Car running after Mother Moline. Funny, I don't see him talking to Mother Moline or driving *her* around in his car. And I know why, too. If you were really Garvina's friend, you know you would call and tell her what that man is trying to do to her grandmother. Somebody needs to do something!"

Three

◆

I think I'm a mammy. I think I have become a mammy."
Garvin pulled down the leg of her gray sweatpants so
that it would match the other leg, and pushed up the
arms of her matching sweatshirt. Funny, the arms wouldn't stay
up and the legs wouldn't stay down. She leaned back on the pillows piled on her matching floral-printed comforter.

"I don't think I want to hear this, Garvin. This sounds like one
of those conversations I really don't want to hear. Could you call
back and I'll just let my answering machine pick up, then you can
do your venting thing—"

"Look, Jonee, all my other friends are out of town. So it looks
like you're elected. You can groan if you want to, but I'm telling
you I realized it today. I need to vent about this. I'm a mammy."

Jonee groaned again on the other end. "Garvin, I really don't
think I'm the one—"

"Listen, girl, I'm having a moment and you're elected. I think
you're enlightened enough to deal with this, okay? Now, let's press
on—just don't try to call me mammy later on…ever."

Jonee sighed loudly.

"Listen, Jonee, yesterday was a really bad day for me. I got that
bomb dropped on me at work…"

"I don't think it's so bad, Garvin. Really." Something about
Jonee's voice sounded petite, and Garvin wondered if her own
voice had that quality. "I can't understand why you're freaking out

over it. It seems like a really great experience; it could be a monumental case."

Garvin held the telephone away from her ear and shook her head as though her friend could see her. "Of course, you would think that. It's not you that's saddled with it. You don't see your career going up in smoke."

"I don't think that's fair and I don't think it's a very apt description, Garvin."

Poking with the fork with her free hand into the container Miz Maizie had left in her desk drawer, Garvin left her conversation with Jonee hanging. She was momentarily distracted by her hope that one more bite of sweet potato pie would appear. When none did, she set the container aside and answered.

"Whatever, Jonee." She paused for effect, then continued. "Then, after finding out that my legal career has been scheduled to crash and burn, I find out that my grandmother has just gone crazy. She's running around with some young gigolo." Garvin reached on her nightstand, grabbed and then throttled her blue-and-red cloth hair roller bag.

"*Meemaw,* Garvin?" Jonee snorted when she laughed. "Your Meemaw? I find that a little hard to believe. No, I find that very hard to believe."

"Well, whether you believe it or not, I heard them myself. She was giggling and whispering to him over the phone. She's never home now when I call, and you know Meemaw is always home. And if *you're* shocked, you can imagine how *I* feel. My Meemaw paying some strange man for a little attention." As she spoke Garvin began to part her hair in sections. She dipped her finger lightly into the jar of hair cream that she kept in her roller bag, then gently rubbed the cream into the lines of scalp that surrounded the section of hair. "I'm going to have to do something, Jonee."

"Garvin, did you ever think that Meemaw was taking care of herself before you were born?"

"Right, Jonee. She says that all the time. But I also know what happens to people when they get older, when they start to get lonely, when they need company." Garvin brushed the section of hair she was holding and then began to roll it on a pink roller. "Speaking of company, I went hunting last night."

"Garvin."

"I put on my most predatory dress. I was working it, girl." Garvin parted off another section of hair and began to repeat the process. "Saw somebody, thought he was worthy prey, went back to my place, and caught the drift way too late that he was not Don Juan. So, I spent the night realizing my ceiling needs to be repainted—"

"Why do you do it then, Garvin?"

"What do you mean, 'Why do I do it?'" Garvin stopped rolling her hair, intent now on the phone, on the conversation.

"I mean, lately you go out and come back saying the same thing. How it wasn't worth your time. It was no good."

"Oh no, I know this is not Jonee talking. I know you are not tripping, like you are little Miss Perfect, like you are some lamb. Don't let me have to remind you, Jonee. If I open your closet door, you know the bones will be at least hip deep."

Garvin could hear Jonee sigh on the other end. She went back to rolling her hair. "That's not what I mean at all, Garvin. It just seems like you walk away from the situation more frustrated than before you started."

"Look, Jonee, we both know the deal. We are big girls. I'm not looking for Prince Charming; if he was coming he would have been here by now. Besides that, I don't need anybody to rescue me, control me, take care of me, sweep me onto his horse riding in *his* direction. I don't need anybody to defend me or to pay my way. I don't need anybody full time working my nerves. I just need a little release. That's all. And it seems like I ought to be able to get that. And for sure I'm not going to let anybody make me feel like I'm wrong about this." She snatched a roller from the bag, but held it midair as she talked.

"Garvin—"

"No, Jonee. I'm not bothering anybody. I'm not making any babies. I'm not on welfare; I'm not sixteen. No crimes are being committed. As the song says, 'It ain't nobody's business if I do.' I don't need anyone trying to make me fit their antiquated notion of what I ought to be doing. Not anyone, not even you.

"And you know how it goes; sometimes it works out, sometimes it doesn't. Besides that, Jonee—"

Her friend's voice sounded frustrated. "Never mind, Garvin. Never mind. I'm sorry I mentioned it. How did we get on this anyway?" Jonee paused as though trying to recollect. "Oh yeah. You were telling me that you were a mammy."

"Yeah, right." Garvin grabbed another roller, paused, and then plunged on, "You know I hate that holier-than-thou stuff, Jonee. And we both know if I opened your closet door, just as many bones—"

"We've already been through that. I said, okay, Garvin. Can we let it go, counselor? You win the argument. Are you going to tell the mammy thing or what?"

"No problem." She took a deep breath, inhaling the spicy perfume of the baked apple pie-scented candle that sat burning in a holder on her vanity. Garvin lowered her arm, resumed rolling her hair, and continued her story where she had left off. "After work and the Meemaw situation, I was just feeling out of it. So I got up, drove to Georgetown, and just walked around. Did some shopping, thinking that would make me feel better. Then I decided I would stop by this little art gallery that I've passed by before. I thought, 'Hey, this will do the trick.' Pick me up a little, you know?" Garvin brushed another section of hair while she cradled the phone between her ear and shoulder. "A little art. A little culture. The finer things in life."

It was tough to keep the antique phone cradled; she had to keep readjusting it. Moments like this made her wonder why she had ever bought it. "But this exhibit, the whole exhibit, was about mammies."

"Mammies?"

"Yeah. Rag dolls, ceramic dolls, pictures, ads, labels. All mammies. And I wasn't sure at that point whether to walk or run out the door. But I'd paid my ten dollars—and you know how I feel about wasting money—so I was locked in."

"Why do I know this is going to be bad, Garvin? Why do I know I'm going to hate this? I really don't think I'm the one to hear this—"

"It was the exhibit from Hades, from the Twilight Zone, or somewhere. Mammies everywhere. I know someone made it up just to torment me. So I figure, this is some sort of racist backlash exhibit, so I am all prepared to hate it." Garvin waved a pink roller wildly in her hand as she spoke. "Then I walk up on this picture of the artist. Of course, just to shatter the emotional defense I have created, the artist is this very righteous looking sister in dreads." Garvin sighed and dropped her arm. "It was a conspiracy. No, it is a conspiracy. I know it. Let's-just-see-how-bad-we-can-make-Garvin-feel Day."

She could hear Jonee rustling on the other end of the line. "Garvin, my dryer just beeped. I really should go before my clothes wrinkle."

"So anyway, I'm hip-deep in this thing, now. There's no turning back. 'Just relax, Garvin,' I tell myself. 'You're liberated. Free your mind.'

"Of course, you know everyone in the gallery is white, except me. And girl, I can feel it. Every time they come to a new mammy, I can feel them looking at me for my take, the African American perspective."

"Garvin, you are tripping."

"No, not really. I can feel it. They are comparing me to the mammies. So I just try to look dignified. I tell myself, 'It's a new millennium; I'm not bound by the chains and fetters of the past.'" She began waving her arm again.

"You know what, Garvin? You're going to have to pay me for this one. There is no way I should have to sit through this one for free." Jonee's voice sounded exasperated, but like one who has been exasperated by the same thing many times before.

"'Okay, I can do this,' I tell myself. I am a modern woman. I shake my hair and lift my chin. I am a 'phenomenal woman,' I tell myself; and in that moment, girl, I am grateful I have that Maya Angelou card to pull out of my pocket.

"Okay, okay, I'm feeling better. Let them deal with my exotic womanhood and know that I am mammy no more." Garvin started rolling her hair again.

"Garvin, this is ridiculous."

"Listen, Jonee, I'm serious."

"Right. I'm not feeling you on this one."

"Just then, when I'm starting to feel better, I pass by this image of a new mammy, a modern mammy, an updated version of mammy. It's encased in glass. And I stop right in front of it, pretending to be interested. Knowing they're watching me. So I do the hair-throwing thing. Then I glimpse my reflection in the glass.

There's my image…me, Garvin…reflected so that it appears right next to the image of the new mammy. And girl, it was me." She tapped on her chest with a roller.

"Garvin, you really have issues. And you know, I don't think I'm the one—"

"I was mammy. She had on the same color lipstick as me. Same hairdo. *Oh mercy,* I thought! Then I realized—"

"Garvin, are you listening to me? I told you I don't want to hear this. I'm feeling really uncomfortable."

"—she, the mammy, would have said the same thing. Some colored mammy hollering out, 'Oh mercy!' just like in one of those black-and-white movies. A mammy, Jonee, I'm a mammy! My grandmother is seventy-five and working out with some pretty boy toy, I'm in my thirties and I'm a mammy. Something is wrong here."

"Garvin, I have to go, now."

"Jonee?"

"Really. I've got a call on the other line. Okay?"

"Okay. Call me; we'll go for Thai food."

"Bye. Maybe I'll see you at work. Not tomorrow, though. I'll be out of town."

Garvin stared at the phone, then at the mirror on the vanity that sat across from her bed. Definitely, mammy.

She reached into the top drawer of her nightstand. Her hand hit an unopened pack of cigarettes. It had been there for six months. Garvin knocked the pack to the side with her hand, found the scarf she was looking for, and then tied it around her head to cover the rollers. She stood and looked at herself in the mirror. She was thin, though. Fashionably thin, even after giving up the cigarettes. Ally McBeal thin, and that definitely wasn't mammy. Not mammy at all. As she turned to admire her rear view, what there was of it, the phone rang.

"Garv? Garv? That you?" The voice on the other end didn't wait for her to speak. "It's me. Ramona."

Four

◆

───────────────

arvin told herself she was not going to get angry—she was not going to let Ramona push her buttons. She could hear Ramona's jewelry rattling on the other end. The absentee had surfaced. She didn't want to hear any of Ramona's stories. She just wouldn't pay attention, that's all.

"Garvin, I need to talk to you."

"I know." She needed to go to bed early so that she could go in early and try to read the Hemings files. She would not let Ramona get her worked up.

"You busy?"

"Mm-hmm." Garvin hoped "I don't want to be bothered" would ooze between the cracks of her nonverbals. "For sure, I know *you're* not. Not busy, I mean. I tried to call you today, but your secretary said you were off today. *Again.*"

"I know. I was. Something happened today, Garvin."

"Right, Ramona. Something is always happening. And you know what? It is none of my business." Garvin's hand began to rub her forehead.

"Stop going off. This is me, Ramona, okay? So don't even go there. Something happened today, Garv. That's what I'm trying to tell you." Ramona paused, something Garvin had never heard her do. "I met a man."

Garvin stopped rubbing her head and hit the bed instead with her free hand. "Wait, Ramona. Are you telling me you took off today because you met a *man?* That is too trifling. Definitely trifling. You know I like a man as much as anybody, but you don't take off from work for something like that."

"Just listen, okay, Garvin? It's not like you think."

"You are not going to work my nerves, Ramona. I mean it."

"Garvin?"

"Okay." She pressed her hand back to her forehead.

"On my way into work this morning, I got off the Metro at Gallery Place, and I drew myself up because you know I hate the way people push and shove and run like they have lost their minds trying to get to the trains downstairs. I just tried to slow down to avoid the crazy people."

Garvin could just imagine Ramona, her high hair, iridescent lipstick, and big earrings. And black lip liner, she couldn't forget the black lip liner.

"Two people in front of me almost got into a fight."

As Ramona talked, Garvin played the movie in her mind…

"'Man, you better not push me!' the woman in front of me yelled at a man jostling by to the right of her, while she stepped on the foot of the man crowding past her. I just watched and tried to avoid it all.

"Then…*wham!* Suddenly I was flat on my back. Then I saw black. The next thing I knew, some people were standing, leaning, and stooping over me. One fool had his big moon face right in my face.

"'Are you all right?'

"Right, I'm on my back, I can feel air blowing up my legs, and I feel like my eyes are walling up in my head. 'Mm-mmm,' I said. I learned how to say 'mm-mmm' from this woman, Audraine, that I used to work with. When people were talking to her, gossiping, all she would say was 'mm-mmm.' That way, no one could say she was for or against, positive or negative. I mean that lesson stayed with me. And even though I was flat on my back, knocked off my feet, and compromised, I had the presence of mind to say, 'Mm-mmm.' It just seemed like one of those moments to me.

"Anyway, there I was with his big moon face hovering over mine, and I realized that people were still rushing by my little group trying to make it to their trains. You know, I never noticed how high those ceilings are or how cold and hard the floor is till I was laying there—it was like a giant concrete cave. I was just considering how inconsiderate people are, when I heard this voice.

"'You people got to move!' First the voice was kind of far away, but it seemed to be getting closer. 'Oh,' the voice said. 'I see, but you know she got to move. You can't leave her there; people trying to get to work.' It was a woman.

"You might think she was heartless, but when I saw her face bend down over mine, just behind the moon face, when I saw her I knew she was just a sister-girl trying to do and keep her job. Her hair was red and she didn't have any roots showing, but those waves looked tired, and I knew where she was coming from. Just another sister trying to keep it real. There she was stuck there wearing that tight, crazy, brown Metro uniform you know nobody would want to wear. I understood.

"I know how it feels to be working and always feel like you could be gone. That somebody is just looking over your shoulder waiting for their opportunity to find you messing up. I knew like she knew that she didn't even have to do anything wrong. Something just had to happen in her vicinity and they would lay it on her doorstep. It didn't have to be under her control or responsibility. I understood.

"She was responsible for that concrete station, and she had to keep things moving. I understood the pressure she was under;

just like she understood me flat on my back, with my eyes walling, and air blowing up my legs. While she and I were trying to have a meeting of the minds, that big moon face just kept getting closer.

"'Here, I'll help you,' it said. Now Garvin, you know I have always been a little self-conscious about my hips and weight, but I just laid there like dead and let that big moon face reach his hands down and pick me up. He owed me.

"'I'm sorry,' he kept saying over and over.

"'Is she all right?' the train station lady asked over his shoulder. She was just checking, just doing her job.

"Moon face just kept saying he was sorry, and started asking if I was okay.

"'Mm-mmm,' I said.

"The train sister looked me over and said, 'You can take her through the handicap gate, if you need to go outside.' She said it like she was really hoping we would go outside, then she moved quickly on to the next nuisance. I understood. She was just trying to keep it real.

"Mr. Moon Face kept saying he was sorry as I tried to get a fix on how I ended up on the floor. About the same time, I checked my face and rubbed my hair—there was no need to look any more foolish than I had to.

"'I'm so sorry; can I at least buy you breakfast?'

"'Mm-mmm,' I said. By now, it was pretty clear that he was the cause that I was knocked out at the Metro. I mean, why turn down breakfast? For sure, I knew I wasn't going to that stupid job after lying out on my back at Gallery Place. 'Will you call my job for me?' I whispered it.

"'Of course, I will. I'm so sorry.' I just leaned my weight on him. I mean, he didn't hold his weight off of me when he knocked me out flat in the subway, did he? He held me up until we got in the booth at the restaurant."

"Wait a minute, wait a minute," Garvin interrupted. The movie in her head froze, stuck on pause. "Are you telling me you went *out* with this guy? Did you get his name? Did you call an ambulance? What is wrong with you, Ramona?"

"Calm down, Garvin. He turned out to be a nice guy. He paid for everything."

Garvin reached into the drawer of the night table near her bed, grabbed the ibuprofen, and popped the lid. "Of course, Ramona. He doesn't want you to sue him, so he's going to make nice until everything's okay—I don't believe you!"

"I knew you were going to act like this, Garvin. I shouldn't have told you."

"No, you needed to tell me. You didn't need breakfast, you needed a lawyer. He could be setting you up. What is moon face's name anyway?"

"His name is Derrick and I think he's a nice guy."

"Well, that qualifies him."

"He asked me out on a date. He's an engineer at the Patent and Trademark Office…and he's a minister."

Garvin shook two caplets into her hand. "Okay, and that's supposed to make me feel better. You are not going on a date with some lunatic stranger. This whole thing could be some elaborate plot he works to get to women."

"Or it might just be something good that came into my life."

She reached for the bottle of water she always kept near her bed at night. "You are not going out with this guy."

"I knew you were going to act this way, Garvin. I shouldn't have called you."

Garvin popped the caplets into her mouth and took a swig of

water. "You know what, Ramona? You're right. I told you I didn't want to hear this, but I believe you called because you wanted me to stop you."

"Maybe I called because I wanted you to be happy for me. Something feels different this time."

"Right, Ramona. Different than all the Jermaines, DeWaynes, and Dantes. I don't think so. You are not going out with this guy! Do you hear me?"

"Bye, Garvin." *Click.*

Garvin hung up the telephone and pounded her pillow until she got tired. Someone was definitely out to get her. Things couldn't get much worse.

Five

arvin startled awake. Her digital alarm clock display blinked on and off in the darkness: It was 4:00 A.M. Her heart pounded, her limbs were paralyzed, and her lungs seemed frozen. She wasn't breathing. *Okay, Garvin, calm down. Breathe. It's okay—breathe.*

It was the same old childhood nightmare. It had been a regular occurrence in her life for so long, so many nights, she couldn't remember when she first started dreaming the dream.

In the dream, the nightmare, she was a little girl and stood safely on a ledge, more like the rim of a canyon. Her feet were firmly planted on the soil, on bright red-orange clay. The sun and the light it cast were the same color as the soil, but the sky was an almost cloudless cobalt blue. There was no wind, just heat—pressing, but not oppressive. What held her attention was not the color, not the stillness, not even the heat. Her eyes were drawn to the canyon and what lay there.

In the midst of the fissure, many feet below the rim of the great canyon, was a single-passenger, biwing, propeller plane. The plane was crumpled, as if it had crashed, and it was burning out of control. On one wing of the plane lay the unconscious pilot, still untouched by the flames.

Even as she lay awake, Garvin could still feel her little girl self's torment. What could a little girl do to save a man? What if the plane exploded just as she reached him? What if she died trying to rescue the man? Were little girls responsible for saving men? Shouldn't she just stay where she was, safe? Where he lay was too far, too deep, too wide.

Yet she could not walk away, and there was no one to cry to for help. It would have been so much easier if there had been someone else there, someone older and braver. Where was God? She was just a little girl. What did He want her to do?

Night after night she stood on the rim of the canyon, watching the plane burn. The dream never ended. She never got any older or any bigger, just night after night she stood on the rim of the canyon anguishing until her chest heaved for air so hard that it woke her up. *It's okay, Garvin. It's just a dream.* She lay still until she regained control of her limbs and her breathing returned to normal.

Garvin was out of the house and on her way to work early. There was no point in trying to fall back asleep, no point in risking another bad dream. One every twenty-four hours was enough. Between worrying about Meemaw, about Ramona, about the Hemings case, it was no wonder.

She stopped for a large decaf on the bottom floor of the large building in which Winkle and Straub rented office space, then headed for her office. Garvin was glad no one else was on the elevator when she boarded it. *Forget all this foolishness.* She was not going to worry anymore.

Meemaw, Ramona, Hemings—they were all grown people, just like she was, and they could take care of themselves. *Just take a few moments of quiet time this morning and get yourself together, Garvin.*

She nodded at the receptionist as she crossed through the doorway that led to Winkle and Straub office space. Kind of like crossing into Oz, only the color was oatmeal. Down the corridor,

past Gooden's office, she made it to her cubicle without convers-
ing with anyone. She sat down, leaned back in her chair, closed
her eyes, and took a deep drink of the cinnamon-flavored coffee.
Garvin loved the smell even more than the taste.

Okay, so what? So what if Meemaw was making a fool of herself with a younger man? She was not Super Garvin, she couldn't
save everybody. So what if Ramona was being used by some con-
ning, fabricating, clerical-collar-wearing creep? Ramona was old
enough to know better. And as for Hemings—she was not about
to risk her career for some modern day African-American Don
Quixote who saw windmills everywhere he worked! Garvin
breathed deeply.

"Excuse me, I hope I'm not interrupting you."

Garvin began to choke on the swallow of coffee that was making its way down her throat. Great. The last thing she wanted was
to look like a fool in front of Gooden.

"Can I get you a napkin?"

*No, Gooden, just let me sit here with coffee all over my mouth and
chin. Thanks!* "No, I have some napkins in my drawer, thanks."
She reached into her lower right drawer. Something about the
man always made her feel caught. Like a little kid. Like he always
suspected her of doing wrong and no matter what she did he
always caught her at moments when she was compromised, when
there was no way she could explain herself.

"Are you sure that you're okay, Garvin? I can come back. It
looked as though you were resting. Perhaps you didn't sleep well."

He was such a creep, and the way light reflected off his big
shiny forehead… "No, no. I was just…" There was no use trying
to explain. Besides, the sooner she got this over with, the sooner
she could have her office to herself again.

"Do you mind if I sit down? This issue is somewhat sensitive."

Garvin motioned to a chair. "No, no, of course. Please sit down."

Gooden dragged the chair closer to her desk. He smiled and looked deeply into her eyes. He wore his most concerned expression, but his eyes were hard, bright, and dead. "If we could take a moment, Garvin, I need to talk to you about the most recent case you tried—the Bowman case."

"Yes." Garvin leaned in, hoping to decipher where Gooden was going before he got there.

He held an official looking folder in his hands. He took one hand away from the folder and then spread it out, in a most sincere gesture, on Garvin's desk. "You must know, of course, that they are most pleased with the outcome of the trial."

Why wouldn't they be? They won 1.5 mil. "Yes?"

"While they were most pleased with the outcome…"

That's where you always got killed…on the other side of the pauses. Always slammed by the "but," the "howbeit ever," the "although." Creamed by the word just on the other side of the conjunction chasm.

Garvin didn't know what was coming, but she felt a sinking feeling. She wasn't on the rim of the canyon anymore—she was definitely heading rapidly for the big crack.

Gooden leaned in further and stage whispered in his most concerned voice. "But, based on a rather exhaustive follow-up interview that I did with the clients, there is some indication that you may have been biased in the way that you interacted with them."

Suddenly, just for a moment, Garvin realized she was observing the conversation her look-alike was having with Gooden from the upper right-hand corner of her cubicle. Gooden was opening and closing his mouth and the look-alike Garvin sat looking shocked. Just momentarily, the two of them seemed so removed, so far beneath her. From that vantage point, it was clear just how really big Gooden's head was.

His lips moved and the sound finally reached her. "As I said, they were pleased with the outcome, but had some reservations about the professionalism with which you treated them."

"Biased? Unprofessional? Based on what?"

"Please, Garvin. I know this is all taking you by surprise," Gooden stage whispered urgently, "but I'm trying to keep this as confidential as possible; it is, after all, very sensitive."

"Based on what?" Garvin always avoided calling him by his name; there was something about calling him *Mr.* that really worked her nerves.

"Based on the interview, as I previously stated. Would it be better if I gave you some time, say a couple of hours before we complete this? You did seem to be resting when I entered." Garvin shook her head. "All right then. Again, this is all based on my findings from the follow-up interview."

"What follow-up interview?" Garvin hoped that Gooden couldn't hear her heart beating. "Is that customary?"

"I'm sure that after you've had some time to think this through, you will recall this policy is clearly documented in the Winkle and Straub Office Policy Guidelines. In fact, I believe Chapter Twenty-one, Paragraph E, Subparagraph One-C, the follow-up interview is documented and authorized. Just to be sure I was using and interpreting it properly, I checked with the chain of command—in fact, I checked as high as Mr. Straub himself."

Garvin felt warm. "I mean, is it customary? I've never heard of a follow-up interview being done, not even after a losing case. Is it normal?"

"Based on the guidelines, it is not *abnormal*. It is to be used at the supervisor's discretion. In an effort to serve Winkle and Straub more effectively, it was my decision—supported by the chain—to randomly conduct follow-up interviews as a way of ensuring quality and to find opportunities for continuous improvement. I made sure I had *everyone's* support for the program before I moved forward. Unfortunately, what I thought was going to be an interview that documented only glorious praise instead seems to have uncovered what appears to be charges of bias. Most unfortunate." Garvin thought she saw a glint in Gooden's eyes as he spoke.

"Gooden! This is a trap."

"Ms. Daniels, I'm certain that you are upset and taken aback by all this, so I won't note for the record that your behavior is bordering on belligerence and unpro—well, at least, inappropriate behavior."

Garvin imagined that was the very language he would use in his private memorandum for record—a memorandum that he would search for opportunity to use in a seemingly innocent but clearly public way.

He had her.

He would also use all the office witnesses, all the listeners who could not hear his stage whisper, but who would happily document her yelling and her apparent lack of propriety in the office. The heat seemed to be overcoming her.

"I'm trying to help you, Garvin. We all are." His stage whisper was a little louder. Those statements would go into the memorandum, too.

She lowered her hands to her lap; she didn't want him to see that they were shaking. "I would like to meet with Mr. Straub." He would get her through this. "I would like to meet with Mr. Straub immediately."

"I'm sure he would love to meet with you too, Garvin. He is most concerned." She was sure she saw a glint in his eyes, maybe a little upturn at the corners of his mouth. "Unfortunately, that isn't possible. Surely you understand he would be the person having to adjudicate this matter—should it come to that—and it's imperative that he maintain all appearance of impartiality. You can sympathize with his position, can't you?

"However, at his direction—so that we might freely investigate and quickly resolve this matter—I am here to notify you that you are being placed on administrative leave for the next ninety days. I need you to initial and date these three documents to indicate that you understand the nature of this administrative leave." Gooden removed three copies of an administrative leave letter from the folder he held and laid them on the desk before her like exquisite, rare jewels. "This is most unfortunate. We are all just sick over it, Garvin. Mr. Straub is most concerned. Winkle and Straub must follow the policies equitably though."

Garvin was sure that Gooden was smiling.

"What about my case load? What am I supposed to do for ninety days?"

Gooden looked her straight in the eye. "You are so conscientious, Garvin. Always worried about your clients. That's why this whole unfortunate incident has shocked us all.

"Mr. Straub—here, you can read it for yourself—" he pointed at one of the copies of the letter that lay before her—"has given you ninety days paid admin. During that time, you will prepare to litigate the Hemings case upon your return. Ms. Jonee Rainat will act as your contact here and work with you as you prepare the case."

"Exactly what did I do?" Garvin heard pleading in her voice and wondered what all the watchers and listeners must be thinking. "What have they accused me of doing? I'm entitled to know that."

"Ms. Daniels, Garvin, you must be sensitive to the fact that we must protect our clients. We mustn't allow them to feel threatened in any way, or suffer even the slightest discomfort for speaking what they perceive to be the truth. I'm sure they are greatly troubled by this matter. We're all greatly troubled by it."

"I'm entitled to know the charges!"

"There are no *charges*, Garvin, simply allegations. This is not a criminal case." Gooden looked at and spoke to Garvin as though she were a simple child. "As this is an administrative matter, it's felt that we should withhold the details of those allegations until there has been a thorough investigation. We want to protect you, the clients, and Winkle and Straub. You can understand that, can't you?"

She was feeling woozy. "Am I being fired?"

Gooden laid a well-manicured hand on top of the copy of the letter nearest to him and leaned toward her. "Garvin, that's a bit premature, don't you think? You don't think we're trying to get rid of you, trying to harm you, do you?" She was sure those words would also go in Gooden's memorandum for record. "Let's stay positive and make the best of this. I'm sure it will be resolved to everyone's satisfaction…and I'm sure that the outcome will ultimately benefit everyone at Winkle and Straub."

Garvin was not going to beg. "I assume this leave begins tomorrow."

"As a matter of fact, as Mr. Straub wanted to give you plenty of time to prepare the Hemings case, your leave begins at 1:00 P.M. today." Gooden gestured and turned toward the doorway of her cubicle. "Several boxes have been prepared." There, in her doorway, were about seven new cardboard boxes, waiting to be filled. *How did they get there?*

"Please feel free to take whatever office supplies you believe you will need."

The heat left her—instead, she was cold. Very, very cold.

Gooden turned back to her, removed a pen from his pocket, and extended it to her. "Now, please initial the letters so that we can quickly put this all behind us."

Six

"iz Maizie, my life is falling apart! I don't know how much more of this I can stand." Garvin paced back and forth while raking her fingers through her hair. As hard as she walked, she could have worn a groove in the floor in front of the stalls.

The older woman stopped cleaning and turned to face her. "Now, you going to have to get ahold of yourself. You going to pull every hair you got right out of your head."

"What am I going to do? I can't believe this is happening to me. I work hard, Miz Maizie...why is this happening to me?"

"You asking the wrong question, honey." Miz Maizie expertly wrestled the mop into the squeezing mechanism on her bucket.

Garvin stopped pacing, but still felt frantic. "What do you mean? What question?"

Miz Maizie stared deep into Garvin's eyes as though looking to find something there. "You not ready to ask the question yet. You not even ready for me to try to tell you what it is."

"I hate that! I hate when people do that. It doesn't help; what am I supposed to do?"

The older woman stopped mopping and smiled what appeared to be a sympathetic smile at Garvin. "I'm sure you do, honey. I'm sure you do hate it. But you in a situation right now that you can't fix by arguing, you can't take control over it. And Who I would tell you to ask what to do, you don't want to ask. So you just gone have to wait it out." Miz Maizie returned to her mopping. "What I can tell you is that it will get better. It's probably gone be worse for a while…then one day, it'll just get better. Now while you stopped, can you move out of the way so I can get to them stalls? Thank you."

"I'll understand it better by and by, right? Well I need to understand right now! Gooden, everybody, they have me right where they've been trying to get me the whole time. I'm going to lose my job! If I try to defend myself, they say I'm belligerent. If I say that I know Gooden is trying to get me fired, they say I'm paranoid. And they're using the very policies put in place to protect people like me *from* bias to *accuse* me of bias. No details, no facts, no statements. Gooden says it and that's that, my career is over."

Garvin's eyes filled with tears. It took all her strength to keep them from falling from her eyes, so she had no strength left to keep her voice from squeaking and quaking when she spoke. "I'm a good lawyer, Miz Maizie. I work hard for my clients and I treat them with respect. I knew they didn't like me, but I thought being a good lawyer…"

"You thought that would be enough to protect you from the people that don't want you here. That it would be enough for them to overlook the reasons they might not like you." Miz Maizie shook her head.

"I'm so embarrassed, Miz Maizie. I'm so humiliated. I can see it in their eyes, how they're so glad this is happening. Glad I've been taken down a peg. Glad that now they can feel like they're better than me. And there's nobody to help me. They even got to Mr. Straub." Garvin covered her face with her hands. She felt like a weak, fragile, defenseless little girl. "What am I going to do?"

Garvin heard Miz Maizie put down her mop and pull off her

gloves. She stepped closer to Garvin and put her arms around her. "I can't tell you about what you going to do later on, baby. But right now, you're going to wash your face. You're going to hold your head up and gather up your things, just like other people have had to do before you. And every step you take, as you walk out the door, you're going to remind yourself that your job is not what makes you who you are. You're going to remind yourself that not everyone here wishes harm to you. You got people in your corner, more people than you think." Garvin wrapped her hands in Miz Maizie's uniform and buried her face there to muffle her sobs.

"You going to remember that the same person you were before you came through that door is the same person who's leaving. Nobody can take that from you unless you let 'em. You going to tell yourself that it's some strong people praying for you—even if you won't pray for yourself—and you gone remember that *I* told you that no weapon formed against you shall prosper. You're going to remember that a lot of good people paid a big price—some blood, some beatings, some prison—for you to be able to get to this place, and you not going to give up because of this little price you might have to pay. You going to walk out of here with dignity and make me even prouder than I was the day you first walked in here. And you going to keep hope in your heart."

Miz Maizie walked Garvin to the sink and splashed cold water on her face. "Besides, Miss Garvin, you know it ain't over till the fat lady sings. And I ain't struck up a tune yet!"

Garvin laughed in spite of herself. She allowed Miz Maizie to wipe her face, and took comfort in the old woman's touch as Miz Maizie straightened her hair.

"Now, you go on. We'll be talking. Besides that, I need to hit that spot right where you standing with the mop and I'll be done.

Move that 'Do not enter' sign out of the way when you go out."

Garvin took a deep breath, held it, stepped to the doorway, and did not look back.

The menu flapped open and shut. Garvin picked at the folder, put it down, then pressed her hand to her forehead. She picked up her glass of water and took a sip, most of which spilled on her blouse. "Great! What else can go wrong?"

"Garvin, you've got to get a grip on yourself. This is going to blow over. And look, at least my trip was cancelled and I'm able to be here for you. Thank God for small favors.

"Besides, you know Mr. Straub has to know that Gooden is up to something." Jonee flipped through her menu. "He didn't get to be the second name in Winkle and Straub by being stupid." Jonee was tiny, even more petite than Garvin, and in her black, tailored suit she looked lost in the red leather seat cushions.

What else could go wrong? Garvin put both of her elbows on the table, rested her face in her palms and slowly shook her head. "Why is this happening?"

"Oh, Garvin, come on."

The waiter stopped at their table and Jonee ordered curry chicken with paneang sauce. "I don't know why I even look at the menu, I always order the same thing," she said to Garvin when the waiter walked away. "Why didn't you order?"

"I can't eat. This is crazy."

"No. It happens to people all the time. Look at the Hemings case."

"This is not *like* the Hemings case."

"How do you know? Have you read it?"

"No, but I'm not like *him.*"

Jonee looked away.

"Do you think that's what this is about? Do you think it's about race?"

"In part."

Garvin shook her head and closed her eyes while Jonee spoke. She couldn't bear to look at her.

"Why is that so unbelievable? Alcoholics get jobs, murderers get jobs, so—racists get jobs too."

"This is 2000."

"And so? You know Gooden has problems. I don't think he likes anyone, not even himself. And yes, I think he has issues with your color, so what? I don't understand why that freaks you out, why it's so unbelievable. It happens all over the world."

"What do you mean?" Garvin looked up at Jonee.

"I remember when I was in Thailand, when I was a little girl, hearing how some Thai people talked about Korean people. Same thing. Same stereotypes. I don't hear it so much anymore. I just don't think it helps to try to pretend it's not there. You shouldn't let it hold you back, but you shouldn't walk around wearing blinders either." Jonee pushed a lock of dark hair behind her ear.

Garvin wanted to be somewhere else. *Anywhere but here.* Anywhere that would remove her from the pain, from the embarrassment, from the failure.

"I've thought about it a lot, Garvin…why you try to deny that it's there. I still haven't figured it out. It's like on some unconscious levels you acknowledge that racism goes on, but then, consciously, you deny it. I'm working on a theory…the meat of it is just still out of my grasp."

"You know what, Jonee?" Garvin looked around the restaurant at the plants, at pictures of exotic fruits and unusual temples. "I don't want to talk about this, about race, about Hemings, about any of it. I have to figure out what I'm going to do about my life."

"Lighten up, Garvin. You act like it's all over. You'll be back. Why would Mr. Straub have assigned you the Hemings case if you weren't coming back?"

"Maybe he's trying to throw the case."

Jonee took a sip of water. "This is starting to sound like a very bad episode of Perry Mason. Look, Garvin, you're getting your check. A very fat check I might add. Think of it as a paid vacation. You can do all the stuff you'd planned to do at your townhouse—"

"This is my *life*, Jonee. This is not high school. I've lost my job and I told you about Ramona going out with the crazy cleric. And then there's Meemaw. She's never home, and I just have a really bad feeling about the whole thing. This is real, not some soap opera—my life is falling apart."

"Right, your Meemaw's gone man crazy."

The women paused, quiet, while the water set Jonee's plate before her.

"Really, Jonee. Watch." Garvin took her cell phone from her purse and dialed Meemaw. The phone rang and rang. "See? I haven't even told her what's happening to me. What is she going to say? Meemaw's going to be devastated. What am I going to do?"

"Why don't you check the messages on your answering machine. There's probably a message from Meemaw waiting for you." Jonee took a bite of the curry chicken, careful to also pick up blanched vegetables and rice on her fork. "Mmm."

Garvin dialed the number and pushed the buttons to access her answering service. She listened intently, then felt as if the blood were draining from her face. She pushed the button so the message would replay and held it out so Jonee could hear.

A muffled voice spoke from the receiver. It sounded as if the person speaking was intentionally disguising his or her voice, as though a handkerchief or some other cloth had been placed over the mouthpiece. "There's trouble...your Meemaw...that man... GoGo Walker...women...his past ...check L.A. papers...a player...better come quick." The telephone line went dead.

Her friend stopped chewing.

"Jonee, I'm sorry, but can you take care of this?" Garvin motioned toward the drinks and the food on the table.

"Sure. You just had tea anyway." Jonee covered her mouth with her napkin.

Garvin slid from the booth. "And I need you to do me a favor." Jonee nodded, her mouth still full. "I need you to check the back issues of the L.A. newspapers—*The Times,* etc. Maybe you should check farther out, like the *San Diego Union Tribune* or the *San Francisco Chronicle.* Hit all of them, okay? Check for the name GoGo Walker. Maybe social-type stuff. Even criminal stuff, okay? You've got my numbers. When you've got something, call me." Garvin stood, stopped next to her friend, then looked down into her eyes.

"I'm going home."

Seven

◆

arvin turned off of Interstate 95, then onto State Highway 421. Eighteen miles blurred past her. It was always the same. Something jolted inside of her when she passed the first dented metal sign: Cape Fear River. She motored over the small bridge and imagined the water rushing beneath her. Garvin recalled, almost verbatim, her teachers' descriptions of the river.

The Cape Fear River and its tributaries are an invaluable natural resource available to we citizens of North Carolina. It is the largest and most industrialized river system in our state and has tributaries in twenty-nine of our one hundred counties. Over a quarter of our state's population resides within the Cape Fear River basin. The Cape Fear River system provides freshwater for business and residential uses, routes for waterborne transportation, various recreational opportunities, critical wildlife and fisheries habitat, as well as a number of other functions and benefits.

That was the classroom definition. But Garvin knew more. The Cape Fear sometimes looked like a sheet of dark glass near sandy beaches. And the Cape Fear, in darker more hidden places, also held secrets. Sometimes its currents, like gnarled hands, reached out for leaves or branches that hung too close, pulling them along.

The water held hidden things, mysterious things, and whispered stories. It cradled things best forgotten. Garvin shuddered—it happened every time she crossed the river.

While the driving rock beat of Lenny Kravitz's "Are You Gonna Go My Way" pumped from the stereo speakers in her Lexus and brought her back to reality, Garvin turned off of the highway onto the main road, Highway 74, that lead to and through Jacks Creek.

As hard as she tried to push the accelerator down, the Atlantis Blue Lexus seemed to slow to the thirty-five miles per hour posted next to the aqua-and-white town limits welcome sign.

She was home.

Another trip through the way-back time machine. She had made short trips home to visit Meemaw, but three whole months... The car seemed to move slower and slower.

On both sides of the road there were fields. Trees draped with Spanish moss bordered the fields. Some of the land was covered with family gardens, full of vegetables, nestled around homes. The homes, dotted here and there, were mostly older. Toys and bikes littered the front yards. Some had fruit trees or pecan trees planted nearby. Her eyes also detected a sporadic outhouse tucked here and there behind some of the homes. Along the road there were ornamental trees with tiny blooms in bright colors—violet, pink, white, and bright blue.

Occasionally there was what looked to be an abandoned wooden barn or shack, unpainted and barely standing. Garvin knew from years in Jacks Creek that the buildings may have looked abandoned, but could easily be home to an individual or family.

No computer, no cable, no Sesame Street, no television. No electricity, no toilet, no well, no water.

No subway, no bus, no cabs. No streetlights, no stoplights, no neon.

Small, rust-covered trailers peeked out from groups of trees. Telephone poles and wire fences were covered, almost unrecognizable beneath rapidly creeping emerald-colored kudzu vines.

Everyone she drove past waved to her—men, women, strangers. She was in the country. Garvin passed a boy, probably no more than ten with a fishing pole propped on his shoulder. Just as likely, in the winter, that pole might be replaced with a rifle as the boy searched for a rabbit or a coon, something to fill his family's pot.

In some of the larger fields, workers picked early summer tobacco. Garvin knew tobacco harvesting would mean more families coming to town to buy clothes and shoes, to get haircuts and go to beauty shops. It would mean more cash for groceries and fewer food stamps. The harvest meant more contracts for car sales—even though those cars might be repossessed during the dormant winter. Harvest meant a respite from the hard poverty that most of Jacks Creek suffered during the cold season. It meant doctor's appointments, dentist's appointments, and medication that had to be put off when times were harder. Tobacco harvest meant more smiles. It also meant that blueberry harvest would soon be at hand.

Blueberry bushes. Some of the fields were planted with what looked to be acres and acres of the fruit plants. *"I get five dollars a flat! A nice shiny, crisp, new five-dollar bill every time I hand the man a flat!"* She could remember the voices of the pickers, all the buzz about the blueberries and all the money that could be made. Garvin recalled conversations among the workers about which grower had the cleanest fields, which ones gave the fairest prices, about how some fields had blueberries so big they looked like grapes—dark fruit so ripe it just rolled off the bush right into the pickers' hands. She could see images of them talking, their heads wrapped in scarves or topped with old broad-brimmed straw hats. Some of the women carried babies they had brought with them to the fields. Sometimes whole families worked in the fields, picking for fast money, immediate money.

Garvin recalled how thirsty the workers would be—after hours and days stooping to pick unprotected under the biting sun, after riding back home on hot overstuffed buses—spending some of their hard-earned money on sodas and juices.

Still, it was five dollars a flat—sometimes six when things went well; sometimes three-fifty when times were hard. Garvin could rarely bring herself to buy blueberries in the city where stores sold a pint of blueberries for more than people—people *she* knew—were paid for picking the whole twelve pints in one flat.

She turned off the CD and gave in to the ebb and flow of Jacks Creek, and to the shadow of her mother's voice.

"I love you, baby…" She thought she could feel her mother's lipstick kisses on her cheek, nose, and forehead.

"Where you going, Mommy?" She'd always been afraid her mother might not come back. Sometimes it was days before she saw her.

"Shh. Not so loud, baby. We don't want to wake up Meemaw, do we? Mommy's not going far. Just going on a little adventure. Just going to meet up with your daddy. I told you, we gonna get married when he comes back home. He said so, and you gone be the flower girl." Garvin could still smell her mother's face powder. "And we're gone have our own house with a fence and a yard so you can play outside." She could feel her mother's hands stroking the hair near her temples. "You wait till you see your daddy. You all look so much alike. Same lips, same pretty hair. It's gone be like a fairy tale. He said he can't wait to see his baby and hold her on his lap."

Garvin still remembered the signal. Late at night, the phone would ring once. Her mother, excited, would come to her with the same breathless story and then slip away into the night.

But not before they sang. Usually, her mother would sing lead, softly so Meemaw wouldn't hear.

And Garvin hummed and sang background waiting, waiting until she could sing her favorite line. *"…no river wide enough to keep me from you!"* The river she imagined, when she sang, was always the Cape Fear.

"Shh, you gonna wake Meemaw!" Her mother would kiss her again and then be gone. Garvin would sit on the porch and wait until Meemaw awakened and then called her inside. She remembered at night, when the house was still, she would slip out of her bed to her knees and pray for God to keep her mother safe and to send her home.

And He always sent her mother back safely—until the night of Garvin's tenth birthday. The old newspaper accounts said her mother was traveling with a man in a car.

Garvin pushed the radio remote and kicked on Foxy 95.9 FM. *It's silly. It's ancient history. My mother was weak.* The fairy tale was over. That was then…but she wasn't about to lose her Meemaw now. She reached down for her pack of cigarettes, removed one, and lit it. *Look, I'll stop again when this is over—Garvin argued against her conscience—right now, I need something.*

She would have to drive to Annapolis to get the ivory-colored interior of her car detailed, to get rid of the smoke, just as soon as she got back to D.C. But she'd worry about that later. The road pulled her closer to Meemaw's house.

Monique looked at the wall clock. It was almost time for seventh period, but she wasn't going. Just one day. Just one day when she could leave school and not have to listen to the snickers or watch the groups whispering—the preps, the geeks, the jocks, the freaks, the yos—and wonder if they were really talking about, pointing at her. *I just need a break. Just an hour.* She would leave early and miss all the eyes, miss having to wonder if it was about her skin or her *little secret.*

She pretended to be solving the trig problems—what was the point anyway? Her life was over, she wasn't going to college… plenty of people had told her as much—but her eyes were really following the long hand on the clock. It was funny, but she had never noticed before how the hand seemed to linger at each tick mark, as if it weren't sure if it wanted to go on to the next one. Finally, after sixty hesitations, it made significant progress—a minute passed. Soon as she heard the irritating buzz that indicated the period was over, she would slip out.

At 2:45 she moved out the classroom door with her other classmates.

"Hey, que pasa, muchachas?"

She almost bumped into Josephina and Carmen as she hurried toward the exit.

"What's happening, girlfriend?" Jo repeated her statement in English.

"Girl, you better look where you going. You about to run somebody down! Where are you in a hurry to? You can't be *that* excited about class." Carmen was still twirling the tip of one of her braids.

Monique hoped that her face was not flushing. "I'm on my way to…" She couldn't think of an answer, so she just let her voice trail into nothing, hoping they wouldn't question her further.

"Whatever." Carmen turned to Josephina—"Come on, Jo"—

then back to Monique. "We've got chem lab. See ya." Monique watched the two girls walk away, then turned quickly back in the direction of the door.

"Hey, Monique!" Lacey's hand grabbed her and pulled Monique out of the throng moving in the direction of the door. It would be too late if she got to the exit when the crowd had thinned. "Did you decide about the party? Are you going? Ricky's definitely going to be there!" Even in the hallway, Lacey couldn't stop moving.

"I don't know, Lacey." Monique looked in the direction of the shifting crowd—it would be thinning soon. "We still got time, right? I gotta go, okay? Okay?" She started moving and inserted herself back among the other students.

"Call me, okay?" She heard Lacey's voice over the top of the stream of bodies. Monique kept easing closer and closer to the left. At the door, she pushed and quickly stepped out.

GoGo opened the door to his BMW convertible for Miz Hightower. Others called her Meemaw, but to him she was always Evangelina, Miz Hightower. She had a lot of class. Why had it taken him so long to see how much sophistication women like Miz Hightower had? How much they had to offer?

"I love this car! I've been thinking it would be just the thing for me. Folks' tongues would really wag then; not that they're not wagging enough now. Then I thought, why buy one? I'll just keep you riding me around in yours." She laughed. "Like the song says, 'Let's give 'em something to talk about!' Whoever thought I would be having so much fun in my seventies!"

GoGo slipped into his seat, which automatically adjusted. "It's almost impossible for me to believe your age. You're a beautiful woman." He reached to turn on the CD player; Brian McKnight began to sing "You Could Be the One."

Evangelina Hightower waved GoGo's comment away with her hand. "Oh, you go on and get out of here. You don't have to pull my leg to get me to ride with you, precious." She cuffed him on the arm and laughed again. There was something about the way she said "precious." She began to adjust her seat. "I just love these things. You know, this is way too much car for one man...I'm going to have to see what I can do about that!" She winked at him. "Well, let's get this show on the road!"

GoGo smiled at her as he started the engine. "My pleasure, Miz Evangelina. My pleasure." He smiled at her, then turned his head as he backed out of her driveway and onto the street. They drove south on Eden Rock.

GoGo blew his horn. "Smitty!" he yelled as they passed the snowball truck just before turning onto Courtney. "School's not out yet, is it?" GoGo nodded toward the girl standing near the play yard fence.

"That poor child. That's Monique." Meemaw waved, but it did not appear that Monique saw her. "She's had a hard time; just looks lost."

"Yep. I see a lot of young people looking that way. Somebody needs to do something." They drove on toward their destination.

"Oh, goodness! Here comes the truck!" Sister Inez abandoned her usual station and started for the door. The whimsical music flowed into the shop, even through the glass window. She stopped and turned around. "Oh, shoot. I forgot my purse." By the time she dug through her purse for her money—which was tied in a knot in a flowered handkerchief—several other women had gathered outside ahead of her.

"We're going to have to get somebody to bring us a snowball. I've already started putting the relaxer in your hair." The client twisted and turned in Big Esther's chair apparently trying to see what was going on outside. "You gonna have to hold still now. I'm trying to be careful to just put this stuff on the new growth. But if you keep moving, I'm liable to mess up." Big Esther was trying to see too.

Women, all shapes, sizes, and shades of brown, were crowding around Smitty's snowball truck. Big Esther could feel her mouth watering. He probably did as much business with grown women as he did with the children, maybe even more. Smitty was a little bitty thing, and that head looked kind of rough. Still, she couldn't deny that her chest pounded a little when he came around.

Big Esther was careful to make straight evenly spaced parallel parts in the client's hair. On the new growth, she carefully combed relaxer cream. She couldn't see everything she wanted to see outside because she had to pay attention to the job at hand. Big Esther looked up from the touch-up she was doing to catch glimpses of what was going on.

The women outside were covered with rollers, hair clamps, beauty capes; some wore plastic bags on their heads. Something about Smitty and his snowballs just called them like the Pied Piper. She could feel her own feet shifting, ready to run out the door along with them. What for? All he had was snowballs. And blueberry syrup.

Esther yelled out the door, "Hey, you all left my door standing wide open. Somebody better come back here and close my door, or I'm locking all of you out." The last person in line—a comb stuck in her head—turned and slowly, constantly looking back over her shoulder, made her way back to close the shop door. "While you here," Big Esther said when the woman came to the door, "get a snowball for me—large—and one for this lady here." The patron with the comb in her hair looked caught, hood-winked, bamboozled.

Big Esther leaned forward over the client in her chair and asked, "What size?"

"Small is fine," said the client. "With blueberry juice, please."

Big Esther stood and nodded. "Yeah, I want blueberry juice, too." She could almost taste the sweet juice on her tongue, the cold press of the ice on her lips, the cool mixture sliding down her throat.

"Esther, you know I can't carry all that." The patron with the comb stuck in her hair whined. "I only got two hands."

"I know *you* ain't *complaining,* Bernice. Not after I worked *you* in *today* after you *missed* your appointment *Saturday* without *calling* to let me know." The patron rolled her eyes. "No point in rolling your eyes. You know I'm right. Take the money out of what you owe me for doing your hair."

"I couldn't call, Esther."

"What you mean, you couldn't call?"

"My phone was off—disconnected. I had to wait until I got paid yesterday."

Big Esther grunted. "Just get us our snowballs and stop making excuses, please."

"I declare." The patron turned to walk back to the truck.

Outside the window, the patron joined the line while Sister Inez wiggled her head, obviously flirting with the snowball man. "Hey!" Big Esther hollered after the woman. "Tell Smitty Big Esther said 'hey!'"

Eight

◆

Garvin pulled into Meemaw's gravel driveway, rocks crunching under the car's wheels, all the way back to just in front of the garage door. She stopped the engine, and sat still in the car. Good thing she wasn't in the clunker she drove in high school; Meemaw would have heard her coming from blocks away.

She felt foolish—what would she say to Meemaw? How would she explain about her job? More to the point, how would she explain arriving in Jacks Creek at her grandmother's door unannounced? She couldn't tell everything—couldn't tell her she was there to bust up her crazy relationship with a younger man, with a gigolo…

Her grandmother was getting older, but she was still feisty.

Meemaw who had raised her and kept her sane. Meemaw who had held her and held back the world. Meemaw who, when Garvin was a child, seemed to know everything she tried to hide. Meemaw, who was her soft spot.

No man was going to do to Meemaw what had been done to Garvin's mother.

Maybe, Garvin thought, she should cover what she was omitting by telling all there was to tell about the case and about her situation at Winkle and Straub. Meemaw would be so concerned about her, Garvin would have GoGo out of the way before her grandmother even noticed he was gone.

She sat in the car for a few more minutes practicing the story. She would have to be good; the story would have to be tight. Meemaw could detect a rotten story from miles away. She looked at her image in the rearview mirror. That was the expression, mildly anxious and a little irritated. She couldn't look as if she were questioning or snooping in any way. Garvin lifted her shoulders, turned, and opened the automobile door. *I'm ready.*

Everything was the same, even the way the large gravel piled higher in the center of the driveway and flattened on the sides. Bushes with small, bright blue flowers grew along the concrete pathway leading from the driveway to the front door. Flaming red gladioli grew from a circular area in the front yard that was built up and surrounded by aging bricks. A familiar concrete birdbath sat just off to the side. The large windows on either side of the door seemed framed with white cotton curtains bordered by ruffles made from the same material. The two windows were bordered at the bottom by green-painted, rectangular pots full of red, white, yellow, and blue flowers.

Garvin stopped at the bottom of the red brick steps that led to Meemaw's door. The wrought-iron railings looked freshly painted. She was home. As she climbed each stair, she imagined more clearly Meemaw's face as she would greet her, the outstretched arms, Meemaw calling her name.

She opened the screen door and first tried the doorknob. Good, Meemaw was at least keeping the doors locked. Garvin pushed the small, rectangular, lighted doorbell. No answer. She pushed again. Maybe Meemaw was in the kitchen, now making her way to the door.

No answer.

Garvin pulled her old keys from the pocket of her jeans. Good thing she had brought them with her. Meemaw must be "indisposed." Garvin smiled. For some reason it had always given her such pleasure to answer the phone and have to report that her Meemaw was "indisposed." Garvin laughed to herself as she turned the key in the lock.

"Meemaw." She stood in the middle of the living room calling. "Meemaw." She stopped to breathe in the place where she had spent her childhood. There was the same furniture, the same knickknacks on the mantle, the same floor lamp.

She called a little louder this time. "Meemaw."

Same well-cared-for lace curtains. It almost seemed to be the same light coming through the window, the same light that shone through all the windows. Garvin closed her eyes, and for a moment, in her mind's eye, sat on Meemaw's lap, her head cradled on Meemaw's bosom. Safe and loved…

She was home.

She opened her eyes; she had to remember the task at hand. At least her grandmother had an answering machine…and the red light was blinking. "Meemaw?" Garvin walked toward the kitchen, then toward Meemaw's bedroom, still calling. She walked quickly back to the kitchen, across the room, and looked out the back window over the sink. Ivy plants on stacked shelves framed the glass.

Maybe Meemaw was outside? Garvin moved to the back door and cracked it open. "Meemaw?" No sign of her.

At the end of the yard was the in-law apartment her grandfather had built years ago. A smaller version of Meemaw's house—still vacant. Garvin couldn't remember much about her grandfather, but she seemed to recollect a conversation between him and Meemaw about the apartment, why it was needed when there was enough room for everyone in the house.

"Evangelina, I got a feeling you might need it someday." As Garvin

recalled it, her grandfather's words had settled the matter. And there it stood.

Garvin looked back from the in-law to the kitchen where she stood. *Where is she?* Meemaw was always home—after school, after work—she could always be counted on. Meemaw was always home. Suddenly, Garvin's mouth twisted with displeasure and her foot began to pat. *GoGo!* Obviously, she hadn't come home a moment too soon. Garvin was sure Meemaw must be with GoGo. *What is she thinking?*

She needed a smoke. Garvin pulled one from the pack in her pocket. She would have to remember to stick them in her purse. She looked around the kitchen—of course, there were no ashtrays. Garvin looked through the cabinets; there were jars of canned tomatoes, string beans, beets, and blueberry preserves—but no ashtrays. She stood over the sink allowing the cold water to run—she would have to make sure she got rid of the evidence. Meemaw didn't allow smoking, especially in her house.

Whatever. I'm a grown woman, for goodness' sake. Garvin snuffed out the butt under the running water and looked for some place to throw it away. She looked at the garbage disposal switch, flicked it on, and dropped the last of the cigarette down the sink. She was a woman, but there was no point in getting Meemaw worked up, at least not until GoGo was out of the picture. Better not to leave any traces.

GoGo! Garvin turned off the water and looked toward the living room. She needed to get moving, she was going to run out of time.

Then she remembered the answering machine—it might hold a clue.

Quickly she moved to sit in a wooden chair that sat in front of the little table that held the machine. How would she explain listening to the messages? No big deal, keep covering with the obvious. She was checking because she was worried about her Meemaw. She pressed the button.

"Hello, Miss Evangelina. Sorry I missed you. I have the ripest, sweetest tomatoes and I was going to bring you a couple on my way home after I lock the store. Sorry I missed you. Of course, you know this is your friend Larry Green."

Well, that was of no help. Garvin had known Mr. Green for years. He was the owner of Green's Grocers, the small neighborhood mom-and-pop grocery store; only Mrs. Green had died years earlier. Garvin couldn't count the number of trips she had made to Mr. Green's for milk, eggs, and stuff. Mr. Green—that was no help at all.

No new-millennium gigolo is going to capture my grandmother. Garvin checked the next message, something about a church women's auxiliary meeting; she skipped past it.

"Miz Evangelina, I was just calling—" Garvin paused the tape. It was Big Esther's voice, it had been years since Garvin talked to her friend—*"to remind you about your appointment this afternoon at four. See you then."*

Esther. Garvin's best friend, sometimes, her only friend—the one who understood, the one she had opened her heart and told her secrets to—but that was long ago. She was in Jacks Creek now to rescue her Meemaw.

What had Esther said? At four. That gave Garvin some time to check things out, to find out just how far things had gotten. But she would have to work efficiently. She listened to all the messages—five all together—and not one of the messages was from GoGo, and not one of them sounded like the mystery voice that had warned her to come. A voice she would have to be careful to listen for while she was in Jacks Creek.

Garvin went out to the car, brought in her luggage, and dropped it in her old bedroom. She lay the case files on the desk that was near the foot of her bed—the same bed and the same desk that had been hers in high school. She stared at the files for a moment. She had started going through them briefly before leaving for Jacks Creek. A sigh escaped her; she would deal with the files later. Right now she had more pressing issues.

Garvin changed into a grungy sweatshirt. She walked to the bathroom, and looking in the bathroom mirror, systematically brushed her hair until it wrapped completely around her head. Then she tied it with a turquoise silk head scarf. She was ready for business. She had been disappointed at first that Meemaw was not home, but actually this had worked for the good—she was free to investigate.

Garvin started back down the hallway to the living room, but could not resist Meemaw's bedroom door. There was Meemaw's bed—the bed where she had spent so many nights crying after her mother… There was Meemaw's dresser and on top of it was the same bouquet talcum powder. Garvin lifted the can to her nose and smelled. Her eyes watered.

He was not going to have her Meemaw.

First she sifted through the laundry hamper, but found nothing suspicious. Then she checked Meemaw's clothing drawers. "GoGo Walker. What kind of name is that?" Garvin mumbled as she looked through leg warmers, sweat pants, gym socks; evidence that Meemaw was really working out. Of course, that didn't prove anything either way. "Trainer, my big toe!" Poor innocent Meemaw, he probably began his seedy seduction by pretending to be a fitness expert.

Garvin found nothing to aid her case, but she would make him sorry he ever laid eyes on her Meemaw all the same. How could something like this happen to Meemaw?

Next Garvin moved to the hall closet just off from the living room. No unusual coats or jackets, but the boxes on the top shelf might hold a clue. She dragged a footstool to the closet, looked around for telephone books, and then stacked three of them on top of the stool. She grabbed the boxes in the front and yanked off the lids. Nothing, just papers lined up neatly and systematically. Just like Meemaw. Garvin closed the boxes and stepped down from her makeshift platform to set the boxes on the ground so she could reach the ones farther in the back.

Back on top of the telephone books—white pages, yellow pages, white pages—Garvin tiptoed and stretched for the rear boxes. They were really far back—another telephone book would help. This was nothing for Meemaw to reach, her much taller grandmother had always seemed to put things just out of her grasp. Garvin stepped down and searched the room for another book in the kitchen closet, in the utility closet, on the TV stand under the TV. *I'm wasting time.* She went back to the living room closet then stepped back onto her stack. She would just have to reach higher.

Garvin stretched higher…reaching…reaching…and gave a little jump. The top book shifted. *Uh-oh!* She knew she was not going to be able to catch herself, and cursed as she fell. Good thing Meemaw was not at home.

Whack! She slammed her back on the hardwood floor; her left elbow hit the wall. Garvin groaned, then surveyed the damage. Nothing broken. The worst of it was that her right arm had hit the boxes and the contents dumped out and scattered on the floor. "Great!"

Garvin picked herself up, then got on her hands and knees to pick up the papers and letters. She was never going to get them back in order. That kid feeling came over her, that panic that she was going to be in trouble. *Funny how you come home and you're a kid again. This is silly.* She was not a kid, not anymore. She was in control of her life—she laid down the law for others, now. Garvin Daniels no longer lived at the mercy and whim of other people—she was in control.

As Garvin moved to pick up the letters, her left foot caught the leg of the coffee table that sat near the couch. *Crash!* A small ivory-colored dove lay on the floor, looking serene despite the fact that it was missing a wing. *Meemaw is going to kill me!*

Garvin scrambled to gather the letters, close them in the boxes, and place the boxes back on the shelves. She put the foot-stool back in place, then grabbed the dewinged dove and stamped into the kitchen.

This is ridiculous! She was a lawyer for goodness' sake—at least for the time being. Garvin pulled out and shoved closed drawers looking for glue. Finally she found a tube and set about repairing the bird. *This is stupid!* She was losing time and making clumsy mistakes. Still, if Meemaw found her bird broken…better to take this time. Keep a cool head.

She still had time to go through the most important spot before she went to meet Meemaw at Big Esther's Beauty Shop.

Garvin made herself delicately apply glue to all the crannies and then carefully reseat the wing. She held the dove up to the light. *Good as new.* She walked back to the living room and placed the turtledove back in its place on the table—maybe just a little bit farther back so the ivy plant leaves covered it, just to give the bird the time it needed to dry. Garvin sniffed the air. Glue, definitely, glue. She marched to the front door and opened it. The screen door would block the bugs, but let in a fresh breeze to clear the air in the room. She sniffed again. Somehow the scent of the flowers outside was more real in Jacks Creek. The place had *something* going for it. Then she turned and looked across the room.

Meemaw's desk—a treasure trove.

She should have started there. If there was going to be evidence anywhere, it would be the desk. She had always wanted to go through Meemaw's desk anyway.

Monique was glad she had decided to come to Miz Hightower's. That man's red convertible wasn't in the driveway, so maybe she would be able to visit with Miz Evangelina, at least for a little while. For a little while she could feel what it must be like, pretend that someone cared for her. Pretend that Miz Hightower might be her grandmother, that her life was different, that nothing had ever happened…

When she reached the area of sidewalk just in front of the driveway, Monique noticed a strange car with D.C. plates. She stopped, then decided to go ahead.

As she walked up the sidewalk she noticed Miz Evangelina's door was open. Miz Hightower never left her door open unless she was outside, and she was nowhere to be seen. Monique climbed the steps quietly, wary that something might be wrong. Cupping her hands around her eyes she leaned forward to look in the screen door.

A woman was on her knees digging through Miz Evangelina's desk compartments. Monique could feel her pulse increase. *I need to look calm.* "Who are you? Where's Miz Hightower?"

Rear in the air and hands flying, the woman did not seem to hear Monique's question. She spoke louder, "Did you hear me? I said, where's Miz Hightower?" Things did not look good.

The woman jumped and turned, papers went flying. She looked guilty—things did not look good. At first she seemed to be thinking of an explanation; then she looked angry. "Who wants to know?"

Monique could feel her breathing getting shallow. "I said, where's Miz Hightower?" It didn't matter how afraid she was. She was not going to let somebody hurt Miz Hightower. The woman in front of her was not very big, but she looked mean. In fact, the woman seemed well practiced in looking mean. She was smaller, but obviously meaner than her older friend. Had she overpowered Miz Hightower?

"And *I* said, who wants to know?" The woman menaced toward the door. Monique had to force herself not to take a step backward—D.C. license plates on the woman's car, her head wrapped in a rag, a ratty sweatshirt—she had heard all the news stories and there was no telling what was going on inside Miz Evangelina's house.

"What have you done to Miz Hightower? What are you doing digging through her desk?" Monique looked into the room, trying to see past the little, mean woman for some hint of Miz Hightower's whereabouts.

"Who am I? I'm her granddaughter."

Monique stared at the woman. *Her granddaughter?* Not! "Well, she never mentioned you to me." Monique watched the woman's expression, looking for signs, wondering if she should just bolt and call the police. The scarf on the woman's head was tied just like on TV.

The woman glared at her. "Why doesn't that surprise me…not *now,* anyway! Not with all that's obviously going on here. I'm not surprised at all that Meemaw never mentioned *me."* The woman pushed open the screen door—forcing Monique to quickly hop to avoid the door—and stepped outside.

Nine

arvin stared up at the girl in front of her. *What else can go wrong?* She would have to get rid of the girl quickly. Nothing was going right. She would have to take control of the situation.

Garvin gave the girl the once-over. The teenager did look like the type Meemaw would take under her wing; she looked like she needed someone. Maybe, just maybe, she could get some information from the girl. Maybe it would be better to play good cop, just for now anyway. She would set the girl straight later on, after she got what she needed—what she needed to get Meemaw out of this situation.

"Look, I'm sorry…" She looked a question at the girl, a question that asked her name.

"Monique."

"Right…Monique. Pretty name." Garvin searched the girl's eyes and forced a smile. "I just drove in from D.C. straight from work and—okay, I'll admit it—I'm a little cranky because of it." She put on her most winning smile, the one she practiced for the juries. "Let's start again, okay?" She reached her hand to Monique. Pretty girl. She just had this look, like all her relatives had died. The teenager slowly raised her hand, still looking wary, and Garvin grasped it and shook. Not too hard, just a warm, friendly shake.

"Miz Hightower, Miz Evangelina, is my Meemaw—my grandmother. I was just going through some things…trying to surprise

her before she got home. You startled me. Sorry I blew up at you."
She couldn't tell if the "good cop" routine was working.

"She never mentioned you."

Garvin was going to have to come up with something to coun-
teract the doubt she saw on the girl's face. *What is she looking at?*
The girl's eyes kept darting back to her hair. What was it?

"Oh, you know Meemaw." Garvin forced a chuckle. "If you
know her at all, you know that when you are with her, she makes
you feel as if you're the only person on the planet." Why was the
child staring at her hair? Garvin smiled and pretended to unself-
consciously reach to smooth her hair. *Shoot! The head rag! How am
I going to play this one off?* Better to keep covering with the obvious.

"Oh, my goodness!" Garvin made good use of the embarrassment she was feeling. "I can't believe I'm standing here with the
rag on my head. You must think I'm crazy." She smiled and really
played it to the hilt, covering her face with her hands. "This is so
embarrassing! I was going through some things, getting some
things in order, and I thought I would wrap my hair to keep the
dust out of it." Garvin pulled the scarf from her hair. "And look
how I'm dressed. No wonder you don't believe me." Garvin tried
another tactic. Most people couldn't stand to say to another person's face that he or she is dishonest. "Come on, I can tell you
don't believe me…you probably think I'm some sort of criminal."
Garvin laughed, keeping her eyes glued to the girl's expression.

"No, I…" The girl looked down. "I don't think you're a criminal."

Garvin took a deep breath. "Actually, Monique—Monique,
right?—actually, I'm an attorney. Can you believe it? Good thing
you're not the kind of person that judges a book by its cover." The
girl gave a slight nod. "You know what? Maybe I should get some
I.D.; I can tell that you are just concerned about my grandmother,

and I appreciate that, Monique. I really do."

"No—" the girl looked away, down, then back at Garvin—
"you don't need I.D., I was just…"

"You were just worried about my grandmother. To tell you the
truth, Monique, so am I. I've been calling and calling and I can't
get her on the phone, so I told the people at my job, 'Look, my
Meemaw comes first—I'm going home!' And gave my car the gas
and burned my way down here; now, I can't find her.

"Listen, Monique, maybe you can help me. Do you have any
idea where she might be? Any ladies she might be with?" Garvin
held her breath.

"Well…" Monique looked unsure. "There's a man who's been
coming over a lot. I've never met him, but I've heard some of the
boys at school say his name. I think it's GoGo. GoGo Walker."

"GoGo?" Garvin forced her voice to sound light. "What kind
of name is that?" *Just wait until I get my hands on him!*

"I don't know, but I see his car over here a lot. I stopped by
today to visit Miz Hightower because…well, she asked me to, and
when I didn't see his car I thought it was okay."

"Well, of course, Monique. I'm sure my grandmother is going
to be so sorry she missed you." Garvin smiled warmly at the girl.
Just wait until I wrap my hands around his throat!

"And I see them a lot, driving around. Him driving her in his
red convertible. He drives a red BMW." Garvin couldn't read the
girl's expression.

*A pimp! A player! My Meemaw is being hustled by a player! I'm
going to kill him.* Garvin made herself grin at the girl. "Isn't that
wonderful! I'm so glad Meemaw has a friend, someone her age
that she can pal around with."

"Well—" Monique bit her lip—"actually, he's not her age. He's
younger, but…" The girl looked away.

Garvin stared at Monique. *She's worried too.* "Younger? Oh well, you know Meemaw, a friend to all mankind." Garvin smiled. *I will kill him when I see him, it would be worth the jail time.* "So, do you know where he works or anything?"

The girl scuffed the toe of her tennis shoe on the brick porch. "Well, I never heard anybody talk about where he works…they just talk about the car, and…"

"And?" *I'm going to torture him before I kill him.* Garvin smiled her most comforting smile at Monique.

"And nothing. That's all I know about him." The girl looked away again.

It will be a slow and painful death. She knew what *they* were talking about—his car and the way he was making a fool of her Meemaw. Not just a player, a big pimp. Garvin had to get rid of this kid before she screamed, she had gotten all the info she was going to get for the day.

"You know what, Monique?" She looked at her watch. "I've really got to run. It's been wonderful meeting you and I am sure I'll be seeing a lot of you. Don't worry, I'll make sure Meemaw knows you came by." Garvin's expression ushered the girl down the steps and closed the door on any further discussion. "But I've got to go, okay? Bye." She went back inside and shut the door abruptly.

This was crazy. How could something like this happen? Garvin walked into the kitchen and sat down; she felt weak. She crumpled in the chair and cried. This was crazy. How could her life be falling apart this way? Her Meemaw! Meemaw was the one who was always dependable, the one who could never be fooled. This was crazy!

And the river, there was always the river.

And her job. Garvin laid her head on her arms and just let the sobs wrack through her body. She had enough worries of her own and here she had to rescue Meemaw, had to be distracted by this when she had enough to worry about—shouldn't have to bother about anything but trying to concentrate on her job. Another series of sobs shook her body. She was just one little woman and this was too much.

And what about Ramona?

Garvin walked to the living room, pulled her cell phone from her purse, and carried it back to the kitchen. She sat down and dialed Ramona's office.

"Good afternoon, Technical Solutions. Ms. Robins speaking. May I help you?"

This time, Garvin didn't bother to return the salutation. "Ramona Kingston, please."

"She's not in. May I take a message?"

"No." Garvin clicked her cell phone off. This was too much. Way too much. Why did everybody expect her to fix everything for them? She had enough problems of her own.

Garvin began to run her hand across her temples. Right now, her Meemaw was the most pressing issue. This snake had obviously tricked his way into Meemaw's life and was making a fool of her. She was not going to let him have her grandmother, use her, destroy her, and then throw her way. He was not going to destroy the one person she had left in the world. She would do whatever she had to do to get him out of Meemaw's life.

Garvin wiped her face. *Whatever* she had to do.

Ten

◆

Garvin drove down Eden Rock in the direction of Big Esther's salon. She would meet Meemaw there.

Actually it was a good place to meet her grandmother; there was no chance that a man like GoGo would have the nerve to sit in the shop with her Meemaw. Big Esther's was the only black beauty shop for miles, and Garvin figured he wouldn't chance coming face to face with one of his other women.

She sat back in her seat and noted the peach and pecan trees that dotted the edges of the road. Jacks Creek had *some* measure of beauty. When she got to the salon, Garvin pulled into a space, parked, walked to the front door, and paused. Her friend had come a long way from the one-room wooden shack in which she had started out doing hair. There was a large, plate glass window with Esther's name on it. Garvin reached for the brass door handle, pushed, and stepped inside.

The feeling of being outside of normal time—of slowing, slowing—stayed with Garvin as she walked through the door. She closed the door softly behind her; no one slammed Esther's door.

Esther had come a long way—she wasn't in the tiny, run-down shack anymore, she had moved up to a storefront. But something about the style of the clock on the wall, something about the macramé plant holders, something about the throw rugs on the linoleum floor, about the water-stained tiles overhead said that

Jacks Creek had fallen behind the pack and seemed to be in no hurry to catch up.

"Check the ones in the back for me." Garvin recognized her friend's voice. The waves gelled into the back of Esther's head cried out "ten years ago." She was a little stouter, but her neck was still slender and graceful. She wore her six feet well. Esther held a rattail comb in one hand and pointed toward a client sitting under an older model hair dryer. The young woman she spoke to, a stranger to Garvin, twisted nonchalantly over to the client and lifted the hood. Except for a quick once-over by the ones who could see her, all the ladies in the shop went on with their conversations as though Garvin weren't there.

"So now that all my business is out in the street—" the younger woman laughed, and so did the rest of the women in the shop—except for one who clicked her tongue where she stood hidden behind the window plants—"who you courting, Esther?"

The women snickered and exchanged looks, then sat forward on their seats, waiting for Esther to answer.

Garvin knew the young woman saw her, even though she did not acknowledge her, had given no clue to Esther that someone was behind her. The young beautician was doing that thing that some country people do—that thing Garvin had forgotten being gone so long from home. She went on with her conversation as though Garvin was not standing there, so that there was time. Plenty of time to acknowledge a stranger, time enough to take in all the details, all the nuances that would fill the young woman in on Garvin's life. A tactic that some unknowing stranger might take for slowness was actually a country-fried, gravy-smothered form of perception.

This might take some time.

"Bit, you know I don't have time for no men." Esther answered the young woman, still unaware of Garvin's presence. "I got a boy and a girl." She nodded her head toward her station. A photo of two children—the littlest one missing two front teeth—peeped out from behind a scattering of rollers, hair clips, and end papers. Peeped from behind a bottle of cola with peanuts resting at the bottom like pearls. "Not to mention that I'm in here almost twenty-four seven doing heads."

Garvin looked around the room while Esther talked. It was definitely the beginning of summer harvesttime. The usual Jacks Creek beauty shop clientele—teachers, preachers' wives, postal workers, store clerks—was supplemented with fieldworkers. Women who usually bought their hair care products, if they bought any, at the Winn Dixie on the aisle that held the health and beauty aids for black people. Women and girls who generally took their beauty treatments at their kitchen sinks or in front of the stove now filled seats in the best and only black beauty shop in town—at least as long as there were tobacco and blueberries.

The women were visitors to town, and their children hid behind their skirts, up under their arms, seemingly afraid to look or speak to the townspeople.

The three couches were full, and there was a head under every dryer. But none of the heads belonged to Meemaw.

While Garvin looked around the room, the girl named Bit smirked at Esther. "Um-hmm." Finally, she changed her gaze and acknowledged Garvin. "Can I help you?" Bit pursed her lips and frowned like something sour was in her mouth.

"I'm looking for my grandmother." It wasn't quite four, and Meemaw was known to run a few minutes behind.

"Garvina? I thought that was you!" A voice came from behind her. "But you so skinny and your hair is another color." Garvin turned to see who owned the voice that came from within the plants by the window. "It's me, Inez. Sister Inez. Sister Inez Zephyr." The woman stepped forward from her hideout.

"Garvina—I mean, Garvin, girl!" Esther's voice broke in before Garvin could think of a comeback for Sister Inez. She turned and found herself face to face with her childhood friend. "What are you doing here?" Esther's almost dimples were in full view.

Now that Garvin had been publicly acknowledged, the clients stared openly and directly at the conversation—unlike what she had become accustomed to in the city.

Esther seemed genuinely glad to see her. "Girl, I can't believe it. I was just thinking about you. What you doing here?"

"Well, I—"

"I'm glad somebody called her!" Sister Inez broke in before Garvin had to speak. "Obviously *somebody's* her friend." She stepped farther away from the plants and looked pointedly at Garvin. "Who called you?"

"Gir-ir-irl!" Esther, rattail comb still in hand and two bobby pins gripped in between her teeth, opened her arms to embrace Garvin, but she spoke to Inez. "If you don't hush your mouth, you going to be walking home with rollers in your head…that's if you got any hair left when you leave here."

Sister Inez drew up, offended. "All I said was—"

Big Esther gave Sister Inez the eye. "All you said was too much."

Sister Inez sank back among the window plants mumbling about being disrespected, unappreciated, and about not coming there again if there was someplace else to go.

Having made short work of her troubles, Esther held her arms open wider and Garvin stepped across about fifteen years and hugged her friend. Grabbing Garvin's hand with the hand that still held the rattail comb, Big Esther grabbed a stool and dragged it close to her station. The clients went back to their conversations. However, Garvin knew they were keeping at least half an eye on her. She sat on the stool Esther offered and rested her feet on the highest rung.

"Is that really Inez Zephyr?" She leaned in to talk softly to Esther—not a whisper, that would be too obvious. Instead Garvin talked softly, careful to keep her facial expression as if they were talking about the weather.

Esther took one the bobby pins from her mouth and used it to pin a curl in place on top of her client's head. "Um-hmm. Same old Inez—foolishness then, foolishness now." She used the other pin to further secure the curl. "Inez looks bad, don't she?" Garvin nodded. "Minding other people's business is hard work. It'll wear you out."

Garvin noticed that Esther's client seemed to be trying not to smile, seemed to be trying to hold her shoulders so they wouldn't shake, seemed to be trying to mind the beauty shop etiquette that said she shouldn't acknowledge that she was overhearing her beautician's conversation with another person.

Garvin looked from the client back to Esther. What did Inez mean? *Did Esther make the mysterious call?* Disguising her voice didn't seem like the kind of thing Esther might do. Still, a lot of time had passed…

"Grab that box of pins for me." Garvin and Esther slipped into a beauty shop ritual, a simple bonding ceremony, a hairdressing practice that affirmed their connection as women. As Esther worked sculpting curls into place, Garvin handed her the pins. It was the same ritual Meemaw had practiced with her, probably the same ritual Esther's mother had practiced with her. Garvin propped her elbows on her knees. It looked as though there were going to be lots of curls; she might as well get comfortable.

Across the room, a patron flopped open a fan magazine. "Girl," she said to no one in particular, "that Denzel is still fine, ain't he?"

Several women nodded in agreement. "He sure is, girl."

The patron showed the picture around the room. "You know that's part of the reason I said yes to marrying Garfield. He reminded me so much of Denzel." She pointed at the picture; some of the other women rolled their eyes. "That's why we named the baby Little Denzel. His daddy just favor Mr. Washington so much!" The patron looked pleased and giggled.

Esther leaned forward and whispered. "Uh-huh…more like Denzel meets the hunchback of Notre Dame." Garvin turned her head and covered her mouth with her arm.

Garvin watched the other women for a while, then thought to ask Esther about the call and watch her face for any telltale signs. "Esther—"

The phone rang. "Wait a minute." Esther grabbed the phone and began to explain that yes, she did do press and curl. She paused as though listening and then explained that yes, she could do touch-ups, but she couldn't take anyone else today. Then she frowned and told the person on the other end that she knew their shop in *Wilmington* took walk-ins, even their shop in Fayetteville might take walk-ins, but she didn't so they were going to have to make an appointment or drive to Wilmington or Fayetteville. "Okay, well you just call back then." Esther smiled at Garvin as she hung up and shook her head. "What were you saying?"

Garvin leaned forward to speak—

The door banged open.

Patrice Lotty walked in the door of Big Esther's beauty shop and all conversation stopped. That is, except for that made-up conversation people keep up so the subject of their attention won't know that she is their focus. Discourse that would keep Miz

Lotty from knowing that in her presence, Garvin had forgotten momentarily what she wanted to ask Esther, that others had probably forgotten their lower back pain or that they had been under the dryer too long, or had forgotten just who they were saying ought to be ashamed for doing psychic telephone hot line commercials.

Instead all eyes seemed focused on Miz Lotty. Her tattered green T-shirt and her burgundy pants fit right in with the salmon-colored walls in Big Esther's. And all heads turned and watched as she walked to Big Esther's station. Miz Lotty didn't seem to notice all the attention. Her focus was on Big Esther.

"I-I-I've got some stuff you might want."

Esther put on her most disapproving look—Garvin had seen it before—still, there was something else in her eyes. Miss Lotty dug around in her bag, while at the same time, from moment to moment, she pulled at the oily, stained pants that sagged around her body. "I've got toothpaste." She pulled several large tubes out of her bag, while she kept her right pinky finger extended. "You know, the kind that whitens." Her diction was perfect except for an exaggerated slowness.

Miss Lotty dropped the tubes back into her bag and then began to scratch through what looked to be three inches of new growth with one stubby index finger, while she kept the pinky extended. She stopped scratching long enough to dig back in the bag. "I got these scrunchies." She pulled up several packs of the brightly colored cloth ponytail holders, then reached in the bag again. "I've got these two gospel tapes."

A couple of the church ladies looked up. "Who?"

"Um, Kirk Franklin." Miss Lotty rubbed her nose as she walked over to them, then pocketed five dollars from both of the ladies as the tapes disappeared discreetly into their purses.

"And I've got these men's underwear."

Sister Inez Zephyr leaned forward from her place in the plants. "What size, Miss Lotty?" Sister Inez reached into her jacket pocket and pulled out her glasses, apparently for a closer look.

"A bunch of sizes, Inez. Some small enough for your boy, and some big enough for your husband."

Several of the ladies in the shop tittered. One snorted. "That's pretty big!" One of them whooped.

"What you laughing at?" Sister Inez looked over the top of her blue-framed glasses at the closest laughing woman. The woman laughed again, louder. Sister Inez looked disgusted and then turned back to Miss Lotty. "How much?"

Miss Lotty scratched her head. "Half."

"Half?" Sister Inez looked indignant. "Miss Lotty, you know I ain't paying half for something you stole. Two—that's what I'll pay."

Miss Lotty looked wounded. "Inez, all the years I knew you, I never thought you would grow up to be such an uncaring person. Inez, you know that isn't fair."

"It ain't fair for you to steal either, Miss Lotty." Sister Inez looked like she knew she was standing on moral high ground.

"These are silk, Inez. There's six pair in this pack. And you know it's hard to get your husband's size."

The other women laughed again. "I know that's the truth," one of them said.

Sister Inez rolled her eyes. "Two, I said."

Miss Lotty looked agitated. Esther cleared her throat. "Just take your stuff and go, Miss Lotty. You know I don't like you coming in here with that stuff anyway."

The woman moved to put the pack of brightly colored men's boxer shorts back into her bag. "Wait a minute." Inez reached out her hand and almost snatched the pack to her chest. "How many packs you got?"

Miss Lotty tugged at her pants, then reached in to dig in the bag. "Five. Five packs."

"Okay, I'll give you four dollars a pack. That's it." Sister Inez frowned at Miss Lotty.

"It isn't fair, but okay." The two women made the exchange and then Miss Patrice Lotty pulled at her pants and headed for the door in a hurry. She stopped and turned. Pinky still raised; she scratched her head, again. "Esther, I'll be back, okay?" She smiled. Two of her teeth were broken. "Looks like I need a touch-up. You just put me on the books, okay?" She pulled at her pants and attempted to straighten her shirt.

"Okay, Miss Lotty. You just say when."

"I'll be back, Esther. For real, I will…you still reading all the time?"

"Yes, ma'am. I'm still reading." Esther's voice sounded sad.

"Okay, I'm going to be back soon. You'll see." Then Miss Lotty turned and hurried out the door. It slammed behind her and the shop was quiet for a moment.

"That is too sad." One of the women broke the silence.

"A shame," another one said.

One woman reached to check the heat control on her hair dryer. "She used to be a good-looking woman. Chile, that crack is eating her up." Another patron kicked one of her crossed legs back and forth. "That stuff is all over the place. First it was in the cities, now it's even here and getting all kinds of people. Look at that. A schoolteacher. It's a shame."

"Miss Lotty…a crackhead," another patron chimed in. A sudden sorrow came over her face when she looked at the woman sitting next to her. "Sorry, Gertie. I wasn't thinking."

"Oh, I know you didn't mean no harm," Gertie told the woman next to her. "It hurts just the same. I never thought it would get my son. Sometimes now, I just wonder." She wiped her brow. "It's killing me too, not just him. Every time I go to visit him at the camp where they got him locked up, it's like I'm locked up too. They pat me down like I'm some criminal. I got to take off my shoes and they pat me all kind of private places like I got a record too; I might as well be there with him. Might as well call me crackhead too." Gertie shook her head. Her right eye twitched, and the corner of her mouth drooped as though being tugged by invisible string.

"He's my only son, my only child, and I love him…he ain't no animal. I wonder," she said, "who's gonna be around to take care of me when I'm old." Her words hung in the air, drifted on dust particles.

"It sure is sad," another client said, finally breaking the silence. She then quickly changed the subject. "I'm hungry; Esther, when is Miz Moline gone take orders?"

Esther stuck the rattail comb in her smock pocket, left the pin curls, and walked to check the client's dryer. "I don't know about that—" she lifted the hood and began to check the rollers at the base of the client's neck—"but what I do know—" she turned to Sister Inez—"is that you are a hypocrite."

"Oh! Oh!" One of the clients exclaimed softly. Esther began to take pins from the woman's rollers, apparently checking to see if the hair was thoroughly dry—too soon and the hair would frizz. She looked ready to pluck.

"Esther, it ain't none of your business, and if it was some other shop in town, I would go there."

Garvin leaned forward on her stool. Esther was puffing up, snatching rollers from the crown of the woman's head and throwing them into a basket near the dryer. "Yeah, well it ain't no other shop, unless you going to follow that other woman that called to Wilmington. And long as you in my shop, you might as well know anything you say is my business. Trying to cheat that woman." Esther looked around the shop. "And church people buying hot gospel music—it's disgraceful." It was getting ugly; the other patrons watched intently. Several of the sisters said, "Amen. You right, Esther."

Sister Inez looked put upon. "She stole that stuff, Esther."

"Yeah, she did, and she's on crack. You just bought stolen goods. How does that make you better?" Sister Inez's mouth just moved open and shut, no words came out. "And you supposed to be something at the church. Miss Lotty is high; what's *your* excuse?"

Garvin looked around the room. Some women had covered their mouths with their hands, some just had big gaping *Os*.

"Never mind, Esther. I'm not gone argue with you. I just came here for you to fix my hair. I don't want to talk about it." Sister Inez moved back to her habitat.

Garvin shook her head. She was really back in Jacks Creek. Another little taste of home.

Esther frowned and looked as though she were going to argue some more. Instead, she felt the rollers at the back of the woman's neck. "Your kitchen is still a little wet. About ten more minutes." She pushed the hood back down, turned the dryer back to hot, pulled the rattail comb from her pocket, and walked back to finish the pin curls.

Esther smoothed the back and the sides of the client's hair and then sighed. "That's why I can't go to church anymore. Hypocrites." She shook her head. "I'm sorry—" she smiled wanly at Garvin— "what were you asking me before everything broke loose?"

Garvin looked at the clock. It was 4:45 in the afternoon. "Meemaw. I'm looking for my Meemaw."

Eleven

---

arvin closed the beauty shop door behind her, walked calmly to her car, and slid into the seat of her Lexus. Behind the gray, smoky glass, she pounded the dashboard several times with the flat of her hand.

"Great!" She yelled aloud to herself when she was sure no one was looking. A whole afternoon wasted. She flipped the vanity mirror on her sun visor down to check her face, then quickly flipped it back into place. "Great!" So Meemaw wasn't at Esther's after all. Obviously had no intention of going there, since, according to Esther, Meemaw had called to cancel her appointment so she could frolic with GoGo. Esther didn't say "frolic," but Garvin knew the deal. *Great!*

"She's with him all the time," the women in the shop had told her. But it was more what they hadn't said out loud…

It was more the expressions on their faces. Expressions that asked what an older woman, a church pillar, was doing running around with a man like that.

Garvin pounded on the dashboard several more times, then sat back in her seat. She could feel the muscles in her jaws clenching.

She sighed. She had to get control of herself. *I have to keep a cool head or I'm going to blow this.* Meemaw might wind up prey to a washed-up ex-football player. Garvin began to imagine her grandmother decked out in chiffon and jewels, sitting coquett- ishly on a couch in a dimly lit room, music playing softly in the background. A man's arm inserted itself into the apparition, and in his hand was what appeared to be a glass of champagne. The phantom Meemaw, wearing hot pink spandex workout clothes, giggled and reached for the glass...

Garvin shook her head to clear the nightmare fantasy. She couldn't let it happen, not to her Meemaw.

Garvin bit her lower lip and looked out the window. She felt like a little kid again. Could feel that same panic rising, threaten- ing to take control. That same helplessness she'd felt when her mother began to laugh too much, to watch the clock, to pace the room, to dab on perfume. She could see her mother toying with her hair until the moment came when she could slip into dark- ness and run to meet the man—the stranger her mother said was her father. And then there was the river.

Garvin pressed a hand to her temple and a deep breath helped her calm down. Emotional outbursts weren't going to change any- thing; she would have to take deliberate action. She turned the ignition switch, pulled out into the road, and headed for Meemaw's house.

Monique watched as Garvin's Lexus sped by.

"Nice car," Lacey pointed at the immaculate LS 400. "Some- day I'm going to be rolling like that." She stopped in the middle of the sidewalk to perform a set of choreographed steps.

Monique shook her head, then grabbed Lacey's arm to turn her toward an alley. "This way." They walked until they stood alongside an unoccupied house. The frame of a window set into the basement of the house was covered with iron bars. Monique checked to make sure no one was watching, then pressed the bottom of the window open with her foot. The window looked as though it had been nailed shut at one time.

"We have to do this quick before anyone comes along. Watch me." Monique kneeled and pushed the window open wider while she turned sideways and slid her legs between the bars. In a swift move she slid her hips between the bars and reached for an iron pipe that was suspended from the basement ceiling. When her grip was sure, she used the pipe to pull her body into the room, then hung there, her legs dangling in the air. She released her grip and landed firmly on her feet amid a cloud of grime.

Still outside, Lacey looked hesitant. Monique beckoned her with a hand wave. "Come on. Hurry up, before someone sees. You can do this, it's easy." Monique watched Lacey kneel down and, in a matter of seconds, the other girl was in the room. The two slapped their hands together to remove dust then began to beat at their clothes. "Wait." Monique felt around until she gripped an old crowbar. She used it to push the window closed behind them.

Still blinded by the darkness, the two girls felt their way in the musty room, bumping into filthy boxes and crippled furniture. Monique, after her eyes had adjusted, pointed to a moldy sofa. "We can sit over there." They stepped on and around pieces of broken glass, making their way toward the couch. A shaft of light struck a small pile of broken, discarded jars, most of them without lids.

Lacey ducked her head and tried to cover her hair with her hands. "I hate bugs, Monique. I hope there's no bugs in here." She stepped gingerly; for once, dancing didn't seem to be on her mind anymore.

"Bugs are the least of it. We probably need to watch out for rats, maybe snakes."

Lacey grabbed Monique's arm as the two made it to their seat. "How did you ever find this place?" Lacey jumped and jerked each time she heard a sound.

"Sol."

The two girls huddled together on the stained love seat in the dank cellar. What had been large, strange, orange and blue flowers on a gray velour background were now unified by a thick layer of greasy grime that covered the sofa. The smell of must and mold was heavy in the air; a swatch of sunlight from just over Monique's right shoulder where she sat on an arm of the couch was their only light.

"This is truly, really truly gross." Startled by a noise, Lacey tightened her grip on Monique's arm. "What was that?"

"Probably just the house settling." Monique looked at Lacey, then back at the window.

Lacey was using her hands to hit her arms, apparently swatting at imaginary bugs. "Why did Sol bring you here?"

Monique bit her bottom lip and then looked at her friend. "You know."

Lacey looked toward the window. "Yeah." Lacey swatted at more insects. "So why are *we* here?"

"I wanted to talk to you about the party."

Lacey's face looked confused, about as close as she seemed to be able to come to looking annoyed. "We could talk about the party anywhere."

"I know, but I wanted to bring you here so you could see…I don't know. I guess it was a dumb idea, but I wanted you to be where we—me and Sol—where we, you know." Monique grabbed her hair and twisted it into a knot. "I just wanted you to know what you were in for at the party."

"Well, I guess I'm gonna do it. I mean, it's no big deal." Lacey picked at the pink frosted fingernail polish that covered her bitten fingernails. She pulled the collar of her shirt up around her ears. No electricity in the hideaway, no light, which also meant no heat. There was a chill in the air despite the warmth outside.

"You don't have to, Lacey." Monique scrunched her body back into the couch each time footsteps or a shadow passed by the window. "I mean, you're right. It's no big deal. We all gotta do it sometime, right?" Monique shrugged her shoulders, laughed, and paused. It wasn't what she meant to say at all. It wasn't why she had pulled her friend away secretly to this room. She didn't know if she would have the courage to say it.

Monique looked back at Lacey. Her friend always wore too much lip liner, probably because she was trying to sneak it on in a hurry after she left her house on the way to school. "It's just that now might not be the right time or anything."

"What do you mean? Are you trying to tell me something about Ricky? Is he dating somebody else? I knew it! I knew it!" Lacey pulled the edges of her collar together to cover her face. "I waited too long. I knew it. What am I so afraid of? I'm such a jerk!" Her words were muffled by the fabric.

Monique extended her hand to touch Lacey's shoulder, then withdrew it before she made contact. She looked around the room.

Sol had brought her here three years ago, had shown her how to sneak through the window. The sofa hadn't been quite as dirty then, but it *had* been dirty, not what she had imagined it would be like. The setting was not at all what she had imagined when she was a little girl. There were no lace curtains and no canopies in the dank cellar.

She had to tell her friend the truth.

"Lacey…look, Lacey, we came here for a reason…all I mean is

you don't have to do it." Monique felt like she was going to choke on the words she just couldn't say. What was Lacey going to say? Who was she to try to tell *anybody* how to live his or her life? "I wouldn't do it."

"You've already done it. What do you mean, Monique? Everybody's doing it. How am I supposed to keep him if I don't? When I say no, I know there are twenty other girls ready to say yes." Lacey's ponytails wiggled as she shook her head back and forth. "Then I see him with other girls, kissing them, laughing with them. Then he ignores me. I must be the only one. And everybody I hear talking about it…they make it sound like, like it's cool, you know." Lacey's expression was wistful. "Before *you* told me it was cool, and I've heard you talking to the other girls sometimes."

Monique felt like she could hardly breathe. "I know, but…" She looked back toward the light. "You know how we do…I just want people to think I'm okay, you know. So I say what I think they want to hear. Do you know what everybody would say if I said this out loud? But what difference does it make anyway? It's not like I'm Miss Popularity." Monique felt like she was going under and fighting for air…needing to say a lot, but afraid she would drown in murky water. "If I was you, I wouldn't. That's all. I wouldn't. I'm trying to be your friend."

"Right." Lacey's words seemed tight. "But you already did. Remember? And who are you to tell me?"

Lacey's words hung in the quiet for a while before Monique convinced herself to speak. "Did you know I got pregnant?" Lacey looked startled. "Yeah, it was before you moved here. But I did. A little girl." She had surfaced for a little while, but Monique could feel her fingers clawing for the surface of the water as the under-tow pulled her down, down. "And I'm not supposed to know where she is. They told me she would be adopted…" Monique could feel air bubbles flowing from her nose, past her eyes, shooting toward the surface. "So I've got this kid. And I can't touch her or talk to her. And I'm supposed to feel better because she's adopted, but it feels like I'm in prison. Or like I'm in hell, and she's on the other side in heaven, you know."

Lacey whispered, "A baby?"

Monique reached her hand to wipe the water away from her face. "And I'm supposed to pretend like I never had a daughter. Like I don't know that people are looking at me and talking about me. And I think, what's the point? How many years am I supposed to live this way? But they told me, they promised she would be with a family."

Lacey sat quietly, head down, picking at her nail polish.

"And Sol, he don't even think about me. Like he don't know me or is finished with me. Sometimes when he's with the other guys he laughs when I walk by, like I'm a joke, like he's finished with me, like I'm trash. You know?" Monique closed her eyes and wondered how much deeper the current would pull her. "Lacey, do you know what I'm saying?"

She looked up and nodded at Monique. "I know what you're saying, but…"

"No, you don't know what I'm saying. You don't know how it is. Even though I did have the baby—I tried to do the right thing, you know? But people still treat me like, like…I don't know. Sometimes—" the water around her seemed to be pushing the last of the air from her lungs—"sometimes, I wonder if I'd had an abortion and hid it, what things would be like. Would people treat me better, would they still smile at me or let me come over to their houses to visit their kids? Would they treat me better if I had covered it up? Maybe they wouldn't talk behind my back, or even to my face, because they wouldn't know. Nobody would know."

Lacey looked uncomfortable. "People like you, Monique. They do." Lacey ducked and swatted at the air as though she felt or heard something buzzing around her head. "This place is creepy." She waved again, then looked at Monique. "Maybe you're overreacting."

"Right. Now that you know, watch and see if you don't see that they treat me different. You know, when they picked people for the Junior Honor Society, they didn't pick me because I had a baby. But you know Denise Johnston? She had an abortion; everybody knows, but they let her in. They even let Sol in. At least I tried to do the right thing."

Lacey picked at her jeans. "What difference does it make, anyway? I mean, who cares about the stupid Honor Society?"

Monique wiped more water away from her face. "I care. And I care that everybody at school knows what happened. And I care because some days it seems like my whole life is over. I care because I had the baby and gave it away and everybody got to see my shame. Funny, it's supposed to be cool to do it, but it seems like it stops being cool when there's inconvenient evidence that you did it. Everybody gets to see my shame."

Monique gasped for air. "And I care because every day...I think about her, I love her even though I can't hold her, and I know I did the right thing. And Denise, she's smiling like everything's okay, but I can see it. I can see the death in her eyes." Monique choked. "But my life, I screwed up my whole life, probably my daughter's too, and I just...I just wouldn't do it if I was you. That's all. I just wouldn't."

"How did it happen? I mean, didn't you try to be safe?"

"I planned to be, but...what's the difference? It just wasn't what I thought; it wasn't like in the books or anything."

The two sat breathing in the darkness. Lacey reached for Monique's hand, and she squeezed back. "The funny thing, Lacey, is that it wasn't so much fun. I don't even know why I did it. I didn't even *want* to do it, but everybody said it was so cool and it was no big deal and I didn't want to look like I was trying to be Miss Untouchable. Sol asked me, and I don't even know why I said yes. *He* didn't even look happy; almost like he didn't want to really do it either. I just thought, hey, it's no big deal.

"But, Lacey, the thing is—when it was over—I wanted to cry. Like something had happened to me or been taken from me." Monique looked into Lacey's eyes, hoping for some sign that she understood. "It happened here—" Monique gestured around the room and Lacey shuddered—"I guess I thought it would be different. Not sneaking away to some place like this. I felt bad, like I was dirty, but I didn't want anybody to see me cry. They were all partying and everything and I didn't want them to talk about me." The water pushed harder against her rib cage. "Big deal. They've been talking about me ever since anyway, you know? And Sol won't really look me in the eye, but I wonder what he feels inside, if he's still the same. He won't look at me, you know? Like I did something wrong to him. Like I made him do something he didn't really want to do." She looked back toward the window. "But sometimes, I think I see on his face the same thing I feel in my heart. Like…I don't know…whatever."

It sounded as if Lacey was crying softly.

"You know what, Lacey? I thought it was no big deal, but since I did it, I feel…I don't even know how to explain it. But one thing for sure, it made a very big deal in my life."

Lacey opened and closed her mouth, cleared her throat, and then said, "You always look cool, Monique. I had no idea. I mean, sometimes I see a few people look at you funny, but I thought that

was because—don't get mad, okay—'cause, you're, you know...
mixed. You know?"

Monique laughed sarcastically. "Yeah, I know. Come on, we
better go." She rose from the couch, started toward the window,
and looked over her shoulder at Lacey while she walked. "Well,
you were close. How they treat me is about parentage—it's just
not about mine."

Twelve

◆

arvin pulled into Meemaw's driveway again. She sat listening while Stephanie Mills's soprano voice floated from the car speakers singing a song about home. A song that asked if God was listening, a plea from a lost and confused girl for divine direction. Garvin closed her eyes. How great it would be if there was really someone that she could pray to, or even sing to. Someone who could tell her exactly what to do, who could reassure her about her career, about her Meemaw, about her friend Ramona...someone who really heard and responded... someone who would take responsibility for the outcome...a happy ending would be nice.

Peck, peck. Garvin jumped in her seat and banged the same elbow against the door that she had cracked when she fell earlier.

She opened her eyes and turned to speak to—no, to *yell* at whoever the crazy person was knocking on her window.

"Meemaw!" She yelled through the window glass and fumbled to open her car door. "Meemaw!"

Her grandmother stepped back as Garvin swung the door open and almost leaped into her arms.

"Baby!" Meemaw laughed. "You don't have to tackle Meemaw. I'm not going anywhere." Garvin wrapped her arms around Meemaw's waist, locking her wrists as if she would not let her go. Meemaw chuckled again, the sound drifting over Garvin's head.

"Meemaw, I'm so happy to be home." Garvin hadn't known

how true the statement was until she said it.

"So I see. I saw you pull up, but it was taking you so long, I thought I better come check on you." Garvin kept holding on to her grandmother. "My baby." Meemaw stroked Garvin's hair. "My little Garvina. Look at Meemaw's little attorney."

Garvin opened her eyes and lifted her chin so that she could look into Meemaw's face. "It's Garvin, Meemaw. Not Garvina. You know I hate that name."

"Excuse me, sweetness." Meemaw's voice took on that tone. That tone that meant she was about to reach for the flyswatter or the brush. The tone that told Garvin that she had come a little too close to stepping over the bounds between parent and child. The tone that told Garvin that her mouth was about to get her backside into trouble—even if she did think she was grown. "You're never too grown to be straightened out," Meemaw had told her many times.

Garvin retreated. "Never mind." She closed her eyes, shook her head, and laid it on her grandmother's chest. Garvin breathed deeply. "Meemaw, you still smell like the same soap."

Her grandmother laughed and began to rub circular patterns on Garvin's back. "Now what did you think I would do? Stop using soap because you left? Just stand still in time. I guess you thought poor Meemaw would just dry up and peg away."

"No, Meemaw. You know what I mean."

"Yes, baby, I'm just teasing. You know me. I like the soap; it's still working, no need to change."

Garvin liked the feel of her grandmother's hand on her back and she wondered what they must look like standing there in the driveway. Where she was dark brown, Meemaw was ivory-colored. Where she was not much more than five feet, Meemaw stood more than a head over her. While her hair was long, chemically straightened, and brown; Meemaw's was close-cropped, naturally straight with only the slightest curl, and jet black with just a tiny bit of gray. She was thin, but Meemaw was big boned—though not quite as full figured as Garvin remembered. She tightened her grip around her grandmother's waist.

"Good thing I didn't just eat. It could be a mess as hard as you're squeezing me." Meemaw's chuckle made her chest rise and fall. Garvin did not loosen her grip. "Of course, I know you remember when you couldn't have wrapped your arms as tight around me. Working out is doing me good—there's a little bit less to love, wouldn't you say?" Garvin just held on. "What GoGo has me doing is really working!"

Garvin thought she would bite her tongue off. She would have liked nothing better than to grill Meemaw and read her the riot act about GoGo, to sit her down and straighten her out. But she would have to resist. Meemaw would never tolerate it, and if Garvin weren't careful, she might blow any opportunity she would have to get the 4-1-1 on GoGo—the vital information that would tell Garvin how to get rid of him. Garvin hugged harder.

"Child, let's go inside and sit down before you cut off my circulation, and you can tell me what brings you running back to Jacks Creek."

The two women walked arm in arm up the front steps and then held hands as they walked through the doorway. "I sure am glad to see you, baby. I thought maybe at Thanksgiving or Christmas, but it sure is good to have you here now." Meemaw motioned Garvin into the kitchen. "When I got home—I was out with GoGo. He has the cutest little car. That man is something else." Meemaw started giggling again, and Garvin fought the urge to upchuck. "He has the cutest little red convertible, and that is a good-looking man, I tell you."

Garvin hoped she had on the poker face she had developed in her years of legal practice. "I know, you told me before."

"Oh, that's right, I did. Well, we have so much fun. We just fly all over town, just wherever we want to go. He's not married, you know."

Most gigolos aren't. Garvin looked around the room for a fly-swatter—Meemaw definitely needed a reality check. She kept right on talking. "You would think some smart woman would have made herself available to be found by now, but I guess he's just been waiting for the right one!" Her grandmother's eyes were twinkling, almost glittering. It was sickening. "Well, enough about me and GoGo."

Yes, enough. Please!

Meemaw walked to the stove and turned the teakettle on low heat. "I saw your bags and I said to myself, 'Let me put on some hot water, I know my baby is going to want some tea.'" Meemaw opened the cabinet and began reaching for boxes of tea. "What kind? I'm going to have something herbal. How about you? Chamomile? Lemon?"

"Cinnamon."

Meemaw reached for the box, extracted a bag, and dropped it into a cup painted with bright red cherries, blueberries, apples, oranges, pears, bananas. She plopped her herbal tea bag into her own cup and brought them to the table. "See here, your favorite cup. Nobody ever uses it but you."

Good. At least there was still something GoGo didn't have access to.

Meemaw stirred her tea. "Okay, so now that I'm sitting, tell me the story. Tell me why you're here."

Garvin looked down to compose her thoughts, then back into Meemaw's eyes. "It's about my job, Meemaw. Everything's falling apart." While they sipped tea, she told the story to her grand-mother in detail. Meemaw shook her head in all the right places. She made clucking noises when Garvin told her about Gooden. Especially when she recounted her conversation with him on the day she left the office.

"That is terrible," Meemaw said at just the right moments.

"So that's why I'm here. I'm on administrative leave while they investigate. I'm *supposed* to work on this case. An EEO case." Garvin could hear the disgust in her own voice.

"Hmm," Meemaw said.

"A man."

"Hmm."

"A black man."

"So I figured." Meemaw gave only the briefest smile. Otherwise, her expression was inscrutable.

"I've just started to get into it, but it seems to be a stereotypical case. According to his complaint, he worked at the same company for years and often filled in at the supervisory level when there was a vacancy. Trained others to do the supervisory job, but was passed over for promotion, blah, blah, blah. He claims that it was because of race—but more likely the others that were hired were more qualified. I'm sure management had some justifiable reason for hiring them over him, and I'll end up looking like a fool in front of the court arguing a case I know there's no chance in—no way I'm going to win."

Meemaw's face gave no clue; she just kept staring Garvin directly in the eye. "It's really something how smart you are." Garvin searched for a hint of sarcasm but found nothing on which she could put her finger. "How you can just look at a case briefly and make a decision just like that—" Meemaw snapped her fingers—"on the man's life."

"Really Meemaw, we see these things all the time." Garvin felt silly for trying to defend herself; Meemaw wasn't accusing her.

Meemaw smiled the same mysterious smile. "I thought you said you didn't know anything about EEO, that this was your first case."

"No, I've never tried an EEO case and it is definitely not my area of expertise. But Meemaw, I hear people talking about these kinds of cases all the time. The courts hate them, and people are sick of them. And to be honest with you, *I'm* sick of people using race as an excuse, as if there are no opportunities. Look at me, I made it."

"Yes, look at you."

"It doesn't make sense to me. If he didn't like it, why didn't he leave? If they were treating him unfairly, why did he stay so long? Being a good employee? Right. So now he's wrecking the whole company and subjecting them to ridicule. What did he think, one day they would change and turn around and say they were sorry? If that was his reasoning, it's pretty weak." Garvin knew she had lost her poker face and instead, looked openly disgusted.

"Hmm," Meemaw said.

"I just hate that victim stuff. It just makes us look bad."

"Who is 'us'?"

"You know what I mean, Meemaw. Black people. It's embarrassing, and it sure makes it harder for somebody like me—I mean for everybody. A case like this is a career buster, and Gooden gave it to me just to bring me down."

"Why do you think that, Garvin?"

"He has it in for me."

Meemaw's eyes bored into her. "Why?"

Garvin shrugged. "I don't know, Meemaw. He just does."

"Well, how do you know?"

Garvin began to rub her temples. This was not going well. She thought to cut off the exchange, to steer the conversation in another direction, but thought better of it when she remembered her plan to obfuscate the real reason for her journey to Jacks Creek. "He assigned me this case for one reason—he knows the case is a joke. Everyone knows it's almost impossible to win an EEO case in the courts now. Then he did that investigation. He never did that to anyone else. *Then* he got me kicked out of the office for three months—which is *why* I'm here. He is out to get me."

Meemaw opened her mouth, as if to speak, but Garvin quickly continued.

"I know he was within his rights as a manager, and I can't really prove anything, but I know what's going on. I mean, I'm not stupid. I know what he's trying to do."

Meemaw sat silent for several seconds, took a sip of tea, then answered. "Number one, baby, there's no need to yell. Don't start exploding up in here. Meemaw needs her peace. Second, maybe it's not about you, Garvina—Garvin. Maybe the man, Hemings, really has a case. Maybe he really needed a good lawyer, and maybe God chose you."

Garvin snickered. "Yeah, right. I doubt I'm on God's list of favorite people."

"God works in mysterious ways—"

"'His wonders to perform.'" Garvin finished the quote. "I just can't see God looking down and choosing me to help anybody. I'm no missionary." If only Meemaw knew...Garvin and God hadn't even been on speaking terms for quite a while.

Meemaw sipped her tea, then smiled broadly. "Maybe I'm wrong. Maybe it is all about you."

Before Garvin could frame a question, the telephone rang.

Meemaw rose from the table—no, she *bolted* for the living room to answer the phone and caught it by the second ring. Garvin could hear her grandmother giggling and whispering into the phone. *This is ridiculous!* She had to resist the urge to stomp into the living room, grab the phone, and tell Mr. Loverman to lay off. She couldn't believe Meemaw had left her alone at the table and was jabbering conspiratorially on the phone with a man who was probably half her age.

Garvin cleared her throat.

Meemaw began to speak aloud into the telephone so that Garvin was able to hear. "My beautiful granddaughter is here. What?" Meemaw hooted. "Oh, I guess I look okay for an old bird." She cackled. "Well, thank you, GoGo. If you say so. I do feel pretty young these days."

Garvin thought she was going to retch. Good thing she was here. She would be able to keep an eye on Meemaw, to keep the snake from slithering up to her doorstep so easily. GoGo could count on it—he would be meeting Garvin. Soon.

"Oh, stop it, now!" Meemaw kept babbling. "What I was trying to tell you is that I need to get her settled. It won't take me long. You can call me back…or hang on the line." Meemaw paused as if she was listening. "All righty then, suit yourself. You hold on, I'll be right back." Garvin could hear Meemaw set the phone on the table.

When she appeared in the kitchen doorway she was beaming. "I hate to rush, but my friend is on the phone. So here—" Meemaw reached for a set of keys hung on a nail next to the door molding—"Take these. The house in the back is ready for you. From the amount of luggage I saw, I figured you were going to be staying a while." Meemaw moved to the back door that led to the little house out back. "I sat your bags out on the steps. You don't have to carry them all over at one time."

Garvin's mouth dropped open. "Mee-Meemaw," she stammered, "I thought I would be staying here—in the house—with you. I-I-I—"

Meemaw cut her off midsentence, grabbed her arm, lifted her from her seat, and started moving Garvin toward the door. "Baby, you know you are welcome. Stay as long as you like. This is your home. But you know how it is when two grown women try to stay in one small house. You are not a little girl, and I can't tell you what to do, how to live your life. That would just cause confusion, wouldn't it?"

Garvin could feel pressure on her arm where Meemaw steered her. "I'm not going to tell you what to do, but you know Meemaw has rules. And I'm not going to bend those rules for anybody. Meemaw don't ever take down for nobody. And you know when you don't get your way, you like to explode, and Meemaw has peace in the house and I need to keep my peace."

Garvin found herself standing outside on the back porch with the screen door between her and her grandmother. "But, Meemaw!"

"Don't worry, baby. Everything's going to work out fine. You are welcome to stay out back as long as you want to; this is your home. It's nice and aired out. I keep the place ready. Your grandpa said we might need it someday." Meemaw beamed at her and then waved her hand as if to say, don't bother. "And don't worry about the cigarettes. I didn't have any trouble digging them up out of the garbage disposal." Garvin could feel her mouth moving open and shut like a fish while Meemaw talked. "I was able to retrieve the telephone messages—Mr. Green says to tell you hello." Meemaw kept waving. "Don't even think about the papers and boxes—I'll have them back in order in no time. And you did a good job on the little dove. I'm sure it's going to mend just fine."

"But, Meemaw!" Garvin could feel herself panicking. What was Meemaw doing? What about her plans? How was she going to—

"Now don't you worry about a thing." Meemaw was closing the door as she spoke. "I'm going to run and get the phone, but you just take your time getting settled." Meemaw smiled, then yelled over her shoulder just before she shut the door, "Don't hang up, GoGo. I'm coming!" She turned back to Garvin, that same twinkle in her eye. "Hmm, baby. We're going to have a good time." She quickly closed the door.

Garvin stood smack-dab in the middle of her confusion. *Should I be crying? Did my grandmother just put me out of the house for a man?* She waited at the door, staring as if Meemaw would come to her senses and beg her to come back inside.

It didn't happen. Garvin snatched up her bags and dragged them, while she stomped down the short pathway to the back house. She heard the door opening behind her.

Meemaw was almost singing. "Garvina, I just wanted to make sure you brought your church clothes. Come Sunday, everybody in this house—" Meemaw smiled—"everybody on this *property* goes to church." Her grandmother nodded, winked, and quickly closed the door.

Garvin threw down her bags and jumped up and down on the sidewalk. This was crazy. *Garvina, not Garvin. I mean, Garvin, not—oh, forget about it!*

Exploding? Exploding? She had reason to explode. She had been kicked out of her own house, and Meemaw was losing her mind over a womanizing jock!

Garvin stood still and took a deep breath to regain her composure. GoGo may be winning now, she cursed under her breath, but he had definitely met his match. He was about to be put out of business. He might be a player, but he hadn't met her. He was about to *get* played. Garvin grabbed her bags and marched toward the smaller house.

He could count on it. Definitely.

Thirteen

◆

Lacey danced ahead of the other three girls. Monique watched her friend's blond hair flying as she bobbed and turned. Lacey looked like she didn't have a care in the world.

Carmen shook her head and pulled at one of her braids. "Girl, do you ever stand still? You must drive you mama crazy!" Lacey smiled and kept dancing.

Josephina laughed. "Every day with you is a *fiesta!*" The girls walked and Lacey danced right past the window of Big Esther's Beauty Shop. "So, Lacey. Did you decide? Are you going to the party?"

Monique looked away, then turned back. Lacey stopped dancing just before she reached the alley that led to the hideaway. She turned to face the other girls. "Not really. I mean, I decided." Monique held her breath. "I've got better stuff to do; I'm not going." Lacey smiled at the three of them, but Monique was sure she saw something extra in the look she gave to her. "I've got good friends. I don't need to hang out with losers." Lacey made an *L* with her index finger and thumb and pressed it to her forehead.

"Girl, I can't believe you did that." Carmen threw her braids over her shoulder. "That is so old and tired." She looked at Monique and Josephina. "That's your friend, *your* girl—she did the loser thing. I can't believe she went there…"

The four girls continued walking until they came to the corner where Carmen and Josephina split from the group to walk toward their homes. As they walked away, Lacey turned to Monique and hugged her. "Thanks, okay?"

Monique could feel her face get warm. "It's no big deal."

Lacey hugged her again. "That's what you taught me; it is a big deal." She looked in the direction of her house. "I gotta go, okay?" She pointed at Monique. "Tomorrow, at school."

Monique nodded and stood watching as Lacey walked, then danced down her street. A touch of melancholy played across the smile on her lips. Head down, she turned and started her solitary walk home.

Meemaw stood near the front door humming and waiting for GoGo to arrive. Monique stepped into view. Always sad, always blue. But at least this once, it looked like the child was going to be the winner, and GoGo was going to miss his opportunity to taste her cookies. *He's going to have to just be satisfied with my sweet presence.* Meemaw laughed to herself then stepped outside onto the porch.

She peeked around some red rose blossoms. "Hey baby, that you? I can't be sure with your head down and everything." Monique stopped and smiled wanly, like something was on her mind. No doubt there was. The home the girl was heading to was no haven. "Come try Meemaw's cookies." She beckoned Monique with her free hand. "You know you are just the prettiest child. Tell me how school's going."

She hugged Monique when the girl came within her grasp, then pointed at the treats. "You take some of these cookies with you so an old woman won't be tempted."

"You don't look old, Miss Evangelina. I've always thought you were really beautiful. I wish my…" The girl shrugged.

"Maybe, but I still don't need all these cookies. I just happened to have them bagged up with some napkins hoping I would run into some sweet person to give them to. You are just the right one. I don't think there's anyone any sweeter."

Meemaw passed the bag to Monique, then put one arm around the girl and took her young face in one hand and kissed her on the cheek. "Why don't you come to church sometime, sweetie? There are lots of young people there. And if you don't want to sit with them, you know you can sit with me." Monique shrugged her shoulders as she bit into a cookie.

Meemaw hugged Monique one last time and then let her go. "You come back and check on me, okay, darling?" She took another bite of the cookie, smiled, and nodded.

Meemaw called to Monique as she watched the child walk away. "Keep your head up." The girl seemed so alone.

"Lord, she needs somebody and Garvin don't know it, but she needs somebody too. I'm not trying to mind Your business, but it looks like a good match to me." Meemaw laughed. "If You think so, I'm going to get out of the way and let You work it out. But You know me, I'm just suggesting."

Meemaw smiled sadly. The child looked like she needed a little sweetness in her life, cookies were just a pleasant dressing for what looked to be a deep wound. Meemaw turned and walked back to the house.

Garvin looked out her front screen door to Meemaw's back door. She would have to stay calm about the whole thing. She had had all night and most of the day to think the situation over. Actually, it could turn out to be the best possible situation. She wouldn't have to worry about Meemaw overhearing her conversations with Jonee; she could smoke if she wanted—like an adult. Garvin snickered to herself. Jacks Creek wasn't exactly full of men, especially not her type, but should she come across some strange and unusual Valentino that just happened to have stopped off in Jacks Creek she wouldn't have to work too hard at making up an excuse for Meemaw. In fact, she looked around the room, if she was discreet this place might do.

She shook her head. Even in Garvin's fantasies, Meemaw had radar.

Yes, being in the smaller house might work out after all. It had been years since she'd been inside. The house layout was roomy and open; she could see the kitchen and bed from where she stood in the simple living room. Only her bathroom and a small sewing and storage room were beyond the kitchen, out of sight around a corner. In front there was a window that gave her a clear view to Meemaw's back door. She was far enough away to have some privacy, close enough to throw some curves in GoGo's path, and—Garvin looked toward the kitchen—close enough to sit for dinner at Meemaw's table. Her stomach growled. Meemaw's cooking would be just the thing right now.

She stepped outside and walked the path to Meemaw's. Garvin pulled the screen door open and the wooden door open. Her grandmother stood on the other side of the threshold dressed in a bright green jogging suit with bold yellow and white accents. Her bright yellow headband matched the suit and the bright yellow high-top tennis shoes she wore.

"Isn't this something? I bet we had the same thing on our minds." Meemaw held a metal, nine-by-fifteen-inch baking dish. "I thought to myself, 'I bet that child is hungry.'" Meemaw smiled. "I know how you love my meat loaf. And guess what? I just happened to have all the ingredients." Meemaw pressed the pan into Garvin's hands then leaned to kiss her on the forehead. "So here's all the stuff to get you started."

Garvin looked at the raw beef and sausage that lay in the pan. "Meemaw, I don't know how—"

"Oh, don't worry about it, baby. This is just as good a time as any to learn. You have enough there that you will definitely have leftovers that you can nibble off of for days." Meemaw looked so pleased. "We come from a cooking family, so I can't wait to see what you turn out. I put one of my recipe cards in there—I've had those cards for years—so be careful with it. I'll get it back from you later." Meemaw pinched Garvin's cheek. "We are going to have a good time. I just know it, don't you?" Meemaw pinched her again and then closed the door.

Garvin stared at the closed door.

It was unbelievable. Absolutely unbelievable. She fumed back down the path and into her house. This was crazy. Garvin slammed the pan on the kitchen counter. She had spent years proudly telling men she was not domestic, now she was supposed to just whip up a little meat loaf! Forget about it. She picked up the pan and walked to the trashcan prepared to dump the contents.

A stained, age-browned, three-by-five card peaked from beneath the onion in the pan. Garvin pulled out the card and begin to read. The ingredients and directions were listed in Meemaw's handwriting: "Crumble one pound of hamburger along with one pound of sausage into a large mixing bowl. Add the finely chopped onion, salt, pepper, and garlic powder. Knead the mixture. Using your hands and praying as you knead seems to improve the taste."

Garvin sighed and set the pan down. *I love you, Meemaw.* On the other side of the card was written a Bible verse. "O taste and see that the LORD is good: blessed is the man that trusteth in him. Psalms 34:8." Beneath that, in smaller print, was what seemed to be a prayer Meemaw had written.

> *"Lord, today I'm feeling about as mixed up as the stuff in this meat loaf. We buried our daughter yesterday and her baby is just about as hurt as a child can be. Help us. Help me remember that You are always good, kind, and sweet. Amen."*

"Meemaw," Garvin said softly. Meemaw who held her when she cried. Meemaw who held back the river.

The sound of a car door shutting—undoubtedly GoGo's car door—startled her back to reality.

Fourteen

◆

A soft summer breeze tickled at the curtains that framed her kitchen window. Garvin looked at the wicker basket that sat on the table in front of her. She picked through the contents—pecans, dark syrup, eggs, butter. Tucked in the fold of a forest green, cloth napkin was another card.

In the week or so she'd been home, she'd found one collection of ingredients and cards after another.

Garvin thought about her friend Ramona—big earrings, high hair. It would be good to talk to her, to hear her jewelry clanking, to hear her complaining about her job. She picked up her cell phone and dialed Ramona's number. "Hello, I'm sorry I'm unable to answer your call. Please leave your name and number." The voice was too peppy, too upbeat to be Ramona. "And remember, if things are looking gray, keep your head up, help is on the way! 'Weeping may endure for a night, but joy cometh in the morning.' Psalm 30:5." *Beep.* Garvin pressed the end button without leaving a message.

Everyone around her was going crazy.

She set the phone down and began to finger the pecans. Ramona hadn't been to work in days, and no one was saying why. She wasn't answering the phone at home. Garvin could just imagine what the people at her office must have been saying. But Ramona was her friend. She was the first friend Garvin made, the first friend who found her when she got to Washington. She was an I'll-fight-for-you kind of friend. Ramona had heart. She didn't go to work, but Ramona had heart.

When Garvin thought of Ramona, she thought she understood why her friend didn't go to work. It was as if Ramona used any excuse not to go in because she felt like she was in a cage. That she was imprisoned by the desires of the people that she worked with—their desires that Ramona would be like them. That no matter how hard she worked, no matter how efficient she was, what they really wanted was for Ramona to be like them. Or at least they wanted her to want to be like them.

It was as though they wanted to be able to say to people, "Yes, we've got a tiger in our office. We hired her, so that proves we're okay. We speak to her, sit next to her, and even let her come to office parties."

But Ramona's coworkers really didn't *want* a tiger in the office, because they really didn't know anything about tigers except what they saw on TV. They weren't sure what a tiger would do.

In essence, what they really wanted was for the tiger to stop being a tiger, to just *look* enough like a tiger that they could keep saying they had one.

But Ramona couldn't—at least, as Garvin saw it. She didn't want to stop being a tiger. Ramona was a tiger that could file and type eighty words a minute. She growled and paced, but she hadn't bitten anyone, didn't intend to bite anyone. She just wanted to be free from the cage, to be free to be who she was, to work as a tiger, to be promoted as a tiger. Tiger Ramona's coworkers were afraid; they wanted her to change. But Ramona was just Ramona.

It must have made Ramona tired at the end of the day. She must have feared that at the end of the day she might not be able to get out of the cage. And there were moments, Garvin had to admit, when—with as few tigerlike qualities as she allowed herself to have—she felt trapped in the same cage.

Garvin redialed and left her number and address on Ramona's recorder, then she reached into the basket and pulled out another card. Obviously at least as old as the first card, it read: "Pecan Pie—pretty much the same as the recipe on the syrup bottle (always use the dark), but with a little bit of extra this and that."

On the back of the card was another Scripture. "How sweet are thy words unto my taste! yea, sweeter than honey to my mouth! Psalm 119:103" and a prayer. *"Thank You, God, that Your Word and Your presence make even bitter things in life go down sweet."* Garvin rubbed her fingers over the words and tried to imagine what could have brought her Meemaw sorrow. She didn't remember her grandmother ever complaining. Funny to learn, in this way, that Meemaw's life had also been touched by sorrow. Meemaw lost her daughter…

Garvin saw now that her own grieving had been so blinding, she hadn't been able to see her grandmother's hurt. She fumbled in her purse for a cigarette and lit it. The phone chirped. She answered.

"Garvin, it's me, Jonee. I've got the scoop."

Garvin sat back in her chair. Hopefully she had the dirt on GoGo Walker. "Okay, let me have it."

"By the way, before I forget, a cleaning woman at Winkle and Straub said to tell you the fat lady hasn't sung yet. She said you would know what she meant."

Miz Maizie. Garvin allowed herself to smile. "Yes, I know."

"Garv, are you smoking?"

Silence.

"That's crazy, Garvin. You worked so hard to quit. You're just going to have to start all over again."

"You don't know what I've been going through. I never even see Meemaw. Maybe for a little while, a quick hug or something, and then she's gone. I don't know how much more I can take. I figure if I can get rid of GoGo—don't you hate that name? Who names their kid GoGo? Who names *himself* GoGo?"

"Well, his name sure didn't seem to stand in the way of any of his activities in L.A."

"But soon as I can get rid of him, the stress will be off of me and—"

"I don't think it's all that bad, Garvin."

She sat at the table gesturing as if Jonee could see her through the cell phone Garvin held in the palm of her hand. "Why *would* you think it was that bad, Jonee? She's not *your* grandmother. Your grandmother is probably snug in bed or knitting in a rocking chair somewhere. Your grandmother is not running all over town with some new young *boyfriend*."

Jonee laughed. "I really think you're blowing this out of proportion."

"Do you know Meemaw isn't cooking anymore? She used to cook all the time. Now she's sneaking out of her house to spend time with this GoGo guy."

"Sneaking? I thought from the number and address you left on my voice mail that the two of you were living in different houses."

"We are, but she never tells me when she's leaving—I just discover she's gone or I hear the car pulling out of the driveway."

Jonee sounded so amused. "It's funny *you* talk about *her* sneaking. Just a couple of days ago I think I remember you leaving me a message in which you said you were glad to be in separate quarters in case you got an opportunity to go hunting...and how many conversations have we had about *you* creeping around?"

"That's not the point, Jonee. And it's really not funny. I'm worried about her—you just don't understand, you don't know about my grandmother." Garvin hoped that Jonee did not hear her voice catch. She rubbed her temples.

"No, I don't know and I don't mean to make fun. But I'm pretty certain Meemaw can take care of herself. She raised you."

"Well, I'm glad you're so confident. But it's been a week now, and a day hasn't gone by when she hasn't been with him."

"Have you said anything to her about it, about him?"

"This is really delicate, Jonee. I could blow everything if I say the wrong thing. You just don't understand."

"Anyway." Jonee's voice sounded cynical. "I have some info for you from the *Times*." Garvin could hear Jonee rustling papers. "It seems like Mr. Walker was quite a heartbreaker when he was in L.A. But before I go into that, I just have to tell you about the weirdest thing that happened to me when I was at the library getting the info."

Garvin inhaled deeply. "Jonee, I don't think I'm in the mood to hear this."

"Well, I've been listening to you moan all morning about what's going on in your life, so you can listen to my little story…*if* you want the Walker information."

Garvin sighed loudly.

"I thought so. So I went to the library to dig up the dirt on Walker. When I leave—with lots of copies at twenty-five cents a pop—I get in my car to drive away. I pull out and I'm sitting at the light."

"In D.C.?"

"No. North County library in Anne Arundel County—I spent the night with my grandmother. So anyway, I pull out onto Ritchie Highway and I'm waiting at the light to turn onto Aquahart Road. You know, where they're building that new bank."

"Mm-hmm." Garvin hoped she sounded as bored as she felt.

"Then out of the corner of my eye I see these two men. One was riding on one of those construction tractor thingies. Only what makes me notice them is that the one is driving really fast, really crazy, and the other one is running to keep up with him. When I turn to get a better look, they look like construction guys and they've got on those camouflage-looking work suits, but my brain tells me something is wrong."

"Jonee—"

"No, wait, I'm serious. I have to tell you this. I keep looking and I finally realize what's wrong—they're kids. Maybe nine years old, and playing around with the equipment. And the one running alongside the tractor looks like at any minute he's going to fall and get crushed by the tractor thingy."

Garvin was growing more impatient. "What does this have to do with GoGo?"

"So instead of going the way I planned, I turn into the shopping center. Now the kids are off the equipment and they're playing in these huge dumpsters that are filled with broken boards and who knows what else."

"I'm not feeling you, Jonee."

"So I start driving around looking for cops because I know this is a disaster just waiting to happen. I couldn't believe it, you know?"

"So what happened?" Maybe she could move Jonee's story along.

"I found some police and let them know. When I drove back by, the kids were gone. I guess somebody got them before they killed themselves."

Smoke curled up from Garvin's cigarette as she massaged her temples. "Jonee, what if their parents were there? What if they were those crazy people who don't want anyone to look twice at their kids, even if they don't want to pay any attention to them? It sounds like an unnecessary risk to me."

"It was so weird though, Garvin. They were little kids and I saw them. I couldn't pretend I didn't see them. And what if one of them got killed or injured? I couldn't live with myself."

"Maybe, but I have enough on my hands with my own life."

"Garvin, that doesn't make sense. Why would you become a lawyer if you didn't want to get involved in other people's lives? When I saw them, I don't know, it was like they were my kids. I didn't know them. They weren't Thai, they weren't even Asian—little blond-haired, blue-eyed kids—but I felt like they were connected to me, that I had to protect them.".

Garvin leaned forward and laid her head in her hands. "Jonee, is something going on with you? Is your biological clock kicking in or something? Or is it that everybody in my life is going crazy—Meemaw, you—and Ramona's never home and she's got this crazy message on her answering machine!" Garvin stubbed out her cigarette, sighed, and leaned back in her chair. "Well, anyway, what did you find out?"

"Garvin, I know everything looks bad now, but it's going to be all right."

"If you say joy will come in the morning, I'm going to scream."

"Huh?"

"Never mind. You were about to tell me what you found out."

"Well, Walker was all over the place. His name showed up in one section or another of the newspaper almost every week. GoGo this and GoGo that. Not a lot of quotes—he seems to be a no-talk, all-action kind of guy. Hard-hitting on and off the field. Always has a woman on his arm, sometimes one on each arm—you know, the model type. A different one each time, no repeat engagements."

Garvin slapped her hand down on the table. "I knew it! I knew it!"

"He was this well-respected, top-notch player—looked like he could play a few more years—then all of a sudden he makes this announcement that he's going to retire. Just out of nowhere. And that's when things start to get interesting."

Jonee had gone fully into briefing mode. "Articles start showing up about him escorting older women, rich widows, always in out of the way places. Where he was a press hound before, now he seems to be ducking the media. After he retired, he stayed around for a while, did some local sports shows. Then he kind of faded into nothing.

"There was one final rumor column speculating about his attachment to these older women, and some possible troubles with his finances."

"Great! He milked all the old women in Cali for money, gets exposed, and worms his way to Meemaw's doorstep! Well, he didn't count on me. Didn't figure on my grandmother having a granddaughter that can match him step for step. He's going to wish he had stayed in L.A."

"Garvin, what are you planning?"

"I'm going to beat him at his own game. He's got a thing for model types? Well, I'm betting that dog won't be able to resist the bone I'm going to throw him. Then I'm going to expose him."

"Garvin, why don't you just tell Meemaw what I told you?"

She shook her head from side to side. "He's got her blinded. She'd just take his side. But this way, if it's right in her face, Meemaw will have to see him for what he is. I've got to go, Jonee. I've got a beauty appointment to make."

Fifteen

◆

arvin flinched and hunched her shoulders, drew her legs to her chest. "You know I'm tender-headed." Garvin faced the mirror and talked to Esther's reflection. Esther frowned and Garvin relaxed...some. She held her hand over her scalp as if to block it, or protect it.

"Garvin, who in Jacks Creek doesn't know that you are tender-headed?" Esther pointed toward her supply closet. "Can somebody reach me the base?" A young girl got up from the chair where she sat near Inez Zephyr by the window.

The girl walked to the closet, a small black purse slung over her shoulder, and began to poke around the shelves. "Where is it?" she called over her shoulder.

"There it is, right there." Esther pointed with the rattail comb. "Right there." She pointed more emphatically. "Right in front of you. If it was a snake, it would bite you."

"The grease, you mean." The girl straightened and held in her hand a large jar of what looked to be petroleum jelly.

Esther nodded. "That's it."

The girl brought the base to Esther. "You should have said grease. If you would have said grease, I would have known what you meant." The girl used a single finger to push her owl eyeglasses up on the bridge of her nose. She made herself at home and sat on the free stool near Esther's station. Her gray knee socks bagged around her ankles.

"It's called base." Esther started methodically making parts in Garvin's hair and applying the base carefully on Garvin's scalp.

The girl watched the process intently. "My name is Matty, Matty Zephyr. Sister Inez is my aunt."

Esther casually bent over and whispered in Garvin's ear. "That figures."

"Are you going to put that all over her head?" The girl talked to Esther as though Garvin were not there.

"Yes, I am." Esther gave the girl her phoniest smile.

"Why?"

"Because her scalp is sensitive, and when I put the relaxer on her hair, her scalp has a tendency to burn in reaction to the chemicals." Garvin could see Esther's reflection look at the sign above her station that said children nine years old and under had to remain with their parents at all times. "How old are you, honey?"

"Ten." The girl pushed her glasses up again. "So if she burns from the chemicals, why does she keep getting it straightened?"

Esther cleared her throat. "So her hair will look nice. She wants to look nice."

"If she doesn't get it straightened, she won't look nice?" The girl started hitting the heel of her right shoe against the bottom rung on the stool.

"Don't do that, honey." Esther's eyes narrowed slightly.

"So I *said*—" the girl enunciated more clearly, as though she thought Esther might not have understood her question the first time—"if she doesn't get her hair straightened, she won't look nice?"

Esther's nerves seemed to be quivering. "No, she could look nice. She just wants to look especially beautiful."

The girl pointed at her own hair. "I wear Senegalese twists. I think they're beautiful."

"Yes, they're beautiful." Esther's smile was getting tighter, and her responses shorter.

"And I don't have to use chemicals that burn my scalp."

"That's nice." Garvin watched Esther carefully apply the cream just above the part, only on the new growth. Almost as soon as the relaxer touched the hair it began to grow limp.

"Don't you think it's funny?"

"What?" Garvin watched Esther's face. It was tight, and she was down to one-word responses.

"Well, maybe more strange than funny. But—" the girl pushed her glasses—"don't you think it's funny that most black women have to straighten their hair to feel beautiful. If most white women burned themselves for their hair to look like ours, we would laugh and call them crazy. Don't you think?"

Esther put her pointing hand on her hip.

"Just think!" The girl slapped her leg and laughed. "What if millions of white women had to get their hair kinked up. If they wouldn't go outside in the rain or wouldn't get in a swimming pool because they didn't want anybody to see them with their hair straight."

Esther didn't laugh. Instead, she dipped her comb into the jar of cream.

The girl stopped laughing. "Sometimes I wonder where that comes from. Who said that God gave us the wrong kind of hair— that God got it a little wrong when He made us?" Matty started swinging her leg again. "Who said that we are only right if we look like someone else?" She tilted her head. "I don't think it's God, do you?"

Esther took her comb out of the jar and just stared at the child like she wanted to kill her.

"Of course," the girl continued, oblivious to Esther's reaction, "now there are a lot of people making money off our hair and how we feel about how we look. A lot of people counting on us feeling like the ugly duckling." She wheezed slightly, shifted on the stool, then adjusted her eyeglasses once more. Everyone turned to look, as though E. F. Hutton had just given the word. Who would have thought that the Zephyr clan could produce a child genius, even an irritating child genius?

Garvin hoped the conversation wouldn't escalate to a fight—especially since it was she sitting in the beauty shop chair with half her head full of relaxer. Esther looked ready to jump.

"Inez? *Inez!* Girl, you better come get her." Instead, Esther gave peace a chance.

Inez peaked out from behind her station and crooked her finger for Matty to come back to her place near the window.

As Matty complied, Esther's image in the mirror spoke to Garvin. "Girl, I was about to lose it!" Garvin laughed, relieved, as Esther continued applying the cream. "Here, hold this." She held the big jar of relaxer that Esther extended to her.

As the comb dipped into the cream, Garvin flinched. "Make sure you just apply it to the roots, to the new growth."

Esther stopped mid-dip and moved so that she was looking directly into Garvin's eyes. "Miss Garvin, this may not be D.C., but trust me, I know how to do a touch-up. Do you see anybody in here with their hair broken off?" Garvin shook her head and slid back in the seat.

She sat still and watched Esther quickly and carefully make parts and apply the chemical-based cream that would straighten her hair. She could hear conversations around the room. Levels of "he said" and "she said" and waves of "Hush, girl!" punctuated by "If I was her I would." Then across the room someone yelped. "Stop! You about to eat all my boiled peanuts!"

"All this gossip. It just makes me sick. And Inez is the worst one of all!" Esther spoke just loudly enough for Garvin to hear. "That's why I don't go to church anymore."

"I wouldn't think that was why."

Garvin looked up. Matty was back on the stool.

Esther stopped and looked as if she were about to take Matty to school, then looked back at Garvin's head and began quickly completing the touch-up. "Well, Miss Matty," she said instead, "what would your opinion be?"

"Well, I wouldn't think that would be the reason. It doesn't make any sense. People gossip in bars and it doesn't stop anybody from going there. People gossip in the grocery store and it doesn't stop anybody from going there. There must be some deeper reason. Gossip just sounds like a convenient excuse."

Esther's head started wagging. "Oh, so you think there's some *deeper* reason? Well, I just figure God wouldn't tolerate all that kind of foolishness, He wouldn't waste His time with people that act that way. He wouldn't be someplace where people like that are."

The girl paused, took off her glasses, wiped them, and replaced them high up on the bridge of her nose. "I think it's just the other way. It proves to me that God really is God, like in the Bible. God is love. And His love is big enough that He loves people like me, people like you, and even people like my Aunt Inez." Matty slid off the stool and went back to her window seat.

The pinched look left Esther's face. She looked several times in Matty's direction. "Come on." She tapped Garvin on the shoulder and led her to the rinse bowl to get the cream out of her hair.

Without saying a word, Esther shampooed twice, applied hair conditioner, and placed a clear plastic bag on Garvin's head that covered all her hair and scalp. "Come on." She began to lead her to a dryer. "We'll just leave the conditioner on for fifteen minutes." She looked again in Matty's direction.

Garvin touched Esther on the arm. "Are you okay?"

"Sure, girl." Esther smiled wanly. "I just…"

From out in the street, the twinkly music of the snowball truck floated into the shop. Women began to quickly move toward the door. "Is it the snowball man?" a patron under a hair dryer asked. Hoods began to fly up in the air and women grabbed purses.

Esther's mood changed. "Come on, girl. Things are looking up." Garvin trailed Esther to the door.

They followed the crowd outside. Parked at the curb was a white truck with *Smitty's Snowballs* painted on the door. A small man worked with a scoop, putting ice into paper cups of different sizes.

"I want a large one," one woman said. "With extra custard flavor."

"You want marshmallow?" The man smiled and winked.

"Just a little bit." The woman blushed.

"We want the blueberry special," another woman pointed to herself and a woman standing near her. "Mediums."

The man filled two medium-sized cups, then reached a dipper into a large, stainless steel pot fitted inside an even larger stainless steel pot containing ice. Each time he opened one of the refrigerated compartments, a quick shot of cold cut through the summer heat. "You want a little soft-serve ice cream in it?" He beamed at the two women, his big eyes focused only on them. They nodded first at each other, then back at the man. "Two women with good taste."

Garvin watched the women, could feel the twitter in the air. The women were so excited they had forgotten to be self-conscious that they were on the street in rollers, in bags, half-curled, half-pressed. They seemed to be unaware of cars that passed by. The man didn't seem to notice their half-done appearances. Instead, he talked to each woman as if she were Queen Esther.

"Hi, Smitty." Garvin watched, surprised at Esther's demeanor when their turn came to stand in front of the little man. "Looks like business is good." She was almost coquettish.

"Yeah." The man ducked his head; he appeared to have lost his gift of gab.

"You know what I want, Smitty. Strawberries." Esther was openly flirting with the man!

"I told you I don't have no strawberries on the cart, Esther. Just blueberries."

"Well, I'm gonna keep asking. One day you're going to have what I want—you're going to get me some strawberries."

The man shook his head and looked like a bashful schoolboy.

"I guess pineapple will do for now. Large." Esther pointed at Garvin. "Give her orange sherbet flavor and vanilla." She turned her eyes away from Smitty for a moment and looked at Garvin. "What size?"

"Small." Garvin couldn't believe Esther's boldness with the man.

"I saw you at the movies with some little bitty woman."

"What woman? I go out a lot...now." The man lifted his head as if he were asserting himself.

"I don't know her name. I've seen her before; she's from another county. But you know what? She was too little for you. A man like you, you know your little-bitty genes are crying out for a big woman. You've got to give your children a chance!"

Garvin was trying to be invisible, but laughter just burst from her.

"What am I missing?"

Garvin turned and looked up into a smiling, dark-skinned face with GQ features.

"What's up, Smitty?" The two men slapped, then grabbed hands. The man looked back at Garvin. He had to be at least six-foot-four, a well-toned wall of a man. "So, what am I missing? I like a good joke."

Garvin stammered, suddenly self-conscious as her hands flew to the bag on her head. "Do I—do I know you?"

"GoGo," the man answered. "GoGo Walker."

Sixteen

◆

unlight hit his face so bright he could not ignore it, couldn't roll over just one more time. GoGo rubbed around his mouth and around his eyes for morning crust, for morning matter: *duck butter.* He laughed a private laugh. It had been a long time since he had heard that one. *Duck butter.* Where did that come from anyway? *Duck butter.* He shook his head, smiling, as he swung his feet to the floor. The things kids came up with.

He scratched the side of his leg through his pajama bottoms. GoGo looked down at what looked to be at least two hundred images of a cartoon beagle, ears flopping, feet pedaling, running all over the red silk background of his pants. He had come a long way…but a long way to where? He wasn't sure if this was a better place or not. From smoldering, steamy, silk men's loungewear to some black-eared, big-nosed beagle.

No, he corrected himself, he was *sure.* He was on his way to a good place.

GoGo stood and stretched, enjoying the morning quiet. He took pleasure in the stretch, in the way he could feel each muscle move, even in being alone, of being quiet. He raised his arms above his head and rotated his shoulders, felt the pull and release of his shoulder and back muscles, then in a fluid motion pulled off his white sleeveless T-shirt and headed for the shower.

Behind the leopard print curtain, steam cleared his nose.

GoGo liked the water hot. He liked lots of soap and long showers, but he would have to cut this one short. He was due to meet Smitty in forty-five minutes. They were going to put a new engine in Smitty's truck. It had been a long time since he'd done anything like that. A long time since they'd talked.

"What's up, home slice?" GoGo emphasized the last two words, stretched them out to mock the hamburger commercials he hated, commercials that always made it look as though black folks were shouting "hallelujah" over fast food.

When GoGo came to stand beside the truck, he popped his friend with the work towel he had brought with him. Smitty stood up and looked like he was trying to scowl at GoGo. He never had been able to pull it off in the past, and it didn't look like he was going to be able to pull it off today. "Man, you play too much. If I hit my head on this hood, man…"

"Yeah, yeah, yeah." GoGo dropped the army green backpack that he carried to the ground. "Still trying to go for bad. *Shorty.*" He threw a fake jab at Smitty and the two of them pretended to spar—the language they had spoken all their lives.

"Okay, okay, man. I don't have time to fool around with you. I got to get this truck fixed. I got work to do. I got to have this truck fixed so I can keep selling my snowballs till I can do something better."

The two men threw a few more jabs, then settled down, both their heads leaning over the truck. "You know my business is going good, GoGo man." Smitty turned the torque wrench. The cranking sound provided background accompaniment to his words. Both men kept their eyes down while they worked.

"So I hear, man. 'Smitty and his snowballs!'" GoGo imitated

the sound of the women's voices.

"That's all right, man. I may not be big time, yet. But I'm getting there."

"Ain't nothing wrong with it, Smitty man. Nothing at all. You doing good. Besides that, big time ain't everything." GoGo cleared his throat, a signal to change the direction of the conversation. They worked for a while in silence. GoGo stood up, shifted his weight on the concrete block on which he stood, and wiped his face. "Anyway, man, where did you get this snowball idea anyway?" He stared briefly at his friend's head then leaned back into the car.

"B-more."

"Huh?"

"Baltimore, man. In the spring and summer people can't wait to get snowballs. From a stand or from a truck. Man, people come pouring out the house like the first thing spring make them think of is snowballs. Grown folks, kids, everybody. The vendors pile this ground-up ice in a cup and squirt flavors on it: cherry, orange, spearmint, chocolate, piña colada. All kinds of flavors. The people go crazy."

GoGo kept looking down into the motor, working with his hands. He could tell from Smitty's voice, though, that he was standing up, moving his hands around like he was excited.

"Sometimes they add marshmallow."

GoGo frowned at the thought. "Marshmallow?"

"No, man. You got to taste it. A little marshmallow on top. Maybe some in the middle. People like it, man. Sometimes they put in a little soft-serve ice cream."

GoGo turned his head a little to see his friend's actions. Smitty seemed still more excited. "Seemed like a quick business I could throw together, bring that taste back home. Only I figured, hey, I got all these blueberry bushes on the land. I can give it my own taste. Add blueberry juice, a little fruit, and make my *own thang*. The people love it. 'Specially the women at the beauty shop. Man, they go crazy for it. It's like it's got special powers over the women!"

GoGo looked up from where he worked. "Yeah, right."

"No, really, man. You should see how they come running: from their houses, from their jobs, 'specially from that beauty shop, man, from Big Esther's. You saw it yourself the other day. 'Specially Big Esther herself. Sometime, man, the way she come running scare me myself."

GoGo stood up and looked across at Smitty. "Why is that?"

Smitty's excitement seemed to suddenly go cold. "What you mean, man? You know why. That's a big woman. A woman like that, she get excited, she could do some damage. *Big* damage." Smitty laughed a little, one of those invitational laughs, like he hoped GoGo would laugh and agree.

"You sure, Smitty? You sure that's what it is?" GoGo watched his friend shift from foot to foot.

"I hate when you do that, GoGo. Like you know something everybody else trying to figure out. Always putting people on the spot. You make it hard to be your friend, man. Real hard, sometimes."

GoGo smiled. Smitty seemed like a worm sticking its own self on the hook. "Is that a threat? I hope that's not a threat, man." GoGo turned his fist sideways and thumped his chest while his face and voice mimicked sorrow. "You know I couldn't take it if you dumped me, man. I thought you were my boy."

"GoGo, man, you play too much. *Way* too much."

"Okay, Smitty, but I just think you're complaining a little too much about Big Esther. Something don't sit right. Besides, it always seemed to me that you liked the healthy girls." GoGo rubbed his head. "In fact, man, it seems like when I think back I remember you talking about a girl named Esther when I would come down to visit my grandmother in the summers. How many Esthers are there in Jacks Creek?"

It looked to GoGo as though Smitty was rubbing the rag he was holding over his hands hard enough to wipe the skin off. "What's it to you anyway? There are several young ladies I keep time with. So why you worrying about me and my true feelings. At least I got *somebody*. Who you with? If I didn't know you all my life, man, I might wonder. *Some* people talking. You ain't with fat or skinny, except maybe some old ones. What's up with *that*? If you want to talk about something—talk about somebody's business—let's talk about yours first."

GoGo straightened from where he leaned over the car. "Hmm." He paused then stepped down from the cinder block. "I guess that's fair." He nodded toward his backpack. "Let's eat while we talk. My stomach is about to touch my back."

The two men walked from the truck in the direction of the sun. GoGo's boots crunched dried grass, leaves, and he stepped on and over rocks as they walked toward a stream that ran across Smitty's property. Just as GoGo remembered—he could hear the stream before he really saw it. There was something about the water that had drawn him, even as a boy.

"You caught anything from that stream lately?"

"I ain't had much time for fishing, GoGo. You know, I been working on my business."

"Yeah, I know how it is. But I'm trying to learn how not to let all the stuff I'm doing to *make* my life better keep me from *living* a better life." The two men walked on in silence until they came to the stream's edge, where they found seats on large rocks nearby. GoGo jerked the backpack open, reached in, and tossed a sandwich to Smitty.

"What is it?" Smitty poked at the opening to the sandwich bag.

"Yeah, right. Like it makes any difference. All of a sudden you got gourmet taste buds?" GoGo laughed. "It don't look like you packed a feast, so it seems like you're gonna have to square with what I brought. Anyway, it's baloney and cheese."

"Baloney?"

"Yeah, like you don't eat baloney. Man, please." GoGo shook his head, smiled at his friend, then looked down at his sandwich. He pulled back the plastic and looked at the lettuce tucked behind the cheese. *Wonder if that qualifies as an attempt at the vegetable and fruit food group.* Between the cheese and mustard, the lettuce was about to go down for the count. Good thing they had decided to eat now.

And also good there were no women around. He wiped his hands on the rag he had tucked back at his waistline. Women would have been disgusted at the thought of the two of them eating without scrubbing the oil off their hands. What was the point? They were holding the sandwiches by the paper and anyway their hands would just be dirty again when they went back to work on the truck. GoGo lifted a bottle of soda to his lips and pulled at the liquid. When he tilted his head back to drink, his sight followed a blackbird flying overhead. He finished the gulp and breathed deeply. Then he belched, like when they were ten—something else women wouldn't understand.

"You know, Smitty, man, there's lots of reasons why I came back here. I made money, so much money…how many limos can you rent before it gets old? Kind of like too much cotton candy."

"I wouldn't know anything about having that much money. I'm just trying to pay my bills." The look on Smitty's face reeked with sarcasm.

GoGo kept talking, didn't miss a beat. Talking was not usually his thing, but it was easier with his friend. "But I made so much money, it lost the thrill. I could tell it was thrilling to other people around me, but it didn't mean much to me. One day, I don't know, it's like I looked up and realized I had messed up." GoGo took another drink and looked toward a bank of trees near the stream. "I didn't know anybody who knew me, who knew who I really was, who weren't more interested in the money and the fame than in me. At least I wasn't sure.

"So since I wasn't sure, I didn't even try to connect. I just did what I thought people were doing to me: I used them for what I could get. Other players, advertising people, whoever, it didn't matter. And women, man."

"Yeah, the women." Smitty nodded his head.

"It's not like you think, Smitty, man. Not even like what I thought it was." GoGo turned to look directly at his friend. "I just used them. I didn't think about them. Sometimes we used each other. Then one day, like I said, I just woke up. Like I just rolled over one morning with a bad taste in my mouth. All I had playing in my head was pictures of these women, like videotape. Something had to change."

GoGo looked at his sandwich. He pulled the bag top over it and crumpled what was left. It didn't look too good anymore. "One minute I didn't care about anybody, and the next minute, I'm examining my whole life. It was crazy. I started trying to figure out who I really was, who I used to be. It got deep. I couldn't make any sense of it."

Smitty laughed. "Maybe it was drugs."

"You know, Smitty, that was about the only thing I didn't do. Funny, but I had this ethic about my body, about being an athlete, something that wouldn't let me defile my body with drugs. It's crazy, you know. I did everything else to my body, but somehow, I just couldn't do that." Smitty looked at GoGo, then quickly turned his head.

"I tried to forget about it. Told myself I was crazy. I tried partying even harder, but in the matter of a month, all day long, man, I could hear my mother's voice and everybody else that had tried to teach me how to live." GoGo shook his head and then swatted at a gnat that kept circling his head. "I couldn't take it, man. When I walked around, when I slept, I couldn't stop thinking about it. And the more I thought, the more I realized how much I had messed things up." He took his hand and bounced it against the top of one of his knees. GoGo caught his breath, as though tired of talking. The water kept churning in the background.

Sometimes it seemed he had to tell the story, even if he didn't want to. "There had to be some way to stop the voices. To stop the guilt. I mean, some of it was easy, like I stopped agreeing to do ads for stuff I didn't believe in just so I could get more money." Smitty grunted, then snorted.

"Okay, man, you may not understand, but I'm telling you. Anyway, most of the stuff I could make right, but the thing about the women, the more I thought about it, the worse it got. Most of them, I wouldn't even know if I saw them again, but somehow I really started seeing what I had done to them. What I had done in their lives."

"What you talking about, GoGo, man? It ain't like they innocent. It ain't like most of them weren't looking for what you were looking for."

"I know. But you know what else? I realized that excuse wasn't going to make the voices stop. I was responsible for what I did. Some of them, you're right, were in it for the thrill. But there were just as many that I knew were on some kind of fantasy trip, like I was going to love them; thought they were going to rescue me, make me settle down. I knew it and I used them anyhow, then I made my exit." GoGo looked up at the sky, then back at his friend. "And you know what else, Smitty? I got a little girl. Eight years old."

"What?"

"Yeah, man, I got a daughter. And I know her when I see her, but that's about all. When I woke up, when I came to myself, she was seven. How am I going to fix that? By the time I woke up, her mama was married and not too interested in having me around messing things up. So I send checks and cards and stuff, but that's about it. Never get any response."

GoGo rubbed the back of his neck. "You know, I thought about all the years I had heard people like Jesse Jackson talk about women and babies and being responsible, and how I had laughed about it. I had enough money to take care of anything that came up. Jesse was talking about young kids on the street, not somebody like me. Then I looked up and realized that money couldn't fix it, couldn't fix my daughter, couldn't fix the women. Shoot, it couldn't fix me."

He hadn't planned to talk to Smitty about this, to sound like some Bible-thumper, but he couldn't stop himself. The words fell. "I started going to church again. I kept driving by this one church and then one day, I finally stopped. Man, I almost shook myself to pieces the first time I walked in the door. For sure I knew a bolt of lightning was going to rock the place with me sitting there. I made sure I got out of there before they started asking for people to join. You know what I mean?" GoGo laughed and swiped at his friend's shoulder. Smitty turned and smiled, then looked back at the stream.

Maybe he was saying too much. Maybe he should stop. But the words tumbled. "It helped some, but the voices just kept on, no matter what I did. In the daytime, in front of people, I tried to look like I had it together. Sometimes I would just break out in a sweat for no reason. Then at night I couldn't sleep. Or if I did, it was nightmares about how I had messed up my life and all these other people's lives." Smitty was silent. *He probably thinks I've lost my mind.*

The words bubbled up from deep on the inside. "One night, I just couldn't take it no more. I wouldn't tell this to nobody but you, man, but I backed myself up into a corner in my own house with all the lights out. I just started shaking all over and I couldn't stop crying. I had messed up bad, not just my life, but my little girl's, everybody's."

Like living water. "For real, Smitty. I know this sounds crazy, but I don't remember falling asleep. I must have though." GoGo closed his eyes and he was back in the moment. "It was like I was dreaming, but these words kept running through my head. 'But he was wounded for our transgressions, he was bruised for our iniquities: the chastisement of our peace was upon him; and with his stripes we are healed.' When I could shake myself fully awake, I was still crying and mouthing the words."

Smitty sat silent, looking uncomfortable.

Like a river of life. "Remember hearing that in church when we were kids?" GoGo shrugged. "Why would that even come to me? Why would I remember that? I don't ever recall memorizing it. And it came to me that it was about me. *I* couldn't fix it. I couldn't make the past right, but *He* could. Thousands of years ago, He already fixed what I had messed up.

"You know, Smitty, I couldn't fix it. I admitted it to myself—all the women, my little girl. I cried and told Him all about it. Everything. How I had used people. And I...I let it go. Decided I would try to do right and let Him work out the details, work out the plan."

Smitty drained the last of his soda from his bottle. He seemed to turn his head as far away as he could from GoGo. "Okay, man. I don't mean to be cold or anything." He cleared his throat. "But I don't see what that has to do with you not having no woman. Okay, so we were both choirboys. And, okay, so you found religion again. Okay, but I don't get it. We're grown men, you know? What are we supposed to do? It's all around us—women—all in our faces."

GoGo rolled his shoulders and turned his head a few times—his neck was feeling tight. "What I'm trying to say is, I know it doesn't make a lot of sense if you think about it in terms of how we live. Yeah, I'm a man and when I try to figure it, it just don't figure. But one thing for sure, my way wasn't working. Definitely wasn't working. Look, who was I kidding? I didn't have it together. So I thought, what have I got to lose? If I try it and it doesn't work, what have I lost? Just one day, I had to admit it to myself. It was scary, man. I never been alone—not in high school, not anytime. And people looked up to me *because* of what I was doing—but whatever. I was going to be alone and get myself together."

Smitty looked at GoGo and raised one eyebrow.

"I survived the first night, Smitty, and for the first time in a long time I slept without fits. So it turned into another and another. And I got the courage to come back to my grandmother's house, to try to remember the lessons she and my mother tried to teach me, to find myself, get myself together. I figured, on the field I know right from wrong—no compromises, no excuses. I just have to apply that in the rest of my life."

Smitty spat on the ground, as though there was a bitter taste in his mouth. "Who are you kidding, man?"

"It's not easy, Smitty, man. Let me be the first to admit it. But I know I'm doing the right thing. It took a long time, but I'm finally realizing that God knows more than I do. Not just more than people knew thousands of years ago, but more than I do right now. So I'm doing this thing, one day at a time. It's not easy. I'm still not strong, so I stay out of the way of women, of temptation. I'm still not together—but I'm trying. That's why the older women, you know? First I hung around them because it was safe for me, they reminded me of my mother. Then I realized I was helping them get in shape, giving them attention they needed. Now I realize they're helping *me* and, mostly, I enjoy their company."

Smitty smirked and shook his head. "Yeah, right."

"Look, man, it's not all about how young, how fine, or whatever. It's about more than that. Some of that stuff was just for show. About getting somebody, having somebody with me whose looks I thought would impress other people. That's what I meant about Big Esther. It's not about all that, about the show. There's a more important connection than that."

"I hear you talking, Gandhi, but I'm just not feeling it. Know what I mean? You been out there, man. Done everything you were big enough to do. Now you want to tell me don't try to get mine. Not to take it, not to make the best of the opportunities in front of me. You got to be crazy…I been invisible all my life. Women didn't even know I was alive. Now they got their eyes on *me*—just watch my smoke."

"Smitty, man, all I'm saying is I'm just realizing that I left little pieces of myself all over the country. Pieces I can never get back, valuable pieces. And I wonder sometimes what I have left to give if I ever meet someone else."

Smitty stood and reached his empty bottle and bag toward GoGo's outstretched hand. Appearing to have a change of mind,

Smitty dropped the items, instead, on the ground, then turned and stomped away. "Enough of this, I got stuff to do."

There was a knock at the door; but before Garvin could rise from the bed, the doorknob turned and Meemaw peeked in the door. "It's just me, baby. Mind if I come in?" Just for a moment, as she entered the room, Meemaw's face against the dark blue seemed surrounded by stars.

Garvin raised up on one elbow and smiled at her grandmother. "I must be really settling in. I'm in the bed before you get home and I leave the door unlocked to boot. Just like old times."

Meemaw smiled and kissed her on the forehead. "Busy day?"

Garvin shrugged. "I spent most of it working on the case and visiting with Esther."

Meemaw sat on the edge of the bed. "I just didn't want to go to bed without letting you know how good that pecan pie was. Girl, I almost hurt myself eating that slice of pie! And the meat loaf tasted like you put your foot in it. My grandbaby can burn!"

Garvin laid her head back on the pillow. "Thanks, Meemaw." The low-wattage bulb in the lamp next to her bed provided a soft circle of light. "Don't you think it's funny, Meemaw, how we describe food being really good—'put your foot in it' and 'burn'— somebody who didn't know would think we were saying something bad." Garvin rubbed Meemaw's arm through the sleeve of her jogging suit. "You have a good time, wherever you were?"

Meemaw smiled. "Yes, I did." Meemaw paused, then added, "Do I hear a little something in your voice, Miss Garvina?"

"It's just that I never see you, Meemaw. It's like you don't have time for me."

"Oh, baby." Meemaw caressed Garvin's face. "You know you

are Meemaw's little lamb." She bent over her and kissed Garvin again.

"What do you all do?"

"Who? What do you mean?" Garvin had the distinct impression that Meemaw was only pretending not to understand the question.

"What do you and GoGo do when you are out?"

"Oh, all kinds of things—talk, ride around, exercise. All kinds of things. I told you, he's my trainer."

"You never bring him over here; we never go anywhere together with him."

Meemaw looked solicitous in a grandmotherly sort of way. "Now, why would I do that? You have your friends, and I don't necessarily expect you to bring them to meet me. Besides, I told you, he's my trainer." Her fingers picked at the flowers embroidered on the sheets.

Garvin looked at her grandmother's face, hoping to read a clue there. "I met him yesterday, did he tell you?"

"Met who, sugar?"

"GoGo, your trainer. Did he mention meeting me?"

Meemaw shrugged and smiled. "I don't believe he did."

"Funny…seems like he would have mentioned me."

"You'll have to ask him about it next time you see him."

"Maybe." Garvin began to pinch at the fabric of Meemaw's suit. "Meemaw, since he's your trainer, do you pay him?" She looked to see if her grandmother would give some sign of being flustered or annoyed.

"Of course, baby. I always taught you a workman is worthy of his hire. That includes trainers." Meemaw laughed at her own joke.

"How much?"

"How much what?"

Garvin felt like tying her grandmother to a chair and turning on the hot white light. "How much money do you pay him for training you?"

"I don't pay him money."

Garvin propped herself up again. "So what *do* you pay him?"

"That's between him and me." Meemaw patted her on the shoulder. "Isn't he the cutest thing?"

Garvin thought her grandmother had done probably the fastest conversation shift she had ever seen.

"Never thought I would think a bald-headed man was cute— you know your granddaddy had a full head of hair all his life— but GoGo definitely is cute. Don't you think he's cute?"

How many times are you going to say cute, Meemaw? There was something striking about him though. GoGo looked like one of those statues of the black warrior angels, only with incredibly kind eyes. "He's all right, but I don't go in for *that* kind of man. I'm kind of surprised that you do."

Meemaw raised one eyebrow. "Why are you sounding angry, Garvina? What do you mean 'that kind of man'?"

She was getting too close to blow it; she would have to be careful. "I'm just tired, Meemaw. That's all. Just tired." She laid her head back down on her pillow.

"You know what, Meemaw should let you go to sleep. We have to be up early in the morning for church. I know you need your sleep. You always did get cranky when you were sleepy. Turn over."

Garvin turned over to her stomach, and Meemaw began to rub circles on her back.

"Meemaw, is church going to be…you know, bumpa-thump?"

Her grandmother laughed softly. "It is what it is. Soft is nice,

165

but I'm just a person that likes it…bumpa-thump! Now hush, little lamb." Meemaw kept making circles with her hand as she sang to her. "'All night, all day, angels watching over me, my Lord. All night, all day, angels watching over me.'"

Garvin sighed, she could feel herself drifting toward sleep, drifting the way she did every night Meemaw sang the song.

"'All night, all day…'"

The feel of the kiss on her cheek made her realize she had fallen asleep. Meemaw's breath was warm and sweet on her face. "I love you, little lamb."

"Me too, Meemaw." She heard the lock click when her grandmother closed the door. She dreamed of Meemaw's embrace, and the river. Always the river.

Seventeen

◆

arvin walked up the worn, wooden steps. Same steps, same wrought-iron railings that were there when she was a child. Same wooden double doors flung wide open, same aisle that led through the sanctuary up to the pulpit. It looked to be the same usher with the same white gloves, white nurse's uniform, and little white cap. In fact the usher—Garvin heard "ursher" in her mind—seemed to be wearing exactly the same badge Garvin remembered from all her years at New Jerusalem.

Same problem getting a seat.

What was she thinking of? She stood in the aisle looking from side to side for an empty seat. It was third Sunday and there was always a crowd when the Chancel Ensemble performed.

The usher held up one finger, then signaled to her right side— a sign to Garvin that there was one seat available in the pew at which the woman pointed. The Ensemble, as they were affection- ately known, always kept the church jumping. The group was just as famous for their soul-stirring ballads as they were for bone- shaking praise and worship. And all the while the accompanist's fingers slid up and down the keyboard, while his right foot kept time.

Garvin could feel that old excitement building inside as she inched past people already sitting in the pew. It had been years, and she had forgotten how much she loved the music.

Of course, some people said it was all a show. Garvin remembered...remembered when there were no robes, no electric pianos, and no synthesizer.

Some folks back then—they always denied it if you tried to pin them down—said some of the women in the choir were just trying to get attention. Some folks watched them and could tell you what kinds of slips the singers wore each Sunday. No one else knew or could see, but some folks said they could see unsuitable colors—red, tangerine, green, even polka dots—peeking from beneath the hems of some of the singers' dresses when they got to shouting. It was all a show, some folks said. They said those women didn't get happy; they were shouting to attract attention and show off their bright, Jezebel slips; they were looking for husbands.

Of course, Meemaw said some folks should keep their mouths shut.

Here Garvin was, though, back in New Jerusalem. Just as she was about to sit, she recognized two men seated to the right and one pew back. "Move over Byrd." She had been classmates with Brian Byrd since third grade.

"Man, maybe we better move. I know lightning is about to strike." Winston Salem nudged his buddy just before he slid over to make room for her. It was elementary school all over again.

"Hardy har har." Garvin scrunched her face up and her lowered voice spit sarcasm. "Like the two of you are a couple of religious giants. Who are you, T. D. Jakes and a chocolate-covered Billy Graham?" Garvin put a hand over her mouth to stifle her laughter at her own joke. *Zing!* She still had it. "Move over," she whispered.

Byrd put his hand over his mouth to muffle the sound and to hide the movement of his lips. "Yeah, like you need some room.

They must not be feeding you in Washington. Now I know why you came back home. You need some cornbread."

The two men snickered quietly and lowered their fists in front of Garvin's knees and gave each other dap, each turning his fist sideways and alternately touching the top of the other man's fist.

Garvin sat down. The wood, the smell of it, was familiar, and she remembered. Remembered a little girl who sat on the front pew on the right-hand side—the side where the wise women of the church sat. She sat on the side and in the pew where the older women played tambourines, and where sometimes an old woman could be heard speaking in a strange, unknown language. There were no other children on that row. But after Garvin's mother had died, the women, the mothers of the church had taken her into their circle—a circle that included Meemaw.

Garvin remembered singing with them and praying with them. She could even feel the wood and metal of the tambourine she'd played. What she remembered most, though, was Meemaw. Meemaw was a lightning rod.

She was a lightning rod, and all eyes watched her—even the pastor. Whenever the spirit blew into the church, it was always Meemaw who felt it first. The air around her would hum and sizzle, spreading electricity to others until the whole church was shouting, singing, and dancing—until everyone was free.

Meemaw was a lightning rod.

The choir called Garvin back from her memories. As they sang, "Blessed be the name, Blessed be the name, Blessed be the name of the Lord!" she found herself spontaneously standing, clapping, and singing along. Garvin looked toward the front pew. Meemaw was still a lightning rod.

After the announcements, after acknowledgment of the visitors, and after the offering, Sister Naomi's nephew—the one who had been delivered from an alcohol habit all of Jacks Creek was sure would kill him—stood and sang the sermonic hymn.

Garvin remembered seeing Reggie staggering along the side of the dirt road that ran by the shop, a local dirt-floor shack with no water. Electricity for the shop was rigged from a hidden line that borrowed from a nearby dwelling, unbeknown to the family that resided in the house. The gut-bucket blues belted out of the shop's every crack and out to the road from early Friday night until Sunday morning. Everything shut down for Sunday morning. That included the liquor concession at the shop. Everyone knew the shop's owner bought beer in town then sold the cans at a 50 percent markup to factory workers and fieldworkers who had money and a burning desire for alcohol.

It was almost unbelievable to see Reggie cleaned up and sober. Folks said he had a monkey on his back for sure. It was easy, even now, to imagine him weaving as he walked sometimes on the road or sometimes on the grass. Garvin had driven by him as he lay crumpled on the ground, occasionally bleeding from a fall, sometimes unconsciousness from overconsumption. It was useless to talk to him on the weekends; he was in a cheap liquor stupor from the time he got off work on Friday until the Sabbath. Her images of him, slouched over or arguing at curbside with one of Rahab's daughters were strong. But she could not deny the powerful testimony in front of her eyes. Here was Reggie in church singing a song that reminded everyone that God was sovereign. Garvin stood to her feet and applauded, even before his song was completely over.

Then Reverend Scott took the pulpit.

Garvin sat down and shifted in her seat. Something about the reverend, particularly after she got to be a teenager, made her want to seek a place during his sermons where his eyes could not find her. Today was no different. It was not that his words were angry, nor that he was full of brimstone; it was, instead, the piercing truth. It was the way the words he spoke always seemed to find her.

"I'm not going to be before you long today."

One of the deacons said, "Take your time, preacher."

Winston and Brian seemed restless and uncomfortable in their seats, too. Garvin smiled. At least she wasn't the only one. She looked around the sanctuary and noticed Meemaw's friend, the girl Monique, hunched in a seat not far from the door.

"I get lots of calls at the office. Most of them start off something like this: 'Reverend, I've got a problem.'

"You know, when I became pastor I wasn't very realistic. I was a young man and I thought my vocation was going to be unfolding the mysteries of the gospel to a congregation that just hung upon my every word. Oh, I'll admit it—" the Pastor joined the congregation as they laughed at the story he related—"my vision was of long hours spent doing biblical research so that I could astound you with my revelatory insight." He shook his head and wiped his brow. "Instead, like many of us, I found that the Lord had another job for me: problem solving." He shrugged his shoulders.

"Let me make sure that I'm talking to the right crowd. Do any of *you* have problems?" It looked as if every person in the congregation raised his or her hand. "Do any of you feel like you have more than your fair share?" Garvin nodded and laughed, as did other people around her. "Do you feel that if you could just get your problems out of the way, you could go on and do some other things, give some service you've been wanting to give, if you just didn't have these problems taking up all your time?" There were lots of nodding heads and waving hands.

"Well, I'm going to tell you about a man who had lots of problems, and we're going to follow his lead, we're going to follow his plan. We're going to come up with our own individual Egypt plans.

"First, though, before I get started, everybody get a little piece of paper and quickly list your problems." The pastor took a sip of water from a glass that had been hidden beneath the podium, then looked back at the congregation. "Why are you all looking at me? You're supposed to be writing."

Garvin reached into her purse for a piece of scratch paper and a pen. She felt foolish. It had been a long time. She wasn't sure the pastor was including her.

"I see you all looking sheepish at each other. Just start writing," the pastor said.

She began to list her problems—her job, Ramona…

"Whew! Some of you got some pretty big pieces of paper! Remember, I said quickly."

Garvin laughed, probably her first deep laugh since she had reached Jacks Creek. Probably her first deep laugh in years.

Reverend Scott looked out over the congregation. "Is everybody ready? You got your problems clearly before you? All right now, don't let me get down the road and somebody say, 'I didn't get mine written down, Pastor.'"

"We're ready, Pastor," one of the deacons hollered.

"All right, now. You heard the man. Let's turn to the story of Joseph in Genesis. You all know the story. He was his father Jacob's favorite son and he had a coat of many colors, you know the fellow—make sure you read the story in Genesis, chapters thirty-seven through fifty. See—" Reverend Scott chuckled—"you thought you had it bad—it took Joseph thirteen whole chapters to get his mess straightened out." The church erupted with laughter.

"Anyway—" he laughed again—"he was bragging to his brothers—showing off. The brother had that pretty coat, and can't you just see him flying around waving it in his brothers' faces? Rubbing it in with his coat. 'Nah-nah-nah-nah-nah-nah, Daddy loves me more than you.'

"Well, his brothers got mad, took his coat, and sold him into slavery." The pastor took another sip of water. "Poor Joseph wound up in the land of Egypt. There he was falsely accused of rape, thrown into prison, and kept there for years." The preacher wiped his forehead.

"Now you are probably thinking the moral of the story is don't get the big head and run your mouth when you got a whole bunch of brothers who are bigger than you." Garvin could feel herself relaxing, could feel her burdens lightening as she chuckled. "Well, you're in the right church, but in the wrong pew!" Garvin looked at Winston and Brian and the three of them laughed out loud along with the other members.

"I mean, that is good advice—" the preacher laughed—"but remember, you still got your problems in your hands. That advice might have worked a week ago, a month ago, even a year ago. But right now, you got trouble—holding it in your hand."

Garvin looked at the piece of paper she held.

"The reason we're talking about Joseph is he was a brother with a lot of problems. Fortunately, he goes from the dungeon to the palace, and I'm going to tell you how he did it, so you can do it too." Reverend Scott put his finger up to his lips and looked around. "Shh! Pay attention now. The man went from living with thieves to sitting on a throne, and we're going to learn how he did it. Why, you ask?" He laughed. "So you all can stop calling me."

Garvin laughed and wondered what had kept her away so long.

"So today, we're going to have problem-solving day. We're going to solve them and we're going to do it quickly. And we're going to do it the way Joseph did it. The brother was in chains and fetters, but even on lockdown, he gives us the solution. You ready?" The preacher chuckled. "You all should see your faces. You're looking like, 'Come on, man!'

"Out of all these chapters, we are going to focus on just four verses from Chapter 40, starting with verse 7: 'And he'—we're talking about Joseph—'asked Pharaoh's officers that were with him in the ward of his lord's house, saying, wherefore look ye so sadly to day? And they said unto him, we have dreamed a dream, and there is no interpreter of it. Do not interpretations belong to God? Tell me them, I pray you.'

"Now, we're going to jump to verse 13. 'Yet within three days shall Pharaoh lift up thine head, and restore thee unto thy place: and thou shalt deliver Pharaoh's cup into his hand, after the former manner when thou wast his butler. But think on me when it shall be well with thee, and show kindness, I pray thee, unto me, and make mention of me unto Pharaoh, and bring me out of this house.'

"Well there it is—there's our solution. Our plan. Our Egypt plan. Do you see it? The plan is simple: Think about somebody else. While you're in your dungeon, while your life as you know it is threatened, think about somebody else. Look around and see who you can help get out of the dungeon. Don't you worry about getting out—let God get you out—you just worry about helping your chosen person. Plant the seed of hope in them that is going to grow and be the way out for you.

"You all look puzzled. Yes, that's what I'm really saying. Don't think about the trouble in your hand. Find somebody and you be their angel, help get rid of the problems they have in their hand."

Garvin looked at her hand, then at Winston and Brian.

"First, I want you to look around the room and find somebody you can help." The reverend smiled. "Go ahead, you can look and still keep listening to me. For some of you this might be kind of hard—it's been a long time since you thought about anyone but yourself. That's all right. Ask the Lord to help you. Ask Him who you can be a blessing to; I guarantee you will receive an answer."

Garvin looked until her eyes lighted on Monique.

"Everybody got somebody in mind? If not, pray on it. You'll know soon. But we're going to move on to the next step. The next step is the easiest and the hardest. Look at your own list."

Garvin looked at Monique, then at the paper in her own hand.

"Now, you're going to get a jar with a lid, put your list inside, and close the lid on tight. You're going to pray to God to take care of your list while you help your chosen person with his or hers. Then you're not going to bother your list, or even think about it, for six months or until that person you're helping gets free, whichever comes soonest."

Garvin sighed; it seemed impossible.

"Go ahead, some of you probably want to cry, or want to kiss your little pieces of paper good-bye. I know it's hard—for some of us our problems are like our children, like our loved ones." He laughed. "For some us, our problems are our children." He shook his head. "But I'm asking you to trust God to be the problem-solver, and I'm asking you to be His angel in someone else's life. Make them feel special, let them know God loves them and hears their prayers."

Reverend Scott went on with his sermon, and Garvin sat back in her seat. She could let Ramona go. She could let the job go— what control did she have anyway? But what about Meemaw? What would happen if she left Meemaw defenseless while GoGo wound himself tighter and tighter around her grandmother?

Garvin fingered the piece of paper in her hand.

What about Meemaw?

Eighteen

---

eemaw laughed as Garvin tiptoed over to smell the contents of the big pot cooking on her stove. Garvin didn't remember being a big fan of crowder peas, but the smell was making her stomach shout. Salty, onion-seasoned, rib-sticking food. The smell drifted to her on a puff of steam. It was good to have Meemaw visiting in her little home for a change.

"Girl, get your nose out of my pot!" Meemaw swatted at her with a dish towel. "You need to check that chicken you have baking in the oven."

Garvin grabbed a pot holder, pulled open the oven door, and bent to poke the chicken with the large fork she held in her hand. It was looking good, just starting to brown.

"Is the water boiling yet?"

Garvin checked the pot; Meemaw had promised to teach her how to make hot water cornbread.

"My baby is going to turn out to be a good cook yet. Your granddaddy would have been so happy to see you in this place— and cooking no less. I do believe that you are going to turn out to be good marriage material after all." Meemaw reached into one of Garvin's cabinets and got a large blue, glass mixing bowl.

"Wait a minute, Meemaw—" Garvin stood at her grandmother's elbow watching intently—"I'm not learning to cook for a man. Basically, I'm learning to cook because you forced me, remember? I'll admit I'm starting to like it, but it definitely has nothing to do with marriage. As a matter of fact, I'm not sure that I'm at all interested in being married."

"Suit yourself." Meemaw shrugged her shoulders. "Hand me a measuring cup, would you?"

"That's all, Meemaw? Just 'suit yourself'?"

"Honey, you are a grown woman. Nothing wrong with being single. Who am I to tell you how to live your life? You have to answer for yourself." Meemaw measured a generous amount of cornmeal into the bowl.

"Meemaw, I already had church today. Why do I feel another sermon coming?"

"Oh hush, child. I *just* said suit *yourself*, remember?" Meemaw searched the countertop with her eyes. "Where's your shortening?"

Garvin went to the pantry, pulled out a large can of butter-flavored shortening, and took it to Meemaw. "I enjoyed church and everything. I'll even admit I feel better—in fact, I'll go so far as to admit that I'm thinking about trying the Egypt plan thing. I thought your friend, that young girl Monique, might be someone I could help."

Meemaw beamed at her. "You don't know how good that makes me feel. That child needs somebody, and you just might be the one… God works in mysterious ways. Isn't that something? Today is your first time back to church in a while and, as far as I know, it's her first time in church ever. Next time I'm over here I'll make sure I let you know how to get in touch with her." Meemaw started humming.

"Well, don't get too happy, Meemaw." Garvin reached into a drawer and handed her a big spoon. "What Reverend Scott said made sense, and he was funny. But that doesn't mean I agree and surrender to *everything*. I am not going to live my life bound by somebody else's rules, some rules some men probably made up long ago to keep women in line."

"Garvina, if you don't want to hear what I have to say, then let's not have this conversation. Let's just enjoy this good time together." Meemaw pointed toward the pantry. "Pass me the salt, sugar."

Garvin talked as she walked to get the salt. "Listen, Meemaw, everybody knows the Bible has been translated over and over again. Everybody knows that many of those men had less than honorable motives." She grabbed the round, blue box with the girl on the cover. "I believe in God, Meemaw. It's just that everybody has to find his or her own way. The way that works best for him or her. Certainly a big God can understand that."

Meemaw laughed and shook her head. "You don't believe God."

"Meemaw, how can you say that? How can you say I don't believe in God?" Garvin wasn't sure if she felt hurt, offended, angry, or all three.

"I said you don't believe God. And I can say it easy, baby. How can you possibly say that you believe God is—God who created the whole universe—then in the next breath say you are big enough to dictate to God the terms of how you are going to serve Him? Like you will pick up your jump rope and go home if God will not play according to your rules. Something is wrong with that picture. Like you think you are big enough to boss God around. Like God can't play if you decide to go home." Meemaw chuckled and shook her head. "Of course, I do remember feeling that way myself some years ago."

Garvin could feel her courtroom instincts kicking in. She tried to calm herself, but it was not working. "Meemaw, it's not God I have the problem with. I don't want you to say I don't believe in God, believe God, or to even think that about me. It's the men who wrote the book that I have a problem with, men who said they were representing God. How do any of us know that they didn't get their own agendas mixed in there with what God says?"

Garvin wiped her hands on her apron. "For example, I can see many years ago why women needed to be married. But in this society, I can take care of myself. I don't need anyone to take care of me and if I choose to have fun, it's of no consequence to anyone. I'm not a kid; I'm certainly not going on welfare. I just don't need anyone telling me how to live my life, especially not based on a Book that has as its foundation a lot of outdated thinking."

Meemaw looked at Garvin and shook her head. "You know what, baby? It's difficult to even have this conversation with you. You know what I believe." Her grandmother nodded her head toward the pot of boiling water. "Get me two cups of that boiling water and pour it in here while I stir." Garvin went to get the water while Meemaw continued talking. "You know why it's difficult to have this conversation? Because you are talking like you are an expert, only you've never read the Book. And I know you, Garvina—you would never let anyone get away with that in the courtroom." Meemaw nodded toward the bowl. "Pour it slowly."

Meemaw began to stir. "Now why would an intelligent woman like you do something like that? Why would you argue about something without ever reading what you're arguing over? My guess is that you are afraid to read the Book—maybe afraid that it will change your life. So you have to make up excuses why it's not worth it for you to read the Bible. All I say is, go ahead and take the challenge: Read the Book, and then we can talk. Don't make up excuses because you're afraid."

"I'm not afraid, Meemaw!"

Her grandmother raised a hand to indicate to her that she was pouring too fast. "You know what, baby? Meemaw was afraid too at one time. I wanted to do what I wanted to do and I wanted to think I was right about it. I didn't want anyone telling me anything that would make me wrong; I was scared." Meemaw kept stirring and the shortening began to melt.

"Scared of what?"

"Scared my life might change. Scared I might have to stop doing what I was doing. Scared if I read it I would be accountable. Sometimes, baby, it's just that we're too smart for our own good. Too impressed with our own selves. Too impressed with how pretty we are or how educated we are; with our cars, with our money, with our jobs. And we think God is impressed too. Sometimes we're too impressed with how good or righteous we think we are; sometimes even with how much we've been hurt or suffered. We're sure God is just overwhelmed by us and we think—we want special permission to live the way we want to live. The rules are for other people, regular people, bad people—not for us."

Meemaw kept stirring. "We say, 'I've been hurt so I ought to be able to eat this huge piece of chocolate and not suffer for it.' Or 'I'm basically an honest person and it's hard to survive in this world, so it's okay for me to hide these rotten apples at the bottom of the basket.' Or 'I'm a good person, a self-sufficient person, a person with self-control; I'm not loose—so it's okay for me to sleep where I want to every once in a while,' or 'Somebody treated me bad, so it's okay for me to do these drugs.'

"We forget that the devil will meet us right where we are, wherever he needs to meet us. He loves whispering excuses to us why it's okay in our special circumstances if we break the rules. Believe me, he whispered the same things to me; that's how I know. Don't you think it's funny that we can look at other people doing wrong and see why they shouldn't do it, but we don't have a clue when it comes to looking at our own sin? But when we disobey God, our actions are saying we don't believe in Him, that we don't respect Him, or that we think He is powerless to do anything about our disobedience."

"Meemaw, I just cannot believe that as busy as God must be, He is concerned about how I live my life."

"He loves you, baby. And He is just as concerned about you as He is about Meemaw."

She lifted some of the mushlike mixture up onto her spoon. "It's getting to be about right. Put some of that grease in the cast-iron skillet and turn it up so it will get hot."

Garvin put several scoops of shortening into the skillet while Meemaw continued talking.

"I'm sorry, baby. Maybe I didn't tell you when you were young how much God loves you." Meemaw stopped stirring and focused her full attention on Garvin. "Maybe I didn't tell your mother clear enough. Maybe I didn't tell you how much God values who you are, what you are to Him. You are precious to Him. He watches over you as if you were His little lamb. He cares how you feel, He cares about what you need, He cares about what you eat, He cares about what you do with your body. Every inch of you, every hair on your head is precious to Him. He wants you to know that you are important to Him. He wants you to be good to yourself in all ways and that includes you not just giving yourself away."

Meemaw stirred, then stopped. "Maybe if you—maybe if people in general—knew how much He cared, they wouldn't just give themselves away like it didn't matter. Maybe we wouldn't overeat, maybe we wouldn't do drugs, maybe we wouldn't give ourselves away. All that stuff is killing us, and He wants us to have abundant life.

"You know something? You know those bankcards everybody uses, the ones where they tell you don't give your special number, your PIN number, away? Well, it just breaks my heart that a man or a woman will give their bodies, themselves, away to people they don't trust or care about. They give themselves away faster than they would give out their PIN number. I believe it breaks God's heart. Eating too much, hating, all the same thing."

Garvin looked away from Meemaw. She stared out the window above the sink. A weeping willow tree swayed in the breeze. "Meemaw, we don't have to talk about this."

"Yes, baby. Yes, we do. We probably should have talked about it long ago. It was hard for my mama to talk to me about virtue and value and probably even harder for her mother. What did they know about it? What could my mother have known about her value? Her grandmother was a slave. What she knew was that when people talked about virtue, about women being on a pedestal, they didn't mean her. That same man that wanted to lynch other men for looking at his wife, that same man who invoked God's name as a defense for his actions, was the same man who ripped my great-great grandmother's virtue from her. No one blinked. The sheriff didn't come; no one hanged." Meemaw raised her elbow to wipe her tears away with her sleeve.

"Meemaw, we don't have to talk about this."

"Yes, we do. Mold growing in the dark won't die until light is shed on it. After slavery, things didn't get much better. Look at my skin." Meemaw held out her ivory-colored hand. "The same thievery was going on. Many of the thieves were folks who were supposed to be good and upstanding, pillars of the community. My daddy and my mama, they knew they better not complain. My daddy better not try to seek justice or defend my mama's honor unless he wanted to swing from the end of a rope. I was the product of someone shaming my mother. My cousin Tommy, the same thing happened to his mama. And it wasn't just my family and it wasn't just in the South, it happened all over. No white man was convicted for violating a black woman. That's why, when I hear folks saying America needs to go back to the way it was...when I hear my good brothers and sisters that I love talk about how the past was so perfect, how holy men were in the past...I wonder if they lived in the same country with me and my people. I wonder if they are blind to what we live with every day." Meemaw dropped her arm. "I don't want the past; I want a new tomorrow."

Meemaw closed her eyes. "Nobody fought over my honor. You don't know it, but before I married your grandpa, what had been happening to other women happened to me. Some man who didn't see me as worth nothing shamed me, took my virtue from me. I was so shamed I didn't tell nobody. I didn't tell your grandpa—didn't tell the man I loved. He couldn't do anything. What could he do? What would have been the good in just one more body floating down the Cape Fear? I hid it from him, made excuses. Shamed myself double."

Meemaw wiped a tear from her cheek, opened her eyes, and then smiled bravely. "That's why I love the Lord. When I didn't feel good about myself, about how I came to be, about how someone tried to take my virtue from me, the Lord loved me. When I wore a coat of shame, the Lord took that filthy coat from me and clothed me with a new coat—a coat colored with salvation and righteousness. He put comfort on me and covered me with praise in front of all men. He gave me new shoes of peace." Meemaw began to swing her arms. "And that's what makes me happy, that's why I shout and sing. Because when I felt I was ugly and had no value, the Lord beautified me with holiness and said I was a jewel in His crown of glory."

Garvin cleared her throat, looked down, then stared out the window at the tree again. The long leaves like teardrops, the bending branches like arms…it was the same tree she had stood up under the cry. The same tree that enfolded her when her mother was gone. Her heart tugged. It touched her to see her grandmother moved from despair to joy.

Meemaw kept stirring, wrapped in an inexplicable peace. "So I have spent all my years discovering that I have value in God's eyes, that He takes pleasure in my purity and virtue. Mine had been stolen. I was angry, and for a while, I just did whatever I felt like doing. I had to learn and to believe that God held who I was in His hands, had to learn that your grandpa had God's love strong enough to forgive me and hold me years later when I told him. I had to learn that if someone did me wrong, if I did wrong, God was ready to help me, to forgive me, to make me whole and take me back. What I know now is that however it is that we come to be less than God would have us to be—maybe it's being loose, maybe it's being a liar, maybe it's being racist, maybe it's being a thief, maybe it's somebody violating us—God loves all of us and wants to restore all of us. He restores us and makes us brand new, and that newness is all He remembers. I was learning myself, so I know I didn't do well explaining it to you and your mama."

A tear slid from Garvin's eye. "You taught me well, Meemaw. You took good care of me. You loved me."

"Well, thank you, baby." Meemaw walked near Garvin and bumped her affectionately with her shoulder. "It's just when I see all these young girls, and grown women for that matter, just giving themselves away—and people arguing over whether they ought to have this or that to keep them safe, or whether they ought to just say no, calling them bad, making them feel unlovable and unforgivable—I get mad. It's the same when I see them arguing over treatment or jail—I get mad. What all those people need to be doing is telling those that are wounded that they are loved, that they are precious, that they have value and great worth. Before they argue, they need to minister to those broken hearts."

Garvin blinked her eyes; she felt tears in the corners. "But, Meemaw, why are the rules just for women? Why do just women have to be pure? It doesn't seem fair that a loving God would make women live up to one standard and then let men do whatever they feel like."

"The standard is for men *and* women. God values men's purity too. Read it for yourself. The Bible talks about Joseph, like we heard today, and how much his father loved him, so much that he gave him a coat of many colors because he valued him. The same way King David valued his daughters who were pure and gave them clothes of many colors. Men give their purity away because they get tricked early in life—they think their purity doesn't mean nothing, that the only value they have is in giving it away. By the time they realize they been tricked, it's too late. And they can't admit they feel like they been used or tricked because they can't admit to being weak. They're men.

"You know Meemaw ain't a preacher, but I believe that means something—those many-colored robes and clothes. I think in a spiritual way, God gives each one of us a coat of many colors, something to let us know that He values us. Sometimes I believe the devil gets jealous of the favor God has given us and the devil tries to take away our favor, our spiritual coat of many colors. He tries to make us feel like we're not worth anything. The sad thing, though, is that sometimes the devil doesn't even have to work to take our coats from us—we just give them away because we think we don't have any value, we don't know what we're giving away.

And I'm not just talking about sex. I'm talking about lying, cheating, drugs, gossip, all the stuff we do that makes us feel less than we are supposed to be."

Garvin turned her eyes from her grandmother. She couldn't explain why she felt so ashamed. This was silly; it was silly to feel ashamed over something perfectly natural. She was a modern woman.

"You know, sweetie, there are things all around us nowadays that tell us that only ignorant or crazy people believe in God, or at least only fanatical people believe that there is a God they have to serve according to His rules. But look at Meemaw. You have known me all my life. Didn't I raise you and take good care of you? Am I crazy? Well, you know I believe in God and that we have to serve Him."

While the grease heated, Meemaw and Garvin washed their hands. Then Meemaw showed Garvin how to form the mixture into small cakes. Meemaw smiled and nodded at Garvin's first efforts. She went to the sink and rewashed her hands. "You go ahead and practice, I'll watch."

The warm mixture felt good in the palms of Garvin's hands. As she formed the cakes, she dropped them into the hot grease. "I want to believe what you're saying, Meemaw. I want to believe it for you—not because it makes sense to me—but to please you. But in my heart I don't buy it. I don't see how—as an adult, self-supporting woman—my discreetly choosing to live the single life I want to live is an offense. I just don't buy it."

Meemaw laid a hand on Garvin's shoulder as she worked. "You know, baby, maybe you are supposed to be single. Nothing wrong with that; that's your choice to make. Be happy, take joy in it. But there are blessings and responsibilities that go with that choice. Being single, you can use your time how you want to, spend more time on your work, be more focused. On the other hand, if you're single you have to be celibate.

God intends love for one special person willing to commit everything to you. Love between a man and a woman is a precious thing. It is a love that transforms and heals; love melts hearts and touches heaven. Those are God's rules, and those rules don't just apply to little girls or welfare mothers; they apply to you too.

We have to trust that He knows best and wants what is best for us. God is a holy God and He cannot bend the rules for you because you are older, because you have a good job, or even because you are a good person with a good heart.

"And, baby, you know you don't live in the world by yourself. People are looking at you. Children are looking at you, whether you want them to or not. And they are not going to wait until they get to be your age to try to do what it is they see you doing. Like children always have, they want to be grown-up right now.

"That's why I always say, don't take down. When you bend the rules the way that it suits you, you make someone else feel like they can bend the rules to suit themselves. I know that's not what you want to hear, but God knows best. Trust me—that's one thing I have learned in seventy-something years. If you want to live happy and live long, follow the rules. And the only place to find the rules is in the Book." Meemaw leaned down and kissed Garvin on the cheek. "Despite what you might think, Garvina, I'm not judging you. How can I judge? I'm struggling myself. You probably think I'm preaching at you, but I'm doing it because I love you."

"I love you too, Meemaw. I know what you want me to believe, I'm just not sure that's how I feel. From my heart, I can't honestly say that I believe all this. But I want to believe it for you."

"Don't do it for me, baby."

Garvin squeezed the corn cake that was in her hand. "Meemaw, I—"

"All Meemaw is saying is try it. Read the Book. He is a forgiving God, a loving God, and a merciful God. But He is also Holy, and His desire is that we follow the rules. He'll help us follow them, by His grace. Read the Book."

Garvin dropped the bread into the fat, then used a scoop to turn the cakes that were already browned on one side. She turned and scooped the last of the hot water cornbread from the bowl into her hands.

Meemaw stroked the side of Garvin's face, as if dusting away cornmeal or flour. "Garvina, every day I struggle to try to live right. You may not believe it, you may not see it, but inside I know it's true. I still have desires—I still want the biggest piece of cake, and sometimes I want to cuss at someone who has hurt my feelings. Some days I just don't feel like being nice. Some days I want my prayers answered first. But the difference is, I know what He wants and I have learned to love Him more than I love myself. So I choose to do what He wants me to do, even though that means that I have to deny myself. And I have learned to do that because I have learned to trust that He really exists and He really does want what's best for me.

"When I look at you, despite all your tough show, I know you are still the same tenderhearted little girl you always were. I know you've toughened up because you think you have to do that to make it through life. It's almost like you've tried to shut your heart down so it can't be hurt. The same thing with men—you want their company and their pleasure, but you don't want to risk your heart, so you put on another tough layer to keep them from your heart. I'm just afraid that in order to be safe, you might be shutting away the very best part of you."

Garvin turned her head toward her grandmother. "I just get tired of hearing the same thing over and over again. I stopped wanting to hear it after I heard it the first time."

Meemaw kissed her forehead. "It's love, baby. I don't talk because I want to nag. I talk because I love you. And sometimes the greatest love is telling people what they don't want to hear."

All this made perfect sense, following the rules and being responsible...until she thought about her grandmother and GoGo. "Meemaw, what about you and—"

A car horn interrupted her.

"Oh my goodness! I forgot that child was coming. I wasn't thinking that I was supposed to meet with him when I came over here." Meemaw hugged Garvin, gave her a quick peck. She looked in the direction of the honking car and then back at Garvin. She pressed her lips again against Garvin's forehead, then turned and moved quickly toward the door. "I was looking forward to eating this meal with you. I promised him, though." Meemaw looked at the door again, then at Garvin. "We'll make it up, but I've got to run now. He needs me."

Her hand grabbed the door handle. "Good thing I left my gym bag sitting by the door." The screen door slammed shut behind her. Garvin ran after her, stopping at the door, her hands full of cornmeal. "Meemaw!" she hollered. It was too late.

Her grandmother was already in the red car, and it was pulling away.

Nineteen

It was going to be a good day. Monique was not going to let anything or anyone ruin it for her. Today was a new day. It was Monday, a new week, a new start. She walked down the hall giving herself a pep talk. *I may have messed things up before. I may have doubted myself, but that is all behind me.* She walked into her first period class and sat down.

Mrs. Williamson motioned for her to step out into the hallway. "Monique, you've got to get yourself together. That's why you're in summer school now. I don't know what's going on with you, but I don't have time for it. You're not doing your homework. You're failing your tests and quizzes. I know you're smarter than this."

It's going to be a good day.

Monique could feel the walls starting to close in around her. It was hopeless; there was no way to start over.

And yet, despite the voices that tried to convince her otherwise, she kept trying to reassure herself. *It's going to be a good day.*

Her teacher took a step closer. "Are you listening to me, Monique? Don't try to tune me out. I know things have been hard for you, but you've got to stop making excuses."

It's going to be a good day.

In spite of her efforts to convince herself—to give herself hope, Monique wanted to run, to run away from the reproach. *Just one day, just one break. I know I messed up, but I just can't take any more…no more criticism.*

But just when she felt ready to scream, to run, Monique spoke hope to herself again. *It's going to be a good day.*

"You're not doing your homework. What kind of life do you think you're going to lead if you don't finish high school? And you need to know that the way you're heading, you are not going to finish. I just don't have time to baby-sit you. I've got other students who need just as much attention as you do. I'm trying to help you. Are you listening to me, Monique...?"

It's going to be a good day...

"Come on, now." Meemaw called over her shoulder to Garvin. As the two walked down the sidewalk on Eden Rock, she tried to act as though she wasn't excited to be going to the mom-and-pop store with her grandmother. After all, they weren't going anyplace special. Just down the street to Mr. Green's, just some place she had been countless times.

That's what she tried to tell herself.

"Come on, Garvina!"

She was about to correct her grandmother, remind her of her new name, but what was the point?

"Come on, now. You know the early bird gets the worm." Meemaw reached back and grabbed Garvin's hand. "Come on here, girl. And stop scuffing your feet."

It had been a long time since anyone called her girl—a long time since she'd *allowed* anyone to call her girl. Despite all her intentions, Garvin smiled.

"What's so special about Mr. Green's, Meemaw?" Garvin tried to keep tension between her and Meemaw's arms, kind of like a puppy on a leash. A postcard picture, only she was thirty-something.

"He gave me a call this morning and said he had something special and that I should come right over. Besides that, he's my friend. Besides *that*—" she smiled at Garvin—"it's some time for us to be together, Miss Fussy. For me to make up for running out on you. Your Meemaw is sorry and I'm sucking up to you."

"It's not that easy, Meemaw. You just dropped me. Ran off like I was nothing."

Meemaw turned and tilted her head in Garvin's direction as they walked. "I just can't explain it now, Garvina...he needs me."

Garvin stopped still. "No, I don't understand it. I don't understand you and this guy." She wanted to kick herself as soon as the words flew from her mouth. Her grandmother stopped walking, turned, and looked as if she were reading Garvin's mind. *If I'm not careful, I'm going to blow the whole thing.* She forced a smile, "I guess I'm just feeling like second fiddle, Meemaw. And I don't like it."

Her grandmother wrapped Garvin in her arms. Began to plant loud kisses on her face. "Oh, Meemaw's little baby." She spoke in between kisses. "I'm sorry. You know I love my Garvina."

"Meemaw!" Garvin acted as if she wanted to pull away, but not so much that she would miss the kisses. The same kisses that had helped her make it through days without her mother.

"Is that better?" Her grandmother's gentle hand tilted her face upward. Garvin nodded and hugged Meemaw. The two resumed their stroll. Meemaw bumped hips with her and Garvin giggled. They held hands, swinging them, right up to their arrival at Mr. Green's door.

An old-fashioned bell above the door announced their arrival, as did the scraping sound of the door on the jamb. "Mr. Green?" Meemaw poked her head inside, then stepped into the store.

Due east and running perpendicular with Eden Rock was Main Street. On Main Street were the courthouse, the large grocery stores, the hospital, the library, the gas company, the department store, and five different churches. Garvin remembered how, as a little girl, she had thought of Main Street as the center of the vanilla side. Eden Rock was the center of the chocolate side. And in her young mind it had been clear that, like Neapolitan ice cream, the two did not mix. She remembered that on Main Street, black people—chocolate people—were not expected to linger long and that one was likely to be inadvertently harmed by people who meant no harm.

She also remembered that she was not clear what had happened to the strawberry; why it was not present.

Mr. Green's store on Eden Rock was a safer place. She had always felt welcome here. It was just as Garvin remembered. Polished, dark wooden floors, linoleum in high traffic areas, cinnamon and orange smells in the air. There were seven rows of shelves, each one chock-full of products. There was an aisle side devoted to cleaning goods and car maintenance products. Another aisle side full of canned foods—cream, soup, peaches, green beans—and yet another with candies, chips, and cookies. That had been her favorite aisle. When Meemaw sent her for cooking starch, for clothes bleach, or even for onions, Garvin always found an excuse to go down the candy aisle. It just always seemed to be the most convenient aisle to walk in or out of the store.

This time she followed Meemaw to the front of the store. The wall was covered with jars of all sizes filled with tomatoes and peppers. On the top shelf was Garvin's favorite: large jars full of kosher dill pickles. One jar, half full, sat on the countertop. A label taped to the jar said *75 cents,* and around the jar were peppermint sticks, cinnamon sticks, and boxes of red hots. Her taste buds remembered the crisp, salty, sour taste of the pickle mingled with the biting sweetness of the candy.

Mr. Green still had a glass display case, and within it was an array of penny candy, three-penny candy, nut chews, Mary Janes, jawbreakers. Garvin's eyes kept returning to the jars.

Meemaw leaned over the counter and called toward the back room. "Mr. Green?"

"Ah, Miss Evangelina!" Garvin recognized Mr. Green's voice, even before he appeared from the rooms at the rear of the store. "What a delight." His hair had grayed and thinned; pink scalp peeked from around the edges of his yarmulke.

Meemaw laughed and patted his hand. "I've got good news for you, Mr. Green. Good news indeed!"

"*You* are good news, Miss Evangelina." Garvin had to fight to keep her mouth closed as Mr. Green lifted Meemaw's hand and pressed a kiss to it. Meemaw giggled—she was giggling a lot these days. Mr. Green lifted his eyes momentarily from her grandmother and focused on her. "Garvin, it's good to see you. Good that you are home for a visit." The expression on her face must have questioned how he knew. "You know how small towns are. We are so overjoyed that you are here, we must run and tell everyone." Mr. Green turned his attention back to Meemaw. "Isn't it so, Evangelina?"

"Oh, I suppose so." Meemaw chuckled again.

He smiled at Garvin. "You have grown into a lovely woman and, God willing, when you are old you will be like your grandmother." His attention returned to Meemaw. "Isn't your grandmother beautiful? She wears her age like fine lace."

Garvin looked at Mr. Green, then back at Meemaw. What was going on? Was the whole town in love with Meemaw? "Sure," she responded.

Meemaw waved her free hand at Mr. Green. "You just say those things to try to make me blush, Mr. Green."

"No." Garvin watched as he squeezed her grandmother's hand. "I say them because they are true. You are a lovely woman, and your presence lights up an old man's life."

Of course, that was it. Mrs. Green had passed on some time ago, so being widowed was something the two older people shared in common. Garvin approved; clearly, Mr. Green was the right age and his intentions were obviously much more honorable than GoGo Walker's.

"When I see you, Miss Evangelina, I remember to smile."

"I like you, too, Mr. Green." Meemaw smiled back at the gentleman. "If only I could convince you of the good news I carry." Meemaw laughed out loud. "I've been trying for years now."

Mr. Green smiled broadly. "You know, if anyone could persuade me, it would be you." He patted her hand, then added, "Come and let me show you. Strawberries, the most enormous strawberries—I held the best ones out for you."

"Oo-oo!" Meemaw followed Mr. Green to the fruits and vegetables section.

Garvin wandered the aisles of the little store while her grandmother and Mr. Green murmured over the fruit, laughed, and exchanged stories. The store still smelled the same. There looked to be the same linoleum on the floor, but as Garvin moved between the aisles and glanced at the older people, it was clear time had passed. Her Meemaw and Mr. Green were older, but they seemed at peace, as though they had found something. As though they had completed some universal task assigned to them and now they were free to marvel over strawberries as big as crab apples. They seemed content to talk about fresh cream and to smell ripened peaches.

She watched as Mr. Green held a strawberry out for Meemaw to bite—her pearly teeth cutting into the crimson fruit—watched them laugh as juice dripped down Meemaw's chin. Garvin could not remember a day, not since childhood anyway, when there was time…when she *allowed* time for…for…she wasn't sure what to call it.

Happiness. Meemaw and Mr. Green seemed to have joy and happiness—something that always seemed beyond her own reach. The door to the shop wouldn't open fast enough. Garvin fought silently with it until she was almost out onto the sidewalk, where she could begin to breathe again. *What's wrong with me?* She gasped for air. She didn't begrudge her grandmother's happiness. Still Meemaw's contentment made her own dissatisfaction so much more obvious. *This is ridiculous, Garvin.*

Soon Meemaw was outside with a bag filled with the large strawberries. "Are you okay, baby? I looked up and you were gone." Meemaw cradled Garvin's face in her hand. "You look a little peaked."

"I'm fine, Meemaw. I'm fine. I just thought about something I need to do, that's all." Garvin forced a brief smile then shook her head so that her face was released from Meemaw's hands. "I-I-I just need to get home, that's all."

Meemaw held Garvin's gaze for several seconds. "All right, baby. Let's go then." The two women made their way home.

Meemaw sat on the wet sand and the water, still warm from the day, washed up over her uncovered feet and barely touched her bottom. She smiled as she thought of her granddaughter and dug her toes into the grains that almost looked like putty. The water was blue with white foam, and there was still just enough daylight that she was able to read. Mist and wind ruffled her hair and kissed her face; she breathed deeply. It had been a lovely afternoon spent with Garvin, and now the beach with GoGo was the perfect ending to the day. Families around them walked along the beach and played Frisbee; the sunbathers had already made their ways indoors.

"Thank you." Meemaw smiled and took more deep breaths. "This was the best idea, coming here to the beach. It was a ways to drive, but I would say it was worth it. How about you?" She let her hair fly, instead using her hands to keep her pages still.

GoGo smiled at her and then looked back at the water. "I never would have taken time to do anything like this when I was in L.A. But look at this…look at this world." A solitary gull flew overhead. "I'm the one who's grateful. Look at all this. And you…you take me as I am. I don't have to act like I'm a star, don't have to keep up some image. But you also don't look at me like I'm crazy, like I've thrown away everything, or like you think I'm up to something."

Meemaw smiled, reached for his hand and squeezed it.

"You know, I thought if I could make it, if I could just go pro I would be free. I could call the tune. But the more I got, the more attention was on me…I was locked in. My life was based on what people expected, what they wanted. And when I just didn't want to be part of it anymore—" GoGo rocked forward a little and then leaned back—"it was like the lifestyle didn't want to let me go. It had me around the neck. I couldn't say what I believed…I don't know how to really explain it. But it was like I had to come back home to find me, to find what I left here looking for."

GoGo shrugged again. "I always seem to do that when I'm with you, Miz Evangelina." Meemaw smiled when he kissed her lightly on the cheek. "Just sort of start running my mouth. I don't want to talk…"

Meemaw bumped his shoulder with hers. "But it's just like fire,

fire shut up in your bones. That's why you can't stop. That's why we get together, you know. So you can talk and do more than just be sorry. Our Lord Jesus Christ needs mighty men of God. It's just my honor to help strengthen you for the great work and battles ahead of you. Come on now, let's turn to Isaiah 61 and you read."

GoGo flipped through the pages of the Bible that rested on his lap. "Out loud?"

"Oh, I think so. Somebody might hear you."

Meemaw laughed while GoGo began reading. "The Spirit of the Lord GOD is upon me; because the LORD hath anointed me to preach good tidings unto the meek; he hath sent me to bind up the brokenhearted, to proclaim liberty to the captives, and the opening of the prison to them that are bound; to proclaim the acceptable year of the LORD, and the day of vengeance of our God; to comfort all that mourn; to appoint unto them that mourn in Zion, to give unto them beauty for ashes, the oil of joy for mourning, the garment of praise for the spirit of heaviness; that they might be called trees of righteousness, the planting of the LORD, that he might be glorified—'"

"Stop right there. That's good enough. Now all this time we're spending together is just for the very purpose you just read. I'm here to teach you more about the good news."

"Yeah, and you've been teaching me. That's for real." GoGo laughed.

"You just got through saying how you felt like you were locked in. Well, now you know you are free."

GoGo nodded.

"Good! Now what you need to know is that that sadness you feel, that sorrow, that shame, that heaviness—well, the Lord has already fought that battle. You've got a new coat to wear, and that's praise!" Meemaw playfully slapped GoGo on the arm. "You're a new creature. You and I both know there's some stuff in your past—and you're not alone, I got some too—but here's some good news: You don't have to try to fix it by yourself. The Lord loves redeeming people and turning their lives around, loves filling people full of joy. I know because *I've* been redeemed."

GoGo smiled. "It's so easy to believe when you say it, I just have to work on keeping it together when you're not around." He rubbed his hand over the pages before him. "Besides that, Miz Evangelina, you know I worry about people talking. Not about me, I'm used to that, but I don't want them talking about you. Sometimes I just want to tell them—"

Meemaw kicked at the tide that washed toward her, then laughed. "Oh baby, they know better. But sometimes people need a little cayenne pepper in their lives. You know how it is. Every Sunday they have fried chicken, same old fried chicken every week. Then they get a little taste for something different. Something with a little more spice. That's all it is, honey. I'm just red pepper. They don't mean no harm. Besides—" she tapped his arm again—"you handsome, but you ain't nowhere near as goodlooking as my husband was." Meemaw giggled. "You got a ways to go."

"Yeah." GoGo smiled, but his eyes did not light. "I know that's the truth." He looked toward the surf. "Sometimes all I can remember is how I blew it. Blew it so bad that, saved or not, I better get used to living alone in this bed I made."

"Please! Don't ruin my time at the beach! I could have stayed at home if you were just going to be a sad sack. If that ain't the biggest bunch of nothing I ever heard. Don't let anybody or anything—not even yourself—tell you that the Lord saved you just to leave you sad and lonely on the shelf. This is just preparation time, I believe. Time for you to get yourself together...and time for Him to work on your mate. Oh, there's somebody for you. It might even be somebody like my granddaughter."

Meemaw glanced sideways to see GoGo's reaction. "She's a good girl, but the Lord is having to do a little work on her too. Garvina—you met her the other day, I believe—can be a little standoffish; sometimes I've seen her be a little reserved. But she's been through a lot. See, a man like you would understand that…but come on, let's get back to our studying. We can talk about Garvina on the way back."

The two took turns reading and explaining Bible verses while the tide slowly rolled in.

Twenty

$\diamond$

arvin sat at the table, the evening sun lighting the room, and fingered the note card Meemaw had given her. Monique Nadir. Meemaw had told her all she knew about the girl—where she lived, how she had watched her growing into a lovely young woman. Then Meemaw told her how she had watched the girl change, had watched her dim until there only seemed to be the tiniest light left, a fragile light.

"Monique needs a little hope, somebody to care, somebody to let her know they see the light that's left. She needs somebody to go out of their way for her," Meemaw had said.

What was she going to be able to tell Monique? It wasn't like her own life was so together—not right now, anyway. Garvin set the card aside and then walked to her answering machine. She had so many problems of her own, she just didn't know if she was ready to take on those that belonged to someone else.

The machine clicked into action. *"Garvin? Guess you're not there. Well, I'll be calling you back. We really need to talk about the case, okay? Time's not standing still. It may not be the kind of case you like, but it's the only case you've got right now. As if you didn't know, this is Jonee. Okay? Call me, okay?"*

Garvin pushed a button and deleted the message.

She looked at the case files lying on the table. What was it that was keeping her from them? She pressed the button for the next message.

"Garv? Garvin? It's me, Ramona." Garvin paused the message. *Ramona?* That was all she needed.

She let the message continue. *"I'm kind of glad you're not there, because I know what you'd be saying. But Garvin, girl, something has happened to me. I guess you know I haven't been at my job. I just can't take it anymore. I needed something different, so I took some time off."*

Time off? Was she crazy?

"You know that guy I met? The minister, Derrick, the one who knocked me down at the metro station? Well, he's been a friend to me, a really good friend."

I'll just bet he has. Garvin would have yelled the words out loud but she was already feeling crazy enough.

"You know, Garvin, I never would have met him if I hadn't got knocked down. Sometimes, I'm thinking, maybe it's better to not try and control everything. Just let stuff happen…well anyway, some people from his church are going on this charity bike ride thing where you ride all over the country—it's just called the Big Ride. Kind of stupid, huh? And he invited me. And I'm going. Actually, I'm gone already."

Garvin's temples began to throb.

"We've been training for weeks and we just started out in Skykomish, Washington. Tomorrow we'll get to Spokane. You wouldn't believe it, Garvin."

I don't believe it.

"All the people—teenagers, old people—just all kinds. We'll be riding for a month and a half until we get back to Washington, D.C. Can you believe it? Girl, I'm so sore, but I'm going to make it. You know this old woman that I share the tent with at night, every night she tells me I'm going to make it. And when she looks at me…I feel…I feel… Anyway, Garvin, be happy for me. And Derrick…I think my whole life might be changing." The receiver clicked.

Garvin ejected the tape and threw it across the room. Everybody in her life, every single person, had gone crazy. What was Ramona doing in the state of Washington of all places? Right. As though a person like her would fit in there. This was stupid. And for what? A man. Running off leaving her job for a man. Garvin grabbed the chair and shook it.

This is it. She had taken about all she could take—Meemaw, Ramona, and her own mother for that matter. Maybe she couldn't get to Washington to save Ramona; maybe she wasn't supposed to. But she was here, and she was not going to let her Meemaw be lost, she wouldn't lose her to a man, to the river. Garvin went to her closet and started sorting through her clothes. Monique would have to wait. Garvin was drawing the line in the sand.

Tomorrow she would begin in earnest; she was going to rescue Meemaw, like Malcolm X said, "by any means necessary."

Twenty-one

◆

GoGo pulled into the parking lot and shut down his convertible. Late morning sunshine like this made paying for the convertible worthwhile. He took the keys from the ignition and placed them under the floor mat. His grown-up toy sure beat all the model cars he had put together on his grandmother's porch when he was young.

He reached for the white towel in the seat next to him. It had been a long time since he had played one-on-one. He could see a cloud of dust in the distance moving toward him. Smitty's truck. GoGo laughed. It was appropriate—Smitty was about to get dusted on the court.

Smitty pulled up and hopped out of his truck. "Come on, let's get this on." He slammed the truck door behind him. "You retired from football and you about to retire from this game too!"

GoGo laughed at his friend—already talking junk before he got his feet on the ground good. "That was low, man." GoGo laughed at his shorter friend. "But I guess you would have to take it there, seeing where you *stand* on things." He removed his watch and threw his towel on a wooden bench at the edge of the court. "Oh, man. I forgot to bring the step stool, Smitty. How you gonna reach the hoop?"

Smitty had dropped his bag next to the bench and was already on the court dribbling the ball. "Stop talking, man. Come on out here on the court. I'll show you how I'm going to reach the hoop.

Talking and procrastinating can only put off your whupping so long. I know you know that—all the whuppings I heard your mama give you!"

GoGo moved smoothly onto the court, then reached to swat the ball from Smitty's hand. In what must have looked to Smitty like one single move, GoGo grabbed the ball and dropped it into the basket from above the rim. "Whup *that!*" he crowed as he landed.

Smitty grabbed the rebound and ran it out to the three-point line. *Whoosh!* Sweet, it went in without touching the net. GoGo shook his head. Other guys wouldn't even have played twenty-one with the height difference, but Smitty hung in there. He had heart. More than that, he was good. At the game. At a lot of things.

The two men played hard, jostling and jarring each other. An occasional yell and a fist in the air punctuated their athletic sparring. Rocks crunched underneath GoGo's and Smitty's feet. GoGo used his arm to swipe at the sweat that rolled from his forehead toward his eyebrows.

Smitty smirked and laughed as he charged for the basket. "You out of shape, man? Ready to give up?"

GoGo moved his body into place to check Smitty's drive. "Not in this lifetime."

They played game after game, neither man seemed willing to surrender, or concede defeat. Early afternoon heat bounced up at them from the surface of the court. Smitty stopped dribbling and used his shirt to swipe grime from his face. "Okay, big man. We're even, but you know I don't like to lose and I don't like ties."

GoGo laughed; Smitty was *definitely* speaking the truth.

"This last basket is for the match. If I go to the hole, if I dunk, the court is mine. You stop me, you're the man."

"Smitty, man, that's like candy from a baby."

"So, let's go."

Smitty's eyes were focused, his breathing heavy as he spun and weaved. GoGo kept him covered, repositioning himself between Smitty and the basket each time his friend moved. He was not going to give this one away. Smitty was going to have to earn it. GoGo smiled, admiring his friend's determination.

In a flash, Smitty darted past him and was in the air. Rising. Rising. Rising. Above the rim, Smitty slammed the ball off the backboard and into the basket. "Now!" Smitty yelled as he landed. "Say my name. Say my name, man!"

GoGo laughed, shook his head, and slapped Smitty's outstretched hand. "How long am I going to have to hear about this one?"

Smitty hooted, danced, and talked big junk as they walked off the court and fell onto the bench, both of them exhausted.

Smitty reached into his bag and threw GoGo a bottle of water. "I whupped you, man! But you still my boy. I don't want to see you dehydrated." The two men laughed. Smitty wiped his face with the brown towel he pulled from his bag. He tilted his head toward GoGo. "It's still a lot of life left in this day. What you say we get cleaned up, drive to the next county, and see what women we can stir up."

GoGo felt his chest tighten. He didn't want to talk about this, to go through the conversation about women again. He had hoped they wouldn't have to go through it, but he should have known better. Smitty didn't like to lose, not basketball and not arguments. "Smitty, Smitty man, we already went through this. I told you how I feel."

"Yeah, right. You told me you were saved, but you didn't say you were dead. You didn't say you didn't like women no more."

"That's the problem, Smitty. I like them maybe too much. You know I still got problems with that, and that's why I run. I still get weak in the knees around women—like around Miz Hightower's granddaughter. Everything about her…troubles…" GoGo dropped his head forward and poured some water from the bottle on the back of his neck.

"I don't get it."

GoGo lifted his head and looked at his friend. "I don't have it *together*, man. I'm just trying to get there. I don't know any other way to cope now. No other way than avoiding and running. That's better than doing what I was doing."

Smitty stomped his foot. "It just makes me mad, man. I'm about to get what I been waiting for all my life, and now you're telling me—"

"I'm not telling you anything, man. I'm just saying how I feel, what I've been through, what I've learned." GoGo shook his head. "And to tell you the truth, I really don't want to go into this now. I just wanted to play ball—"

"You may not be trying to preach to me, but that's what it feels like. Look, man, you already been there. Since high school, you had any woman you wanted. And now you want to tell me don't get mine." Smitty took a drink of water, swished it in his mouth, and then spit it on the ground.

"You been my best friend since we were kids. I love you, man. But I can't be your brother and not tell you the truth. You can stop now before you get as wrapped up in it as I was."

Smitty shook his towel, then snapped it in the air. "Yeah, right. Man, everybody is looking for fun. Why not me?"

"'Cause I look back and ask myself, was it really fun? What was I doing? Man, I didn't even want a woman to look at me like she might really be thinking about commitment. And don't even say the *m* word." GoGo stretched his arms above his head. "But I ask myself, what was I trying to stay away from?" He took a deep breath. "You know, I told myself I was being honest so that made it okay. I would tell them I didn't want nothing but a good time. But I knew the deal—I could see it in their eyes. I was saying 'no commitment'; they were thinking, 'Oh, he's just afraid to say he loves me.' I was saying, 'I'm not marrying anybody'; they were thinking 'He wants to marry me; he's hinting to me that he wants to marry me.'"

Smitty shook his head. "So what, man? You told them the truth. They were stupid."

"Maybe. But that don't make it right. I knew what they were thinking, but I did it anyway. After all, I had told them, right? And it was a game—a game to see how many I could hit. But now I look back and wonder what it was all about, what I was trying to do. You don't have to go through that, Smitty man."

Smitty squinted, dropped his eyes, and hunched his shoulders.

This was not what GoGo wanted. He wanted to try to do right, but he didn't want to argue with his friend, to strain their friendship. He didn't want to talk about this to Smitty, but something inside made him continue. "And the other thing I think about, man, is that I avoided the women I was really attracted to. I don't mean physical, I mean deep-on-the-inside attracted to, 'cause I didn't want to lose the game. I got trophy girls. And you know, man, it was like power. I could be with a trophy girl and say, 'You know, I like blond braids.' And the next time I saw the trophy girl, she would have blond braids. Or I could say I like short hair, and the next thing I know, trophy girl has short hair." It was almost as if he was compelled, against his will, to confess to his friend. "The thing was, I didn't even care what it was they did.

Sometimes I wouldn't even remember what I had said to them, because I was off to the next round of the game. In fact, their being willing to change who they were made me not even want to be with them—they were looking good on the outside and hollow on the inside."

Smitty lifted his head. His eyes seemed to search GoGo's. "So why is that *your* fault, man? You didn't make them change."

GoGo rubbed his head again with the towel. "I look back and try to figure out, was the trophy girl wrong for being stupid, for having no self-respect? Or was I wrong for taking advantage of that? Probably both." He pressed his friend further. "That's what I mean about Big Esther. Seems like she might be the kind of woman that you like on the inside, not just a trophy girl."

He wanted to be sure that he made the point with Smitty. "You're not saying you don't want to be with her because you think the other fellas will be all over you, are you? 'Cause as I recollect, you always did like your pork chops with a little extra meat." GoGo laughed, hoping to lighten things. "In fact, man, I've thought about it some more and I'm sure it was Esther you used to talk about in the summertime when I would come to stay with my grandmother." Smitty groaned. "Don't get mad, man. You started this." GoGo laughed again, hoping Smitty was going to let up.

His friend's nose was sweating—always a sure sign that he was getting torqued off. "Do you know how that feels, GoGo man? Everybody else around me got somebody. Nobody notices me— I'm invisible. I got to fake like I got somebody too or else like I don't care." Smitty kept pressing his point. "It's easy for you to talk, man. The ladies always had their eyes on you. You always had somebody."

"Not really, Smitty. I never *really* had anybody, just bodies. Didn't think it mattered, didn't think it was important, but now I know better. Now man, now I wish I was where you are. When you meet the right person you bring just who you are, not ten, twenty, or a hundred different women to the union. I gave so many pieces of me away, what do I have left?

"I didn't consider that God might have someone for me, that He might have a plan for me, might be thinking about me. Now how am I going to meet somebody when all I can do to stay right is run?"

Smitty sat back, quiet, thoughtful. A smile spread across his face. "You know what, GoGo? You think too much. Not to mention that *now* you talk too much." Smitty jumped to his feet. "Of course, that—and not having any game—is how you ended up losing today. The loser pays for lunch, right? I want steak."

GoGo and Smitty grabbed their towels and bags and began moving back to their vehicles. "You're my boy, Smitty man. I don't want this to come between us. I know you're sick of talking about it."

Smitty stopped walking. "You got that right." He cleared his throat, then looked up at GoGo, a quick smile on his face. "I'm ready to eat."

GoGo dodged while Smitty tried to pop him with the towel, then stopped just short of his car. "It's funny though, you know, Smitty? There was a time when you're right, when I didn't have to look too hard. Now...all that's over now."

"What do you mean, man?"

"I mean, when I *wasn't* serious, women were throwing themselves at me. Now that *I'm* ready, nobody seems to see me. Nobody knows me, nobody's interested. Nobody's chasing after me anymore, and to tell you the truth, I don't know how to take it. But I guess she'll come along, the right one. I'll know her when I see her, I guess."

In the distance, a car door slammed. "The right one?" Smitty laughed and pointed. "It looks like she's already on the way."

It was way too easy finding him. So stereotypical. Of course, he would be at the basketball court.

Garvin stepped from her Lexus and pulled her shades down to cover her eyes from the afternoon sun. There were plenty of trees in the area, but none near the court. She threw her hair a couple of times, until the wind lifted it. She was definitely painting a picture; she was on a mission. Her lime green and navy blue spandex workout attire was more fashion than workout, more alluring than practical. Her biking shorts were pinching the backs of her thighs, and the straps of her racer back tank leotard were threatening to leave skid marks. It was all for a good cause, she reminded herself. If she could get GoGo to start slobbering, to begin showing his true colors, his charade with Meemaw would be over.

They were looking—both Smitty and GoGo. She had their attention. Garvin switched and swayed in a way that would have made Marilyn Monroe blush. Smitty was obviously giving her the once-over, but it was GoGo she wanted to snare.

Garvin walked with purpose. "Hello," she breathed her words at the two men when she got close enough to see the whites of their eyes. Garvin zeroed in on GoGo. "Hello, Mr. Walker." She made every move she knew, sent him every note of invitation she had ever seen on television and in the movies, pulled every twist she had ever practiced at a club. Surely the grass must have begun to burn in the place where she stood. The birds seemed to be doing an unusual amount of twittering, some even doing strange, unusual calls.

Smitty seemed amused, but GoGo seemed…almost nervous. He fumbled, then dropped the ball he carried. He kept looking at Smitty like he was confused. GoGo grabbed the towel around his neck and wiped his forehead, then looked around as though he were trapped, as though he were looking for a way of escape. Smitty recovered the ball and smiled even bigger.

Garvin extended her hand and grasped GoGo's hand. "I apologize if I seemed a little reluctant when we first met." His palm felt warm and moist—probably from the game they were playing—but it also seemed to tremble, just slightly. Garvin wrapped her other hand around his, so that her two hands enfolded his. "But of course, I'm sure you understand. I was startled and not at my best…" Garvin let the words drip from her mouth like honey. "I was compromised."

GoGo seemed to almost snatch his hand out of hers. Garvin stepped closer. "But I know you are a friend of my grandmother's and I have just been *dying* to meet you." A step closer—Joan Collins would have been proud.

Garvin turned her head suddenly. She thought she heard Smitty laughing. When she turned back, GoGo had backed away from her two paces. Garvin stepped closer so that GoGo could smell the cinnamon on her breath—she had read in some magazine that it was the one fragrance men could not resist. "I think it would be wonderful if you and I became friends." She stepped closer and lifted her sunglasses so that she could cast a spell with her eyes. "Close friends." She winked at him. "I'm sure my grandmother would approve."

GoGo's mouth just opened and closed. He wasn't acting at all the way she would have expected. Of course, lately all his moves had been on older women. He was probably just out of practice. "I'm sure we have a great deal in common," she purred.

Smitty bounced the ball a couple of times, held it to his hip, and then laughed loudly in GoGo's direction.

For every step she took forward, GoGo seemed to be taking two back. She realized that they were standing near the park bench, near the court. "How about a little one-on-one?" She made her lips pout suggestively.

He bent slightly, and grabbed his watch. "Look what time it is," he said almost too loudly. "I've got an appointment." He looked over her shoulder at Smitty, who was laughing hysterically, and then back at her. "Nice meeting you." He brushed past her and headed in the direction of his car.

She walked—almost ran—behind him trying to regain his attention. This wasn't making sense. "Do you like to dance?" It was hard to drip honey and trot at the same time. "You know there's a banquet coming up soon. And there'll be dancing for those who like to." She smiled coquettishly as he slid behind the wheel of his car.

"Sometimes. I mean, sometimes."

Why was he acting so nervous? "Good." She leaned on the car. "I'll be looking for you. We'll hook up." She batted her eyes at him, gave him the pouty mouth again.

"Well, I mean, sometimes. Not really. Sometimes." GoGo started his engine.

What would ever make anyone think this guy was some sort of exotic playboy? He seemed like a bumbling oaf! If it weren't for saving Meemaw, he wouldn't get within fifty feet of Garvin. She was going to make sure, though, that Meemaw was safe—no matter how goofy this guy was. She struck her most tempting pose. "I'll be seeing you soon. Very soon."

Funny though, he hadn't seemed this wimpy outside of Esther's beauty shop. He had seemed charismatic and in control. Still, for Meemaw… "We shouldn't waste any time getting to know each other." She winked again. "The sooner the better." She flashed him a Lil' Kim smile.

"I-I've got to go." Just as she was about to lean her hip on his fender, GoGo pulled out of his parking space, almost burning rubber. Gravel and a cloud of dust flew from beneath his wheels. Garvin stumbled slightly, straightened herself, and then looked around. Behind her, Smitty laughed, stopping occasionally to bend and grab his stomach, while he packed up his gear. As she turned to frown at him, she saw Monique and Lacey staring at her from where they stood on the basketball court. Garvin nodded, walked quickly to her car, and drove away.

When she pulled into the driveway, Meemaw was in the backyard raking grass. Garvin turned off the ignition and crossed the yard. The sun had softened, and its reflection, along with the greenery and flowers, framed her grandmother. The rake in her hands made a soft scraping sound as she moved it back and forth. "Meemaw, let me do that for you. You don't have to rake or anything."

Garvin reached her hands around the rough wooden handle. Meemaw held on to the garden instrument. "I like doing this. Get away now." Garvin's grandmother fanned at her with one hand, then raised her eyebrows. "What is that gitup you got on? That thing is tight enough to squeeze the ever-loving life out of you." Meemaw shook her head.

"I just went to…to practice, to get some exercise, Meemaw."

Meemaw shook her head, then turned away smiling. She pointed toward the steps. "See my jar?" There on the steps were two jars. One was empty; the other contained a small piece of paper. Meemaw glanced at Garvin, again. "I had the hardest time thinking of something to put in the jar. I've gotten to be so content in my old age. I guess things that used to upset me just don't seem so important anymore. Don't seem worth worrying about." Meemaw gently relaxed her grip on the rake. "You know, like worrying about a husband or a boyfriend. 'Oh Lord, please send me a boyfriend! Please send me a husband!'" Meemaw waggled her head and snickered. "I don't have to worry about that now, do I?" She snorted.

Garvin's hands dropped from the rake. "Meemaw!"

"Oh, please!" Meemaw laughed and shook her head. "You think your Meemaw never prayed for a man?" She laughed again. "It's just that I've learned that what's for me is for me…and I don't worry about problems. I've learned that most times what looks to be a disaster is just an opportunity for the Lord to show off just how good He is."

"Meemaw—"

"Did you fill up your jar yet?" She started talking as though she had not heard Garvin. "I got my problem in the jar." Meemaw's eyes twinkled.

"I've got problems…that's not my problem. It's trying to decide which one or ones to put in the jar."

Meemaw looked Garvin up and down, then shook her head. "I can't get over that outfit, sister girl. That's trouble right there. Maybe you need to put that outfit in the jar." She pointed at Garvin, giggled, and shook her head again. "Anyway, why not put them all—all your problems—in the jar?"

"I just can't, Meemaw. One of them…some of them, I can't let go."

Meemaw raked a little more. "You must not have heard what the man, what Reverend Scott was saying when he was preaching." She hit the rake on the ground to knock off some of the grass that had knotted itself around the teeth. "What about the person you're helping? I already picked out the person that I'm helping."

"I've definitely chosen Monique. I just haven't talked to her yet." Garvin didn't tell her grandmother that she had just seen the girl in the park.

Meemaw raked a little, then smiled at Garvin. "I've already got started." She did a little shimmy.

"Meemaw, what is *wrong* with you? What would somebody think if they saw you?" Garvin wished she could just sweep her grandmother into her car and drive away.

"Well, I'm sure if somebody saw her, he or she would be delighted."

Garvin turned to see Mr. Green standing behind her. He held a small, green, plastic net bag full of fresh peaches. "I'm sure the fortunate person would say 'What a handsome woman.'"

Garvin wanted to scream. *Great!* This was all she needed. Meemaw and Mr. Green were just friends, at least. But she had had about all she could take today of Meemaw's fan club. Now she would have to stand here and listen to the old grocer moon over her grandmother. Garvin folded her arms.

"Baby? Garvin? Are you listening to me?"

"Yes, Meemaw." Garvin turned her attention to her grandmother.

"Why don't you grab that empty jar and you can take it and put your papers in it. Leave me and Mr. Green here to talk. I've got to tell him some good news! Go on now."

Garvin could feel her mouth drop open. She closed it. This was so humiliating; she was being treated as if she were a little child. Garvin marched up the steps, grabbed the jar, and headed for her little house.

"Don't butt in on grown folks' conversations," she could hear

Meemaw whispering to her when she was a little girl. She was being sent away like a little kid! *What more can happen to humiliate me?*

Garvin gripped the jar tightly as she strode to her own front door.

Twenty-two

◆

Still wearing her blue, silk head scarf, Garvin tucked an old green-and-yellow chenille bathrobe tightly around her body while she stood in her kitchen. The robe had been her mother's. Garvin held it closed with one hand. It was late morning, and she could hear mowers and music outside, sounds of activity.

"I don't have a lot of time, Jonee; I have to go meet this kid, this young woman. She got pregnant…anyway, it's too messy to go into."

Garvin stubbed out a less than half-smoked cigarette with one hand—the ash on it was almost an inch long—while she held the cell phone to her ear with her other hand. She leaned forward against her kitchen sink. Morning sunlight felt good across her face. "It's related to this project we're doing at church. You know Meemaw's funny about that kind of stuff; everybody in her house *has* to go to church. She kind of wants me to do this project with the girl, so…"

Why did I say that? Why am I trying to make it sound as if it were all Meemaw's idea?

"Anyway, it's something I want to do. Something I feel like I can do, something to help out. I talked about it Sunday before last, another Sunday has come and gone…so I called her, and we're going to do it today."

"You don't have to explain anything to me, Garvin. Okay? It's me, Jonee."

"Besides the kid, I got this crazy call from Ramona. She's on some kind of bike-a-thon. And I still haven't been able to find out who made the mystery call about Meemaw—not that that's the biggest of my problems—and I finally approached the Walker guy—"

"Without the beauty shop hair bag, I hope."

"Very funny, Jonee. Yes, without the bag. I found him on a basketball court and I can't figure it out. It's almost like he was running from me."

"Maybe your bad hair day scared him more than you could ever have imagined."

Garvin shifted her stance and rubbed one large, puppy-dog house slipper on top of the other. "That's the thing I think I like about you most, Jonee; it's great knowing that I can always count on you for support." She pulled at the silk head scarf wrapped around her head. "It's just that the way he acted, almost like he was panicked, didn't fit with who he really is." Garvin shrugged her shoulders as if Jonee could see. "Maybe he thought I was coming to bust him about Meemaw." Garvin walked to the refrigerator, peeked inside, then shut the door. "I just don't understand it. I wore my tightest, most skeezerlike workout deal, and he practically ran from me."

Jonee laughed out loud. "Maybe he's had an L.S.E.—a life-changing spiritual event."

Garvin joined in the laughter. "Right." She smiled into the receiver and walked from the kitchen area to sit down at the table. "Speaking of men, there are none around here."

"Come on, Garvin."

"No, really. It's almost enough to make me understand why

women would be throwing themselves at somebody like Walker. Just almost, though. A guy like that couldn't get within ten feet of me, even with the self-imposed drought I'm experiencing." Jonee didn't respond.

The Hemings case folders where scattered on the table in front of Garvin, along with legal pads and pencils. "I guess we should get down to business."

"Have you had time to review the files?"

Garvin pulled the largest file closer to her. "Yeah, okay. So here's this guy Hemings and, according to him, he was tops in his class. He's hardworking, blah, blah, blah. He's done this residency at a very prestigious hospital. His life is peaches and cream, until he actually starts to interact with patients at this HMO where he's now employed. He alleges that the patients question his knowledge—"

She could hear Jonee flipping papers. "Right. Hemings alleges that patients regularly ask to see other physicians, and that he finds himself regularly calling in less-qualified, less-knowledgeable doctors to assuage his patients' fears. His statement says he felt 'humiliated.'"

"Great, Jonee." Garvin lifted the folder, then dropped it back onto the table. "But I don't see how his employers are supposed to be held accountable for that. They don't control the patients' fears and misconceptions."

"It's more than just that, Garvin. He says that his employers did or said nothing to try to foster confidence in his abilities. Dr. Hemings seems to feel that they could have reassured the patients about his abilities and tactfully made them aware that their behaviors and fears were groundless. Instead, he says, they did nothing to support him."

Garvin thumped the folder and frowned. "So the credentials

committee at the hospital—that's the group that reviews doctor's licenses, applications, and references to see if they're qualified or maintaining their qualifications, right?"

"Right."

"The credentials committee is getting letters from these same patients, negative letters that question Dr. Hemings's competence. Letters that question his even being on staff."

"Right. And the ironic thing is that because of his *credentials,* he's also a member of that very committee, so he knows the ins and outs of how it works."

"See, Jonee, it's that very thing that makes me want to just tell this guy to take a hike. Really. He's on this prestigious and influential committee. Why would the organization appoint him if they were trying to do him in, if they didn't want him on staff? Why would they have hired him in the first place? I just don't buy it." Garvin picked up a pencil and began to tap on the notepad.

"Come on, Garvin. You know it's not that simple. What he says is that he sat on the credentials committee—the very committee that's supposed to be the internal watchdog, supposed to make sure that everything the docs do is on the up-and-up—and saw them regularly turn their heads and make excuses for the doctors on staff when patients made complaints or when issues came up in surgery or something. You know, the docs-protecting-other-docs kind of thing. It was the usual behavior."

"Anyway—" she frowned and began to doodle on the yellow, lined paper—"so a department head position comes open. He believes he's the most qualified candidate, but they pass him over. He makes a stink, and they whip out the derogatory letters that they have on file."

"Letters he believes they should have removed and never posted in his professional file."

Garvin thumped the pencil on the pad. "Here's another one of those issues that irks me. It's as if he's expecting special treatment. The administrative regulations clearly state that letters of that kind should have been on file."

It sounded as though Jonee was flipping pages again. "Come on, Garvin. Give the guy a break. The allegations in the letters were vague at best; there was no substantiation of why the patients were uncomfortable. Hemings has been on the credentials committee and he's seen the committee look the other way when a patient gets burned during a tonsillectomy or when a doc gets a little careless with a scalpel. Now, in his case…suddenly, they want to go by the book."

"They're entitled to; they're supposed to follow the rules, Jonee."

"Right, but not selectively. If they bend the rules for others and only toe the line for him, that's clearly treating him different. I don't understand why you can't see that."

"I'm just sick of people expecting special treatment and then *filing complaints* because they don't get it."

"What special treatment? He's saying they didn't treat him like everyone else, and honestly, Garvin, to my way of thinking, if they treat everyone else special and then just treat him average, they are still treating him differently. And I find it suspect that they only trot out these letters when he challenges their selection for the department head position. He's got these bogus letters in his file—"

"Bogus, Jonee? Bogus? I think that's a bit strong."

"Okay, *suspect* letters where patients are questioning the standard of care that Hemings is providing, and the organization didn't check to find out why the patients were complaining. Don't you think that if they really had concerns they would have investigated? And wouldn't they have been negligent to allow him to continue to practice if they actually thought there was some substance to the patients' allegations?"

Garvin sighed and sat back in her chair. "Okay, so your boyfriend, Dr. Hemings—"

"*Garvin.*" Jonee seemed to be losing patience.

"Okay. Sorry. So Hemings's complaint seems to indicate that he thinks that he's the best, the most qualified. You know, though, Jonee, when I look through his reviews and compare them to the other docs, his appraisals are not so hot. Not bad, just not good enough for somebody who says he's such a hotshot."

"Right. But if you look at his folder, you'll also see that it has letters from renowned visiting specialists who have clamored over his knowledge and skills."

Garvin rubbed her forehead. "That's their opinion, but they weren't with him on a daily basis like the people at his own hospital."

"True. Still, it makes me wonder."

"Wonder what? Wonder if the whole staff was prejudiced! Come on, Jonee. That's a bit much."

"Maybe. But that's not what he's saying anyway." Another telephone rang in the background. "Hemings is saying that there was at least a subtle climate of racial intolerance in the organization, that it accounts for him being the only black employee on staff and for his problems. That maybe his coworkers weren't even aware of it or how their actions helped to create, or at least perpetuate, the situation. But nothing was done about it and that contributed to his nonselection for the department head position and to the depression he suffered while employed there."

"The organization says, however, that his performance was substandard." Garvin began to draw boxes on the paper and to mark them over and over until the borders were thick and black.

"And they have documentation to prove it. They say that instead of being tough on him, they've been carrying him because they feared—were held hostage by, in fact—just this kind of action on his part. It's funny to me, Jonee. If things were so bad, why did he stay? There are other HMOs. If they hated him so much, why did they hire him? Why did he get paid so much money? Why didn't he complain before now?"

She could hear Jonee flipping through more pages. "Garvin, you've seen the copies of his journal pages. He kept copious notes about what was going on, about their usual procedures and practices, about slights he felt he was suffering. Why didn't he complain? You know what happens to complainers."

Garvin began to poke the notepad emphatically with her pointer finger. "I just don't buy it. I won't. Nobody does these kinds of things to people anymore. The company says he just wanted a job he wasn't qualified for. And you know what, Jonee? I believe them. It's the new millennium, and nobody does this kind of stuff. Companies sure don't do it and get away with it. He wanted them to bend the rules so that he would qualify. And finally, when he filed his complaint, they were forced to confront the one thing they had feared and dreaded most. The managers then felt it was imperative to get his poor performance documented. The responsible thing for them to do was to have a hearing to air and evaluate their findings, even if he did holler EEO. That's what the managers did." The boxes were getting darker.

"Come on, Garvin. It's just as plausible that they trumped up these charges to get back at Hemings because he complained, because he upset the applecart. And you *know* that people can and *do* get away with just these kinds of infractions. EEO cases, no matter how good they are, just don't win in the courts. Juries don't want to hear them. People don't want to believe that these things really happen anymore. They don't want to hear that maybe where they work—or their ordinary, everyday actions in their homes—might be part of the problem." Jonee paused. "And you, Garvin, of all people ought to understand firsthand about organizations selectively enforcing policy."

Garvin rubbed one of her temples. "Right."

"I believe him. And I don't care if you do think I'm a bleeding heart."

"Wrong camp?"

"Huh?"

"You said 'bleeding heart' like you think 'liberal' is a bad word to me, and 'conservative' is a good word. Actually, I think when you say 'conservative' to most black people, you haven't said a good thing. When you say conservative to me, I think of people that stood in doorways to keep black kids from integrating schools. Not necessarily a good thing…but anyway, I don't want to talk politics or labels. And I sure don't want to talk about my own issues. I know what happened with *me*. I'm saying I don't believe *this*. I don't believe Hemings. There's nothing I've read that makes me want to go into a courtroom and go for somebody's jugular on his behalf."

"Don't you find that a little hypocritical, Garvin? You got the bad end of the stick, but that couldn't possibly happen to anyone else. And you don't want to believe that there could be a pattern of this kind of thing happening to people." The telephone rang again in the background. Jonee sounded as though she had moved her mouth away from the phone and was telling someone she couldn't talk right then, to take a message.

"Sorry, Garvin. I'm back. Look, I see this kind of stuff. I can't understand why you don't. Or why you won't admit you see it. Maybe it's denial. The other day I was in the store with my grandmother, just waiting while she shopped. There were two women behind the customer service counter. This black woman was standing at the counter and a white woman with a child came to the counter. Both of the clerks started helping the white woman, while the black woman just stood there. I know five minutes passed before either one of the clerks said anything to the black woman. I was embarrassed and I wasn't even involved. I wondered how the black woman must have felt. Then I wondered if the clerks even saw that anything was wrong with what happened.

"It was subtle, Garvin. They didn't call her any names, they didn't yell for her to get out of the store. It was just very clear that they were uncomfortable having to interact with her. I would say that's prejudice in action. I'm sure the clerks would have disagreed."

"I still don't buy it. I'm sure there were reasonable excuses for why they behaved the way they did." Garvin started drawing spirals.

"You know what? I think you don't buy it because it's easier for you to believe that *everyone* hates you because you are so much smarter than they, which is pretty illogical. How logical is it that everyone hates you and is jealous of you? Just you. Somehow, though, that's easier to believe than accepting that a few people hate you because of something you can't control. Maybe you don't want to buy it because it means that you are separated from the group and you would rather deny racism's existence than to have to acknowledge that you are being rejected. Maybe it's because if racism really does still exist, that might mean there are situations you can't control and where you can't win.

"But maybe, just maybe, it's because you don't want to care. Because you don't want to be involved in anything that makes you feel emotional or that pulls your heartstrings; makes your heart feel vulnerable.

"Whatever the case, this guy is entitled to legal representation. He's paying for it. And you can't let your personal issues get in the way of delivering a rock-solid case. Was he treated different? I think so. Were management's excuses for not promoting him just a sham? I think so. Did they hold the hearings to discredit him and punish him for complaining? I think so. And that's the case you have to make. Okay, so the papers don't build a fire in your belly...maybe you need to meet with him."

"Jonee, don't be ridiculous. He's probably just some jerk—"

"Call him, Garvin. Meet with him. Maybe he can say something to you that will get a fire started."

Garvin sat on the bench in the park across from the Jacks Creek children's home and waited. She was dressed business casual so that she would present the proper image. Thoughts of Meemaw, of Ramona, of her conversation with Jonee about Hemings played at the edges of her mind. *Why am I even here?* She had enough to deal with in her own life. She had better things to do.

Tall trees around the bench provided shade and almost made a canopy, only dots of sunlight were visible on her legs and on the bench. It was remarkably cool. Children's voices and laughter drifted across the street and kept her company while she waited for Monique. This place had seemed as good as any—quiet, open, neutral turf. Garvin had contacted Monique through her counselor at school about meeting and suggested the location. The girl had been silent for a few seconds and then agreed, sounding about as excited as a rock.

What am I supposed to talk to this kid about? What was the point anyway? Garvin knew you couldn't change anyone. They had to want to change, otherwise it was pointless. She had had enough proof of that in her own life. Garvin checked her watch, then picked up her appointment book—maroon with gold leaf trim— and began to take notes. Breezes gently stirred the pages. She should focus on something measurable, some clear target, a change that they both could see. Just talk to Monique about her career goals, about her working future.

Garvin flipped through more pages in her book and then snapped it shut. She pulled her cell phone out of her purse to check for messages—nothing. Leaning forward on the bench so she could see, Garvin spotted Monique walking on the sidewalk in her direction. It was clear from the way she walked, the way she held her head down, that the girl wasn't too excited. *How did I get myself into this?*

Monique kept looking toward the children's home, pants dragging, hair flying in all directions, face unhappy. Garvin watched until, finally, the girl stood in front of her. *This was probably the best idea I've had all year.* Garvin tried not to look cynical.

"Hi." She should probably be proper, set the example. "Hello. I'm Garvin, Garvin Daniels." She rose and extended her hand to Monique. "We met at my grandmother's, Miz Evangelina's."

"Hi."

My, my, we are off to a good start. It's going so well. This was clearly one of those take-charge moments. "I just thought we should meet today to establish a plan, a schedule of meetings. Primarily, I believe we should focus on your career goals and opportunities."

Monique was silent.

Great! This is definitely a wise use of my time. Garvin spoke into the silence. "Perhaps, I can arrange for a battery of tests that would give me some indication of your aptitudes and interests." She forced herself to smile.

Monique remained silent. She simply stared at the playground across the street.

Garvin pulled out her calendar. "Perhaps we should meet once a week. Fortunately, I happen to be here spending some time with my grandmother and have some free time to devote to this...to you. Normally, I would never be able to afford the luxury of doing something like this." Garvin made herself continue to smile.

Monique turned her gaze to Garvin. The girl stared so intensely Garvin felt as though it almost burned. Seconds passed.

Garvin cleared her throat. "Maybe we can also decide where we're going to meet—"

"Why?" Monique's voice was level, pressing.

"So that we can have everything planned and established. So that we can be more efficient." Garvin held her pen poised to write.

"No, I mean why? Why are you doing this? You said it was about the church project. What made you choose me? I don't even go to that church, or any church for that matter. I visited one time...so why me? What's in it for you?" Monique paused. "Are you trying to get me to join? Because if you are, I'm not even sure I believe. And you didn't look too comfortable there yourself, anyway."

Garvin opened and closed her mouth. *Why am I here taking this stuff off of some punk kid? I'm not the one here for help. I knew this was a stupid idea.* She took another deep breath; there was no way she was going to fail on the first meeting. The smile was beginning to hurt. "My grandmother, my whole family, has attended that church for years. But to be honest with you, I live in D.C. and normally I wouldn't have time for...but anyway I'm here, and my grandmother is fond of you, so… It's a perfect opportunity to mentor."

Monique focused her attention across the street again. "So we're meeting so you can help me get a good job? So I can be like you?"

"Well, clearly, Monique, we want a target or goal that's observable and measurable." She was sounding like a strategic planner. "The kind of work you do and having career goals is of great importance. The goals you set for yourself now will determine your sphere of influence, where you can live, how you can live." She pointed at her car. "Even simple things like what kind of car you drive and how you dress."

Monique answered Garvin's comments with another burning stare. "You mean, if I get a good job I'll be able to dress like you were the other day on the basketball court?"

"Listen…" *This is crazy. Why am I even out here? I don't have to justify myself to some kid, to defend myself against her insinuations.* Who was she, anyway, to point fingers? Garvin looked down at her appointment book and composed herself. "Maybe…maybe we should just set the appointment for our next meeting and then…then each of us can come to the meeting with a list of expectations, what we expect or want from these visits. We will be able to tell each other what we want from this temporary relationship."

Thank God for the word "temporary."

Garvin chose a day and a time. She was surprised when Monique agreed. She wrote the meeting information on the back of one of her business cards and handed it to the girl. "Same place, right?"

Monique nodded, then turned her attention back to the playground.

Garvin gathered her things and began walking to the car. Music from Smitty's snowball truck played in the distance.

Monique sat on the bench and wondered…

Did Garvin see that she was drowning?

The Lexus pulled out of the parking lot and onto the street. Monique stared across the street, hoping to catch glimpses of her destiny. Her heart ached. What was the point in hoping? How much money would she have to make to buy a new reputation? What kind of car would she have to buy? What kind of house would she have to buy to recover what she had lost? What would she have to wear so that people would forget? What would she have to have, what would she have to do, to get her baby back?

It felt hopeless. Monique sighed. *It's going to be a good day.* The words felt pointless. She felt foolish saying them, but there was something inside—something that somehow felt bigger than her, something strong that would not let her go, something greater that would not let her give up hope.

It's going to be a good day.

Twenty-three

E
sther sat at Meemaw's kitchen table, her hands folded. Meemaw rubbed the nape of her neck and smiled at Esther. "I don't know if there's anything I like as much as a clean scalp and beauty-shop-done hair. Child, the way you use your fingers and nails to get down in there and scrub, that is something else." Still smiling, Meemaw continued to touch her hair. "Nothing I like better."

"Except maybe strawberries…big ones," Garvin interjected.

"Oh hush!" Meemaw snapped a dish towel at Garvin, then turned her attention back to Esther. "That shop is something else, Esther. Inez Zephyr is still a card. And when that snowball truck came by—" Meemaw placed her hand on her heart—"I thought those women were going to stampede. Smitty has turned out to be an all right little fellow." Meemaw wagged her head at Esther. "You have turned out to be some kind of beautician. Some kind of businesswoman for that matter." She turned so that her gaze included Garvin. "I'm so proud of the two of you. A big-time beautician and a big-time lawyer!"

Garvin could feel herself blushing, but she said nothing. Meemaw leaned over and kissed her on the forehead. "Now you're getting so you can cook too!"

"Humph!" Garvin pulled a pair of red pot holders from one of Meemaw's drawers.

Meemaw chuckled, poured a glass of iced tea, and handed it

to Esther. "And I'm so glad you were able to come here to eat supper with us. We got our hair done and now we get good company to boot, right Garvina?"

Garvin paused, but simply answered, "Yes, ma'am." Still ten. She was still ten. Though Esther's back was to her, she could just feel amusement radiating off of her. Garvin pulled pots and bowls from Meemaw's refrigerator.

Meemaw pointed in Esther's direction. "Why don't you pull your shoes off and put your feet up, baby. All that time you spend on your feet, you need to rest. You have to take care of yourself now, so that you'll still be some good later on." She smiled in Garvin's direction. "Me and Garvina got it all under control."

Garvin pouted. "Mostly me, since Meemaw doesn't cook anymore. She just has to be available and beautiful for all her gentlemen callers. I'm surprised we haven't seen Mr. Green or *Mr. Walker* today."

Meemaw chuckled. "Well, I thought I would set aside a little free time to just be with *you*."

"You haven't had very much time for me since I've been here, Meemaw."

Esther settled her feet on the chair she had dragged in front of her. "That feels good." She grinned. "Garvin, you are whining and sounding like you are jealous."

"Oh, don't pay any mind to Garvina. You know how it is with only children—just acting a little spoiled. She knows I love her."

"That's why I'm the one heating up the leftovers. That's why I'm the one that cooked the food in the first place."

Her grandmother leaned to pinch Garvin's cheek. "And Meemaw is so proud of her baby." She spoke in baby talk. "Yes, I am."

Esther cackled. "I just wish I had a camera. This is definitely a

Kodak moment." She crossed her ankles. "Speaking of kids, you know when I called my mama before we left the shop, she was just clucking and cooing over my two kids. Funny, I don't remember her sounding that way when I was a kid. But she was making those happy hen noises, and I could hear the kids in the background just laughing up a storm. They just love to spend the weekend with their grandparents—they love being spoiled rotten." Esther sipped her tea. "The house is sure going to be quiet without them, though. But I'm determined to relax and enjoy myself. Look, it's just Friday night; I've got Saturday and Sunday afternoon ahead of me and already I got a lawyer fixing me dinner!"

"Ha! Ha! Ha! You and Meemaw need to take your comedy routine on the road. It's wasted here in Jacks Creek. Think of all the people you're depriving."

"Oh, Garvina." Meemaw came to rub her back, and even though she fought to resist, Garvin could feel her muscles relaxing. She tiptoed and kissed Meemaw's cheek.

She turned back to the stove to stir the pots she was heating—stewed chicken, rice, Southern-style fried cabbage. She had to admit it; Meemaw's note cards were paying off. Still she was not going to give up—sometimes a little pity felt good. "And since I'm cooking at my place, I had to drag all these pots over here…"

Meemaw clucked her tongue while Esther laughed. "Well, Meemaw has something I think will make up for all your hard work, you poor thing." She reached into the freezer and removed a rubber storage container. Meemaw popped the lid and took out a large, deep-dish pie. "In about an hour, we'll be tasting peaches!"

Esther slapped her hand down on the table. "That's what I'm talking about!" Garvin tried not to let them see how delighted she was about the pie. She lifted the pot lid to stir the warming rice.

"Miz Evangelina, you know you sure do look good. Really."

"Well, thank you, Esther." Meemaw did a little shake dance.

"I just don't see how you eat this good and still look good."

"Well, you know, I kind of figured it out. I can have it all, I just don't have to have it all at one time." Meemaw and Esther laughed together. "I just have a little bit of what I want, and I have learned to turn down one thing so that I can have another. I don't have to experience it all."

"I never thought of it that way."

"I just figured it's no different, no less of a sin worrying about food all the time than eating food all the time. You just have to get the food to submit to you, rather than you submitting to the food." Meemaw's eyes sparkled. "Plus it helps to exercise and to have a good workout partner."

"Well all right," Esther said.

"Excuse me." Meemaw said and reached over Garvin's head into the cabinet above the stove. She grabbed her problem jar and showed it to Esther. "Did Garvin tell you what we're doing at church?"

Esther shook her head. "No, ma'am."

Meemaw smiled and shook her jar as she explained the Egypt plan to Esther. "So you see, I've got my problem here in the jar, and I've got the lid on tight." She beamed impishly. "And I've already started working on my project to help out. So far, things are looking good."

Esther laughed and looked in Garvin's direction. "Girl, the way you talk all the time, your jar must be jam-packed."

Garvin sniffed. "Not really. I only have one problem in my jar, thank you very much."

"Then you must not be following directions; I thought the pastor said to put *all* your problems in the jar."

"Anyway, Esther—" Garvin lifted the lid and breathed in the

aroma of the chicken—"I've started my help project, but I'm not so sure how it's going."

Esther leaned forward. "So what or who is your project?"

Garvin nodded her head toward her grandmother. "Meemaw kind of helped me decide. I'm supposed to be helping Monique."

"Monique? Light-skinned Monique?"

"Yes, but I'm not so sure she wants to be helped. Things were a little strained when we met."

A shot of warmth hit Garvin as Meemaw slipped the pie into the preheated oven. "You're going to have to be patient. Nobody's paid any attention to her before. You can't expect her to know how to feel about it, or how to act, right away."

"Maybe. But she seemed kind of angry and she kept staring off into the distance like she was in another place. I've been thinking that maybe I need to pick someone else to help, someone that wants to be helped."

"I never knew you to be the kind that would give up so easy." Meemaw picked up Esther's glass and refilled it. "She showed up, didn't she? Don't you think that means something?"

Esther nodded. "Yep, it surprises me. I see her with her little group of friends, I've seen her pass by the shop, and I've seen her on the street. She never speaks and just seems to avoid eye contact. But with the kind of folks and family she comes from…"

"I don't remember her or her folks from when I was here. Of course she would have been a baby."

Esther uncrossed her legs and swung them down from the chair. "No, they moved in after you left. They live over across the railroad tracks—keep stuff stirred up all the time. And people say her daddy—"

Meemaw cleared her throat. "You know, it doesn't help to do what's happening now. If somebody wants to help the child, talking about her and her family is not the way." She had the don't-push-me expression on her face. "She is a sweet child. I know because I speak to her. Maybe she would speak if she felt welcome, if someone invited her in." Meemaw turned to Garvin. "That might be something good for you all to do one day—go to the beauty salon."

Garvin shrugged her shoulders.

"You know," Meemaw continued, "when I look at her I can't help but believe that somebody was out of place, weren't where they were meant to be. I can't help but believe that someone is not doing what God called him or her to do."

She pulled up a chair and sat next to her grandmother. "What do you mean?"

"I mean somebody was out of their place. You know, maybe somebody was supposed to be one of her schoolteachers. Maybe that person always felt like he wanted to be a teacher, but he didn't become a teacher because he figured men don't teach or teachers don't make enough money. God's plan for him was to teach, but instead the man is doing something else. Like maybe he's somewhere being a manager, a bad manager, and making everybody around him miserable.

"Or maybe somebody, some woman, was supposed to be Monique's school counselor. Maybe that woman became a high school counselor, but when it came time to select a job, she didn't take the job in Jacks Creek. Maybe the woman, who God really meant to be a counselor in Jacks Creek, was worried about money, or where she could get more promotion or recognition, so she went somewhere else. Now that woman is sitting at her desk bored to tears because nobody needs her where she is. She's in the right job, but still out of the will of God."

Esther took a big gulp of tea. "Miz Evangelina, that's deep. You know what, Miz Evangelina? You need to be on a talk show."

"Maybe so. If I was on one, you know what I would tell them?" She looked alternately at Garvin and Esther. "I would tell them that they talk all the time about purpose, but they are missing the point. You know I'm not a preacher, but I don't think our purpose or our gifts are just supposed to be to make *us* happy or famous or rich or whatever. I think we are given them to serve other people." She nodded her head. "We're not supposed to find our own blessing; we get blessed by finding out and doing what we're supposed to do to serve and bless other people."

Garvin pushed her chair back from the table. *Why am I feeling uncomfortable?* "I need to check the rice." She walked to the stove.

Meemaw laughed. "Look at me, for example. I worked for years in the textile factory. I fussed and complained every night I came home from work. My husband kept trying and trying to get me to stay at home—but *my* mother worked, *her* mother worked." Meemaw shrugged and chuckled. "I was a frustrated woman. Finally it occurred to me to pray to God about it. I stopped working at the factory, came home, and been happy ever since."

Garvin turned to look at Meemaw. Each day with her unfolded something she had not known.

"Now don't get me wrong," Meemaw said. "I'm definitely not saying every woman ought to stay at home. Everybody's got their own opinions on that, and like I said, women in my family have worked for years and years, during slavery and after. But a woman or man that feels a quickening on the inside that they're supposed to be a doctor, they need to heed that call. Then they need to go a step further and ask the Lord where they need to be, where *He* wants them to be. 'Cause I figure, there might be somebody just like Monique waiting for someone who's never going to come."

"Umph!" Esther leaned back in her seat. "Like we've all got a part in the plan."

Meemaw nodded. "You've got to keep pressing in, Garvina. Talk to her on her level; ask her what she wants, what she needs, what she likes. Monique's been hurt and it's not easy for her to trust. You just keep pressing."

Meemaw smiled and her eyes were full of wisdom. "I'm sure that we are all where we are for a reason. Even when we leave here, it's for a reason." She held Esther's gaze. "That was hard for me to understand when I lost my husband and I just kind of gave up, but then I woke up out of my sleep. I've got work to do here. You've got work here too, Esther; and so does Garvin. Something's coming." Meemaw closed her eyes and breathed deeply. "It's just a sweet mystery watching it all unfold."

The memory of spicy peaches lingered on Garvin's tongue as she walked the path to her front door. Garvin looked up in the heavens, at the stars. From the corner of her eye she caught a blink of light. First one, two, then many fireflies. She began to follow them. In the darkness she reached for one, reaching until she caught it. She cupped her hand so that she could peek at the insect, then realized that her neck and shoulders had relaxed.

Garvin held the lightning bug in her hand and for a moment she danced, raising her arms and spinning in circles as she had as a child with her mother. She could almost hear her mother's voice...

"Aren't they beautiful? Almost like God made flying jewels—fairy dust against the dark sky—little emeralds with wings, like stars lighting the river." Amazement had lit her mother's face. "Come on, let's run and get a jar."

Garvin moved into her small living room and danced into her

kitchen, to her pantry, and grabbed her jar. She opened the lid and released the firefly into the jar. She quickly closed the lid and watched the insect fly about, over and under the scrap of paper, around Garvin's problem.

She needed to make air holes. Garvin went to her kitchen drawer full of her grandfather's old screwdrivers and batteries and at the back found what she was looking for: an old ice pick. It was the same pick her mother had used to make holes in lids for her all those years ago, and it made the same puncturing sound. Garvin punched four holes and replaced the ice pick.

There in the very back of the drawer was a small, velvet box. How could it be? Garvin lifted the box from the drawer and opened it. Her mother's brooch. She fingered the multicolored stones. She had almost forgotten about it, had thought it lost. She pressed it softly to her lips. It was a treasure. She closed the box and then walked to place it in the drawer of the small table near her bed. Garvin kissed her index finger, pressed it to the box, then closed the nightstand drawer. She drifted, dancing back to her dining table.

Garvin set her jar in the middle of the rosewood surface and leaned forward, resting her chin on her folded arms. She began to remember and hum a tune her mother sang to her long ago. It was a Temptations ballad, a song about fireflies, about how their natural light could give comfort. It was almost as though she could smell her mother, the bouquet powder she wore and the cream she used on her face. Garvin could almost feel the warmth of her, as though she were present. "Mama," she said and began to weep.

After several minutes Garvin raised her head and wiped her tears. *This is not good.* She needed something to distract her. She picked up her phone and dialed the number to check the messages on her telephone in D.C.

She punched the proper codes and then listened. There was one message from a long-distance telephone company that promised her savings. *Delete.* One from a businessman she had met on a trip to Denver. "Just stopping through," he said. "I enjoyed our night, our time together. Thought we might hook up—" *Delete.* Fat lot of good that would do her in Jacks Creek. She clicked for the next message.

"Garvin? Garv? It's me, Ramona. We're in Billings, Montana." Something about her friend's voice sounded different. Garvin listened to her update about the preacher, about the other riders, about the mountains they had climbed, about blisters, about the sunsets, even about prayers and songs under the vast Montana skies.

Garvin saved the message and hung up the telephone. In her mind, she imagined Ramona on a bike, climbing a steep hill, muscles straining as she fought to tackle the incline. Thigh muscles and calves quivering with effort and her hair plastered to her forehead by sweat beneath her bicycle helmet. She imagined Ramona staring at a trail up the mountain that looked impossible to climb, wanting to stop but determined to continue. Straining, straining...she wanted to stop, she wanted to continue. The more she pedaled, the farther away the summit seemed.

Garvin could see Ramona almost leaning into the handlebars; she could hear the quiet of the Montana mountainside contrasting with Ramona's rhythmic panting. Tall trees, pungent evergreens, lined the road and wisely observed her progress. And Ramona kept pressing the alternating pedals downward. There was no time to rest. Then there she was at the apex, with no wind and no strength left, about to surrender and tumble back down the distance she had come...but a hand appeared. Because the sun was at his back, only his silhouette was visible. His strong hand

grabbed hers and Ramona's...no, Garvin felt breathless and surrendered to the hand that lifted her and drew her closer...
closer...closer, until she recognized his face, his strong features,
his smile—

No!

Not only no, but... There had to be some stronger word!

Garvin pushed back from the table. She was not going to let
this happen to her, to Meemaw! She was not going to be weak.
She had already seen what being weak would get you—what it
had gotten her mother.

Garvin shook her head. She was not on a mountain; she was
in Jacks Creek, sitting in darkness. She looked at the closet door
where her bag hung on the handle. The bag that held her shoes,
pink shoes in the dark at the bottom of her bag. Memories
pressed in and she imagined herself standing along the Cape Fear,
near the place where they had found her mother. In the dark
water, beyond the banks, she could see a pink shoe gently flowing
with the river. Too far away for her to reach, the shoe—her
mother's shoe—drifted among the memories and stories of other
lives, other lights snuffed then left to the currents. As the shoe
moved it disturbed the water and stories, old stories drifted up
from the bottom...stories Meemaw had told her, stories she had
overheard as a small child sitting on her grandfather's knee. And
even now she was not sure how or why the memory of her
mother's shoe and the memory of the men were connected.

Garvin could feel the rumble of her grandfather's voice where
her head lay against his chest. She could remember the dark,
dimly lit room. His breathing was slow and easy. *"That's how it
happened,"* he would say, his voice just above a whisper as he sat
talking with the other men. *"That's what they told me—I was just a
little one then. Said my uncle was one of the men, one of the ones*

floatin' on the river. The Cape Fear ran red. Back in 1898 in Wilmington."

The other men had listened while her grandfather spoke. Some nodding, some shaking their heads. *"Before that night, colored men was doing good after the war—owning businesses, holding good-paying jobs, serving in political office. My daddy told me some white men was mad—mad about the war, mad about Reconstruction, mad about black prosperity. One man in particular, Alfred Waddell— he used to be in the Confederacy—made speeches about taking back the city. Told white folks they should choke the Cape Fear with carcasses if they had to, so they could take the city back from "subjection to an inferior race…men of African origin."*

Garvin remembered that her grandfather's arm had tightened around her, just slightly, as he leaned forward. *"November it was. That's when Alex Manly told the truth and men died."* Her grandfather's voice dropped to a whisper. *"Bodies floating on the river."* He leaned back in the old cane-back seat.

"See, Manly was the editor of the only race paper in Wilmington back then, the Daily Record. This white woman, Miss Felton, was going around saying how colored men ought to be lynched for raping white women. People say Manly wrote a story in the paper. Manly said white folks didn't hold no special court on morals—said white men and white women was just as likely during that time to be having hushed-up, nighttime relations with black people—said most of the so-called rapes, was just that: so-called."

Garvin remembered her grandfather shaking his head. *"Man, the old people said the white folks went crazy. Waddell made some crazy speech about a White Declaration of Independence. Thirty years after the Civil War ended, they formed a mob, a militia, and burned down the offices of the Daily Record. They run Manley out of town and forced the white mayor of Wilmington, Dr. Silas Wright, out of office. Waddell took over—it was a coup right here in the United States, some folks said. Burned up lots of what the colored folks had built up, run many colored people out of Wilmington.*

"That night, November 10…many a man lost his life. I've heard different numbers all my life—some say nine, some say more…some say the Cape Fear ran red with black blood."

Her grandfather had sat quiet at this point. Sorrow seemed to enfold him and the other men. His voice was heavy when he spoke again. *"My daddy said his own brother, the body of his own big brother, was one of the ones ridin' the Cape Fear. A trail of crimson flowing upstream."* Her grandfather's jaws had tightened. *"Some folks say it never happened—it ain't in no history book, even though that was the beginning of Jim Crow voting law in North Carolina. One thing for sure, my uncle is gone…things ain't never been the same. Not for my family. Not for colored folks."* He shook his head. *"Not for the river."*

She had heard the story many times before her grandfather died. But at some point she could not remember—as she imagined the horror of murdered men in the Cape Fear—she had also begun to imagine a single pink shoe, sometimes swirling, sometimes drifting among them. Another water memory: a little girl on the bank…too deep…too wide.

It was too much! She was not a little girl and right now there was no river that threatened her. It was not the Cape Fear—it was Garvin's mother's own weakness that killed her—weakness for a man, most likely a man like GoGo Walker.

Garvin grabbed the jar, stormed to the door, opened the lid, and almost threw the firefly out of the jar. Forget that. Forget the bug; forget the song. Shoot! Forget the Temptations! *I have to stay focused, to remember why I'm here. Not to cook, not to mentor some girl, some juvenile delinquent. Not to sit around eating pie and singing sappy songs.*

She was there to get her Meemaw out of the hands of a pimping leech.

The pastor spoke about an Egyptian plan? She had a *seduction* plan. Garvin closed the door and slammed the lock into place. She set the jar back on the table and went to scavenge for a cigarette. Tomorrow was Saturday, and he would be easy to find.

She knew the plan—it was temptation—and she was not going to fail.

Twenty-four

◆

GoGo sat in the barber's chair getting a shave—a head shave. He closed his eyes and listened to the fellas shouting about the welterweight boxing match that played over the television set mounted on the wall. Outside the sounds of car horns, revving engines, and folks on Saturday errands created a backdrop for the happenings in Bailey and Bill's Barbershop.

It was good sometimes just to be in the presence of men. The barbershop was men's domain—no women allowed. Men held bottles of soda and bags of chips while they pointed and gestured. A sign up on the wall also reminded the men that there was "No Cussing Allowed."

The company was good, but GoGo was not paying much attention to the match. For some reason, boxing was not his game. He had been in his share of fights on the grid and off, but he was not proud of them.

Maybe it was what his grandparents had told him. "Be a David," his grandmother would say. "Not a Saul. Saul fought when he didn't need to, when he thought he was up against somebody weaker than him. He used his fighting, his being a bully, to try to make himself into a man. A bully ain't no man." She would shake her head.

GoGo could hear the sound of the razor scraping over his scalp.

His grandmother had hated bullies. "David fought when it was the Lord's will. Sometimes he even hid away rather than fight. But when nobody brave could be found, when somebody really needed to step up and be a hero, there would be little old David. When the Lord needed him, when it counted, he stood up." He could see her wiping off the kitchen table and nodding. "Walk like David."

Most of the time, his grandfather would look and act as if he were oblivious to the conversations GoGo had with his grandmother. Then all of a sudden, the voice would speak.

"Mama's right. Saul wasn't worth nothing. He was a bully, was what he was. And you know the thing about a bully? When nobody needs him, he's running around threatening people, hurting weaker people, boasting about he ain't afraid to die. Funny thing is, when you need somebody to be brave and stand up, you can't find the bully nowhere. He's worried about getting killed. He'll tell you he's not gone risk his life. Bullies and Sauls ain't worth much, I don't expect. Even New Testament Saul wasn't worth much until he got a new mind and changed his name." Granddaddy went back to looking preoccupied. "Just fight when you need to—walk like David."

"Aww, man!" The men in the barbershop hollered in unison, and brought GoGo back from his musings.

Bailey, who often introduced himself as Barbershop Owner Number One, cautioned the men. "Y'all be careful. Simmer down now! You don't want me to cut this here man's head."

GoGo opened his eyes.

The fellas went right on talking. Some Saturdays in the barbershop were quiet. Men kept their thoughts to themselves. This wasn't one of those Saturdays; the brothers were on the wild, they were looking for barbershop blood, for a casualty to the dozens.

Brian Byrd and Winston Salem were right in the middle of the mix, while William—aka Owner Number Two—sat in one of the barber chairs with a broom in his hand, keeping an eye on things.

Another patron waded into the fray. "These ain't nothing but amateurs, man, please!"

"I don't see *you* fighting, Dion man." Byrd dropped right into the middle of the conversation. The guys took turns howling and ribbing Dion.

"You don't *want* to see *me* fight, man." He flexed his muscles. "I'll put some knots upside your head, my brother. You better be glad I'm showing some restraint." Dion threw another jibe as the game escalated.

Dion's phone rang. It was his wife. "Yes, baby. What's wrong?" GoGo laughed to himself as Dion spoke into the phone; his voice had dropped a few decibels. The other brothers were quiet, listening for some sport better than boxing.

"Yes, doll." It was so quiet in the shop that GoGo could hear some faint squawking coming from the line. In fact, he was pretty sure the other men could also hear. He could see them sharpening their arrows. Dion was going to be the target.

Dion nodded and spoke into the mouthpiece. "Okay then, honey. Whatever you think. See you soon, okay?" He hung up the phone.

Winston Salem struck first. "Man, I thought you were fists of fury, but you're more like mittens of meekness."

Dion attempted to defend himself. "Come on, man. You know how it is. I'm on lockdown. I'm trying to get out of the doghouse."

The men all groaned at one time and nodded their condolences—not for long, though. It was Saturday; the brothers needed sport.

Byrd struck the second blow. "But man, you just got through talking big. You threatened me, man. I was feeling threatened." Byrd thumped his chest. "Now I know what to do. In the future, I just need to dial your house and tell *Mama* all about it! It looks like Marsha got you in check—that girl always was tough. Even in school, she could fight like a man."

GoGo looked between Byrd, Dion, and Winston Salem. Clearly the attack was on.

Winston Salem nodded. "Sure could. Remember that boy that stole her purse? She caught him and beat him down like a man. He left town right after that."

"Never been heard from again." Byrd was enjoying himself as the other men in the shop laughed. He cast a wary eye on Dion. "If you leave town in a hurry, we'll know what happened." The fellas hooted and slapped hands. GoGo laughed. But not too hard—there was still a razor on his head and the joke wasn't funny enough to risk being maimed.

"So, Pro man, what's this I hear about you building a kind of center or something for the young people?" Apparently Dion wanted to change the subject.

GoGo was willing to help a brother get off the hot seat. "Yeah, a youth center. Something to keep them off the streets. I want to get a sports league started, do some coaching. You know, I figured it would be some way to give back to the community."

"Sounds like a good idea to me, man."

"I'm getting the money together. I've got most of it, Smitty and different people are donating, plus I'm using all the money I get from doing the personal training thing to go toward the center. Once I can get enough money together—"

The door banged open. Kind of like the sheriff had come to town.

Everyone stopped midlaugh.

It was Garvin, Miz Evangelina's granddaughter. "Did I hear you say money?"

She strutted—no, it was more of a winding saunter—up to GoGo's chair and seemed to ignore the other men. Their mouths were open. She wore slinky strapped white sandals and a dress that was more less than more. It was short and clingy, molded to every curve, with spaghetti straps. "I thought I might find you here," Garvin said while she twirled a piece of her hair, brushed it against her cheeks. She pushed her lips into a sex symbol pout.

GoGo's heart started pounding, and he wasn't sure whether to be flattered or frightened—this was clearly not the reserved, cool woman her grandmother had told him about—not today and not the last time he had seen her. The blade scraping his scalp kept him from looking left and right. However, what was clear was that every eye in the shop was on the two of them. Something about her was making him think cat.

Garvin stepped closer and seemed to purr. "I need to talk to you." She smiled but something in her manner was insistent, demanding. *"Now."* It almost sounded like an order—honey-wrapped, but still an order. There was nothing as bad as a woman fronting you off in public, especially in front of a group of men, especially in the barbershop—it was supposed to be a safe place. She didn't look like she was there to harm him—or maybe she did. She looked like she was sending an invitation, a beautiful and sexy invitation he would have been more than ready to accept not very long ago…but there was something else going on. And whatever it was, it was making him uneasy.

Owner Number Two had put on his coke-bottle eyeglasses. His back stooped with age, he suddenly got into motion and was sweeping away clouds of hair. Owner Number Two seemed to be moving in for a closer look.

GoGo knew he should be enjoying this, but something just didn't feel right.

Garvin tossed her hair. "For some reason, I've been unable to catch up with you…but I do want to *thank you* for making so much time for my grandmother." Everything she said seemed to insinuate something else. She placed one hand on her hip.

Owner Number Two was sweeping closer, and Owner Number One had stopped breathing. With his peripheral vision, GoGo could see that the guys were leaning forward, so far they were about to fall out of their chairs.

He tried to clear the knot out of his throat. "It's kind of difficult to talk here." His voice sounded tight in his ears. It was funny how soon you could lose years of practiced coolness. "Maybe later. After…" He gestured toward his head. The fellas all seemed to lean back in unison. For some reason, he could feel the arrows were being sharpened for him.

Owner Number One spoke up. The clippers began to hum, and GoGo could feel the vibrations as they moved over the edges of his scalp. "Well, he'll be done in no time. I'll be dusting him off soon." GoGo could hear the patronizing smile in the old man's voice.

Garvin moistened her lips. "No problem. I'll wait outside for you." She kept her attention focused on him. She smiled, but something in her eyes told him the smile was forced. "I'm parked near your car." She stood staring, smoldering in front of him, for a moment. Then Garvin turned and sauntered toward the door, twisting just as she had entered.

Owner Number Two let out one long, trill whistle.

GoGo exhaled involuntarily. Owner Number One shut off the clippers and loosened the cape around his neck, shook the fine hairs to the floor, and then refastened the cape. "Yes sir, I'm going to have you out of here in no time!"

The guys were all smiling, especially Dion, who probably could feel the shift of attention away from him.

Owner Number Two stopped sweeping and leaned on his broom. "Pro man, it looks like you in trouble. And I ain't sure if that's good or if it's bad."

Winston Salem piped up, smiling, "You not kidding. She good looking—a little skinny for my taste, but I went to school with her, and man, that girl is crazy."

Byrd shook his head and held out his hand so that Winston Salem could give him five. "Crazy man. And ain't nothing worse than a crazy woman. A crazy woman won't leave you alone." GoGo could see the arrows flying across the room.

Dion let one fly. "Crazy?" GoGo couldn't tell if he was the new target or if the men were telling the truth. "You mean, like a stalker?"

The S word. GoGo could feel his breathing going shallow, but he tried to keep his exterior calm. Not a stalker? Not one of those women who would not leave you alone, who waited outside your apartment, who called every ten minutes only to hang up? Not one of those women who called your new girlfriend's house and showed up on her doorstep? They had to be pulling his leg. That was not what Miz Evangelina had described. Of course, nothing about Garvin had been what Miz Evangelina described.

Dion shrugged and looked around the room. "It seemed to me that she kind of liked him."

Byrd turned to face him. "Right, Dion man. Like you would know. You were without a woman for years. But now that you're married, now that you got a little somethin', you're the Love Doctor."

"I'm just saying…"

GoGo thought he caught a quick glimpse of Winston Salem elbowing Dion, as if to let Dion know that he was messing up their sport. GoGo relaxed a little; the fellas were just having some fun.

"That's part of why she had to leave town," Byrd said. "We sat next to her in church a few Sundays ago." He pointed between himself and Winston Salem. "Garvin was just the same…maybe worse. She lives in D.C. now."

"What were you two knuckleheads doing in church?" Dion waited for the laughter to die down and then continued. "Man, it's stuff like that that makes me glad I'm married." Dion shook his head. He had obviously decided to join in the fun. "The last time I was in D.C., before I got married, I got tangled up with a stalker. That crazy woman dented up my car, busted up the windshield, broke out the headlights. You know I hated that." He looked to the other men for understanding. "You can act as crazy as you want to. Shoot! Hit me, but don't hit my *car!*"

GoGo had managed, almost unbelievably, to avoid any really crazy women, any stalkers. How ironic that now, now when he was finally getting himself together, that the guys would even kid around about him having to face a crazy woman now. Miz Evangelina's granddaughter…and in Jacks Creek of all places.

Byrd interrupted his thoughts. "Pro man, what did you do to her? She was trying to play sweet, but man, I think she is planning to do the Delilah to you." The men looked at GoGo's bald cranium and erupted into laughter." Owner Number One picked up a round, long-bristled brush, shook on some talcum powder, and began to dust GoGo's head with it.

"Must be something," Winston Salem added. "I could see it in her eyes. I know her. I'm telling you she had to leave town because she almost killed a man. She's got it in for you. No doubt."

They had to be kidding. GoGo settled back into his seat. They were laying it on just a little *too* thick. "Right. As if any one of you know anything about women."

Owner Number One finished dusting and then used a cotton ball to apply skin bracer around the edges of GoGo's scalp. He removed the cape and beamed at GoGo. "Fine job if I do say so myself."

GoGo looked in the mirror and admired the barber's work. There was nothing to worry about. The fellas were just pulling his leg. He walked to the counter and handed a ten-dollar bill to Owner Number Two.

The old man peeked over his thick eyeglasses. "You better be careful, young brother."

GoGo was determined to look calm. After all, it was a brother's obligation to look cool under fire. A line of sweat trickled down his back. There was nothing worse than a crazy woman, a stalker. *They have to be just pulling my leg.*

Owner Number Two looked out the door. "You be careful," he repeated.

"Yeah, that's right." Owner Number One offered his two cents. "That girl"—to GoGo it sounded more like *gull*—"has always been a handful. 'Course her mama was a speedball too." He sat down for a breather in his barber chair. "You didn't hear it from me, though."

GoGo walked to the door and stood, his hand on the knob.

Monique walked west from Main Street until she reached Eden Rock. She wasn't sure which was better. On Main Street people used code words to tell her she was not invited; on Eden Rock they were more direct.

On Main Street she was just a little too dark, and people treated her like a failure. She would have believed it was the baby, but it had been happening long before, even before she had learned all her letters from Sesame Street. Sometimes she felt that she had failed because she had not managed to keep herself from being stained—she was too dark. Or maybe she was too close to white and blurred the invisible line.

On Eden Rock people let her know that she was no more successful than they were. Monique wasn't sure why. And no one had talked about it except to say that what she felt and saw didn't exist and that she shouldn't let it hold her back. No one talked about it—no one except her grandmother, who when she drank too much called Monique names to remind her of her imperfection.

Not talking about it didn't help.

Monique walked past Big Esther's Beauty Salon. Holding the straps of her book bag, she kept her head lowered. For brief moments she stole glances at the images—the posters of beautiful, brown-skinned women looking out from the salon—though she was careful not to make eye contact with Sister Inez Zephyr. Monique wondered what it felt like to be welcomed inside, to have "hey, girl" conversations, and to share "and then I told him" testimonies spoken from under hair dryers and over washing bowls. Wondered how it felt not to be in between worlds, to have ownership in one or another. To know on which side of the playground to sit, at which lunch table to sit. Wondered what it felt like not to be rejected because people were sure she was going to think she was better because she was lighter. Monique wondered what it felt like to land, to have some place, some flock where she fit in.

She kept her head lowered until she passed Esther's, passed

the street where she might turn to walk to the Jacks Creek Boys'
and Girls' Home, passed other businesses until she stood almost
in front of the barbershop. She noticed Garvin sitting—she
seemed to be stewing—in her car.

Bang! Almost in front of her face, the barbershop screen door
opened and out bolted GoGo Walker, almost running past
Garvin's car to his own. Monique stood transfixed, while laughter—laughter like someone had just gotten the short end—came
pouring out of the shop door in his wake.

The sound of the barbershop door brought Garvin back from her
daydreams. Daydreams and schemes of how she was going to
ruin GoGo Walker. She quickly opened her door and called his
name. It was time to make her fantasies real.

"Excuse me. *Excuse* me."

He kept walking.

"I need to talk to you." Garvin stepped from around her door,
quickly closed it, and began tipping down the sidewalk toward
the passenger side of the BMW. GoGo was in his car and turning
the ignition. "Hey! What the—" Garvin's heel stuck in a crack in
the sidewalk. "Hey! Wait a minute."

Walker pulled away from the curb and made a U-turn on
Eden Rock.

Garvin jerked to pull her heel free. *If he thinks...* She yanked
harder. *Not today! Not this girl!* She kicked the shoe off her foot,
bent to grab it, and ripped the heel off in the process. "Oh no! Not
me! Not today!" She stormed—albeit in wobbling fashion—back
to her car. She gunned the engine, made a U-turn, and took off
after him. This was definitely not over.

◆

Monique watched Garvin fumble back to her car, yank the door open, and pull away. A lot of help the woman was going to be to her. Monique shook her head. Issues.

She crossed the street and began the walk toward her home. She kicked at gravel on the side of the road.

At the top of the hill ahead of her, there were abandoned railroad tracks. When Monique reached them she stepped on the old wooden track ties and stopped for a moment to kick at one of them with the toe of her shoe. She raised her head and looked ahead at her grandmother's front yard.

From where Monique stood, the tract was almost pretty. The abandoned car and tricycle in the front looked like hulking iron beasts—maybe mother and child nestled beneath a large shade tree. Grass grew right up to the edges of the grooves and fissures that covered the land. Farther away, in the midst of the grassland, wildflowers—pink, blue, purple, yellow—started and danced in time with the rhythm of the summer breezes.

Monique stopped and breathed deeply, then continued to cover the distance to her home, her grandmother's home. As she got closer, she could see old paper wrappers, plastic bottles, and tin cans mashed flat into the deep tire tracks that cut gashes in the yard. She could no longer avoid seeing the missing wheels and the rust that blemished the cast-off automobile and tricycle. Broken glass dotted the ground. Monique began to hum, no tune in particular; just whatever notes came to her.

She hummed louder.

Over her humming, she could hear her grandmother's angry voice. Monique thought she could see it flashing from the doorway, then out of random dark windows. Monique was not close enough yet to make out the words, but the mood was familiar.

Closer still, she could decipher some words. "Didn't you hear what I said?" Monique could feel as well as hear the contempt in her grandmother's voice. Then a familiar crash. She stopped and willed herself not to hear. Another crash. "I thought I told you not to…you little…" She could feel herself losing air. She stopped. Maybe it wasn't too late, maybe no one had seen her. She turned and walked quickly back to the top of the hill…back to where her home still looked safe.

She slipped the book bag from her shoulders, opened it, and withdrew a small multicolored pastel jar. Monique twisted the lid slightly so that she could remove it and then peeked inside. She closed her eyes, lifted her head, and whispered soft words that the wind carried away before they could be heard.

She replaced the jar, lifted the book bag, and walked quickly. Faster. Finally running—almost out of breath, afraid to look over her shoulder—back toward town. Back toward the fence. Back toward the playground. Maybe there were children still playing.

Maybe there was hope…

Twenty-five

◆

The early morning sky almost matched the color of her car. All signs of the Cape Fear River were in her rearview mirror. Garvin shifted gears and lifted her cigarette to her mouth. For now, she would have to leave all thoughts of Jacks Creek—Meemaw, GoGo, Monique—behind her, she had a job to do. It was a new day. Garvin inhaled deeply. Smoke curled around her face.

"What's going on with the inquiry?"

She rapidly picked up speed as she merged with traffic onto Interstate 95. It felt good to hit the highway. To hurtle from Jacks Creek into the real world...sixty-five...seventy...eighty miles per hour...to return to life as she had known it.

"I know it's been a while, but you know I can't go into it, Garvin." Over the cell phone, Jonee's voice had that I-don't-want-to-talk-about-it sound. "It's going. Okay? Let's just get *this* case done. I think that's what we have to focus on." She was talking like an attorney.

I might as well face it—it's over. My career is dead and buried. Where am I going to get a job? How am I going to be able to explain why I left Winkle and Straub?

Jonee's voice cut into Garvin's thoughts. "Anyway, I don't think you have to worry about it. And I think you're doing the best thing now—meeting with Hemings."

"Maybe. Whatever the case, I'm going to talk to him, go by my place, and then get back on the road tomorrow. Meemaw reminded me that I have to be back for the Independence Day banquet."

"Banquet? You never seemed to me like the picnic, ants, and fireworks kind of woman."

"I know, but…you know I've been remembering about the banquet and I always liked the fireworks. It's just that in the city it gets so congested and so commercial."

"Are you getting sentimental on me, Garvin?"

Why am I feeling defensive? "Actually, Meemaw wants me there—and it will be an opportunity to corner Mr. Walker. You know, Jonee, I just don't get it. Something isn't making sense. It's almost like the guy is running from me."

"Oh no! Not someone who's able to resist your charms."

"Very funny, Jonee."

Garvin checked her mirrors and then switched lanes without benefit of her turn signal. She mouthed a few choice words at the honking motorist behind her. Yep, she was back in the world. "Anyway, Hemings and I are supposed to meet around twelvish. But one good thing, no matter how it turns out—even if he is a jerk—Hemings and I are meeting in Severna Park at the Breakfast Shoppe. He lives near there, so I thought, hey, why not…a Belgian waffle covered with fruit or a backpacker's pie. Late breakfast, brunch—it sounds pretty good to me."

Jonee laughed. "Sure, Garvin. Like you'll eat any of it, Miss Seaweed and Bean Sprouts USA."

"You'd be surprised. I think Meemaw is rubbing off on me." Garvin stubbed out her cigarette.

The tree limbs seemed to open up like fingers, parting so that the universe could see the treasure hidden inside. Pale morning light wrapped around Meemaw's shoulders. She and Mr. Green sat on her front porch steps sipping coffee from large mugs. She loved the warmth and hugged the cup with both hands.

"You know I have to make the most of this one cup." She took another sip and let it rest on her tongue. "There was a time when I drank coffee from sunup to sundown. Not anymore. So I tell myself I better make this cup last."

Mr. Green's eyes seemed to be focused in the distance. He nodded.

The two sat quietly, each one leaning on a stair railing, watching what little traffic there was moving up and down the street. Even summer school was out, the children were sleeping in, and the pace of life seemed to have slowed beyond what was usual. Meemaw looked up; there was a daylight moon. "It's good to not be in a hurry, don't you think? Not to have to run and scuffle. To be done proving yourself."

Mr. Green shrugged. "Sometimes. Then other times I would give it up to just have my wife present with me. I never imagined I would have to learn to love the world without her in it."

Meemaw turned her head to look at her friend. "You're right, Mr. Green. It's hard sometimes."

"Why do you still call me Mr. Green after all these years? We're friends, aren't we?"

"Yes, of course we're friends. But old habits die hard."

"Sometimes I think you do it to keep a wall between us."

Meemaw paused. "Maybe so." She tasted the coffee. "I always thought my husband and I would go together, but when he left before me, I figured the Lord had made a big mistake. Every day, though, I know more and more that there's a reason I'm still here." She reached out to touch his arm. "And life is getting to be pretty good. God has never left me, and I've got a good and loyal friend."

She nodded her head toward Mr. Green. "My body's feeling strong and vital."

Mr. Green snorted.

"What is that supposed to mean, Mr. Green?"

"Nothing. You are a grown woman, Evangelina. You lead your own life." He shrugged his shoulders. "If I start interfering, I won't be your friend for long. Herschel Green has never been known to be a busybody."

Meemaw was tickled. "If I didn't know better, if I didn't know you had better sense, I might think you were jealous."

"That wouldn't be smart. After all, I am constantly reminded by you that we are just friends. No need for a woman like you to give any thought to an old man like me…especially when you have younger men—a younger *man,* so smitten by you."

"Oh, go on! Get away from here, Mr. Green!"

"Honestly, Evangelina. There have been moments when I thought to pick up the phone and call you, or call *someone* myself. But you are grown, as you say, and you don't need a meddling old man like me. I have had one love, and there is no reason for me to be greedy and think that I would have a chance for two."

Meemaw's laugh was like spring rain as she reached to pat Mr. Green's hand. "Oh, Mr. Green, I have been knowing you a long time. We've been knowing each other a long time. Despite some trouble, some sorrow, I've been a happy woman; I raised a child and a grandchild and I had a good husband. He was more than good, and I'm not looking for anyone else. Who could step in behind a man like that?

"You're as good a friend as I could have. And ain't it something? You and I both remember a time when you and I couldn't have been friends. People might look at us sideways now, but we know a time when I would have been beat down and you would have been run out of town for daring to say that you thought a woman like me was beautiful."

Meemaw smiled. "You just mooning. You know I know you, and I know when something's the matter. I think you are just feeling a little lonely."

Mr. Green sighed. "As usual, you are right. You know me so well, my friend. My children...I hardly ever see them. I know they love me and I know they're busy, but...when it gets to be this time of year, I think of the fireworks and the picnics and the good times...and then I begin to worry if they are still keeping the old ways."

Meemaw shook her head. "You want them to know all that you know, to be devout like you, when they haven't had the same time to learn life's lessons. You have to give them time. When change comes, it all sort of comes at once, just like summer."

Mr. Green patted her hand.

"You are just an old worrywart, Mr. Green. But guess what?"

He smiled as though he knew what was coming. "What, beautiful Evangelina?"

"Good news, Mr. Green. Good news! I need to tell you about this glass jar I got to put my problems in; and then come on and let me tell you the story, the good news!"

Her old friend laughed. "If anyone could persuade me, it would be you."

The two sat talking while birds circled and danced overhead as though they wanted to be near, and the tree boughs bent low as though they too wanted to hear the word.

Garvin pulled off of Ritchie Highway into the strip mall parking lot just a few minutes before twelve. Her tires bumped over broken asphalt—the outward setting wasn't pretty, no trees, no flowers, no shrubs, just glass storefronts—but the food was good.

Great timing. There was no line in the Breakfast Shoppe, and she was seated right away.

"How you been?"

If Garvin remembered correctly, the friendly waitress that seated her was the owner's daughter. The woman's dark hair was the same color as her mother's. "It's been a while, huh?" Garvin accepted the menu she extended. "No rush. Take your time." There was no sign of Dr. Hemings.

The atmosphere inside was relaxing and homey—wooden picnic tables covered with oilcloth table coverings. The walls were covered with old-fashioned sifters and graters. Even older pictures, advertisements, and cooking utensils decorated the small, un-air conditioned, family-owned restaurant. Two ceiling fans kept the small restaurant cool. A chalkboard over the counter announced that fruit-topped Belgian waffles were one of the daily specials. The shop was known throughout the region for sumptuous, leisurely breakfasts cooked the generous, old-fashioned way.

Garvin surrendered to her gastrointestinal fantasies and focused on the menu. About the time she settled on a half-portion of the backpacker's pie—a baked concoction of potatoes, tomatoes, broccoli, onions, cheese, and meat—she looked up to see a man standing next to her table.

"Ms. Daniels?"

Garvin nodded.

"I'm Brian Hemings—Dr. Hemings."

She pointed at the bench across from her. "Great timing. I was just about to put in my order." Hemings—*Dr.* Hemings appeared to be in his early forties, balding slightly, and, unlike she had imagined, seemed to have a gentle air about him. Garvin noticed that he was courteous, almost deferential to the waitress. Something about his manner reminded her of her grandfather—a gentle warrior. They ordered, and then he began his story.

"I almost hate to retell the story. Each time is like reliving it, and I always wonder...I always doubt that people will believe me. I always think that people will think I'm some kind of jerk, a loser, you know?"

Garvin hoped she was not blushing.

"But I guess I need to talk about it. My therapist thinks so anyway...and so does my family. This has been torment for them." His laughter was forced. "I have twins, college freshmen, and I don't think they're going to be begging to come back home any time soon." He picked at his cuticles. "And my wife...well, we'll both just be glad when this is over, one way or another."

The doctor leaned and reached for a large leather satchel that sat on the floor next to their table. He placed it on the bench next to him. "I brought my bag of papers—my therapist says that it's compulsive behavior, that I carry my credentials and my proof as a way of defending myself...and maybe convincing myself that...I don't know." Hemings lapsed into silence, his hands patting the black bag.

He was not loud or boastful. He didn't even seem particularly assertive. The doctor was not what she had expected.

"I didn't want to do this, you know? People think this is easy, that it's easy to complain or go through this kind of procedure. You're a lawyer and you probably sit through these kinds of actions, these cases all the time—but it's very difficult to be in the middle of it. To have your life on hold, to have your future in someone else's hands. It's probably difficult for you to relate. I just didn't know what else to do...I just couldn't live with the way things were anymore. Does that make sense to you?"

Garvin nodded. She understood just a little too well. "Why don't you start at the beginning? We've got lots of time."

As he talked about his education, his early career with the firm, Dr. Hemings dug into his bag and pulled out papers to corroborate his story—diplomas, transcripts, performance evaluations. "I worked hard. Long hours. I studied and worked harder—just like I'm sure your parents told you, doubly hard just like all our parents told us. The staff, the chiefs in organization, always told me I was a good worker, a dedicated professional, an excellent doctor—until I wanted a promotion, until I wanted to be department head. Then suddenly I was transformed into this nuisance, this thing." Garvin noticed that Dr. Hemings's left eye began to twitch. He cleared his throat and took a sip of water. "Do you mind if we talk about something else, just for a minute, until I can compose myself."

The man was either an incredible actor or something tragic had happened to him. Garvin made small talk about her trip from North Carolina, about the Breakfast Shoppe. When he was ready to begin again, he nodded.

In excruciating detail, he gave her dates, times, and names. He pulled a worn journal from his bag and showed it to her. "Whenever I begin to doubt that it happened, when they accuse me of creating this whole mess myself, my journal keeps me sane. It is my memory."

The fan above them stirred the air. Garvin listened and thought of Winkle and Straub. She thought of Ramona and of the things that Jonee had told her. Why had she expected the worst? Why could she believe and know her own pain, but doubt the truth of his? Something like shame began to creep up her neck, to warm her ears, to burn her face.

"I'm a good doctor. It's what I was meant to do—to help people, to help them heal. Sometimes in all this, I begin to doubt myself and I wonder if I'm wrong, if maybe I just want some vainglory. But deep inside—" he placed his hand over his heart—"I know who I am. I'm a good doctor. No, I'm an excellent doctor and I have compassion, I know how to treat people. If it wasn't for people's hang-ups and all the excuses they give themselves why their management staff is all white, or maybe all men—I'm the best man for the job. I have been for all the years they used me to train someone who knew less than me. I was the man every year that they passed over me. And I know that someone has to tear down the walls. Not just for me, but for them too. They're captive on the other side of the same walls that are used to keep me fenced. And it's been going on so long, I don't even think they're conscious of what they're doing. It's hurting all of us.

"I don't know if you believe in God, Ms. Daniels, but I do. In my heart, I'm convinced God wants these walls torn down. It's time now that all of us—our dreams and visions, ought to be multicolored. It's time to dream in Technicolor, or else we're only hearing a piece of God's message. I feel it in my heart, down in my gut. And if I don't do it—if we don't do it—the work will be left for my children and for their children. Here am I, Lord; send me."

The air felt electric around the table. As Dr. Hemings collected his papers, the smiling waitress walked into the charged atmosphere and set their steaming plates in front of them. "Enjoy," she said. Garvin nodded her thanks and Dr. Hemings spoke and smiled politely.

"Dig in," Garvin counseled Hemings as the waitress walked away. She loaded up her own fork with hot potatoes and stringy cheddar cheese. "You've got an uphill battle and you're going to need your strength. But, Doctor—" Garvin looked deeply into his eyes—"you've got one pit bull of a lawyer on your case."

They sat eating and talking strategy well into the afternoon.

Miss Flossie leaned forward in the chair and stared at her image in the mirror. She pointed at the center of her forehead with a crimson-painted, finely shaped fingernail. "That's where I want it. Right there." Her eyebrows were drawn into two high arches, and rhinestones dangled from her ears.

"All right, Miss Flossie." There was no point in arguing. Esther had been trying to get the old woman to let go of the harsh black dye and the pin curls for years. Miss Flossie wasn't about to change. Her legs were crossed and her stockings were knotted just below her bony knees. Bright red-painted toenails peeked out the end of her sandals. "The mens likes pin curls, 'specially the one in the middle of my forehead." Esther used two bobby pins and fastened the curl into place.

Miss Flossie dug around in her purse and pulled out a black, triangle-shaped hair net. "Now tie this on so it will keep."

"Yes, ma'am." Miss Flossie had been around. Her name had been on a lot of tongues, not professionally, but in an amateurish sort of way. She had never been married, but she evidently knew a lot about what the "mens" liked. For years, Miss Flossie had made appointments so she would be in the shop when there were few other women present. Nowadays, it seemed that advanced age had freed her and conferred a respectability of sorts upon her. Miss Flossie now came whenever she pleased. Esther could feel the woman watching her in the mirror.

"You know, Big Esther, I don't have no regrets. I've been on this earth and in this town seventy-nine years." Some people would have argued and said it was eighty-nine years. "I don't regret a thing. But I will say that if I had it to do over again, there's some things I might do different." Esther looked up to meet the old woman's eyes in the mirror. "Sometimes I chose to do it hard when I didn't have to. Like I was proving to everybody and to myself that I could do it by myself, I didn't need no man—except for what I wanted him for."

Miss Flossie dug in her bag and pulled out a wine-colored, lace-edged handkerchief. When she waved it, the scent of perfume teased the air around her. "Sometimes when a man wanted me to lean on him, I told him to get about his business. I wasn't going to depend on no man, and then he let me down or make a fool out of me. I could take care of myself. But now… Anyway, I don't have no regrets." Miss Flossie waved the handkerchief again. "Just don't make your life harder than it has to be…it's all right to take a chance. You still a good-looking woman, lots of mens likes thick womens, and you got a lot of life ahead of you. Take a chance. Makes life interesting."

In the distance, the music of the snowball truck lilted in the air. The women in the shop came alive. Esther smiled at the older woman's image. "Thank you, Miss Flossie." She looked toward the door. "Excuse me, I've got something to take care of."

Twenty-six

◆

She ran over the strategy in her mind. Garvin could envision how she and Jonee would pick the huge rock, the wall, apart. Brick by brick, until it came tumbling down. Her adrenaline was pumping. It was good to be back in the saddle, to be doing what she was meant to do. She could see the wall tumbling down.

Garvin could still see the hope in Hemings's eyes as she shook his hand before he turned and walked away. What was it inside of her that made her not want to believe in people like Hemings? That made her not want to believe in other people? What made her willing to believe the worst, but unwilling to believe the best? What made her afraid to hope and believe in their goodness?

Garvin stood outside of the door of her condominium. The key still fit, still slid easily into the lock, but she did not turn it. It felt as though there was a wall—a door she should not go through. She felt something, she felt it inching upon her, and it told her not to look to the right or to the left. Her hands felt clammy and dampness broke out at her temples. What frightened her was not the darkness. Darkness, the night…that was familiar. It was not fear of the light, of the glow from the street lamp. It was not a fear that she would be seen…

Not a rational fear or a textbook fear, but a real fear nonetheless. It was a fear of something translucent, almost transparent—something murky, gray, and swirling. A fear of something that was jealous of color, that spread itself on red, and layer after layer, made the red disappear. A something that layered itself on white until it was able to impose itself and masquerade as the presence of all color. A something that slathered itself on black until the contrast was gone, and what once was strong now appeared ashen gray. A malevolent something that spread itself on yellow, on blue, on brown, on green and sought to strangle their pigment.

It was an almost tangible thing, a living/dead thing that did not want her to believe. It pulsed.

It was the same something that hated change, that hated divergence, that hated distinction, that hated anything that was not like it, not murky and gray. And that thing crawled up Garvin's legs, up her thighs and hips, around her waist, up her spine, coiled around her neck and threatened to choke her. It was something that told her that it was not really there, that told her she should not scream, even as it tightened its grip on her throat. It was something that would kill her, it told her, and leave no trace or clue. It made the small hairs on the back of her neck stand on end as it slithered through even her thoughts. She could not turn the key.

It was a thing, a great wickedness, that told her that if she opened her heart, if she dared to love or trust, that somehow she would die. It was a once living presence that held her bound on the other side of the door. A wickedness that had for years fed her one drink too many and sent her strange men to keep her docile while she lived within its captivity. It was the same wickedness that left her lonely and crying at night, but a wickedness that promised her something far worse if she should dare to break through the wall.

It was a menace that made her cling to strange facts and unwilling to believe in mystery. A menace that allowed her to glory in glamour and fashion, but made her doubt inner beauty. The thing was a menace that allowed her to believe in God, but inspired fear that He was impotent. What coiled around her was the same menace that believed in religion, but doubted the spirit.

It slid in the crack between her lips and whispered as it inched into her ears that she should not breathe too deeply, that she should not try to speak. It told her not to move, not to open the door. It warned her to forget her plans and told her why they would not work, how it would sabotage those plans and leave her alone and foolish. It was malevolent.

It was all powerful, it told her. Only a great wickedness would steal her hope, keep her love locked away behind a door. Only a great wickedness would threaten her desire to live more, love more, be more. The thing whispered of its power and yet told her it was not there.

Garvin was frozen.

If the phone had not rung, she might never have turned the key.

"Hello." She whispered into the phone, afraid to touch the light switch. Afraid of what was not there, of what she might see. "Hello."

"Hello, Garvin? Garv? It's me. Are you okay?"

It was Ramona. Until that moment, Garvin didn't know that love and hate could exist so strong in the same instant. It was good to hear her friend's voice, to hear it live, to connect with someone who had always fought for her—been willing to stand against any odds. In the same instance, her dislike for her friend was intense. Maybe it was that Ramona was tangible, she was real. She was living, breathing, an outlet for her fear.

"Garvin, are you there? Are you okay, girl? Every time I try to call I always get your machine. But it's just so beautiful up here…and you were just so heavy on my mind. I just thought I would try to call. Garvin, are you all right, girl?"

"Sure, I'm fine."

"I tried to call you at Winkle and Straub, but they were kind of closed-mouthed, kind of funny acting. Are you okay?"

"Just think, you trying to call me. That's a switch, huh? Payback is a big dog."

"Garvin, what is wrong with you?"

"Nothing. I'm chilly, as you might say. Everything is cool."

"Garvin?"

"So you are off riding a bicycle, huh? I'm sure the people at your job are feeling very supportive."

Ramona laughed. "Yeah, well…"

"So what is this marathon thing you're doing? Some sort of charity thing?"

"Yeah. It's called the Big Ride, Garvin, for the American Lung Association. Girl, it is just fearless to see all these people."

"Funny, I was just imagining you on the ride. You know, running from place to place trying to find a nail shop, trying to find some place to get your hair done. I mean, how many black beauty salons could there be in Montana? You must need a special person to ride along with you just to keep up with your earrings." Garvin laughed; Ramona was silent. "You know what else I thought about? About how much you hate being around white folks and there you are in the middle of nowhere. And you and your preacher friend are probably the only black folks on the Big Ride, right?"

"Pretty much." Garvin could barely hear Ramona's reply.

"I'll just bet they are overwhelmed. You are quite a bit of African Americana for their minds."

"Garvin, why are you talking like this? What's wrong with you?"

She plunged deeper. "Did your priest turn out to be a King

Solomon yet? A player?" Ramona didn't respond. "Well, you know what? Don't call me when you need a ride home from your little lark in the woods. You are on your own. You've ruined your job and I've told you over and over again about these crazy ideas, about you running after these foolish men, you are going to get yourself killed—"

"Garvin, stop it. We love each other, remember? We're friends. What's the matter with you?"

"Nothing." She felt like she was going to explode—or maybe implode.

"You're *my friend,* Garvin. But it's funny, you're also the one who keeps telling me to be afraid, that I can't be someone else or change my life or do something else. You were the main one who always criticized me for who I was, now you criticize me for changing."

"Ramona, I—"

"No, *you* listen to *me*. We've been friends for years and we have always had each other's backs, no matter what. I teased you about acting too white; you fussed at me about being too ghetto— even though I knew you didn't want me to change. How would you know who you are if you didn't have me to look at, to measure against? But this is something more, Garvin. I can feel it. Love is not supposed to keep us bound up. We're supposed to be free. And I didn't know what that meant until I was riding through this world. Until this man loved me, not physically, but in a way that freed me. And I've been calling you because I needed to tell you. To share this freedom with you."

It was not just a conversation that Ramona needed, that Garvin needed—it was a cleansing, a baptism. And so Garvin was a good friend and allowed the words to wash over her, over them. She let Ramona's spirit flow.

"I've been raised all my life in D.C. and I love my people, love my family. But I woke up and I was in a camp outside of Billings, Montana. I realized I was not who I was yesterday or even who I tried to be every other day of my life. It scares me the same way every morning, to be a new person each day. To realize that there's somebody deep on the inside of me trying to come out and that she might not fit in, she might not be what everyone expects me to be.

"What will happen if I stop being what everyone else expects me to be and they fall apart, because I'm not there to hold up my side of the image they have built for themselves?

"What happens if I stop wearing big earrings and straightening and dying my hair? Who is depending on me staying the same? What if I choose to stop being hard? What if I choose to believe someone could love me? What if I choose to love? What if I choose to believe that there is a God and that He loves me?

"What if I'm not around-the-way anymore? What if I choose my own way, my own path? What if I choose to be an around-the-way girl who rides in bike marathons and has old white people for friends? Who would be freaked out if they saw the white people holding my hands and praying with me while I wore big earrings and orange lipstick? Whose mind would that mess up?

"What if I woke up one day and realized nappy hair was exotic and desirable, and that combing kinky hair was sensual and pleasurable? What if one day I enjoyed combing my hair? What if I was happy for my skin? Whose plan would that destroy?

"What if I get saved and marry the preacher? Who's going to stop speaking to me, who's going to stop being my friend? What if I choose to let this man love me? What if I miss this opportunity? What if I give it up just so people won't talk about me? What if I stay who I am so that my family will feel comfortable with how they've always felt about me? What if I abort the change so that my friends won't feel uncomfortable? Can I even go back now that I've started? Who am I supposed to be?

"I don't know the answers, Garvin. I don't even know what it is that I'm really feeling. And I can't understand this peace that I have—even with all the questions running through my head—and the way these people have allowed themselves to love me. Oh, not everybody. There are lots of white people that look at me like they are trying to figure out how I got here. But this man, Derrick, and lots of these people…they're trying. I feel embraced."

Garvin could hear tears in Ramona's voice.

"And I want you to be happy for me, Garvin. I need you to be happy for what has happened to me. I need to know that even if my whole life changes, that your love is real and that you will still love me."

Garvin laid her head in her hands and wept.

"I don't have the answers. Sometimes I feel pulled in both directions, like I'm new me and old me. I'm trying to figure it out myself, girl. But Garvin, you're my girl. For all your fussing, I know when it comes down to it you'll be there. And I just felt like if I could talk to you…something about this would make sense to you. I just need you to be happy for me. I need to take a chance."

What if I take a chance? "Thank you. Thank you, Ramona." The two women talked until daybreak.

Twenty-seven

───────────◆───────────

The water was very still and the birds were just beginning to come to life. GoGo cast his hook into the greenish brown water. Trees overhung the lake and tall grass jutted sporadically from the water. Smitty sat hunched over his pole at the other end of the boat. The water smelled pregnant with fish, and there were frequent ripples and bubbles as if they had come to nibble at the water's surface.

The two men had been sitting in the same spot since before daybreak. They already had three good-sized spot and two croakers. It was good fishing weather, and it was quiet, except every once in a while GoGo was sure he heard Smitty humming.

There was something about fishing this way, something about the water that calmed him. Water was at the center of some of his best memories from when he was a little boy. He could remember his father steering the motorboat, cutting through the water, and how much he wanted to stick his hands over the side of the boat into the wake. GoGo could remember wriggling his toes in the same muddy, brown Mississippi water that somehow found its way into the bottom of the boat. "Nasty water," his father would say when he was clearing it out later on, but it was sweet water to GoGo. That was when they lived in Missouri, before his father left.

It had been his job to watch the boat on its trailer, where it was hitched to the back of his father's truck. No one gave him the job, but he knew that if he didn't keep his eye on the boat, it might come loose and slip away. Sometimes he watched as they rode to the Mississippi; sometimes he watched as they traveled to a lake. No matter. He kept his eye on the boat and it never came apart. It was his job. He did it well.

Too bad he didn't do such a good job watching his parents' marriage.

Smitty snatched his pole out of the water. "That's what I'm talking about." A fish emerged from the lake, flapping and jerking so that its fins caught the light. Smitty looked back over his shoulder. "That makes four for me, right?" He had on his best Riddler smile. "Not that anybody's counting."

"Right man." GoGo turned his eyes back to the water. "It's not like this is Bass Master's or something. It's not like this is a competition." He knew better. Everything was a competition. "I probably would be catching more if it were quiet out here." GoGo heard Smitty's line drop back into the water. *Maybe I'm on the wrong side of the boat.*

He was sure he heard it this time. "What are you humming?"

Smitty yanked his pole again. Another fish. Then sang out loud, "The Bobby McFerrin song." Smitty hummed then sang, "Don't worry, be *happy!*" He put a worm on his hook while he sang and then plopped it into the water.

This was not like Smitty. Something was up. "What are you so happy about?"

Smitty hummed a little more before he answered. "Too many fish for me to cook myself. I might have to get somebody to help me out." Smitty smiled over his shoulder. "What's up with me? You'll find out soon enough."

"I hope it's not what I think, man."

Smitty shrugged.

"Man!"

Smitty shrugged again, and then sang-whispered, "Don't worry, be happy!"

GoGo tried to put his mind back on fishing. Smitty was a grown man; he couldn't make his choices for him—some days he had doubts about his own choices. He'd better concentrate on fishing. Pretty soon, the heat was going to drive the fish lower in the water and them off the lake. He tugged at his line to check it; maybe he had a bite. *Not a chance.* He reached into his bag for his shades and put them on with one hand.

Smitty stretched. "Anyway, man, while you're worried about me, you need to know that somebody's got their laser beam on you. *Somebody's* got a plan to get *you.*"

"Yeah?"

"Yeah."

"So are you planning to tell me about it?"

Smitty shrugged and continued his humming. "I didn't want to scare the fish away."

GoGo jerked in his line. "What's the point? I'm not getting anything anyway."

"Maybe you're nervous. You know, maybe the fish can see your line shaking." Smitty seemed to be having a good time.

"Okay, so what's the deal?" GoGo could feel his chest starting to get tight.

"Your girl, Garvin. She's after you."

"Right. She's a piranha; I'm fresh meat. Who doesn't know that?"

"Maybe, but you don't know why."

Fishing and the water were supposed to make him calm, right? It wasn't working. "Because she's crazy and a stalker. She's fine—she keeps crossing my mind—but she's crazy and she's a stalker."

"No, she's not, GoGo man. She might be a little full of herself. She might be a control freak. But she's not a stalker. Where did you hear that?"

"At the barbershop, from Byrd and Winston Salem and the other guys. They said they went to school with her."

"You listen to those two knuckleheads? Man, everybody in Jacks Creek went to school together. But she's no stalker, man. She's after you 'cause she thinks you're out to do her grandmother in. She even got ahold of some stuff from the L.A. newspapers when you were a player—you know old sins die hard."

"I knew some other people had been speculating, but I didn't think her own granddaughter…"

"Yep."

GoGo pulled off his shades. "What are you talking about, Smitty man? How do you know this?"

"I got connections on the inside." Smitty resumed whistling the song.

"You know what, man? I've heard there are snakes in this water, but I would be willing to risk it just to flip this sucker and get you to quit with the song." GoGo began to rock in the boat.

"Cut it out, man. You know I don't swim. Quit acting crazy."

"Okay then, tell the story."

"My source says that Garvin will do anything she has to to get you away from her grandmother, including throwing herself in your path. She plans on *playing* the *player,* baby! That way she figures she can show you up to her grandmother. And she's not going to let anything stop her. In other words, if she catches hold of you, your fish is fried." Smitty fell out laughing.

"How do you know all this?"

"Don't worry about that. I'm not giving up my information source. Maybe you should be trying to figure out, *Mr. Player of the*

Last Decade, how you're going to keep yourself...*pure!*" Smitty hooted. "Man, I never thought I would see this day come."

"Right, man. Thanks for the support." GoGo wiped sweat away from his brow. It was getting hot sooner than he had expected. "So, all these times..."

"Yep!"

"Well, how do I...man!"

"Funny thing is, my source thinks Garvin's working her plan with just a little *too* much gusto. She thinks maybe Garvin's got a little crush on you, and maybe she's not even admitting it to herself."

GoGo looked out over the water. "Yeah. Whatever."

"You look nervous, GoGo man. This is so *sweet!*"

"You *would* think this is funny, Smitty. You've been thinking that what I'm trying to do has been a joke from the jump."

"What's funny is that everybody in this town jumps to conclusions. You think Garvin's a stalker. She thinks her grandmother is a playee and you're the player. Now you think I'm hating, making assumptions about me. You're wrong. Always been wrong. 'Course, I always did let people think what they wanted."

"Yeah, Smitty man, but you don't know how it feels to be trying to be straight and to know that somebody, especially a fine somebody, is out to pull you down."

"Maybe not the way you do, GoGo. But here's something I'll bet you never knew—I never have, man."

GoGo turned to look Smitty in his face.

"Yeah, man. I'm saying what you think I'm saying. I never have, man. I'm a virgin. For years nobody noticed me, and I was just too shy to push my way to the front. Then, man, I was eighteen, twenty, twenty-five. Who was I going to tell? You know what men would think—I didn't even feel like I could tell you. Man, especially you.

"Dated outsiders, women from outside of the county, to try to keep up my reputation. I felt ashamed to tell any woman. What would she think?" Smitty's face broke into a smile. "Then I just blurted it out. Man, I found out somebody is really excited about it. She's a good woman. I just took a chance and told her—I was tired of carrying it around. Man, you would have thought I was Denzel."

"Is she…"

"Nah, but she said she was glad because she wants to start over. She said we should wait and do it the right way. Get to know each other, see how it goes, and do it the right way. I thought women would be turned off, but my stock price just leaped about two hundred points!"

GoGo almost leaped to his feet, but realized quickly that they were in the water. "Smitty man! My dog! This is freaky…this whole thing is freaky! It's got to be a God thing…"

"Yeah, I guess so, GoGo man. We're going to start going back to church too. She said she's not doing it any other way. I'm not sure how I feel about it, but I'm willing to listen, you know?"

"Man…" GoGo threw back his head and laughed. "This is too much." It didn't even matter anymore that he had only caught two fish. His laughter stopped short. "Now what about me? I told you I'm still weak in this. And the thing is, I'm attracted to her…very attracted to her…and what if she catches me in the wrong situation?"

The two men looked at each other. "Run!"

Their laughter echoed off the trees.

The Independence Day banquet was packed. All kinds of people there—teachers, maids, insurance salesmen, children, women, and men. The church ladies were having a particularly good time since the church men always cooked every year. All of Jacks Creek was there—all of those who frequented Eden Rock—from the youngest to the oldest. The music played loudly and was part of the meal, but the center of the banquet was the table of food.

Meemaw looked down at her plate. She didn't remember a year in her life when she had come to the banquet and seen so little food and so much plate. She laughed to herself. She had picked her favorites: barbecued chicken, a dab of potato salad, and a good helping of collard greens. She looked back at the table. A hunk of that watermelon was going to be calling her name in a minute, but she was going to leave the cake alone. Meemaw bowed her head slightly and began to thank God for what she did have on her plate. Then she asked Him to help her not to long for, or maybe even to help her forget about, what she didn't have. *Thank You, Lord, for satisfying my mouth with good things so that my youth is renewed like the eagle's.*

They had decorated the room so pretty. Different colored lights were strung from the ceiling of the large log cabin. Red-checkered tablecloths and red, white, blue, and gold balloons in all the corners—the balloons weren't plants, but they ought to provide suitable coverage for Sister Inez to collect information. It was even good that the floor was concrete; it would be easy to hose down at cleanup time. Meemaw looked up and smiled across the room at Smitty. That child was looking awful moony tonight.

Miss Flossie rearranged her pin curl. She looked down the table at Evangelina and shook her head. Why would anybody come to a banquet and not taste a little bit of everything worth having? The child was foolish…she always had been a Goody Two-shoes. Miss

Flossie stood up, plate in hand; she was going to do some damage to that banquet table.

When GoGo walked by, Miss Flossie forgot all about the food. That was one good-looking man. *Maybe I need to start working out.* She still had a whole lot of life left in her, and it might be safe to try to talk to him now that his grandmother was gone. She followed GoGo with her eyes until Barbershop Owner Number Two came into view. Now he, old William, had been her good friend for years.

She caught his eye and winked. He looked away like he was scared somebody was going to catch him. *Forget you then! And don't come sniffing around me later, with your bent-over self.* He was too old anyway. Miss Flossie looked around the room to see what else struck her fancy. Winston Salem wasn't looking too bad tonight, and Byrd might do in a pinch. No need to worry about Owner Number Two—there were too many fish in the sea.

Esther stood at the end of the banquet table watching Miss Flossie. She was a funny old woman. It was kind of sad though to see how man crazy she was. Miss Flossie hadn't been able to get any food all night because she was too busy watching the men.

The smell of barbecued ribs called Esther back to her own plate. She had been looking forward to this all day. Esther grabbed the tongs and laid a couple of ribs on her plate. Now that was silly. Might as well get two more so she wouldn't have to make another trip back to the table. Esther pushed the ribs over so she could fit a piece of chicken and a good scoop of potato salad on her plate. Those men could make some serious potato salad! It was the kind she liked—yellow with mustard and egg yolks.

She used the greens spoon to nudge the potato salad over to

make room for the fried collard greens. Esther frowned at the okra and passed it by for a piece of butter-soaked corn on the cob. She laid the golden corn on top of the greens so it wouldn't get any red barbecue sauce on it. Oh mercy! The baked beans looked good—caramelized syrup all along the edges! Esther figured she would get some of them later when she came back to make take-home plates for the kids who were staying at Big Mama's house. She would have to remember to get the plates after she finished her cake and ice cream.

Using her napkin, Esther grabbed a piece of cornbread. She smiled back over her shoulder at Miss Lotty. The woman looked good. Some of her family members must have cleaned her up and persuaded her to come. That was the good thing about the Independence Day banquet, you were liable to see anybody there. "I love this cornbread, Miss Lotty. I can't wait to tear it up." Esther found her a good seat where she wouldn't have to walk such a long distance back to the banquet table.

Miss Lotty watched Esther walk away from the banquet table. It was like watching two boys fighting under her skirt. The child always had a tendency to eat too much. It just didn't make sense to Miss Lotty how somebody could love food so much that they just let themselves go.

Miss Lotty kept her eye on the door. She reached for some corn on the cob. Most of the food was just way too greasy for her taste. It was unhealthy. Miss Lotty rubbed her nose and kept her eye on the door. She felt her pocket to make sure the twenty-dollar bill that her niece had given her was still there. Miss Lotty almost dropped a piece of cornbread trying to keep an eye on the door. She had to pay attention. Everybody and his brother came to the banquet. She was starting to feel a little shaky, but any minute a connection—a little ready rock—might come through the door. Just a little something to take off the edge.

The picnic was Jacks Creek at its finest. Garvin sat hunched in a chair near the punch bowl. It was a good place to scout the room. Meemaw seemed to be occupied. GoGo had spoken to her briefly, but Monique had sat down beside her and the two seemed intent upon their conversation. Garvin kept her eye on GoGo.

She took a sip of the punch. It was tart and sweet. Garvin thought about her conversation with Ramona and smiled. She imagined Ramona, the preacher, and his parishioners. Ramona, of all people, with a preacher. God must have a sense of humor. *Her* partner in crime with a minister? What else was God going to do, fix her up with a choirboy?

She should never have mentioned anything to Ramona about Walker, though. Her friend had gone off on this tangent about GoGo. But that was crazy. Ramona was just feeling romantic— probably the elevation was getting to her—but she was way off base. Sure, GoGo was her type, but then he was everybody's type—even Meemaw's. And the main thing was, she had a job to do. She was on a mission and nothing was going to get in the way of what she had to do. Nothing.

Garvin had on her black predatory dress, the dress she used in the city when she was hunting—short, black spandex with spaghetti straps. It did the job in the city, but it was a little much for Jacks Creek. Meemaw had looked at her like she had lost her mind when they had met to get in the car. She had seen a lot of leering eyes since she got to the banquet, but the important thing was that she was sure the dress would do the job on GoGo Walker.

That was if she could get close to him.

For some reason he seemed to be dodging her. But it was going to work. A plan was a plan. She looked at her watch. The fireworks would start soon.

Children ran back and forth in the cabin. "I know I told you to sit down." All the mothers seemed to be saying the same thing. Fathers were casting stern glances. It was a beautiful picture of family life in the community and Garvin was glad that she was there.

"Come on, they're starting the fireworks." People began to move toward the door and Garvin made sure she could see GoGo Walker as he shifted with the crowd. She watched his shoulders and the rust-colored plaid shirt he was wearing. Followed him outside into the warm summer night. He seemed to weave in and out among the trees. Fireflies danced among the colored lanterns and lit his movements. Garvin had thought that the problem would be getting Meemaw away from him. Instead it was Smitty that seemed to be GoGo's constant companion. She could hear them laughing over the noise of the crowd. Overhead, from the other side of the lake, fireworks exploded—bursts of red, yellow, blue, orange, and green.

The crowd moved toward the bleacher stand made of old wooden boards, the same stand where people came to sit and listen to summer evening concerts. Smitty moved out of view, and Garvin saw GoGo step up onto the bleachers and take a seat. People quickly filled in spots around him.

"Oo-oo!" An especially big and bright explosion filled the sky. Garvin took the opportunity to make her move.

"Excuse me. Excuse me." There was no way to be modest as she climbed in the dress she was wearing. Spandex wasn't forgiving. Besides, modesty wasn't the plan—at least not with Mr. Walker. She wiggled into place next to him and hoped the wooden bench beneath her wouldn't splinter.

"So, I finally get to talk to you," Garvin purred in GoGo's direction. "I know it couldn't possibly be, but sometimes I feel like you are trying to avoid me."

GoGo looked around as if he were in a panic.

"Ah! Ah!" What looked like a blue blossom exploded in the sky.

"I would like for us to spend some time together." Garvin leaned on him. "I haven't had much company since I left D.C."

"Hey, Garvin!"

Smitty was making his way through the people sitting on the benches. "Oops, sorry." He looked and then pointed between Garvin and GoGo. "You think I can squeeze in there?" Smitty didn't wait for an answer but stepped up and turned to sit. Most of him landed in Garvin's lap. "Sorry, I guess I'm a little bigger than I thought I was."

"I guess so!" Garvin was piqued. The man must be crazy.

"No problem, Smitty. Here." GoGo hopped off the end of the row. "Take my seat. I need to stand anyway." He walked away while Garvin sat lodged in the stand.

"Doesn't this remind you of high school? Wow, it's really snug up here." When the band across the lake began to play patriotic songs, Smitty sang as loud as he could while Garvin boiled. If Smitty could have read Garvin's mind, she was sure he would have been surprised at the personal fireworks display going off in her head.

The last display was spectacular—an American flag with all kinds of multicolored explosions around it.

"Can I help you down?"

Garvin wanted to slap Smitty's hand out of the way. She had spent the whole stupid show locked in the bleachers. Who knew where GoGo was by now?

For some reason, Smitty seemed particularly amused. "You be careful now." Garvin brushed past him and kept searching, in around the trees, until she came upon GoGo. She could have been mistaken, but it seemed that when he looked back and saw her he suddenly inserted himself in a conversation Barbershop Owner Number One was having with his family.

That was okay. She would bide her time.

"Hey, Garvin." It was Smitty, again. "We just seem to keep running into each other." He grabbed her hand and spun her around several times. By the time he stopped, GoGo was long gone.

"Hey, Smitty! Come settle this argument." Winston Salem's call, several yards away, diverted Smitty's attention, and Garvin used the opportunity to get away. She used tree trunks and barbecue grills to shield herself from Smitty's sight as she ran and sneaked about looking for GoGo. Garvin could feel herself getting winded—the cigarettes were going to have to go.

There he is! She ran toward the men's bathroom. A small cinder block building, it was painted the same putrid green as Miz Maizie's janitor uniform. Garvin stood just to the right, her back plastered against the wall near the door opening. The rat was cornered; there was no other way in or out of the building. And she was determined to go in if she had to.

She could hear him breathing, almost panting as though he were afraid, and knew that he was coming toward the door. When his foot stepped through the opening, she pounced.

"So, GoGo." She got close, close enough to feel his heart pounding. "I've never had to work so hard to connect with a man." Garvin reached for the hem of her very short dress and gave it a small, suggestive tug. "Now, to carry on with the conversation we started earlier."

Garvin reached for one of GoGo's hands and placed it on one

of her shoulders. "I think we need to spend some time together. And sooner…" She placed an arm around his waist and used her other hand to press the back of his head so that his face moved closer to hers. "Sooner is much, much better than later."

Walker's lips moved open and closed until they made contact with hers. Finally, he stopped struggling. She felt both of his hands move to the small of her back. His hands were strong. His lips were soft, firm, and moist. Garvin stood on her tiptoes so it would be easier to kiss him. She leaned forward and felt herself surrendering. At least it was going to be a sweet, spicy sacrifice.

"Miss Garvin?"

It couldn't be. Not now. Not when she was so close.

"Miss Garvin?"

She reluctantly stepped back, turned her head, and then opened her eyes. It was Monique. The girl had the strangest look in her eyes. Garvin thought she saw disapproval there…but there was something else. Whatever it was, it quickly turned to defiance.

"Miz Evangelina, your grandmother, is waiting for you. She's tired and she wants to go home." The girl looked between GoGo and Garvin. "Now."

For some reason, Garvin felt naked in front of the girl and pulled at the hem of her dress. This was just great. The kid always seemed to show up at the wrong time. "I'm coming. Okay, Monique? Just give me a minute." She felt like an idiot.

"GoGo man, I thought I had lost you." Smitty stepped around the side of the little building. "We need to go, all right?"

Garvin turned to look at GoGo. He stared into her eyes, looked at Monique, then back at Smitty. He didn't say a word, just walked away with his friend. Garvin turned to talk to Monique, but the girl was already hurrying away, her form difficult to make out in the darkness.

"Monique. Monique, wait." This was stupid. This whole thing was stupid. And what was that look Walker gave her? And what were these feelings she was having? "Wait, Monique."

Garvin ran and she caught up with Monique under the last string of lights, just before the parking lot. "Monique, what's wrong? What's the matter?"

The force of the girl's response surprised her. "What difference does it make to *you*? I'm just an experiment. Something to kill some extra time. Something you're doing to make yourself feel good, so you can use me to wave around and tell people you're 'giving back to the community.' As long as we keep our appointments, as long as we stay on schedule, what do *you* care?"

"Would I be running after you like a crazy person if I didn't care? I asked you what's the matter? What do you want from me? What is wrong with you?"

"What's wrong with me? You don't want to know, you might get your hands dirty."

"I asked you what's wrong."

"What's wrong? I had a baby, that's what's wrong."

"I know that, Monique, but it's not the end of your life—"

"How would you know? You get to jet around and do whatever you feel like and nobody points at you. What do you know about life ending?"

"Maybe I've been through some hard things too, Monique. Maybe you don't know what I've been through."

"How could I know, Miss Garvin? You don't talk to me. Not like I'm a person, you just talk to me like I'm another appointment. Whenever we meet, you always come off like you're so straight and perfect—like I should try to be like you. But when I see you around, what you're doing is what got me in trouble in the first place. And…what do you care about how I feel, anyway?"

"Monique—"

The girl laid her hand over her heart. "Everybody paints this picture of me, like I'm trash. You even make me feel that way sometimes. But I don't get it, Miss Garvin. I don't see the difference between what I did and what I see you doing—at least I never threw myself at anybody. What makes it okay for you? Money? Your job? Oh, just forget about it." Monique turned to walk away.

"Wait, Monique. You don't understand. There's a reason…"

Monique turned back. "Funny, that's not good enough when I say it. Maybe it's because everybody thinks I'm nothing anyway, so they can point fingers at me that they won't point at themselves."

"Monique, lower your voice. People are looking."

"So what? They look at me all the time anyway."

"Monique, this isn't helping. What do you want from me?"

The girl stepped closer and whispered fiercely. "What do I want? I want a fair chance…I want my baby!"

"You know that's impossible. Your baby was adopted. You told me yourself that you gave her up for adoption."

Tears began to flow from Monique's eyes. "But it never happened. That's what they promised, but something happened. She's here. She's in Jacks Creek. She's at the Boys' and Girls' Home. I know it's her."

"Monique, you're just imagining this. You want it to be her."

"No, I know it's her. I know she's my baby. The first time I saw her I knew her. I saw her on a playground at the park. She was with a bunch of little kids and they were holding this rope to keep them all together.

"I followed them…followed her. She had on these little red rubber boots and she kept trying to step in the puddles, and I know she's mine. Her eyes…" Monique was gasping for air. "I *know* she is. And when I look at her through the fence, through the bars around the place where she lives, I feel like I'm in prison. Like both of us are in prison. And I want my baby. If everybody is going to hate me and talk about me, I ought to at least have my baby. Nobody wants either one of us, but we can love each other."

"Monique, I—"

"You know the playground? I go there so I can see her. And I can look at her, but I can't touch her. And she's there with nobody. Just like me, outside with nobody. And it was all for nothing—do you know some people think I killed her? You want to do something for me? Get me back my baby!" The girl turned and started to run.

"Monique! *Monique!*"

Garvin felt Meemaw's hand on her shoulder. "Just let her go. Give her time."

Garvin shook her head. "Meemaw, she's got some crazy idea that her baby didn't get adopted. That the little girl is in the Jacks Creek Boys' and Girls' Home."

Meemaw started walking in the direction of the car. "How do you know it's crazy, Garvin?"

They opened the car doors, slid onto the seats, and Garvin eased the car out of the parking lot and onto the road. "I just don't know what to do about this."

Meemaw looked out the window. "You're going to have to figure this one out for yourself."

"I'm willing to help. But this is way over my head. I don't want to get involved in all this. I didn't make her get pregnant; no one raped her; she has to take responsibility for herself. She was acting like a grown person—she can't suddenly turn into a helpless little girl."

Garvin could feel Meemaw's steady gaze. "You're right. She

made a bad decision, she used poor judgment, and she did wrong. And that makes you uncomfortable, doesn't it? You can't abide people behaving in a way that seems weak, or in a way where their heart rules their heads—especially if the outcome is messy."

"I don't think that's fair."

Meemaw looked back out the window. "We all stumble for different reasons. Remember when we were talking about virtue before? I said some people were like Joseph and my grandparents—other people or even just life tried to steal their value, their virtue, and their worth. Well, some people are like your mother and Monique. They give it away looking for love. Hoping it will be enough to make somebody love them, or just pay attention to them. Hoping that they can pay someone to make them feel special and valued. Some people don't know any better. No one has ever told them what their value is. But sometimes, Garvin, there are people that give it away out of fear, anger, or hardened hearts. They tell themselves they are going to give it away before someone can take it, so they can keep control of the situation. They devalue themselves so no one can have a chance to steal something precious from them. To tell you the truth, it seems to me that the end result is the same. What good does pointing fingers do? All the situations need Jesus' touch."

Garvin hit her turn signal. "Meemaw, you're always making excuses for Monique. It's almost like you want to coddle her. Well, I feel like she made her own bed."

"You're right. I do feel sorry for her. Sorry because she's in pain, and just like most of us she tried to fix it herself. Only she got caught and got exposed in a public way doing something that everybody frowns on. Most of us just don't get caught—at least not publicly."

"Well, I disagree. And I have enough problems in my own life—I don't have time to fool with someone who just wants to feel sorry for herself."

"Maybe Monique's problem is just a little too close to your own."

Garvin pulled into the driveway and shut off the car. "What do you mean by that, Meemaw?"

"Both of you are full of pain. You just try to cover yours up with anger. You act like you're mad at God. What it really is, is hurt. You just got too much pride to let it be that you are hurt. Being hurt might mean that you are weak. Instead, you just trying to cover it up with other things—being in control, being mean, acting up 'cause you mad, because you're hurt so you think the rules are supposed to be bent for you."

Garvin could feel her eyes watering.

"When people are hurt like you and Monique, I can see the pain—the dead thing they're holding on to, the thing they're covering up—almost a mile away. People disguise it with all sorts of things: overeating, not eating, sleeping around, racism, fear, weakness, lying, stealing, pride, fighting."

"Meemaw, I don't need this lecture." Garvin reached for her car door.

"Don't you open that door. You always want to run when it gets too close, but we're going to have this out, right here tonight!"

Meemaw touched Garvin's arm. "People think they are protecting themselves, but those disguises are all just big blinking blue lights that say 'pain.' They keep covering and covering until the disguise has taken over their lives; they look in the mirror and don't see themselves anymore, don't even know who they are. Then they're mad at what the disguise has done to them.

"Getting mad won't help. When you get mad you're just kissing the devil, and he's happy about it. The devil wants to date you. He wants to date you for a long time. He wants you in the same hopeless position that he's in.

"Garvina, you can't let go of the disguise, and you can't help Monique until you are willing to let go of your own hurt. You know, baby, I was hurt too. I didn't have no idea how angry I was, how hurt I was. Why didn't He protect me? Why did He let my baby die? Why did He let my husband die? One day, though, I looked around me and inside me and I tried to recall the day I stopped living. The day I stopped looking at the stars and at the clouds. The day I stopped breathing and when I found that day, I found the hurt. I looked at that hurt and held it in my hand."

Garvin cried openly now. The tears burned her face.

Meemaw reached for her hand. "I cried and prayed about it, then I knew it wasn't mine to keep, that if I held on to it, it would just keep rotting and making me sick. I gave it to Him. Then one day I woke up and I could smell the earth again. I started to remember about the flowers and how good it felt to have rain on my face."

Meemaw pulled Garvin's head onto her shoulder. "Bad things happen sometimes, but He promises they won't prosper. We're the only ones that can make bad things prosper; if we keep meditating on them like they were not yesterday, but right here today. If we keep covering over that bad thing with ugly memories, we just make it worse.

"We don't serve a God who doesn't care about us. He gave up His throne to make it up to us. He endured the cross, bled, and died so that He could redeem us and protect us from whatever tried to harm us. He paid the price for your tears, for your anger, for your hurt. Give it to Him, He paid for it. Let Him have it. Let go."

Garvin reached her arms to Meemaw, almost crawled into her lap. In Garvin's mind, she saw the river—the Cape Fear flowing red, and her mother's shoe.

"Whatever it is that you are letting continue to break your heart, whatever dead thing you're holding on to, that's what has power over you. We hold on to bad things forever, nurse them forever. Good things we let go, let them be snatched away in a few minutes. Even if we write it down, most times we forget. Let it go and let Him in."

Garvin gasped for air. "My job…my mommy. I tried so hard, tried to do everything right. Tried to speak right, walk right, talk right. What's the matter with me, Meemaw? Now I've lost everything, even my job. Why me, Meemaw? Why don't they like me?"

"Garvina, you listen to me good. Some people try to cover up their hurt with control. They control everything around them, won't let anything in to hurt them, until one day they realize they have succeeded—they are alone. Nobody can get in—not even God— and they can't get out, and they're still hurt. If they let Him in, He'll take that hurt away then put life where that dead thing was.

"Nobody can love you, Garvina. You won't let them. I try 'cause I already love you. You're my baby. But you don't give other people no reason to even try. You won't even crack that door— everybody ain't mean, wrong, and out to get you, sugar.

"Let Him love you. Don't you know when He looks down and sees you His heart skips a beat. 'There's my baby, look at her,' He says. He knows everything in your life ain't been right, but you can't fix it—only He can. God sees you, baby. And He cares."

Garvin's body wracked with sobs.

Meemaw rocked her until she stopped crying. Her grandmother wiped her tears. "You and Monique are both hurt. You have to decide. Can you do anything to help the child? Are you willing? Are you willing to go out of your way? And Garvin, nobody can decide that but you.

"If you're going to help Monique, you're going to have to tell her what you know out of love, out of your broken heart. Being holier-than-thou, pointing fingers, and being judgmental never saved anybody. But an honest and true testimony—where you show your own scars and tell how your own wounds were healed—that's a testimony that saves. And only you can choose whether you're going to do that.

"But first you have to allow light into your own soul."

Twenty-eight

Garvin spun around in Esther's chair. The lights were out, the shop was closed, and Esther was packing her bag. The shadows in the shop cut across Garvin's midsection so that she was alternately feet in the light, then head in the light. Her eyes sometimes focused on the front window, sometimes on Esther. She felt like a child spinning in the chair.

"Why do we have to dress like this, Garvin, if we're just going to take a look at things? We look like Power Ranger rejects." Esther wore spandex bike pants and top, so that she was covered wrist to ankle in neon green and hot pink, with black and yellow accents. Her shoes matched.

"You'll see and you'll be glad you're wearing it." Garvin wore a similar outfit, but hers was red and white, with red, white, and blue shoes. "This is it, Esther. This is my last try. I didn't come here for all this. Someone called me and told me Meemaw was in trouble, that this guy was trying to inhale her, so I came. I still don't know who called and I still haven't been able to get in between the two of them. Now I've got this Monique thing—I mean, I agreed to help, but I didn't sign up for all this."

Garvin stopped turning and looked in Esther's direction. "The other day, I almost had GoGo in front of the barbershop. But he got away. I jumped in my car, had my foot on the gas—" Garvin raised her foot in the air as though she was pushing on an imaginary pedal—"my foot was tingling and I could see myself thrashing him once I caught up with him…so I was after him, then a policeman was after me, and it cost me sixty-five bucks…

Then at the picnic—girl, I thought I had him! But everything just went crazy."

She shook her head. "This is it, Esther. This is it."

Esther continued packing her bag. "Garvin, you are still trying to control life, to make it come to you like you the big bad boss. It just doesn't work that way." The shadows of four teenage passersby cut through the light in the shop. She sighed.

Then a smile crossed her face. "Remember when we were like them, when we were in high school? Music, records, clothes. Eight tracks!" Garvin laughed. Suddenly Esther began to roll her shoulders, as though she heard drums. "Remember afros? Dashikis? Remember African dancing class?"

Garvin doubled over. "Eight tracks? You know you just went way too far."

Esther stopped dancing and stood still. "Thinking about the old times, looking at the kids, makes me laugh. But there are times when I see a young person, like that child, Monique—and not just her, but some of the other children, too—it breaks my heart. When I see them, it makes me think about my own." She pointed at the picture on her station.

"You know, Garvin, whatever they see me do, they want to do the same thing. If I drink grape soda, girl, they've got to drink grape soda too. If I wear a hat, they want to wear hats too. I read; they read. I think that's just how they learn. And they're not waiting until they're grown to try to do what they see me do; they want to do it right now."

Garvin spun in the chair again. "Your kids are cute—good kids."

"The point I'm trying to make, Miss Garvin, is that when they mimic us doing something we like, or something we think is good, we pinch their cheeks and jump for joy. And we don't waste no time taking credit for teaching them. But if it's something we don't like, or something we do that makes us uncomfortable, all of a sudden we want to point at them and act like we don't know how they got that way. Like me, I know I eat too much and my kids do too—ain't no point in pretending that they didn't learn that from me.

"And I'll be real with you, Garvin. When I see kids like Monique. When I see these little fast girls running around here and these mannish boys, I feel like we had something to do with it."

Garvin stopped spinning and shook her head. "You may feel that way, but we aren't parents to any one of them. I don't have any kids, and until Monique, I tried to avoid interacting with any. Maybe you did, but I know I didn't sign up to be a role model and you can't put that responsibility on me."

"Come on, Garvin. That may sound good, but you know we don't have to be parents for kids to want to try to be like us. All we have to do is live in the world. And living, whether we like it or not, gives us responsibilities.

"Think about how we used to watch Miss Flossie. All these little girls looking at her and wanting the attention we saw her getting from men. Those of us that had somebody to tell us that wasn't the way to get that attention were blessed. Some of the other girls tried to follow her and didn't realize until it was too late that it was the wrong way.

"Think about how we used to watch Miz Evangelina in church and pretended to shout like she did." Esther grabbed a pair of hot curlers and stuck them in the bag. "Anyway, you may not think so, Garvin. But in my heart, I think we have something to do with it—so do our parents and their parents. But we can't deny our part. I think we have to own up to them and be willing to tell them how we went wrong. I think we should try to help fix it, but we can't fix it if we keep on intentionally doing things we know are wrong. Who are they going to look at to learn the right way?"

Garvin laughed. "This would sound like a religious conversion to me—" she waved her hands in the air—"except you don't go to church anymore, remember?"

"I'm serious, Garvin." Esther shifted her weight onto one hip. "Remember when Inez Zephyr's niece was in here? She really made me think. And she was right. Ever since my husband died, I have been mad. I just said, 'I'll take care of my own self. I can't count on God. And I'm not going to love another man just so God can take him away too.' But I don't want to live my life halfway, like I've buried half of me with him. What am I teaching my kids? And it's too hard trying to do it all by myself. I want to let myself be happy again before it's too late. I want to open my heart to other people. There's no guarantee that I won't get hurt again, that I won't get the wind knocked out of me. But it's too hard trying to be mad all the time. I need God, Garvin. And if He has somebody else for me, I need him too."

Garvin sat quietly until Esther was finished packing. The two women left the shop and locked the door.

"Esther, are you sure you want to take two cars?"

"Yes. I'm not exactly sure what craziness this is that you have me involved in, but I told you I can only give you an hour and a half. I've got to pick up my kids and I've got other stuff to do. If we're not done in that time, I'm leaving you. Do you understand what I'm saying, Lucy Ricardo?"

"I've got to try one last time. Meemaw is still running around with Walker. I can't even count how many times they've been out since the banquet. He's still coming by just as bold as you please.

I've tailed them a couple of times by myself and I know they're going out Orchard Road. There was this building, a bunch of cars—expensive cars, and blaring music."

Esther shook her head and put her arm around Garvin's shoulders. "Did you ever think that they might really be doing what they said? Just working out."

"Maybe. Sometimes. But other times she comes home and her socks are clean and her workout clothes are dry."

Esther stepped away, laughing. "Garvin! I can't believe you. You are checking up on your Meemaw. You are sick, girl!"

"I'm not going to let him have my Meemaw."

Esther gave Garvin the eye. "You sure that's all this is about? You sure you not a little sweet on GoGo yourself? Somebody told me they saw you and him in a lip lock at the banquet. Maybe he put the whammy on you, and you are just obsessing and projecting that Meemaw is feeling the same thing."

Garvin felt her face get warm. "That's the problem in Jacks Creek—everybody minding everybody else's business."

Esther started walking toward her car. "What is that saying about the pot calling the kettle black?"

"Esther…"

"Okay, Garvin. We can stand out here arguing if you want to, but I told you one hour and thirty minutes, and you've already spent ten."

The two women got in their cars, Garvin leading the way, and drove until they reached Orchard Road. High, brilliant green grass grew along the sides of the quiet, rural road. Garvin turned on her blinker, pulled over, and ran back to Esther's window when she parked her car. "Okay, the building is about a mile ahead. We can park here and walk the rest of the way."

"*Walk?*"

"I don't want them to hear the car."

Esther did not look pleased. "You didn't say anything to me about walking. You know I'm not Jane Fonda. And I told you I had somewhere to go—you're going to have me sweating my hair. Don't you think a quarter of a mile away would be good enough?"

"Come on, Esther."

They walked along the side of the road for a short distance. Then Garvin waved for Esther to follow her into the high grass.

"Oh no, no, no! Now you want me to walk through this crazy grass? What if we come upon a snake? Garvin, you know I hate snakes!"

She giggled at her friend. "Come on, Esther."

Esther kept looking from side to side. "What's that? What's that rattling sound? Oh, Lord! Help me! Garvin, I knew I shouldn't have let you talk me into coming."

Garvin put her hand to her chest. She was laughing so hard that she was gasping for air. "Esther, girl, you are crazy. There are no rattlers in this area."

"You sure?"

"Come on, Esther."

She and Garvin continued wading through the grass. "What if this is like that Stephen King book?"

"What Stephen King book?"

"You know."

"There's no corn here, just grass."

The pair kept making their way through the waist-high, sometimes shoulder-high plants. Suddenly Esther began to sing—punctuating the song with strange noises—and to dance with abandon. "Remember this move?"

"Esther?"

"I just felt free all of a sudden. Remember what I said about

African dance class. Come on, Garvin. You remember."

In spite of herself, Garvin began to go through the motions, humming and laughing until the two of them were out of breath.

"Esther, girl, you are still crazy. I haven't laughed so hard in a long time."

"You too, Garvin." They linked arms and continued walking.

Garvin pointed. "See, there it is!" The ribbed, galvanized steel building rose before them. "Come on, let's run."

"Garvin, you know I don't run." Esther panted behind her.

When they reached the clearing, the parking lot was indeed full of expensive, full-sized cars. "See, I told you. Meemaw is just one among many. He's got a harem of rich, golden-aged women."

"Garvin, I think you are taking this all wrong." Esther pointed in the direction of music that pumped from speakers. "That's Fred Hammond singing 'I Want to Know Your Ways.'"

"I don't care who it is. I'm going to find out what's going on and then I'm going in to get my Meemaw."

"This is crazy. We need to go. It's going to take us another half hour just to wade back through that grass."

"You go back if you want to, Esther." With every word, Garvin moved closer and closer to the building. She stopped and lifted a finger. "Listen to *that* music. You can't convince me a bunch of old people are dancing to that."

"What? That's Vickie Winans singing 'I Hear Music in the Air.'"

Garvin resumed walking. "I don't care; I'm going."

Esther stopped. "I'm not going, Garvin. Come on, let's go. You're just going to end up being embarrassed."

"I'm not turning back now."

"Well, I am."

"Go on then." Garvin turned back to see Esther marching toward the high grass. "Esther?"

"I told you. I'm going back. This is crazy. I've got to get my kids…and I've got something to do."

"Esther!" Garvin stomped her foot. "You quitter. Just wait, I'm going to pay you back." Esther waved a hand behind her and disappeared into the grass.

Traitor! Garvin crossed the rest of the way to the building, careful not to make a lot of noise on the rocks in the parking lot. As she got closer, she could hear people laughing and *whooping* in time with the music—it sounded like a disco. There was a window in the back door that she could peek through. But that might be too obvious.

She circled the building. There were windows on the side, but they were too high for her to reach alone.

Traitor!

Garvin looked about for something to stand on—there were three industrial-sized paint cans, empty ones. Quietly as she could she dragged them up under the center window. Two of them, she stacked and tested to make sure they were stable. She set the third can next to the first two. Garvin stepped up on the single can, then used it to reach the top of the two stacked cans. She was in place and able to see!

She pressed her two hands and face to the window. Inside were gray-haired men and women, some more or less gray than others. They were stepping, clapping, bouncing, and gyrating to the music. Garvin recognized Kirk Franklin's song "Revolution."

GoGo Walker was in front of the group wearing a head mike and calling the moves. "Step right, step, step. Step left, step, step." Meemaw was on the front row laughing and smiling. She looked like a young girl.

Garvin stepped a little to the right on her perch for a better view. GoGo was pumping his knees. "Now tap, now tap, now turn—right face!" The whole class was looking at her. Garvin froze, then thought to duck. She closed her eyes…then she felt herself falling. *This is not going to be good.*

Her ankle twisted underneath her when she landed.

She kept her eyes closed. Maybe she would be invisible. Garvin could hear feet running toward her. "Are you okay?" She didn't have to open her eyes to know that it was *him* leaning over her. Garvin kept her eyes closed and her mouth shut. Maybe they would think she had a concussion. She could fake amnesia.

More feet arrived behind him. "Garvina, are you alive?"

If she could just keep her eyes closed.

"Garvina?"

"Ow!" Her eyes flew open. Meemaw had pinched her!

"Girl, I thought you were dead. What are you doing out here?" Meemaw looked like she was torn between concern and anger. If Garvin just didn't say anything, maybe concern would win out.

"She fell pretty hard." It was his voice again. Then he leaned over Garvin's face. "Are you feeling sharp pain anywhere?"

Smart question.

GoGo felt her arms. She wanted to shout and tell him not to touch her. He felt her legs and ankles. She moaned.

"Don't move, Garvina. Hush." Meemaw was leaning over GoGo's shoulder.

GoGo talked over his shoulder to Meemaw. "I don't think she's broken anything, but her ankle is definitely sprained. We need to get her home right away and keep her off that foot." Others had gathered and were whispering behind their hands.

Meemaw leaned farther forward. "How did you get here, Garvina?"

She felt so foolish in front of all the people. "In my car."

"Well, where is it, baby?"

"Don't worry about it, Meemaw. I can get myself home." She raised up on her elbows.

GoGo shook his head. "Not on this ankle." She wanted to glare at him, but that might tip the scales in favor of Meemaw's anger.

"Where is your car, baby?"

"About a mile up the road."

Meemaw opened her mouth, frowned, and then closed it. "You know what? There's no point in even going into it right now." She laid her hand on GoGo's shoulder. "You take her home for me."

"Yes, ma'am."

"And I'll get my stuff together, then pick up Garvina's car and drive it home." Meemaw walked away shaking her head. She looked at one of her friends. "See, I told you, you don't have problems...that's why I got all this gray hair. Lord, have mercy."

GoGo swept Garvin into his arms. "Let me know if I hurt you." He carried her to his car, opened the door, and sat her on the front seat. "Wait just a minute." Garvin turned to see him lift a Bible and what looked like a study guide and put them into the trunk of his car. They must be Meemaw's.

GoGo came back and lifted her again. "We got to be careful of that ankle." He got her settled in the backseat and elevated her foot with a towel. He slid behind the wheel and drove carefully, seemingly even avoiding bumps in the road. Garvin must have fallen asleep, because the next thing she knew, he was carrying her up the walkway to her house. "Your key," he said.

She handed it to him; he opened the door and carried her over the threshold.

He set her down in one chair and brought another to prop up her foot. Garvin could hear him rummaging in the kitchen. Then he appeared with a foot tub, which he filled with hot running water. GoGo carried the water into the living room and set it near her chair. He dug in his bag and pulled out a jar full of white crystals. He shook some of them into the tub and stirred it with his hand. "Epsom salts. It should help the swelling." He gently took her foot off the chair and placed it in the tub. "Let's let that soak a while." Garvin was too tired to fight. The water was soothing.

Looking over her shoulder, she saw him looking out the door. He appeared to be looking at the sky. When he noticed her looking at him, GoGo opened the door wider and smiled. "More fresh air, right?"

He dug into his bag again and pulled out a towel and a jar of ointment. He sat across from her and placed the towel on his lap. "Give me your foot." She hesitated. "Come on, Garvin, it will make your ankle feel better."

She placed her foot on the towel, and he used two fingers to dip some ointment from the jar. The aroma was sweet and spicy. The scent became stronger as he rubbed his hands together to warm the salve.

Garvin was afraid for him to touch the tender area, but the caress of GoGo's fingertips was light and gentle on the places where she was sore. As she began to relax, his hands moved skillfully, kneading the perfumed oil into her skin and soft tissues. Garvin felt herself sinking into his massaging hands. The balm pressed and stroked away the stiffness and numbness in her joint.

As the sun began to set, the room darkened. The only light in the room was an early moonlight and the flickering of a firefly that had somehow found its way inside. "Do you have candles?" Garvin nodded and pointed limply toward the counter where her problem jar sat. "Do you mind if I light one or two?"

She couldn't think clearly enough to respond. She closed her eyes and hoped that drool wasn't dripping from the sides of her mouth.

GoGo lifted her foot and placed it gently on the chair while he lit candles and set them around the room. The breeze she felt told Garvin that he had opened the front door even wider. She heard his footsteps coming nearer. Lifting her foot, he sat and quietly resumed his ministrations. It was easy to see why so many women had been enticed by him.

The silence, the flickering candles, his hands…it all intoxicated her and loosened her lips. "This is wonderful…this is magic…but why *GoGo?* It doesn't sound like a Casanova kind of name."

He cleared his throat and laughed softly. "It's not. You'll have to blame my grandmother. It's a Bible name, like Isaiah. Only she named me *Abed-nego.* As in Shadrach, Meshach, and Abednego in the fiery furnace. None of the kids could say it, so it became GoGo…and that stuck."

"That's funny. Somebody like you with a biblical name."

"Maybe…maybe not." They lapsed back into silence. The shadows and the sweet, aromatic relief enfolded them. Garvin could feel herself giving in to abandon and his voice, almost like a song, added to the atmosphere around her.

"'*I am black, but comely, O ye daughters of Jerusalem, as the tents of Kedar, as the curtains of Solomon.*'"

Garvin wasn't sure if she was awake, or if it was a dream.

"'*I am the rose of Sharon, and the lily of the valleys. As the lily among thorns, so is my love among the daughters. As the apple tree among the trees of the wood, so is my beloved among the sons. I sat down under his shadow with great delight, and his fruit was sweet to my taste.*

"'*He brought me to the banqueting house, and his banner over me was love.*'"

Garvin could feel herself drifting in and out. GoGo's voice was a hymn, a prayer.

"'My beloved spake, and said unto me, Rise up, my love, my fair one, and come away. For, lo, the winter is past, the rain is over and gone; The flowers appear on the earth; the time of the singing of birds is come, and the voice of the turtle is heard in our land;

"'The fig tree putteth forth her green figs, and the vines with the tender grape give a good smell. Arise, my love, my fair one, and come away.

"'O my dove, that art in the clefts of the rock, in the secret places of the stairs, let me see thy countenance, let me hear thy voice; for sweet is thy voice, and thy countenance is comely.'"

GoGo spoke a divine love sonnet to Garvin—a song that caressed her and blessed her; a song that affirmed her beauty and her worth.

"'Behold, thou art fair, my love; behold, thou art fair; thou hast doves' eyes within thy locks: thy hair is as a flock of goats, that appear from mount Gilead.

"'Thy teeth are like a flock of sheep that are even shorn, which came up from the washing; whereof every one bear twins, and none is barren among them. Thy lips are like a thread of scarlet, and thy speech is comely: thy temples are like a piece of a pomegranate within thy locks. Thy neck is like the tower of David builded for an armoury, whereon there hang a thousand bucklers, all shields of mighty men.'"

She could feel his strong hands squeezing and strengthening her ankle.

"'Thou hast ravished my heart, my sister, my spouse; thou hast ravished my heart with one of thine eyes, with one chain of thy neck.

"'How fair is thy love, my sister, my spouse! how much better is thy love than wine! and the smell of thine ointments than all spices!

"'Thy lips, O my spouse, drop as the honeycomb: honey and milk are under thy tongue; and the smell of thy garments is like the smell of Lebanon. A garden enclosed is my sister, my spouse; a spring shut up, a *fountain sealed. Thy plants are an orchard of pomegranates, with pleasant fruits; camphire, with spikenard, spikenard and saffron; calamus and cinnamon, with all trees of frankincense; myrrh and aloes, with all the chief spices: a fountain of gardens, a well of living waters, and streams from Lebanon.*

"'Awake, O north wind; and come, thou south; blow upon my garden, that the spices thereof may flow out. Let my beloved come into his garden, and eat his pleasant fruits.'"

She surrendered, and then he lifted her, carrying her to the bed.

"'Come, my beloved, let us go forth into the field; let us lodge in the villages. Let us get up early to the vineyards; let us see if the vine flourish, whether the tender grape appear, and the pomegranates bud forth: there will I give thee my loves. The mandrakes give a smell, and at our gates are all manner of pleasant fruits, new and old, which I have laid up for thee, O my beloved.'"

Garvin felt him undoing the sheet and blanket beneath her…and then he covered her. He leaned over her, and she could feel the warmth of his breath on her face. Her lips parted slightly and waited for the kiss.

"You're a beautiful woman, Garvin. And you're probably too far asleep to remember this, but I know what you've been thinking of me. You're wrong. I'm trying to learn to live my life in a way that honors God. That might sound crazy to somebody like you—but I've tried the other way." He kissed her softly. His lips were full and they pressed firmly on hers. She was too close to unconsciousness to respond. "Maybe it's not too late for us to try, for you to get to know who I really am—who I am now. I have surrendered who I am to the Lord. My life has changed, and if I love you, I will only do so if I can also give you and God honor."

His song continued.

"'*Set me as a seal upon thine heart, as a seal upon thine arm: for love is strong as death; jealousy is cruel as the grave: the coals thereof are coals of fire, which hath a most vehement flame.*

"'*Many waters cannot quench love, neither can the floods drown it....*'"

Garvin heard GoGo blow out the candles…and then the door closed behind him.

"Baby?"

Garvin struggled to respond to Meemaw's call. "Ma'am?"

Meemaw leaned over her, and Garvin could feel her grandmother's smile in the darkness. "How's your ankle, sugar?"

"Much better." She wiped her eyes. "Where were you, Meemaw?"

"Oh, I came by and peeked in, and saw that you were in good hands. Mr. Green came by, and we sat out front sipping tea.

"Abed-nego is a good man. I knew his people for years." Meemaw laughed softly. "I was real tickled that *you* thought he was courting *me*. Did he tell you we've been studying the Bible together? That's part of what I pay him for helping me. It's hard for somebody as far out there as he was to make a change—I figured it was up to him to know when he was ready to show people that he's a new creature. In the meantime—" Meemaw chuckled again—"I don't mind giving people a little something to talk about. Maybe they'll be ashamed enough of their judging spirits when it's over to do something about changing."

"Meemaw?"

"Hush now, Garvina. You get some sleep. We got plenty of time to talk in the morning."

Garvin's sleep was deep and full of images of Ramona, of mountains, of fireflies, of Abed-nego, of Meemaw, of Esther, of

Monique, and of vessels of many, many colors.

"Help me, Lord," she whispered in her dreams.

Twenty-nine

---

*I*f spring is the time of renewal and rebirth, then summer is the time of change and radical transformation. It is a time of pubescence and rapid growth, so that little ones become giants all in the matter of a few days. Summer is the time when that which did not appear, unexpectedly becomes. Young, yellow flowers become ripened red tomatoes and exotic-looking flowers become huge juicy watermelons.

On the surface, summer often seems indolent and lazy, but it is, by necessity, deceiving. It drowsily and without announcement or fanfare is the season of profound metamorphosis, of hothouse growth that closes the door on tender beginnings while ushering in abundant life. Summer is the time of graduation, matriculation, and relocation. It is a change of scenery, and sometimes, a change of heart and mind. If spring is to be celebrated, then summer should be pondered as a time of lemonade, great mystery, and awe.

Sometime in the midst of her recuperation, Garvin realized there had been no dreams of rivers too wide, no canyons too deep, no dreams of her mother's shoe. The change was sudden— and welcome. As she healed, she opened the Word, opened the life that had been closed for so long. Meemaw and friends had brought her comfort, and as they visited, she provided them with missing pieces—the true and full story of why she was in Jacks Creek.

Sunshine and summer smells filled the room. Garvin's blue, silk lounging suit was cool enough to allow the breeze from the overhead fan to touch her skin. She lifted the loaf-shaped wicker basket to her nose. The zucchini bread smelled delicious. Tucked in a fold of the peach-colored cloth napkin that lined the basket was another three-by-five card and a knife.

One good thing about being ordered to bed: Meemaw was cooking for her again. It had been a parade of Garvin's favorites— apple pie, broccoli casserole, fried catfish. Thanks to GoGo, her ankle was fine. It was her severely sprained back that had gotten the best of her. Still, things were looking up, seemed to be working for the good.

Garvin removed the worn card, looked over the recipe, and then read the Scripture handwritten on the back.

"My son, forget not my law; but let thine heart keep my commandments: For length of days, and long life, and peace, shall they add to thee. Let not mercy and truth forsake thee: bind them about thy neck; write them upon the table of thine heart: So shalt thou find favour and good understanding in the sight of God and man. Trust in the LORD with all thine heart; and lean not unto thine own understanding. In all thy ways acknowledge him, and he shall direct thy paths (Proverbs 3:1–6)."

Underneath was another of Meemaw's prayers: "Thank You, God, for a new day. Thank You for new hope."

"Amen," Garvin whispered. She sniffed the bread again and then cut a slice. She poured decaf coffee and cream into her cup. Washington was calling to her, the law was calling, but right now it all seemed so far away. Garvin picked up her cell phone and dialed Jonee.

By the time the receptionist had put Jonee on the phone, Garvin had devoured almost half of her bread.

"Garvin, how are you? Are you feeling any better? Are you up to this? I can get us more time, if you need it." Jonee had a million questions.

Garvin laughed. "You're speeding, girl. But here are the answers. I'm fine, I don't feel anywhere near as sore as I did. The doctor says I'm going to be good as new, but reminded me not to play private eye anymore. Yes, not only am I up to it, but I'm fired up. And more time is what I don't want. I feel like I've been out of action long enough. This back thing has had me in bed for more than three weeks. It's been good for me being here, but I feel like I have unfinished business in D.C."

"All right then. So what's the plan?"

Garvin picked her working folder up from the chair where it lay near her, and laid it on the table in front of her. "As I see it, we've got two briefs to prepare, two motions to respond to, and unfortunately, not very much time to do it in. I feel bad for saddling you with all this. But if you can take care of them, I can prepare to take the depositions and to head the settlement conference."

"The settlement conference is next Friday. Are you *sure* you're up to it?"

"Definitely. I don't care what I have to do, I'm determined to get there. And between you and me, I feel like we shouldn't entertain any serious ideas of settling—we need to meet those suckers in court!"

"Wow, Garvin! You need to be put on bedrest more often."

Garvin took a sip of coffee and then laughed. "You should try it sometime. Actually, I'm sure it helped. But it was the meeting with Hemings—I just couldn't deny what I saw in front of me. I felt my litigator's teeth start sharpening." She picked at the bread on her plate. "But one thing I've thought about, Jonee, is you. Why you were so willing to believe him."

"Come on, Garvin. Do you think racism is just a black-and-white issue? Do you really think I don't get called names, that people don't make nasty remarks? And it's not just white people—it's black people, other Asians. It's not race-specific, it's a human issue. I just know that denial is not the answer. It's like alcoholism or any other *ism,* admitting there's a problem is half the battle. Denial is part of the sickness. People know that now about alcoholism. We just don't seem to have learned that lesson about racism and stuff.

"Anyway, cruel taskmistress, I need to get started on the stuff, okay? I've got a few folks helping out on this, a couple of summer interns, so I should be good to go. I'm glad to hear you're feeling like you're back to yourself. And I'll alert folks that you'll be coming in. Mr. Straub may want to meet with you before the conference, so you should probably plan on getting in here early on Friday."

"Will do. Thanks, Jonee. And give my love to Miz Maizie."

"If I haven't mentioned it every time we talk, she always tells me to give you her love. I'm sure she'll be glad to see you."

Garvin clicked off her phone and polished off her bread and coffee. She got up from the table and then walked carefully back to her bed. She was feeling much better, but it made more sense to be careful than to risk a setback.

She fluffed her pillows and then swung her feet from the floor to the bed. She promised herself she wouldn't be doing any more climbing—particularly on stacks of things—anytime soon.

There was a brief knock at the door. "Hey, girl!" Esther stepped inside with her two children. "Are you supposed to be sitting up?"

"Yes, Nurse Esther. The doctor says it's okay for short periods of time at first, and then a little longer each day." Garvin smiled at the boy and girl. "Man, you two guys are getting big." The boy raised his arms as if to make muscles. "I'm impressed."

Esther dragged a chair over from the table, while her daughter sat on the side of the bed. "I feel really bad about leaving you,

Garvin. I should have stayed with you."

Garvin laughed. "Why? There just would have been two of us embarrassed and on bedrest." She smiled at her friend. "Everything's fine. I should have listened to you." Garvin touched Esther's hand. "But it's all working for the good."

The woman nodded. Her son sat at the table, staring at Garvin's glass jar. "What's this?" He pointed with a stubby finger.

"It's my problem jar. You put your problems in the jar and then leave them there for God to solve them, while you help someone else."

"You just got *one* problem, Auntie Garvin?" The little boy sounded incredulous. "My mama would have a whole jar full!"

Garvin and Esther looked at each other and laughed. "No, I have more than one problem. You're mama's just smarter than me. I had to take a fall before I realized I still had too many problems in my hands."

The little girl snuggled closer. Esther leaned and touched the girl on her leg. "Be careful of Auntie Garvin's back, baby."

Garvin began to play with the little girl's barrettes, rearranging them, retwisting them. She looked at Esther. "She's just fine. I'm enjoying it."

The little girl kissed Garvin's cheek and then looked at her mother. "Mommy, when are we going to get our snowballs?"

Esther blushed. "Hush, baby. Grown folks are talking. Soon. We'll get your snowball soon."

"I want the strawberry one, the special kind."

"Hush now, baby. Mama told you to be quiet."

Garvin raised an eyebrow. "Esther, you're supposed to be on vacation, aren't you? You need to take some time off to spend with the kids."

"I am, Garvin." Her friend looked uncomfortable.

"Well, then how…?" Suddenly Garvin smiled.

"A lot has happened since you have been down. You know me and the kids started going back to church."

Garvin nodded. "Meemaw told me."

"And, well, Smitty's started going back to his family church—it's the same one GoGo belongs to. And we're not rushing anything, kind of taking it slow. Sometimes the four of us do things together. You know, just one day at a time."

Garvin chuckled. "You and Smitty, huh? I guess that's kind of been in the works for years. But I thought he didn't make strawberry snowballs."

"Well, now he does."

She reached and slapped Esther's knee. "Go on with your bad self!" Garvin kissed the little girl's forehead. "So when did all this start?"

"You know the day I left you hanging?"

"You mean the appointment—that was *Smitty?*"

Esther nodded. "Come on, kids. We better let Auntie Garvin get some rest."

"And what about the snowballs?" The two children spoke at almost the same time.

"Soon, I promise."

Garvin offered Esther and the children some bread. Esther cut thin slices for each of them, wrapped them in napkins, and then rewrapped the loaf. They took turns hugging Garvin and then waved as they went out the door.

Garvin slid down so that she could lay her head on her pillow. She reached into her nightstand drawer and wrapped her fingers around the case that held her mother's multicolored brooch. She opened the case and studied the individual gems, then snapped the case shut and hid it away under her pillow, and drifted into sweet daydreams of her mother.

The two of them sat together on the front steps of the house sipping iced tea. "Look at this." Her mother had reached into her pocket and showed her the piece of jewelry. "Look how pretty it is. Someday it's going to be yours. I like to just pull it out sometimes and look at it. But someday it'll be yours and you wear it or do with it what you want." They had finished their tea and then gone in search of nectar from wild honeysuckle blossoms.

Garvin didn't remember falling asleep, but the knock at the front door wakened her. She raised her head and looked. "Come in, Monique."

"Miss Garvin, I saw your grandmother out front and she said you wanted to see me. If this is not a good time, I can come back."

She sat up in the bed. "Come closer." Garvin swung her legs to the floor, moved to make room, and patted a spot on the bed next to her. "We need to talk." While squash ripened on the vine, Garvin told Monique the story of her own birth, of her mother, and what Meemaw had taught her about virtue and the coat of many colors. "I've got a lot of lessons to learn myself, a lot of things to try to undo in my own life, but maybe we can learn the lessons together. Maybe we can start together."

Garvin reached under her pillow and removed the box that contained her mother's brooch. "I don't have a coat of many colors to give you. I don't have a dress or robe like Tamar." She opened the little box. "But my mother gave this to me, maybe it will help you remember who you really are."

Monique ran her fingers over the brightly colored stones. "Are you sure you want to give this to *me?*" There were tears in her eyes.

Garvin pressed lightly on the jewelry in the girl's hand. "We've got to stop trying to be tough, stop trying to build walls to protect ourselves." Monique turned her head away while Garvin continued. "You know, I always have to be strong, in control. I can't let anyone see me being weak. And you know what? I finally realized that my need to always be strong is my biggest weakness. I had to come home to learn that if I can allow myself to be weak, I can find strength. It's when I allow myself to be vulnerable; to admit to God and others that I am weak, that I need help; that's when I truly find strength.

"You are not a mistake that someone made, Monique." Garvin gently raised her hand and turned Monique's face toward hers. "You are not even a mistake that *you* made. I'm not a mistake. People may look at us with shame and they may point fingers at you, or me, or people like my mother. But God is not like that." Garvin got gingerly up from the bed and picked up her Bible from the table. "Listen. Just since I've been here in bed I found this, in Isaiah 54:

"'Fear not; for thou shalt not be ashamed: neither be thou confounded; for thou shalt not be put to shame: for thou shalt forget the shame of thy youth, and shalt not remember the reproach of thy widowhood anymore.

"'For thy Maker is thine husband; the LORD of hosts is his name; and thy Redeemer the Holy One of Israel; The God of the whole earth shall he be called.

"'For the LORD hath called thee as a woman forsaken and grieved in spirit, and a wife of youth, when thou wast refused, saith thy God.'

"When I read it, Monique, I knew Isaiah was talking about women and girls like me and you. God was saying that His mercy and His love are for us. That He knows that we have been brokenhearted, that we have felt like we could never be forgiven, that we could never lift up our heads. That we would have to live in shame all our lives because of what we did, or because of what our mothers or fathers did. But God says that we are not single, we are not shameful, we are not orphans. He says that He is willing to marry us and take away our shame. He even wants to take away the memory of our shame, and to be our Father if we will let Him." Garvin's face glowed as she continued reading.

"'O thou afflicted, tossed with tempest, and not comforted, behold, I will lay thy stones with fair colours, and lay thy foundations with sapphires.

"'And I will make thy windows of agates, and thy gates of carbuncles, and all thy borders of pleasant stones. And all thy children shall be taught of the LORD; and great shall be the peace of thy children.'

"I just never wanted to let anyone in, Monique. I didn't want to get hurt again. I didn't want to love someone else just to be hurt again. But the promise is for us, whether we gave ourselves away or whether we were taken. And whether I was strong enough to say it before or not, I do care. Maybe you can look at the stones, at the colors in the brooch, and remember the verses—remember who you are."

The two women hugged, and Garvin rocked Monique while she cried. And while they sat, Garvin told her about the calls she had made. Calls that confirmed Monique's suspicions.

"As best I could find out, when the family found out about your little girl's heritage they 'respectfully declined,' saying it wasn't a 'viable' option for them. She's been in Jacks Creek ever since.

"I had to do some heavy negotiating, but the family services judge agreed. I can't make any promises, Monique. But he's granted permission for you to see your daughter and visit with her Thursday, just before I leave for Washington. That is, with the stipulation that you don't tell her who she is or who you are. That's the best I could do."

Monique's voice was a whisper. "Thank you. Thank you."

"And Monique, you're not going to believe it. Her name is Destiny."

"Well, don't you two look like you've heard some good news!" Meemaw peeked in the door. "I just wanted to bring these to you." In her arms were a large bunch of pale pink roses. Garvin reached for the roses and took the small card from Meemaw's hands. "Well don't leave me in suspense."

She tore the note open.

Garvin,
I wanted to give you time to think and heal. Maybe we can
begin again. How about an early dinner on Thursday?
Abed-nego

Meemaw pressed her hands to her face. "This has turned out to be some summer."

Thirty

$\blacklozenge$

he blue Lexus pulled into a parking space across from the Jacks Creek Boys' and Girls' Home. Monique, sitting on the passenger's side, opened her book bag and pulled out her small clay jar. "I-I wanted you to have this. It's the only thing I have to give you. Something to say thanks. It's my problem jar. My paper's still in there." She looked at Garvin. "I just wanted a home, a home for me and my baby."

Garvin cupped the small earthenware vessel in her hands. She rubbed Monique's shoulder. "I can't make any promises, Monique. But at least this is a start." Garvin took a deep breath. "Come on, let's go."

They crossed the street and walked inside the building. The front hallway was hushed and carpeted, and the walls were covered with dark, cherry-stained wood.

"Can I help you?" A tall stately woman appeared from behind one of the office doors and examined them over the top of her half-eyeglasses.

"I'm Garvin Daniels, and this is Monique Bryan. We're here for a meeting with Destiny."

"Oh, yes. I'm Mrs. Winn." The woman extended her hand to Garvin, but continued to eye Monique. "I must tell you that I really have some reservations about this."

Garvin's mouth was more of a line than a smile. "I appreciate your concerns, Mrs. Winn. But the matter has already been settled.

Monique's visit with Destiny has already been arranged. And unless you're prepared to share your reservations with the family court judge, we really should get the meeting started."

Mrs. Winn opened two heavy, wooden double doors at the end of the short corridor. When they stepped through the doors, the walls were no longer wooden, but were painted a sterile beige color. The carpet had changed to speckled linoleum tile squares. The doors were now aluminum fire doors. As they walked the hallways, as they passed doorways, they could sometimes hear the voices of children, or adults whose voices sounded as if they were speaking to children. They continued walking until Mrs. Winn stopped and pointed. "You may wait here." She turned and walked away.

The room had three doors—one off the corridor that they had walked down, one to their left as they entered the room, and a third door that appeared to open to the courtyard outside. Garvin leaned against the jamb of the corridor doorway, while Monique sat in a chair that faced the second door.

"It's going to be okay."

Monique shrugged. "I must look as nervous as I feel."

"Anybody would."

The side door opened. It was Mrs. Winn, and holding her hand was the prettiest little girl. Destiny.

She was tiny and her hair was a darker, more golden in color than Monique's, but it was the same texture. The little girl's eyes were exactly the same as Monique's, only more innocent. Destiny held a patchwork stuffed kitten in her hands.

Mrs. Winn's voice had a nasal quality. "Destiny, this is Ms. Daniels. And this is Monique, she's here to visit you."

Monique looked frozen. Her voice squeaked. "Hello."

Destiny stood silent and stared. Monique began to tremble.

The little girl walked to her and touched her hand. She blinked and tilted her head.

"Hello." Destiny leaned against Monique, pressed her kitten into Monique's hands, and hugged her. "His name is Space Cat." A single tear slid down the teenager's face.

"Mrs. Winn, why don't you and I speak privately and give these two young people some time together?"

The other woman stammered. "I-I'm not sure about this."

"We'll be nearby. You and I can talk and allow them this short time." Garvin pointed the way, and the two of them stepped into the hall.

Monique did most of the talking and most of the smiling. Destiny was quiet, but she was more than willing to play with puzzles and to color using the crayons and paper that were in the room. She was also willing to hug, and it seemed as though she felt it was her duty to cheer and comfort Monique.

The meeting was bittersweet. *I might not ever get to see her again.* She tousled Destiny's hair. Her eyes were drawn to the third door.

Monique and Destiny built a tower of blocks. "Do you like to build?" Destiny nodded affirmatively.

The door looked as though it opened onto the courtyard—the courtyard that led to the street. *I might not ever see her again.* It would be easy enough. There was no alarm on the door. "Do you like to play outside?"

Destiny nodded again. "Yes."

"Would you like to play outside with me?" It was crazy to take this kind of risk. It was stupid. Mrs. Winn was right outside. *I might not ever see her again. I might not ever hold my daughter again.*

Monique looked at the other doors, then back at the door that led outside. *I might not ever see her again. We might not ever hug each other again.* "We have to be very quiet, okay?" Destiny put a finger to her lips. "Let's go." Monique was surprised at how quickly, how easily, how quietly the door opened. Her heart was pounding. "Let's run, okay, Destiny?" In seconds Monique and Destiny were out of the courtyard and standing on the curb, waiting for a break in the traffic.

Oh God, please help me!

Meemaw and Mr. Green sat on her front steps drinking tall glasses of lemonade. Each glass had a strawberry floating near the bottom, and another berry decorating the rim of the glass. Meemaw offered her friend more blueberry crunch—baked, sweetened blueberries mixed with walnuts and covered with a crunchy topping. Mr. Green patted his stomach and shook his head.

Meemaw smiled. "It looks like a happy ending to me."

Mr. Green shook his head. "I'm not so sure."

"You just worry too much. What could go wrong? Your kids ask you to visit them. They pay for the ticket, and all you can do is fret."

Mr. Green's eyebrows knit together. "What about the store?"

"Well, Mr. Green, you are a very important person in Jacks Creek. But I believe—" she nudged him—"if we work real hard, we can make it without you for a few days while you take the first vacation you've been on in at least twenty years."

He shook his head. "I'm just not sure, Evangelina."

"You are the most fretful person. How can you be so fretful and still be my best friend?"

Mr. Green's eyes twinkled. "Oh that's easy, my beautiful

Evangelina; it's because I know that you will bring me good news." The two laughed, talked, and sipped their lemonade.

Monique looked down at Destiny. It would be foolish to think that she could take care of her. This was not the way. *Help me, God.* Maybe she might never have Destiny, might never hold her again, but she couldn't let her daughter suffer or put her in danger.

She stooped and hugged Destiny like she might never hug her again, then kissed her daughter on the cheek. "Come on, Destiny." The little girl grabbed her extended hand. "We better go back. We don't want anybody to be worried, right?" Destiny nodded and clutched Space Cat to her chest. *If we hurry maybe nobody will notice that we were gone.*

Monique's hands were clammy. As she approached the door, it occurred to her that the door might be locked from the inside. She reached out and grabbed the knob.

It turned! She and Destiny stepped back inside.

"Monique!" Garvin looked frantic.

"I told you so," Mrs. Winn said smugly.

Thirty-one

◆

——————————————————

*A*ny word from the settlement conference?" Garvin spoke into her cell phone as she buzzed through downtown traffic trying to find the least crowded route to the mall—as though there was such a thing as a good route in D.C. There were tourists everywhere.

Jonee sounded preoccupied. "They're saying it's going to be at least a day or two more."

Garvin turned onto Constitution Avenue. "Great. Hurry up and wait, right?"

"Garvin, are you sure you ought to be doing this? The meeting this afternoon is really important, and I don't think you should be late."

"I'll be there, Jonee. Stop worrying. I know it's important, but I wouldn't miss this for the world."

"Okay, Garvin." Jonee laughed. "I'll save you a seat."

"Yeah right." Garvin pushed the disconnect button. "Parking space. Come on parking space," Garvin whispered to herself. Ten feet ahead of her, a car with Oregon plates pulled out of a space. She whipped her car into place—there was still time on the meter. "Woo-woo-woo! Yes!" Garvin added a quarter and then began the dash for the mall. She felt free, almost as though she were flying. Garvin ran past the temporary platform and microphones that had been assembled.

At the other end of the mall there was a sea of bicycles coming in her direction. Garvin ran faster and began calling her friend's name. "Ramona! Ramona!" Two riders passed Garvin on either side, and then she was wading, running the midst of the riders. There were bikes of all colors and types. A sea of spokes, wheels, and helmets. Some of the two-wheelers displayed flags, others had squeaking horns.

"Ramona! Ramona!" How was she ever going to find her? There were hundreds of riders. Garvin stopped and turned to look at the banner over the podium. "Welcome Big Riders" was painted in giant-sized, capital letters. She started running again. There were so many of them, the bicycles had slowed, and the riders were walking them. "Ramona!"

"Garvin?"

She scanned the crowd and pulled off her shades so that she could see better. "Ramona?" Garvin spotted her friend waving excitedly at her. Ramona still had on her riding helmet and stood under the shade of a large tree.

Garvin began to wade sideways through the bicycles. "Excuse me, excuse me." As she got closer, Ramona stepped off of her bike and began to jump up and down while she shouted her name. "*Garvin!*"

When she broke through the last column of bicycles, Ramona abandoned hers and ran to meet Garvin.

The two friends grabbed hands and began to jump up and down. They stopped to hug and then started jumping again. A small crowd had gathered around them. Ramona stopped jumping so that she could make introductions. It was her church group. She turned to a man who looked to be in his midthirties. "Garvin, this is Derrick."

Garvin leaned to whisper in Ramona's ear. "The face from the train station?"

"The same," Ramona whispered back. She stepped closer so that she could link arms with him. "Minister Derrick Dauid, the engineer and my husband-to-be."

He smiled shyly.

"No!"

"Yes!"

"No!"

"Yes!" The two women began to squeal and hug each other. Minister Dauid stood to the side smiling. "Ramona." The two women stopped jumping to acknowledge him. "You two look like you have a lot of catching up to do. Why don't you go ahead? I'll help these folks and get our bikes packed up. I've got plenty to do, we can just meet back here." Ramona kissed him on the cheek.

Something about her friend had changed; there was a new quietness, a new assurance. They grabbed hands and ran away like schoolgirls.

"Garvin, you wouldn't believe the things I saw. It was awesome. Mountains, waterfalls like in the movies, and streams so clear you could see the bottom. I never knew my body could do the things it's done. Or that I could do the things I've done, for that matter. It was the first time I knew what it meant to have your spirit soar. Garvin, I got to see spacious skies, to see amber waves, to see purple mountain's majesty, to see the fruited plain. And it was the first time in my life that I felt like America was mine.

"And Derrick...I can't even describe how good he is, how kind, and how he makes me feel. And just how I feel about myself. It's okay, who I am—it's okay to be me. I'm ashamed to admit it, but there were times when I enjoyed the experience so much, I forgot it was about the charity and not about me."

Garvin squeezed her friend's hand. "Maybe it was about both."

"I've been so excited about me, you haven't had time to get a word in."

While Ramona drank water from a squeeze bottle, Garvin told her about Gooden and about her job. "I still don't know how it's going to work out, but one thing I do know, the job does not make up who I am. My value doesn't come from the job, or clothes, or men. It's deeper than that, you know?"

She told her about Meemaw and Jacks Creek. "I thought I was going home to rescue Meemaw, but I think she rescued me. And Jacks Creek was like home, but sometimes it was like Oz—like some strange place I had never experienced before." Garvin told Ramona about the jars, about Byrd and Winston Salem, and about Esther and Smitty. "Who would have ever thought that Esther would break down and fall in love? And with Smitty, of all people—I guess opposites do attract."

Ramona smiled. "Yes, I guess I would say so."

She told her about Monique. "My heart just sank. She's a sweet kid, and man, to have it end like that. At least I was able to convince the judge to make her a ward of the state and to let Meemaw be her foster parent." Garvin slapped her friend on the leg. "And she's staying in my old room. You *know* that's love—I don't want to share my Meemaw with anybody, not to mention my room. I just hope it's going to work out…"

Then Garvin told Ramona about GoGo. "I guess he turned out to be the biggest surprise of all. Funny, I spent the whole summer chasing this guy down because I thought he was trying to make my grandmother. Only it turned out that he was the pure one, and I was the one trying to ruin him. He sent me flowers and we were going to go out to dinner before I left, but with the situation with Monique…I just felt like she needed me more. Whatever's supposed to be, will be." Garvin looked off toward the capitol building. "It wasn't purple mountain's majesty, but Jacks Creek has me believing there's no place like home."

The two women walked and talked. "Look." Garvin pointed to a dress shop. "Come on, let's peek inside." Everything was the same—and everything was changed.

Garvin pulled into her garage parking space, made it into the office, into the conference room, and into her seat just before the clock announced it was two o'clock in the afternoon. Jonee sat in one of the straphanger seats—those seats for support staff, chairs not at the main table, but methodically spaced along the walls of the room. She nodded and gave Garvin a secreted thumbs-up.

Mr. Straub walked into the room, in the customary way of leaders, several minutes after the official meeting start time. He sat on the other end of the table from Garvin. Several attendants surrounded him, giving him papers and whispering information. Straub cleared his throat to indicate the meeting was to begin. It was obvious that his black suit was custom tailored. His gray hair was immaculately groomed, and appeared more silver than gray. His nails were freshly manicured and the skin on his face looked as though he treated himself to facials regularly. Before he spoke, he smiled at Garvin.

A good sign—I think.

"It's good to see you, Ms. Daniels. You look healthy and well rested."

"Good to see you too, sir." The table must have been at least twenty feet long.

His face sobered. "As you know, Ms. Daniels, Winkle and Straub takes our commitment to customer satisfaction very, very seriously. In order to institutionalize that commitment, we have designed a set of policies that we apply equitably and fairly to *all* employees." He scanned the faces of the employees in the room. "Each employee gets a copy of those policies and is required to initial that they have received them when their employment is initiated here." An attendant handed him a set of papers. "These documents indicate that you were no exception. Is that correct?"

Never let them see you sweat. "Yes, that's correct."

"Following those policies, your supervisor, Mr. Gooden, initiated an investigation—"

An attendant leaned forward and stage-whispered to Mr. Straub, "It was a follow-up interview, sir."

Mr. Straub looked annoyed. "Mr. Gooden initiated a series of *follow-up interviews.* And you were informed of those interviews after the fact. Is that correct?" Another attendant handed Mr. Straub another set of papers.

"Yes, that's correct, Mr. Straub."

"At the same time you were notified, Mr. Gooden also informed you that—" Mr. Straub looked at the attendant who had informed him about the interviews—"Winkle and Straub was initiating an *investigation* into allegations of bias in your handling of at least one particular case. Is that correct, Ms. Daniels?" More documents were laid in front of Mr. Straub.

"Yes, sir. That is correct."

More papers. "You were notified that you would be on administrative leave until this matter was resolved."

"Yes, I was."

An attendant produced more papers. Mr. Straub waved them away. "Ms. Daniels, you have been more than patient throughout this ordeal, and I trust that it has not been too painful for you. I know how important your career is to you, and it has long been my conviction that you are an excellent lawyer of unswerving integrity. You have on occasion been a bit direct in your dealings with others, but I have not found that such behavior could be construed as bias. In fact, during this investigation—you will note that I felt compelled to become fully involved in this matter myself—it surfaced that the clients in question had not alleged bias, but had referred to your 'bedside manner.' They assured me that they were more than satisfied with your service and the outcome. And I must say that your directness and candor are traits that I often see in others who are also candidates for partnership."

Garvin could feel her muscles relaxing.

"You will note, Ms. Daniels, that Mr. Gooden is not present at this meeting. In fact, he is not present in the office. He is now on administrative leave having found himself the focus of an unfortunate investigation into allegations of bias."

It was all Garvin could do not to smile, not to dance. She thought about Meemaw shouting in church! It was Garvin now who felt like a lightning rod!

"Sadly, it seems a trusted employee overheard him conspiring with several other employees to use Winkle and Straub policies for his own ends." Mr. Straub shook his head and then quickly stood. "Welcome back, Ms. Daniels. You may consider this matter concluded in your favor. All references will be removed from your personnel records."

Thank You, God! A phrase came to her—"Like fire shut up in my bones!" *Lord, help me hold my seat!*

Garvin nodded as Mr. Straub continued. "By the way, you will find that the personal items you left here have been moved to Mr. Gooden's office." He nodded to all in attendance and then quickly left the room.

◆

Monique sat in a chair near the window beyond the reach of the moonlight. How much more could she have done wrong? It was a stupid move. What had made her try to run away with Destiny?

She ran her hands through her hair, then stopped and shook it when she came to a point where the tangled curls wouldn't let her go any farther. Monique thought over her life. For each memory there was a "what if." She pulled at the threads in the outer seams of her jeans.

Destiny. She would probably never see her daughter again. Monique used her hand to muffle her sobs. She had stolen the baby—almost. But it was *her* baby. The two thoughts chased each other.

Outside, the sky was India ink and the moon's reflection was bright, but in the room, there was just enough light to reveal outlines, shapes. In the darkness, through her tears, Monique looked around the room. On the tallest dresser there was a modern version of a hurricane lamp. In the unlit room, the lace doily the lamp sat on seemed to disappear into the wood of the chifforobe.

Monique sighed and wiped her tears. She had been living at Miz Evangelina's for a week, and tomorrow was the hearing. She grabbed her hair and twisted it into a knot, then let it go. There was no reason to hope. *Please God, forgive me. Please God, help me.*

From the chair, she crossed the room to the door of the small adjoining bathroom. Monique flipped the light switch which was thick with years of paint. Standing in front of the face bowl, she stared at her image in the mirror. Hazel eyes. The same eyes as Destiny, only her own were rimmed with red. Silent tears fell again. Hope was gone. Monique reached into her pocket for the pin Miss Garvin had given her. The words Miss Garvin had spoken came back to her.

"*O thou afflicted, tossed with tempest, and not comforted, behold, I will lay thy stones with fair colours, and lay thy foundations with sapphires.*

"*And I will make thy windows of agates, and thy gates of carbuncles, and all thy borders of pleasant stones. And all thy children shall be taught of the* LORD*; and great shall be the peace of thy children.*"

Somehow she had to believe it was going to be all right. *God, please take care of my baby.*

She turned on the light and noticed a box on her bed. The return address said Washington, D.C. The note card was from Garvin: "Sorry I couldn't be there. Here's a little extra support." She pulled back the layers of tissue paper—it was a coat of many colors.

Monique hugged it to her chest until she fell asleep.

Thirty-two

◆

No one is watching.

In the middle of her office, Garvin did a victory dance, gave a little step of praise. When she finished, she looked around the room, then sank into the chair behind her new desk. She swiveled in the leather office chair and could just feel her back saying thank you. She closed her eyes. *Thank You, God.* He had taken care of her battle. *Now Lord, please help Monique.*

She leaned forward and took a sip of her coffee. "Welcome back, Ms. Daniels." People had been popping in and out all day, welcoming her back, congratulating her, wishing her well. Part of her wanted to answer with a snide, cutting remark, but she reminded herself that she was better than that; she was new.

"Is now a good time?" Jonee was at the door.

"Sure."

"Good news, litigator. The trial is on!" Garvin stood and the two women slapped hands.

"Is Hemings ready?"

Jonee nodded. "He says full steam ahead."

"He knows the risk?"

"Garvin, you know me. I'm the conservative one, I've tried to warn him fifty ways, but he says he has nothing to lose."

Garvin nodded. "Okay then. Give me just a minute."

Jonee ducked back outside the office, then Garvin walked down the hall to the ladies' room and pushed open the door.

Miz Maizie stood at the counter, just as she had stood all those months ago, cleaning the mirror.

"Well, look who is back." The older woman smiled broadly. "And you don't look no worse for the wear to me. Your cheeks even looking a little rosy."

Garvin crossed the room and threw her arms around her. "Thank you so much, Miz Maizie. You don't know how much you helped me keep it together when I had to leave here." She kissed the older woman.

"That's what friends and family are for, right?" Miz Maizie squeezed Garvin and then turned back to her cleaning. "Speaking of friends, I hear you got your old friend's office."

Garvin shook her head. "I can't figure that one out to save me, Miz Maizie."

The old woman winked at her. "I guess the fat lady sang." Miz Maizie started humming.

"Miz Maizie—"

"Yeah, I'm the 'trusted employee.'" She laughed so hard she almost started wheezing. "That Gooden was a bad one." Miz Maizie laughed again. "Sometimes, I crack my own self up." Garvin hugged the woman again, while Miz Maizie held her side until she caught her breath. "A nasty snake, that's what he was. I would hear him plotting against people. Talking over the phone about what he was going to do and who he was going to do it to and when he was going to do it to them. I just started taking notes—he had the cleanest office in Winkle and Straub. By the time I finished writing, his little goose was cooked. I took the information I had to Mr. Straub, and that was that." She snapped her finger through the rubber gloves, then turned back to her work using her nail to scratch at a stubborn spot. "That Gooden was a numskull."

Garvin held on while the old woman worked, kissed her cheek. "Miz Maizie, you saved my life."

"No, baby, I didn't save you, I just helped you out a little."

"You're right, Miz Maizie. Somebody else saved me." Garvin squeezed her again.

"Take it easy there, girl. You acting awful touchy-feely." Miz Maizie stopped all attempts at cleaning. "You didn't go home and fall in love, did you?"

Garvin blushed.

Miz Maizie pulled off her gloves. "Well, don't try to hold it back. I spilled my guts, now you got to spill yours."

Garvin told Miz Maizie about GoGo and all that had transpired that summer. "So, I don't know when I'll see him again. Or even if I'll see him again. And I don't know how things are going to work out with Monique."

"Oh, you got to do better than that. Look how *this* situation turned out. You thought it was the end of the world, now look. You better learn how to encourage yourself, girl. How to look at the things God has done in your life in the past and let that be your reassurance for the future. Keep a prayer in your heart. Remember, it ain't over until it's over."

Garvin walked back to her office, and in her heart, kept whispering prayers for Monique.

Thirty-three

◆

Mr. Green stood at the end of Meemaw's driveway. "If you need me, Evangelina, you just have to say the word and I will come. I closed down the store for my vacation and I will close it again so that I can be at an old friend's side."

Meemaw kept her eyes on the front door of her house, but touched Mr. Green's forearm. "You know that I appreciate that. You know that I do. But you keep your hand to the plow. Somebody bigger than both of us in control of this situation now."

"What do you think will happen to her? Do you think they will press charges against her? Goodness knows she has been through enough in her young life."

"I don't know, Mr. Green. I'm just hoping and believing for the best."

Monique stepped through the front doorway wearing the multicolored jacket that Garvin had sent to her.

Mr. Green spoke gently to Monique. "It's a little warm for that jack—"

Meemaw nudged him. "Hush now, Mr. Green. Leave the girl alone. She just needs a little extra reassurance." She told him about the coat of many colors and the note that Garvin had sent to Monique.

While they were talking, GoGo pulled up in his car. He got out and opened the doors for Monique and Meemaw. Monique kept her head down, but Meemaw talked as if she already knew the outcome. "We sure do appreciate this ride. We shouldn't be in your way long today."

GoGo nodded. "You're not in my way, Miz Evangelina. There's no place else I would be today but with you two ladies." He smiled at Monique's image in the rearview mirror. "Nice jacket, Monique. I like it."

For a moment the girl brightened. "You do? Miss Garvin sent it to me. I thought it might be too warm, but…" She was silent for the rest of the ride.

While GoGo parked, Meemaw and Monique found the hearing room and sat on a waiting bench outside the door. Young men in leg irons and manacles passed them by, and with each one that passed, Monique seemed to fold more and more in upon herself. Meemaw put her arm about the girl and just kept praying silently. GoGo arrived as the bailiff unlocked the hearing room door.

There was a wooden table in the center of the small room, and Monique sat on one side between Meemaw and GoGo. Shortly after they were seated, Mrs. Winn arrived with stacks of papers and folders up under her arms. She staked off the other side of the table, nodded curtly to Meemaw and GoGo, then glared at Monique.

The family court judge arrived from his offices and waved for them to keep their seats. He had only a yellow notepad and a pen in his hands. His gray hair was slightly disheveled and looked as though he had just run his hand through it. His spectacles balanced on the end of his nose. After introductions he began, "First, I would like to make it clear that this is not a trial, it's a hearing. An informal inquiry so that all concerned can decide what is the best way to proceed. As I understand it—" he looked at his notes—"there are two minors involved."

"Yes, and *this* young lady—" Mrs. Winn's face looked pinched— "attempted to steal a child that was in my care."

The judge patted her hand. "Mrs. Winn, we've known each other for a long time, and I appreciate how protective you are of your kids. But I need you to try to turn that passion down just a smidgen so folks don't get too flamed up. Is that all right?" He looked at Monique. "All right, young lady, let me hear from you first."

"Judge, your Honor…"

"You don't have to worry about all that. I'm not trying to impress anybody, just tell me your story."

Monique tearfully told him the story of her daughter's delivery, of the adoption agreement, and her subsequent discovery of Destiny at the Jacks Creek Boys' and Girls' Home. "I knew it was my baby, your Honor. And I went by every day to see her. Then Miss Garvin, Garvin Daniels, helped arrange for me to get to see her. And I don't know what happened. I mean, I was thinking that I was never going to see her again." She dropped her head. "I know what I did was stupid. I realized it once I was outside. That's why I came back—it's just that I couldn't stand the thought that I would never see her again."

Mrs. Winn jumped to her feet. "I object, your Honor. As a matter of fact, if you recall, I objected from the beginning."

"I do recall, Mrs. Winn."

"Based upon years of experience, I felt in the beginning that this girl was not a suitable visitor or influence for the child."

The judge nodded. "I do remember your objections, Mrs. Winn. And I do value your opinion. But first, why don't you just sit down. Now we're trying to do this calmly, right, everybody? It's a hearing, not a trial." He nodded at everyone around the table.

"Mrs. Winn, I never fail to tell you, do I, how much I appreciate the job you do at the home. But there are several irregularities that kind of make this case muddy in my mind. Now, if a girl like this just walked in off the street and snatched a child, well, that would just be open and shut, wouldn't it? I'd be at home right now eating smothered pork chops and this young lady would be on her way to the woodshed." The judge nodded at GoGo. "My wife just makes the best smothered pork chops in Jacks Creek.

"Here's where the waters get muddy. Now our own records make it clear that when this girl, Monique, signed her baby over for adoption, it was written on paper that her baby was going to be adopted right away by a specific family. Then that fell through. Wasn't our fault. Wasn't her fault. But nobody told Monique that the agreement had fallen through. In all honesty—" the judge shrugged his shoulders and met Meemaw's eyes—"I can't say for certain that we legally had to tell her. But I'm even less sure what we should have done morally."

He laid his hands flat on the table. "This is where it gets even muddier for me, Mrs. Winn. We have a birth mother who finds out through happenstance that her baby has not been adopted and just so happens she knows where the baby is and is powerless to do anything about it. All she can do is watch her day after day behind iron bars. Can you imagine that, Mrs. Winn? Now while I don't condone what she did, I can't imagine how tortured she must have felt day after day after day." The judge leaned back and shook his head. "I just can't say how I would have behaved under those circumstances. It wasn't responsible of her to try to take the child, but at least she had the presence of mind to try to bring her back."

Mrs. Winn was steaming. "Your Honor—"

"Wait, wait, now. Since the state made the adoption agreement and that agreement was nullified, I'm just not sure we have a leg to stand on with this stealing thing. Besides that, we have to consider the damage that we've already done to this young lady. Not intentionally, but still, same difference."

Mrs. Winn jumped to her feet again. "Judge, your Honor, you are not going to give that baby to this-this-this *child!*"

The judge leaned back in his chair and smiled at the woman. "You know, Mrs. Winn, I can always count on you for good advice. Here, have a sit down. You're right. This child here needs to be able to learn how to be an adult and how to take care of a child. She's not ready. Don't you agree?"

Mrs. Winn nodded emphatically.

"I think the little girl, Destiny, needs to be in foster care. Settled in with some fine, upstanding family with lots of community support. And this girl, Monique, needs to learn how to be a mother." The judge patted Mrs. Winn's hand. "I knew I needed to have you here, Mrs. Winn. I knew you would have the answer. Now this girl, Monique, is already in the kind of foster home that we were just talking about. I'm going to recommend, and I know this is highly unusual but we all agree it's a highly unusual case, that the little girl, Destiny, be referred to the same wonderful foster care home so the two of them can get to know each other in a supervised, structured environment."

"Praise the Lord!" Meemaw jumped to her feet before she remembered where she was.

"I want to thank you fine people for your help, especially you, Mrs. Winn. This hearing is adjourned."

"But, your Honor…" Mrs. Winn fumbled with her papers.

The judge smiled and walked to the door of his office. "Would you all please wait outside and I'll have the bailiff give you a copy of my handwritten order." He shook Mrs. Winn's hand last. "I'll be sure to give your love to my wife."

◆

GoGo smiled and threw his fist in the air on his way to get his parked car. *Yes!*

"Mr. Walker?" GoGo recognized the judge's voice and turned to face him. "You're a friend of Ms. Daniel's, as I understand it." The judge smiled. "News travels fast in small towns."

"So I see."

"Well, she is one heck of a lawyer. She's got teeth that won't let go."

GoGo laughed. "She can be determined. That's true."

"Well, you tell her for me that we need somebody here like her. The children need her. There's plenty more children in Jacks Creek just like Monique and they need somebody on their side. You tell her I've got a juvenile advocacy position on staff and she's got a standing offer. I can't touch the salary she's making in Washington, but the hours are good and my wife makes a mean sweet potato pie." The two men laughed together. The judge put his hand on GoGo's shoulder. "Son, let me give you a little advice. That young woman is a keeper. Don't let her get away—and I'm not just saying that because I want to hire her." The judge got into his car and kept laughing as he drove away.

Garvin and Jonee waded though stacks of paper and folders on the conference room table. Planted amongst them, like modern-day flowers, were plastic containers with the remains of deli sandwiches, empty potato chip bags, and empty cola cans. Taped to the wall behind the table—their wall of strategy—was a timeline of events for the Hemings case.

"He really kept his cool during his deposition. I think Hemings is ready." Garvin leaned back in her seat, tapped her index finger on a stack of files in front of her. "You know, I think we've been missing the point. We keep trying to figure out who's best—black, white, yellow, red, brown—but I think God is trying to tell us He made us in many colors because He loves us, He values us. Many colors is a gift given to someone loved."

Jonee looked surprised, opened her mouth to speak, but was interrupted when one of the summer interns stuck her head in the conference room door. "My goodness. I can't believe how you guys have trashed this place."

Garvin laughed. "It's the night before battle."

"I'm tempted to not even give you this." The intern was pushing a cart with two levels. Flaps hung from the first shelf that hid the contents of the lower shelf. She kneeled and reached inside. She carefully pulled out a bouquet of roses. Each one a different color. "These are for you, Garvin. And this too." She handed her a large box tied with red ribbon. Garvin untied the ribbon and shook the box so that the top fell off.

Jonee leaned over stacks of papers to see. "What is it?"

There was a note on top of the tissue paper that read, "Open First."

You won't know until you get home just how much you did for Monique. The flowers are from me, to thank you for what you did for her, for Destiny, for all of us.

Now open the tissue paper.

It was a multicolored coat.

Fall is coming and I thought you might need this to keep warm and to help you to remember to think about us starting over again.

*By the way, the family court judge wants you to know that
you have a standing job offer with the court as a juvenile advo-
cate. Pay is bad, hours good, pie the best.*

*At the bottom of the box you will find a set of floor plans for
a house with a foundation of many colors. The plans are on
hold until some future date when I can convince you to say "I
do."*

Abed-nego

Garvin dropped the note and looked around the room. Her
career, her office, her car…it was all that she had worked for. She
closed her eyes and remembered the river, the shoe. She laid her
hand on her heart, and remembered Meemaw, Monique, GoGo,
Smitty, and Ramona. She opened her eyes.

"Jonee, we've got to get to work. I can't think about this now.
We've got a case to win. But once that's over—" she grinned—
"I've got to go see a man about a house."

Epilogue

◆

now covered Meemaw's porch and all her bushes, except for spots where bright lights were glowing in the dusk. The air was brisk, and steam puffed from Garvin's mouth. The turkey she held in her arms warmed her, but it was heavy and the weight pressed through her mittens, rubbing against the ring on her finger. She leaned to peek inside the house.

There was a large Christmas tree trimmed with multicolored lights, balls, and icicles. Monique sat in a chair near the tree, reading to Destiny, who snuggled against her. It was good to see them happy.

Garvin shifted and leaned against the doorbell. Inside, she could hear Meemaw's voice, hear her moving toward the door.

A car door shut behind her. "I told you I would carry that."

She turned to see a walking mound of presents—presents for Destiny, Monique, and Meemaw. Even presents for Esther and Smitty and their kids.

Garvin Walker smiled at the mound that muffled her husband's voice. "Anymore, sweetie, and I think you'd collapse."

It had taken a long time. But finally, she was home.

Dear Readers,

I am dedicating *Ain't No River* to all the unwed mothers and fathers, and their babies. It's dedicated to all the players, all the playees, to the adulterers, to the fornicators who have had enough. *Ain't No River* is dedicated to those who have struggled having, or even just thought about abortion. This book is for people caught up in careers and lifestyles that have taken control of their lives. This book is for all the addicts of any kind who are ready to leave the guilt behind and go to another level. For all of us who are striving to be what God is calling us to be—now that ought to include just about everybody!

Ain't No River was a difficult book for me to write, because I too was some of these things. But God is faithful to forgive. This book has strong medicine and strong anointing, but is stuffed with characters full of humor, warmth, and redeeming love—characters that struggle just like you and me. I write it out of the love in my heart, divine and redeeming love that has transformed me. Indeed, He has done marvelous things!

I believe that the Lord has invited me to write not because I am perfect, but because I was broken, wounded, and struggling. He invites me to write, because I am willing to share and show my own scars, that someone else might be saved. Remember, no matter what we've done in the past—today is a new day. "Surely the arm of the LORD is not too short to save, nor his ear too dull to hear" (Isaiah 59:1, NIV).

You know I love you. And no matter where this book finds you, God loves you more.

Sharon Ewell Foster

sharonewelfoster@aol.com

MEEMAW'S RECIPE FOR CLASSIC PECAN PIE

(The basic recipe was provided courtesy of Best Foods, the owner of the Karo® trademark, but Meemaw always added a pinch of cinnamon and some ground nutmeg to her pie. The added spice truly brings the flavor home.)

3 eggs, slightly beaten
1 cup sugar
1 cup Karo® light or dark corn syrup
2 tablespoons margarine or butter, melted
1 teaspoon vanilla
1 1/4 cups pecans
1 (9-inch) unbaked or frozen deep-dish pie crust*

1. Preheat oven to 350°F.
2. In medium bowl with fork beat eggs slightly. Add sugar, corn syrup, margarine, and vanilla; stir until blended. Stir in pecans. Pour into pie crust.
3. Bake 50 to 55 minutes or until knife inserted halfway between center and edge comes out clean. Cool on wire rack.

* To use prepared frozen pie crust: Use 9-inch deep-dish pie crust. Do not thaw. Preheat oven and a cookie sheet. Pour filling into frozen crust; bake on cookie sheet. (Insulated cookie sheet is not recommended.)

Scripture Verses on Which the Story of *Ain't No River* Is Based.

Now Israel loved Joseph more than all his children, because he was the son of his old age: and he made him a coat of many colours. And it came to pass, when Joseph was come unto his brethren, that they stript Joseph out of his coat, his coat of many colours that was on him.

GENESIS 37:3, 23

And she had a garment of divers colours upon her: for with such robes were the king's [David] daughters that were virgins apparelled. Then his servant brought her out, and bolted the door after her. And Tamar put ashes on her head, and rent her garment of divers colours that was on her, and laid her hand on her head, and went on crying.

And Absalom her brother said unto her, "Hath Amnon thy brother been with thee? but hold now thy peace, my sister: he is thy brother; regard not this thing." So Tamar remained desolate in her brother Absalom's house.

2 SAMUEL 13:18–20

O thou afflicted, tossed with tempest, and not comforted, behold, I will lay thy stones with fair colours, and lay thy foundations with sapphires. And I will make thy windows of agates, and thy gates of carbuncles, and all thy borders of pleasant stones. And all thy children shall be taught of the LORD; and great shall be the peace of thy children.

ISAIAH 54:11–13

All thing are lawful for me, but all things are not helpful. All things are lawful for me, but I will not be brought under the power of any.... Flee sexual immorality. Every sin that a man does is outside the body, but he who commits sexual immorality sins against his own body. Or do you not know that your body is the temple of the Holy Spirit who is in you, whom you have from God, and you are not your own? For you were bought at a price; therefore glorify God in your body and in your spirit, which are God's.

1 CORINTHIANS 6:12, 18–20, NKJV

And the building of the wall of it was of jasper: and the city was pure gold, like unto clear glass. And the foundations of the wall of the city were garnished with all manner of precious stones. The first foundation was jasper; the second, sapphire; the third, a chalcedony; the fourth, an emerald; The fifth, sardonyx; the sixth, sardius; the seventh, chrysolyte; the eighth, beryl; the ninth, a topaz; the tenth, a chrysoprasus; the eleventh, a jacinth; the twelfth, an amethyst. And the twelve gates were twelve pearls: every several gate was of one pearl: and the street of the city was pure gold, as it were transparent glass.

And I saw no temple therein: for the Lord God Almighty and the Lamb are the temple of it. And the city had no need of the sun, neither of the moon, to shine in it: for the glory of God did lighten it, and the Lamb is the light thereof. And the nations of them which are saved shall walk in the light of it: and the kings of the earth do bring their glory and honour into it. And the gates of it shall not be shut at all by day: for there shall be no night there. And they shall bring the glory and honour of the nations into it. And there shall in no wise enter into it any thing that defileth, neither whatsoever worketh abomination, or maketh a lie: but they which are written in the Lamb's book of life.

REVELATION 21:18–27

And he shewed me a pure river of water of life, clear as crystal, proceeding out of the throne of God and of the Lamb.

REVELATION 22:1

A single moment can change everything...

Passing by Samaria

a novel

A National Bestseller!

Sharon Ewell Foster

The date is 1919—a time of unrest and drastic change. For Alena, though, life in Mississippi is perfect, and she prays she will never leave her home. That prayer is shattered when she makes a horrible discovery—a discovery that leads her to challenge all she believes. From a quiet, country setting, Alena is catapulted to Chicago, the "city of broad shoulders." There, amidst riots, misplaced love, and post-war confusion, this outspoken young woman struggles to find herself and the one true thing that will save her...

ISBN 1-57673-615-6